'It was nice kn
I'll know you r
means certain

'Gah!' said Sa
Churl.

But his brothers chaffed him about his recklessness until it was time to board the slave-powered ferry for the trip north to the city of his destiny. Once aboard, Sarazin did not sit. It was too crowded, there were no seats — and his buttocks were raw from the saddle. Padded with greasy raw wool he had managed to ride — but only just.

Lod continued to josh him about drinking riverwater. Had he really made a bad mistake? He thought to ask Jarl about it — but Jarl had vanished. Sarazin, desolated, feared him gone for good. Thus it happens in legend. The old swordmaster trains the youth who is fated to dare all on a perilous quest for power or treasure. Then the master dies, retires or vanishes, leaving youth to battle unaided against the evil wizard, the red dragon, the pit of claws, the halfelven enemy or whatever it is.

Momentarily, Sarazin was half-convinced he had indeed embarked on a life of legend. After all, he had always known he was meant for great things. But, as he realized in a moment of utter panic, he was far from ready to dare such a destiny unaided.

Also by Hugh Cook

THE WIZARDS AND THE WARRIORS
THE WORDSMITHS AND THE WARGUILD
THE WOMEN AND THE WARLORDS
THE WALRUS AND THE WARWOLF

and published by Corgi Books

THE WICKED AND
THE WITLESS

Hugh Cook

CORGI BOOKS

THE WICKED AND THE WITLESS

A CORGI BOOK   0 552 13439 2

Originally published in Great Britain by Colin Smythe Limited

PRINTING HISTORY
Colin Smythe edition published 1989
Corgi edition published 1989

This book is set in 10/11pt Paladium.

Corgi Books are published by Transworld Publishers Ltd.,
61-63 Uxbridge Road, Ealing, London W5 5SA, in Australia by
Transworld Publishers (Australia) Pty. Ltd., 15-23 Helles
Avenue, Moorebank, NSW 2170, and in New Zealand by Transworld
Publishers (N.Z.) Ltd., Cnr. Moselle and Waipareira Avenues,
Henderson, Auckland.

Reproduced, printed and bound in Great Britain by
Hazell Watson & Viney Limited
Member of BPCC plc
Aylesbury, Bucks, England

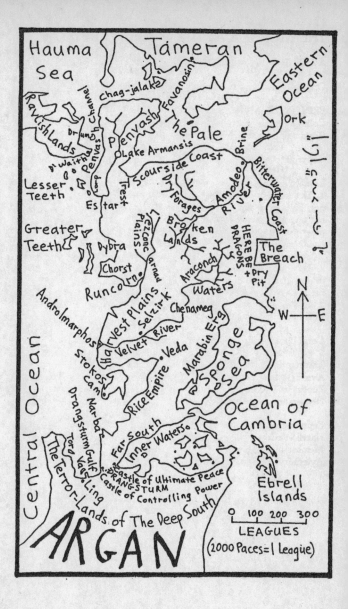

Hauma Sea

Tameran

Eastern Ocean

Ravish Lands

Chanwell

Drum

Chag-jalak

Favanosin

The Pale

Ork

d'Waith

Penvas

Penvash

Lake Armansis

Brine

Bitterwater Coast

Lesser Teeth

Estar

Trest

Scourside Coast

Dry Forages

Amadeo

River

HERE BE DRAGONS

The Breach

Greater Teeth

Dybra

Zezanc Plains

arnad

Broken Lands

Araconch

Dry Pit

Chorst

Runcorn

Waters

Central Ocean

Androlmarphos

Harvest Plains

Selzirk

Chenameg

N

W   E

Velvet River

Marabin Era

Sponge Sea

S

Stokos

Cam

Veda

Narba

Rice Empire

Far South

Inner Waters

Ocean of Cambria

Drangsturm Gulf

Tors

Vaslit

Ling

Castle of Ultimate Peace

DRANGSTURM

Castle of Controlling Power

Ebrell Islands

The Terror-Lands of The Deep South

0   100 200 300

LEAGUES

(2000 Paces = 1 League)

ARGAN

CHAPTER ONE

Rice Empire: Argan's most densely populated nation; supports over a million souls on landstrip roughly three hundred leagues long and a hundred wide between Ashun Mountains and Central Ocean.

Population pressures relieved by mass marketing of slaves to Provincial Endergeneer (to the south) and wars with more lightly populated Harvest Plains (to the north).
Capital: Galtras Laven
Ruler: Lord Regan
Language: Geltic

In winter in Alliance 4324 Sean Sarazin was again wounded in combat. His lastest injury began life as a slight scratch which threatened to heal without trace. However, by diligently rubbing it with salt, he won a scar which would mark his face for a lifetime.

He was intensely proud when girlfriends cherished his scar with delicate fingers and spoke in bated breath of the horror, the pain, the fear. The elegant Jaluba, who was somewhat more than a girlfriend, also admired it. Then made an extremely improper joke about a wound of her own.

Another thing happened that winter: Sean Kelebes Sarazin turned twenty-two. With youth now well and truly over, he wrote elegant, allusive lyrics about falling leaves, mortal flowers and death inevitable. Friends lauded his genius when he poeticised in tea shops and boulevard cafés.

In a more private place devoted to private places,

Sarazin recited his poems to Jaluba also. Whereupon she, with a giggle, damanded poetry in praise of aspects of her anatomy which, though Sarazin admired their elegance, cannot be discussed with propriety.

There was wine on Jaluba's breath when she made her demand. And wine on Sarazin's also. Therefore, let wine be blamed for the fact that he complied with her wishes. Or tried to. In truth, the task proved difficult indeed, for he had no stock of appropriate images on hand.

When writing on love, battle or mortality one drew upon a hoard of hundreds of standard phrases. Such versification was almost effortless. But when Sarazin sought to extol Jaluba's biology, only the witless obscenity of the coarser taverns came to mind. This he did not care to use.

'You will have to inspire me,' he said.

And Jaluba did her best to comply.

Sarazin sought inspiration in wine also, which led Lord Regan to remark on the following morn:

'You look somewhat drawn. What ails you?'

'Nothing serious, my lord,' answered Sarazin. 'A slight touch of *weltschmerz* — nothing more.'

'Ah! *Weltschmerz*!' said Lord Regan. 'I knew it well in my youth. But sorrow for the world is an abuse of talent which maturity avoids. After all, those in pain have chosen to suffer. Concern for such is an error.'

'It was but a trifling indulgence, my lord,' said Sarazin. 'I sorrowed in a poetical sense merely, not a political sense.'

'Good, good,' said Lord Regan.

The two were strolling in the Sunrise Gardens. Green grass. Blue sky. Warm sun. Winter snow on the heights of the Ashun mountains to the east. Sage age instructing youth. Was there a poem to be won from the occasion?

'Remember,' said Lord Regan, 'that—'

A peacock screamed near at hand, and Lord Regan began again:

'Remember, we create ourselves. Always remember that. We have free will so we are entirely responsible for ourselves. Everything happens to us by our own choice. Never forget that.'

'I never will, my lord,' said Sarazin.

'In the final analysis,' said Lord Regan, 'you can have whatever you want. You can be whatever you want to be. You can win whatever you want to win.'

'I believe it, my lord,' said Sarazin.

'Some people become victims,' said Lord Regan. 'This only happens because they have a victim mentality. Feeling themselves to be victims, they behave in a way which makes them just that.'

'My lord's wisdom is all-encompassing,' said Sarazin, truly impressed by the depth of Lord Regan's philosophy.

Shortly thereafter, Lord Regan quit Voice and returned to his capital, Galtras Laven. But he left Sean Sarazin a birthday present. A sword of firelight steel forged on the island of Stokos. A blade so beautiful that Sarazin wept when he first set eyes on it.

Thereafter, he trained more fiercely than ever before. Working by candlelight deep in the night, sweating, panting, pleasurably fatigued, he admired himself in the magnificent mirrors which graced his quarters. He liked what he saw. Muscles glistening, scars menacing, blade glittering.

— *Lord Regan was right.*

— *We do create ourselves.*

Thus thinking, Sarazin strove to shape muscle and ability both. This he loved as much as boulevard delights or his hours of bliss with Jaluba, she of the honey-soft lips, the luxurious fur.

What he liked less was steadily mounting pressure from his tutor, Epelthin Elkin, who worked him harder than ever before, drilling him ruthlessly in the Galish of the Salt Road and the Churl of far-distant Selzirk. Dull, boring, tedious, repetitive work. Unendurable! Sarazin demanded explanations but got none.

Then his combat instructor, Thodric Jarl, announced that they would at last begin True Battle Training. Sarazin

11

exulted, for this glamorous training would at least give him a break from scholarship's rigours. Shortly, he exulted no longer. Here is an example of what he had to endure:

Armed with a shield almost too heavy to hold and an unwieldy blade of blunt bronze, clad in armour and a helm so massive he could scarcely see or hear, Sarazin was ordered into a waist-deep bog then left to defend himself against three aggressive thugs armed with sticks and clubs.

That particular exercise had to be called off when Sarazin tripped, fell, was swallowed by the bog's oily mud, then found it impossible to surface because of the weight of armour oppressing him. He had nightmares about it for days afterwards.

Then, early in spring, Lord Regan returned to Voice to give Sarazin the most startling news of his life.

'You know,' said Lord Regan, 'though you are not of my line, I look on you almost as a son.'

'My lord has always been generous,' said Sarazin.

'I had . . . I must confess, I had plans for you. Yet it is not to be. Certain internal political pressures make it impossible for you to remain within my realm. I am returning you to Selzirk.'

That news left Sarazin incapable of speech.

Once he had gathered his wits he asked:

'My Lord . . . might I know the nature of the pressures which have forced this decision?'

'Alas!' said Lord Regan. 'That I may not speak of. Not here. Not now. But this I promise you: all will become clear to you in the fulness of time.'

When Lord Regan again departed for Galtras Laven, Sarazin's instructors drove him all the harder. He would leave for Selzirk early in summer, so had but a single season to prepare himself for the challenges awaiting in the city of his birth.

At first, Sean Sarazin despaired. He loved life in Voice, the elegant three-aqueduct city where he enjoyed popularity, prestige, luxurious quarters and (the world would be well lost for such a woman) Jaluba's charms. In

Selzirk he would be alone, lonely, totally isolated, without friends, without income, in a filthy foreign city which spoke an alien language.

'Cheer up!' said Thodric Jarl. 'Your mother rules in Selzirk.'

'Yes,' said Sarazin, 'but the Constitution of the Harvest Plains says—'

'What are you?' said Jarl. 'A lawyer? Test your ability and see where it gets you.'

'Easy for you to talk!' said Sarazin bitterly. 'You're not being sent into exile.'

'No,' said Jarl. 'I'm not. But I'm coming regardless.'

'You — you can't!' said a much-startled Sarazin. 'What could I offer? I could scarcely pay you. My mother might find you a position, but I couldn't guarantee it.'

'I'm a mercenary,' said Jarl, 'but I'm loyal to those who deserve loyalty. You're not much yet, but I see great things for you, Sean Sarazin. I'll chance my fate with yours.'

Jarl gave but little praise and that seldom. So this open-hearted declaration made Sean Sarazin dizzy with glorious pride. When Epelthin Elkin declared that he too would go north, Sarazin's ego knew no limits. He must really be something to have won the loyalty of two such men.

However, Sarazin never thought to tell Jarl that Elkin was to accompany them to Selzirk. Elkin already knew all about Jarl, but Jarl had to find out about Elkin the hard way.

Jarl and Elkin first men in the gravel-strewn Great Square where horses were being readied for their departure from Voice.

'Who are you?' said the bulky-bearded Rovac warrior, his manner as blunt as his sword was sharp. Mark that he wore that sword in public in open defiance of the law.

'My name,' said the old scholar, whose beard was as grey as Jarl's but wisp-frail in comparison, 'is Epelthin Elkin. Sarazin's tutor.'

'You'll find him fair lettered already,' said Jarl. 'An old

13

servitor has learnt him his books, while I've taught him the more important things myself. Where is the rest of Selzirk's embassy?'

'You mistake my identity,' said old man Elkin.

His arms were folded, hands warm-muffed by the voluminous sleeves of a gorgeous green and purple robe which fell almost to his open-weave sandals.

'If you're not a tutor,' said Jarl, standing arms akimbo, feet shoulder-wide, 'what are you? A pox doctor? In that case—'

Abruptly, Jarl broke off, slapped a horse fly, then swore at slaves seen overloading baggage animals. Then went to kick arse, boot-crunching across the gravel as if he had twelve leagues or more to cover by sunset. Slaves fell to their knees in fear.

'Sir,' said the slavemaster, intervening on behalf of his charges. 'It's not their fault. We don't have enough pack horses.'

'What's this rubbish, then?' said Jarl, kicking at a heap of goatskin travel bags.

'Those belong to Sarazin's tutor, the old man Elkin.'

'By the knives!' exclaimed Jarl. 'Why so much baggage? He should have left this rubbish in Selzirk. Anyway — it came with the embassy, it can go back with the embassy.'

'Sir—'

'Don't answer back!' shouted Jarl, murder-voiced.

The slavemaster quailed. Jarl kicked the goatskins again. Hard. Then, as a new shade joined the shadow-conference on the ground, turned to find himself facing Epelthin Elkin.

'I would be pleased,' said Elkin, in sour displeasure, 'if you would be gentle with those bags. Within lie codicological treasures of antiquity considerable and value greater.'

'Which you should have left in Selzirk,' said Jarl.

'As I meant to say before anger distracted you,' said Elkin, 'I am not from Selzirk but from Voice. I have tutored Sarazin through all the years he has spent here as hostage.'

'We have never met,' said Jarl.

14

'And the sky is blue,' retorted Elkin, by way of insult.

They glared at each other. Dislike at first sight! Jarl thought to speak his mind — but several slaves were in earshot. To natives of Voice, slaves were invisible unless misbehaving. Jarl, worrying lest they overhear, thus proved himself an alien.

'Come!' he said, striding away to the shade trees flourishing green at the edge of the Great Square.

Thodric Jarl was forty-four. Elkin, though much, much older, matched his pace. Once under the trees Jarl looked up and around, then, satisfied as to privacy, turned on Elkin.

'Know this, old man,' said Jarl. 'I go north at Lord Regan's hest.' That was all he could safely say of his commission from Lord Regan, who had actually recruited him as a spy. 'Understand? You interfere with me, you could be dead by sunset.'

'I, too,' said Elkin heavily, 'am commanded by Lord Regan.'

'What?' said Jarl, taken aback. 'You? What use is a dodderer like you?'

This was unfair. Though ancient, Elkin was scarcely infirm. Grey-headed, yes (his hair pulled back and plaited into a single pigtail hanging almost to his waist) but upright. His mahogany skin walnut wrinkled, yet his bloodshot blue eyes sharp still — 'a knife to undress a virgin' as the local bawdry had it.

'Well?' said Jarl, no reply being forthcoming from Epelthin Elkin. 'Tell! What wants Lord Regan from you?'

'Allow me to think. Perchance the library of memory holds words rude enough to match the discourtesy of a Rovac warrior.'

'Etiquette cannot breed horses,' said Jarl. 'We've few mounts and many leagues to cover, so you must ditch your rubbish.'

'You organised the horses!' said Elkin. 'A sorry hash you've made of the job. I made my requirements known long in advance. If there aren't enough horses—'

15

'I organised nothing! But nevertheless must straighten out our problems. You, for instance.'

The argument threatened to get out of hand, for both Jarl and Elkin were capable of displays of the most monstrous bad temper. But before they could provoke each other further, four leather-clad horsemen cantered into the Great Square.

'It must be the embassy,' said Jarl, for only foreigners like himself would wear iron-studded battle leathers in the Rice Empire, where the hides of brute beasts were thought unclean, and wearing such verged on obscenity.

Indeed, this was Selzirk's embassy: Sarazin's brothers Celadon, Peguero, and Jarnel, plus a prince of Chenameg named Lod. But, being crass young men with no sense of etiquette, they did not introduce themselves when Jarl and Elkin approached. Instead:

'Ho!' said Lod, in Galish. 'Where's this Sarazin?'

'Never mind that,' said Jarl, his own Galish equally shy of protocol. 'Have you a pack horse spare?'

'Soldiers and baggage beasts await on the outskirts of town,' said Celadon. 'But, before I say more — name yourself, old man.'

Celadon, then aged twenty, was looking directly at Jarl, who, from the majesty of his forty-four years, replied:

'Maturity is always old age to a young fool. But don't talk of me as an ancient, boy, or I'll bruise your arse with the flat of my blade.'

'The hair dates the man,' said Celadon, with affected carelessness.

'Thus I was born,' said Jarl. 'Like the grey of my eyes it is common enough on Rovac, which is where I hail from. Would'st like to test age and honour at swordpoint?'

'Not with a nameless stranger,' said Celadon. 'I myself am Celadon, son of Farfalla, who is kingmaker of the Harvest Plains.'

'Know that I am Thodric Jarl, son of Oric Slaughter-house, blood of the clan of the bear,' said Jarl, sword-blood grim.

16

'Clan of the bear?' said Lod, laughing. 'A bad-tempered bear, I warrant. Yet should we be the dogs to bait it? Pray, friends, are we not diplomats? 'Twould be rash to bloody the streets of Voice. And tragic to boot should some of the blood be our own!'

While Celadon and Jarl both had sword-sharp tempers, neither wanted combat. Celadon had been warned by his mother not to rape, maim or kill in Voice, and Jarl was hesitant to imperil his mission to Selzirk. Thus both apologised, albeit grudgingly. Then Lod again asked after Sarazin.

'He'll be here soon,' said Jarl.

Wrong! For Sarazin was delayed saying goodbye to Jaluba, she of the pink lips and the bedroom eyes, she who was but sixteen years of age. In the interests of decency, the less which is said of their long goodbye the better.

CHAPTER TWO

Name: Sean Kelebes Sarazin (who will one day win himself the name Watashi). To his mother (in dreams and letters, for they have been parted for years) he is Sarazin Sky.
Mother: Farfalla, kingmaker of the Harvest Plains.
Father: Fox, a farrier of Selzirk.
Brothers: Celadon, Peguero and Jarnel (all Farfalla's children); Benthorn (a half-brother sired by Fox on the washerwoman Bizzie).

When Sean Sarazin finally condescended to appear, Jarl berated him for wearing silks instead of battle-leathers, and for coming to the Great Square unarmed.

'Swords,' said Sarazin, in a cool, supercilious voice, 'are banned from the streets of Voice.'

17

'I am armed!' said Jarl. 'So are your brothers.'

'These sworders?' said Sarazin, eyeing the four leather-clad strangers with disfavour. 'My brothers? Which are you?'

'I am Lod of Chenameg, sib of Chenameg's heir, Prince Tarkal,' answered the youth Sarazin had addressed. 'This is—'

'Introductions later. First, let's get you dressed!'

Jarl's command lacked legal force, but Sarazin, unable to resist his authority, was soon leather-clad and armed with the worth-rich blade of firelight steel given to him earlier that year by the Rice Empire's Lord Regan. Meanwhile, Lod had fetched one of the embassy's spare baggage animals.

'Good!' said Jarl, on Lod's return. 'Well, load up, mount up and let's be off. I'm sick of pissing around.'

'We did have formal greetings from Farfalla to Lord Regan,' said Celadon. 'After days on the road we did hope, indeed, to sleep tonight in proper beds.'

'Well, you're shit out of luck,' said Jarl. 'Lord Regan quit Voice days ago. Business in the capital demanded his presence. But he left me orders to ride for Selzirk immediately you arrived.'

'Surely Sarazin has friends who want to see him off,' said Lod. 'Shouldn't we at least await their arrival?'

'Oh, I farewelled my friends yesterday,' said Sarazin carelessly.

And, all lobbying for delay having failed, they left the fair city of Voice forthwith — with Sarazin downcast, for Lod had chanced on a sore point. Though legally a hostage, Sarazin had ever been Lord Regan's pet, and hence popular always. But exile to Selzirk must inevitably end his influence with Lord Regan — so he had lately found himself unfriended. Except by Jaluba.

Ah, the luscious Jaluba, mistress of the thousand voluptuous perfumes, queen of the lubricous arts . . .

Sarazin left Voice with her taste on his lips, her murmuring passion still hot in memory. He regretted this

18

(surely permanent) parting, but told himself that, while Jaluba was fun, he was growing too old for idle fancies of the flesh.

—*My career, that's the thing.*

For a full season he had indulged himself with dreams of ambition fulfilled. Now he planned — oh giddy thought! — eventually to make himself master of the Harvest Plains. His next woman would therefore have to be a princess of the Favoured Blood. He deserved — and needed — no less. But . . . would she love him as Jaluba did?

Of course! How could any princess resist him? He was so elegant, intelligent, poised, talented and cultivated. A man of discretion, wise in the ways of the world — and a doughty warrior to boot.

Sarazin assessed his virtues thus as he rode in the front of the expedition where horsedust was minimal. He had taken the prime position as of right, for he planned to live by Lord Regan's doctrine:

'They deserve the best who take it.'

There Jarl found him, and remonstrated with him, saying:

'Why were you late? I told you to be ready to move at dawn.'

'At sunrise,' said Sarazin, a dreamy smile on his lips, 'I was warm in Jaluba's arms.'

'That whore!' said Jarl.

'The most recent of my duelling scars,' said Sarazin, frowning, 'was acquired when—'

'I know, I know!' said Jarl impatiently. 'Some fool of a brag called Jaluba a whore so you took to your sword for her honour. Very well! But mark this — once you've left the Rice Empire you'll find men don't play such games of cuts.'

'An affair of swords is never a game,' protested Sarazin.

'Come!' said Jarl. 'I saw you salt that little nick to make a better scar. Believe me, where we're going you'll get no scratches needing such enlargement. For duels in Selzirk are to the death.'

19

'Who says?' said Sarazin.

'Celadon. Your brother. We've talked already, while you rode dreaming of a bitch of a girl with cream in her cunt and perfume drenched from neck to arsehole.'

'You wrong her,' said Sarazin angrily, feeling that Jarl demeaned him by speaking so crudely of the flesh with which he had pleasured. 'She is but sixteen, yet her soul is as subtle as her body is supple.'

'Not any old whore, then, but a desirable whore. But none the better for that! And you a fool to waste money on appetite.'

'You wanted her yourself,' said Sarazin, stung. 'You begged for her favours. She told me! But she found you unworthy.'

'Ah!' said Jarl, unruffled by this revelation. 'I bet the bitch giggled when she said it. Then bit you for passion with her sharp little teeth. So you thought her in love with you, then emptied your purse on account of it.'

'A woman cannot live on air, any more than a horse.'

'Right! Neither can I. Hence fled from her prices extortionate. After all, meat is meat, and liver goes cheap at the shambles.'

'You're gross,' said Sarazin, disgusted.

'True,' said Jarl. 'Cruel, coarse, gross and violent, steeped in the evil of the world, a master of murder, a lord of deceit. I've had five kinds of pox, the cures of which near killed me. Have you? I know the stench of a battlefield twenty days after defeat. Do you? I know—'

'Yes, yes,' said Sarazin. 'You know the colour of every sunset for the last ten thousand years. I thought Elkin the elder, but find myself mistaken. Well then, speak, dear Master of the Depths of Ancient Wisdoms. Speak! I'm all ears.'

'No,' said Jarl, 'you're all cock, for such is the condition of your age. Very well. In Selzirk find yourself a gash then shaft it. But know what you pay for. You can buy flesh, but you can never buy love.'

'I know, I know.'

So spoke Sarazin, not daring to dispute the world's ruling wisdom. Yet secretly he felt Jaluba truly loved him. After all, she had never asked him directly for money. Delayed payments would see her chiding her little dog for appetites which would eat them into ruin. But she had never soiled their love by bartering herself frankly for cash.

'Right, then!' said Jarl. 'Don't let whores bankrupt you. Watch your gambling, too. I know Lord Regan has covered your debts in the past, though he cursed you for a fool at the time. In Selzirk you'll not meet with such indulgence from your mother.'

'I am her eldest son,' said Sarazin.

'Maybe. But she has the reputation of being the hardest woman in all of Argan. Which is only to be expected, for a woman must be twice as tough as a man to win half the respect.'

'You say.'

'I know! Just as I know you've every chance of ending up face down dead in the Velvet River. In Voice, privilege has protected you from life's harder lessons. You'll have no such protection in Selzirk. So remember: don't drink with strangers, don't gamble with strangers, don't—'

'When is this lecture going to finish?' demanded Sarazin.

'When I'm satisfied you can walk the streets of Selzirk for a day and a night without losing your head,' retorted Jarl.

He was not satisfied for quite some time.

Jarl, frustrated by the slow-paced baggage-animals, refused to allow a halt for lunch. Nobody was game enough to challenge him. With lectures finished, he grilled the foreigners about life in Selzirk, and it was long before Celadon was free to satisfy his own curiosity about Sarazin, who was weary and saddle-sore, unused to riding so far without a break.

To his surprise, Celadon found his kinsman had great difficulty speaking their native Churl. They therefore conversed in the Galish Trading Tongue.

'You're glad to be free again, doubtless,' said Celadon.

'I suppose I am,' said Sarazin cautiously.

A career as a royal hostage was the only life Sarazin knew. He had enjoyed it. After all, he had always had good food, fine clothes, ready cash and comfort; his wit had won applause at parties; he had hunted, hawked, trained with the sword, visited the theatre, slept with courtesans, flirted with girlfriends and dabbled in scholarship.

He had lived, then, as a man of good breeding should. From the warnings Jarl had given him, he suspected life in Selzirk was going to be a shock to the system. But, he thought, forewarned is forearmed. Then realised Celadon was talking to him.

'. . . which might be fun.'

'What might be?' said Sarazin.

'Weren't you listening?' said Celadon.

'Brother,' said Sarazin, 'your speech is so fair it warrants a second hearing.'

Such graciousness would have won him instant pardon amongst the sophisticates of Voice. But Celadon spat, then muttered something uncomplimentary in incomprehensible Churl. They were not getting off to a good start.

'I was talking,' said Celadon, as Peguero and Jarnel rode up alongside them, 'of the pleasures open to free men. It can't have been pleasant living as a prisoner.'

'It's been a tolerable life,' said Sarazin, diplomat enough not to confess that he wished himself a captive still. 'I've had my studies, my sword-work, my poetry.'

'Poetry?' said Celadon. 'Dry stuff, dry stuff! The soldiering life, that's the thing!'

'You speak of war?' said Sarazin.

'Oh, a little hand-to-hand is fun on occasion,' said Celadon. 'But a little's enough for a lifetime, thank you very much. It's the career which matters.'

In fantasy, Sarazin had oft imagined winning glory with his sword. Leading armies into battle. Raising his standard on fields of victory. If he was fated to war, he was sure he would love it. And would do brilliantly. But to be a

22

professional soldier in peacetime? That, surely, was a dull, narrow life.

'Pray tell the merits of this . . . this career,' said Sarazin.

'Comradeship,' said Celadon, without a moment's hesitation.

'He means,' said Jarnel, forgetting, in his enthusiasm, to speak Galish, 'we get together every night and get pissed as newts.'

'Pissed?' said Sarazin, struggling to make sense of Jarnel's Churl. 'Newts?'

All three of his brothers laughed.

'Drunk,' said Peguero. 'He means we get drunk.'

'Oh,' said Sarazin. 'I've been drunk once or twice myself.'

'Well, when you join us in the army, you can get drunk every night of the year,' said Celadon.

'Why should I want to do that?' said Sarazin.

It was an honest question which sought a straight-forward answer. But his brothers merely laughed.

'We'll take you to the recruiter as soon as we hit Selzirk,' said Peguero. 'You'll be bedded down in the cavalry barracks that very same night.'

Sarazin hoped Peguero was joking. If by chance he spoke in earnest, then he was out of luck, for Sarazin had no desire whatsoever to join the army, having decided that what interested him was the governance of the Harvest Plains.

Hé was Farfalla's son, and Farfalla was the kingmaker, therefore — why should he not aspire?

Thus Sean Kelebes Sarazin met his brothers, departed from the cool and shady city of Voice (city of the thousand wines, the seven shades of laughter) and descended to the lowlands. Though it was but early summer, it proved uncommonly hot. The days were ruled by heat, dust and horseflies, while whining mosquitoes tormented fever-dreams by night.

23

On the dusty coastal plain, they picked up the Salt Road and thereafter followed it north. They met Galish kafilas, and, for the first time he could remember, Sarazin saw (and smelt) camels. To his surprise, they did not walk like horses, but instead moved both the legs on one flank simultaneously.

'Mammoths walk likewise,' said Jarl.

'Mammoths?'

'Beasts of the Cold West, like the elephants of Yestron, only with shaggy fur and greater tusks.'

'Oh,' said Sarazin, all eloquence lost to him.

In that time of bewilderment he saw and heard of many people, things and places all totally new to him. One such wonder was the blood-red battlements of Veda, ancient city of the sages. Epelthin Elkin spoke of miraculous artworks housed within — masterpieces by artists such as Aromsky, Keremansky and X-nox the Dissident.

'Did you train within the walls of Veda, then?' said Jarl, curious about the old scholar's provenance.

'My training began at my mother's knee,' said Elkin. 'She taught me certain basics of politeness entirely unknown to the Rovac.'

'I said nothing impolite!' said Jarl. 'Not this time, anyway. Are you ashamed of your breeding?'

'If you must know,' said Elkin. 'I was born a bastard on Burntos. My mother was a kitchen wench. I was fathered, I suppose, by a soldier of the Landguard. I was but five when my mother moved to Narba, where I was raised as a scholar.'

'Your mother a skivvy, yet indulged you in scholarship?' said Jarl.

'There's money in such in Narba,' said Elkin. 'The scholars are scribes, accountants and translators for traders dealing with peoples as various as Orfus pirates and the master of Hexagon.'

Then, while Veda's walls slowly receded into the distance, Elkin bored them at length with details of his doings in Narba.

As the free city of Veda lay by the shores of the Central Ocean on the border between the Rice Empire and the Harvest Plains, Sarazin was shortly in the motherland he had left at the age of four. It was low, dull, monotonous countryside, patchworked with fields worked by peasants from adobe villages.

In Voice, in the foothills of the Ashun Mountains, Sarazin had ever had the heights in view. He missed them. He was depressed and oppressed by the flatness, heat, dust and fatigue of their travels, by the nagging friction between Jarl and Elkin, by his brothers' inane booze-talk and clumsy bawdry. He longed for cool water, mountain breezes, a plane tree's shade and the prospect of an evening of intelligent conversation and sophisticated dalliance.

But dusk daily brought him the company of Thodric Jarl, who harassed him with questions.

'How many leagues have we come today? How many watering holes did we pass? That Galish kafila going south — was it battle-ready? What was its fighting strength? How many men could you quarter in this village? How many could this village feed? For how long?'

Nightly, Sarazin dreamt of dust, camels and muddy water holes; he woke every morning to regret the ever-increasing distance between himself and Voice.

—*Ah, Jaluba! Will I ever see you again?*

CHAPTER THREE

It is 4324 years since wizards and heroes made their famous Alliance. In this time the continent Argan has seen:

1. The Long War, ending in the year 269 when the Alliance finally drove the monsters of the Swarms from Argan North;

2. The building of the castle-guarded flame trench Drangsturm to protect Argan North against the Swarms;
3. The Short War, ending in 374 when wizards defeated heroes and set themselves up as rulers of all of Argan North;
4. The protracted power struggle which destroyed the Empire of Wizards, allowing smaller nations to arise in Argan.

As they neared Selzirk, regrets gave way to excitement. Soon Sarazin would be in the city where, after dreaming about it for years, he would have at last a chance of real power. Powerful foes would oppose his rise to the rule of the Harvest Plains, but at least he was guaranteed support from his mother. For surely Farfalla would approve his ambition once she learnt of it. Surely she would not want power to die out of the family with her death.

Surely not.

By the time they reached the confluence of the Velvet River and the Shouda Flow, some seven days after passing Veda's bloodwalls, Sarazin was all eagerness. Just across the river lay the walls and towers of Selzirk the Fair, capital of the Harvest Plains, sovereign city of Argan's most powerful nation.

Improvising a rite of homecoming, Sarazin dismounted, walked to the river's edge — sun-cracked mud crunkling beneath his feet — knelt, cupped water in his hands, then drank of the mud-flavoured fluid. Closed his eyes. Let hot sun beat upon his eyelids. Committed the moment to memory. Straightened up. Stood. Saw a corpse leisuring downstream, a gash-beak black crow as banquet-class passenger. And laughed with sudden joy, feeling his youth, his strength, his life.

Again he scanned the riverdistant city, seeking landmarks. In the eastern (upriver) quarter rose an ancient wizard castle, now Farfalla's palace. Nine towers it had.

Those of the eight orders of wizards were sealed against trespass by magic, but the gatehouse keep, an extraordinary tower soaring seventy storeys skywards, was at Farfalla's disposal. He could also see the High Court, a modern building (a mere three hundred years old) rising clear of the palace battlements (which were, if he remembered his lessons correctly, some four storeys high).

Sarazin smiled, then walked back to his horse. Then noticed his brothers staring at him. But it was Lod of Chenameg who spoke.

'It was nice knowing you, Sarazin my friend, but I fear I'll know you no longer. To drink from the Velvet River means certain death by nightfall.'

'Gah!' said Sarazin, in a rare display of perfect idiomatic Churl.

But his brothers chaffed him about his recklessness until it was time to board the slave-powered ferry for the trip north to the city of his destiny. Once aboard, Sarazin did not sit. It was too crowded, there were no seats — and his buttocks were raw from the saddle. Padded with greasy raw wool he had managed to ride — but only just.

Lod continued to josh him about drinking riverwater. Had he really made a bad mistake? He thought to ask Jarl about it — but Jarl had vanished. Sarazin, desolated, feared him gone for good. Thus it happens in legend. The old swordmaster trains the youth who is fated to dare all on a perilous quest for power or treasure. Then the master dies, retires or vanishes, leaving youth to battle unaided against the evil wizard, the red dragon, the pit of claws, the halfelven enemy or whatever it is.

Momentarily, Sarazin was half-convinced he had indeed embarked on a life of legend. After all, he had always known he was meant for great things. But, as he realised in a moment of utter panic, he was far from ready to dare such a destiny unaided.

Thodric Jarl, hemmed in by horses, heaped baggage and

a rabble of peasants, dourly pondered Sarazin's chances. Jarl's good advice, thrice repeated, might save him from a few of early manhood's egregious errors. But Selzirk's politics would probably prove lethal.

While Sarazin lived, Jarl had an easy living. He would draw a spy's pay from the Rice Empire, and might win some position in Selzirk itself. But when the boy died? He'd manage, but . . . he was getting too old for new cities, new languages, new beginnings. At age forty-five — yesterday had been his birthday, and, while he had mentioned it to nobody, he was keeping count — he wanted to settle down. He had seen all, had done all, and had been everywhere. Long ago.

—Voice was good. The same again would be more than enough.

Yes. A quiet life, a steady routine and good pay. The soft years in Voice had been the best of his life. He had been furious when Lord Regan had ordered him north with Sarazin.

—When Sarazin dies, what then? Rovac, maybe?

No. Though Jarl oft toyed with notions of returning home to Rovac, far west in the Central Ocean's wastelands, he knew such thoughts were idle. In youth, he had made eighty-nine death-feud enemies amongst the Rovac, for his temper had been formidable even by the standards of those formidable mercenary killers. Plus he had known, all too well, how to hold a grudge.

Some of those enemies would doubtless be dead by now; others, like the accursed oathbreaker Rolf Thelemite, would never dare show themselves in Rovac. But enough would remain. If Jarl went home, it would be killing for certain. Worse, amongst those who would go against him with sword, there would be some he longed to count as friends.

—We quarrelled over nothing when we were young. But then, that is youth, isn't it? And I had no mentor to teach me better. I had to learn everything the hard way.

Nearby, Elkin was complaining. His foot had been trodden on.

'Why don't you get some boots?' said Jarl.

'Because,' said Elkin, who had worn open-weave sandals throughout their journey, 'I hate the smell of dirty socks.'

What was Elkin's mission in Selzirk? Had he truly come north at Lord Regan's command? If so, did the Rice Empire's ruler want him as just one more spy in the city? Or as what? Who would know? Not Sarazin, that was for certain. He knew nothing — not even that Jarl was coming north as a spy.

—*My lord perhaps plays a deep and subtle game. But what game? Logic may tell, for I know power by face and backside both. Perhaps Lord Regan reserves the truth to test my powers of divination. Mayhap the mystery is a test.*

'You'll love Selzirk,' said Lod. 'Why, its very brothels are grander than my father's palace in Shin.'

'Shin?' said Sarazin.

'Chenameg's capital,' said Lod, with amusement. 'Have you not studied the world? I thought this Elkin lettered you.'

'Many years have we spent in scholarship,' said Sarazin. 'We have studied languages, philosophy, botany and poetry.'

'Ah,' said Lod, 'but now you are out and about in the world, you must learn your geography.'

And he launched into an impromptu disquisition on the Chenameg Kingdom. This Sarazin ignored, having found Lod to be a fanciful fellow, given to extravagant embroidery of any truth unfortunate enough to fall to his possession.

'Here we are,' said Lod, as the ferry came alongside one of the wharves of Jone, the dockside quarter. 'What are you staring at?'

'There's a hole in the wall!' said Sarazin, outraged.

True enough. A section a hundred paces long was missing from Ol Ilkeen, the outer battle-wall of Selzirk.

'That is no hole,' said Lod. 'That is but the river gate. In time of war the gate wardens will close it with heaps of horseshit and such.'

'This is scandalous!' said Sarazin.

'A military obscenity, perhaps,' agreed Lod, 'but this is no time to be prudish. You've other things to think of. Soon you'll see your mother. Your brother Benthorn, too. How long since you saw him last?'

'Pardon?' said Sarazin.

'Benthorn,' said Lod. 'When did you see him last?'

How embarrassing! Were Chenameg's sons entirely ignorant of etiquette? Knowledge of Benthorn had reached Sarazin even in Voice; he knew well enough the fellow was a hunchbacked moron who worked on a dung cart and was reputed to be both an atheist and a child molester.

'Aren't three brothers enough?' said Sarazin, hinting to Lod that he should drop the subject.

'Do you jest?' said Lod. 'Or do you mean to disown Benthorn?'

'Oh, him,' said Sarazin, seeing Lod was not to be deterred. 'He's but a half-brother. In any case, how can I own or disown him when I know nothing of him? I was but four when I was taken from my mother's arms to be exiled as a hostage.'

'Then I'll tell you what I know of him,' said Lod.

But Sarazin was spared this further embarrassment, for the loading ramps of the ferry were in place, and conversation became impossible in the chaotic imbroglio as travellers, peasants, soldiers, horses, dogs, pigs, chickens and baggage were disembarked.

Sarazin was scarcely off the ferry when he was separated from his brothers, his horse, his tutors. His brothers could fend for themselves — but his steed?

'My horse!' he cried. 'It's gone!'

'Relax,' said Lod. 'Celadon's got your horse. Let him worry it to the palace. We'll be there on foot before him. Come — the press will ease once we're clear of the wharves. But guard your purse!'

'My purse? Ah — that's gone already! No matter. It held but a bent bronze triner.'

True: the last of Sarazin's cash had been spent in Voice

buying favours from Jaluba, she of the passionate lips, the gauze-veiled (and sometimes unveiled) breasts.

Already Lod was hustling Sarazin onward. Despite Lod's predictions, the crush grew no less once they cleared the wharves. Sarazin was shocked by the heat, stench and crowds of the city in summer, by the ill-mannered jostling, the hawkers bawling in Churl, the inordinate amount of dung on the streets.

'Tell me,' said he, pressing himself against a wall as three dozen muck-stained heifers shouldered past with a clatter of hooves, 'is there no law against herding cattle through Selzirk?'

'There are laws against all dung-dropping animals,' said Lod, 'not discounting our noble servant the horse. But none such can be enforced, for our rulers fear the wrath of those who love dogs. Those irrationals would rise in rage, if not in revolution — and who could tell where that would end?'

Sarazin thought this nonsense, but had already learnt not to expect logic from Lod.

'Are there laws against trees, too? And outdoor cafés? I see none such, though this is surely the weather for dining alfresco.'

'Trees?' said Lod, highly amused. 'Trees would go for firewood. As for tables and chairs! Outside? In daylight? They'd not last a morning. Taverns and theatres alike have bouncers at the door, not just to keep people out but to keep their furniture in. Come, friend Sarazin. Onward!'

Soon they shouldered into the intolerable crush at Kesh, a gate-tower chokepoint at the junction of the Four Worlds of Selzirk. Here people poured into a courtyard from gates opening to the quarters of Jone, Santrim, Unkrana and Wake. Locked in by sweat and shoulders, Sarazin felt his feet leave the ground.

'Lod?' he said. Then shouted: 'Lod? Lod, where are you?'

The crowd convulsed, squeezing his ribs. He was being choked. Crushed. Cracked like a dove's egg in a black-smith's vice. Jarl had warned him of a thousand things. But never of this. He was going to die, strength helpless,

31

weapons useless. He tried to scream, but could not. And he would not have been heard in the uproar.

Then the crunch-crush crowd collapsed, broke up, eased out. He gained, gasping, the freedom to breathe. His feet touched the ground, he saw daylight, he blundered towards it. Then was pushed, shouldered, buffeted, sent staggering by the on-bustling crowd. Stepped in something soft which sklished beneath his boot. His dung-greased boots slipped, slid, almost sent him sprawling.

He won his balance. And gained, at last, the freedom of a quiet sidestreet where he could breathe in peace. There was bright blood splashed on his swordhand's thumb-knuckle where skin had been backpeeled by collision. He put it to his lips. Kissed the red stuff. Sucked, and was comforted.

'Sarazin!' said Lod, slapping him on the back. 'I thought I'd lost you. Welcome to Santrim. You know the city's layout? Your mother's palace is—'

'I know all about that,' said Sarazin, cutting him off. 'Give me credit for something, at least.'

'I do, I do,' said Lod, with a careless wave of his hand. 'For being the consort of clouds, the friend of dragons, the—'

'Give it a rest!' said Sarazin, who was tired, disorientated, and fed up with the low-grade verbal pyrotechnics which Lod thought of as wit. Lod took no offence. He had already spotted his next source of excitement.

'Look,' he said. 'There's a dung cart.'

'We do have dung carts in Voice, you know,' said Sarazin. 'Even though dogs, pigs, sheep and oxen are banned from the streets of that city.'

Nevertheless, Lod danced up alongside the horse-drawn dung cart to chat to the fellow who followed it, pitchfork in hand.

'Sarazin!' cried Lod. 'Come here!'

'Why?'

32

'I want you to meet someone,' said Lod, grinning.

Sarazin feared this must be his half-brother Benthorn. Very shortly, as they were introduced, Sarazin realised he was right.

'Pleased to meet you,' said Sarazin, clenching his right fist: not to kill but to greet.

This ancient rite, though still practised in Voice, had near fallen out of memory in Selzirk. But Benthorn had studied both past and present upper-class mores in detail, for he had an intense interest in power. So the brothers, to Lod's evident amusement, touched fists in the old manner. As skin grazed skin, Sarazin visioned his father Fox sweating over the woman Bizzie, shaft sunk to the hilt in her gash, his breathing harsh, summer's sweat beaded on his brow. The reek of an overloaded chamber pot hot around them.

—*That happened.*

When Sarazin had been eight months in the womb, something like that had definitely happened, causing the first rupture between Farfalla and Fox. While those two had gone on to produce another three sons, the breach between them had never been entirely mended: and they were now estranged.

How had Bizzie gained her hold over Fox? Sarazin had no idea. But here was evidence of their liaison: passion's most unromantic child, the dung-smelling Benthorn with his fat, sweaty face. Sarazin tried to get his measure, but found himself struggling just to understand his Churl. Realising this, Benthorn took the lead and switched to Galish. It made no difference. Sarazin — tired, dizzy, faint — was incapable of character analysis.

While Lod had rightly guessed that Sarazin was shamed by Benthorn's very existence, Sarazin was too well-bred to display his distaste for his half-brother and his work, the pestering flies, the heavy smell of high-heaped dung. He even commiserated with Benthorn when he learnt of the heavy taxes levied upon dung carts.

'A foolish policy,' said Sarazin, 'when the city streets are knee-deep in excrement. I will talk to my mother about it.'

'Farfalla would doubtless order change if she could,' said Benthorn, 'even though all levies on dung carts are hers by law. But change in this case is impossible.'

'Why so?' said Sarazin.

And was taken aback when Benthorn responded by shouting:

'Get away, you!'

But Sarazin's half-brother was merely scaring off some street urchins who were raiding his dung cart for ammunition for gang warfare. Benthorn went on to explain:

'Brother mine, the dung cart tax is enshrined in the Constitution. Before then, anyone with a mule and a pair of wheels could afford to enter the manure business. Carts in hundreds crowded the city. Their owners formed factions which warred with each other. The Framers thought high taxes might diminish a menace which threatened the very foundation of law and order.'

'But the Constitution was written thousands of years ago,' protested Sarazin. 'Times have changed.'

'Yet the Constitution itself can never change,' said Benthorn, 'for it is the foundation of our world. To talk otherwise is treason.'

'And to think otherwise?' said Sarazin. 'Is that treason?'

'That,' said Benthorn, 'is a subject worthy of discussion.'

'But not now,' said Lod, who had lost interest in the conversation since the half-brothers had failed to amuse him by baiting each other. 'Come, let's be going. Sarazin has urgent business at the palace.'

'I'll see you around, then,' said Benthorn, lapsing into Churl.

'What?' said Sarazin.

'He means,' said Lod, in Galish, 'that you'll meet again.'

'I'm sure we will,' said Sarazin.

At least Benthorn was not — contrary to rumour! — a kyphotic imbecile. Maybe he was even innocent of child molesting. Still, Sarazin never wanted to see him again. Right now, he wanted to meet the mother he had not seen since the age of four. The kingmaker. A Power in the land:

consecrated in sacred ceremony as one of the Favoured Blood, and therefore fit to rule.

As Argan's peoples knew well, Argan's nations must forever be ruled by nobles of aristocratic lineage. Only those of the Favoured Blood could preserve the world from revolution, anarchy, war absolute, or, worse still, democracy (a bizarre political perversion practised by the Orfus pirates of the Greater Teeth). Sarazin, as the son of such a noble, thought power should come to him as of right.

CHAPTER FOUR

Kingmaker: one selected for life by Regency bureaucrats to appoint regional governors ('kings'). The kingmaker derives great power from the Constitution — power only the Regency's unanimous vote can restrict. Such a vote came early in Farfalla's reign, leaving her as little more than a figurehead.

Sarazin's letters had oft betrayed aristocratic pretensions suggestive of treasonable political ambition. Farfalla, shuddering to imagine her first-begotten's fate if the Regency learnt of this, was dismayed to hear that Sarazin, intercepted at her palace gates by Plovey of the Regency, was coming to their reunion accompanied by that formidable bureaucrat.

'Tell Plovey I wish to see my son alone,' said Farfalla.

Her servants went. Told. And returned to say Plovey would have none of it.

'Delay them, then!' said Farfalla. 'On any excuse, delay!'

A delay was contrived until Jarl, Elkin and Sarazin's brothers had arrived. By then, Farfalla had packed her throne room with guards and servants, hoping this crowd of strangers would inhibit Sarazin, making him wary of speaking his mind.

—*Gods! If he says too much to Plovey, he's dead.*

Fortunately Sarazin — weary, footsore, and tired of grappling with the complexities of Churl — had rebuffed that keen-minded bureaucrat's diligent efforts to initiate a conversation. And, once brought into Farfalla's presence, Sarazin behaved as noblesse oblige compelled him to: after exchanging formal greetings with his mother, he pleaded his case of his loyal retainers.

'My lady,' said he, in Churl only fluent because this was a much-rehearsed speech, 'these are my tutors, constant companions of my captivity in Voice. This is Thodric Jarl, a Rovac warrior: my swordmaster.'

'What mention is made of me?' said Jarl in curt, loud-voiced Galish.

'Do you speak no Churl?' said Farfalla, in a Galish as good as his own.

'None,' said Jarl, 'for till six days ago I had never set foot in the Harvest Plains.'

'Then my translator will render all which has gone before into a tongue you can understand,' said Farfalla. 'Also, he will translate what is spoken hereafter.'

Jarl gave a low-sweeping courtly bow mastered years before in the city of Chi'ash-lan in the Cold West. As the translator set to work, Farfalla noted a tight smile on Plovey's lips.

What did that smile mean? Fear? Quite possibly. And if Plovey feared friendship between a Rovac warleader and the kingmaker of the Harvest Plains he might act to end it. So Farfalla had best keep her distance from Jarl, lest her friendship prove his destruction. Only fools, slaves and criminals could safely befriend the kingmaker.

Belatedly, she realised Sarazin had resumed his speech:

'. . . is Epelthin Elkin, a scholar, who has tutored me most marvellously in the ways of words.'

Sarazin was praising Elkin at length. And Jarl? Lemons

36

without sugar! The Rovac warrior had no love for the scholar. And Plovey? Fidgeting. Bored by Sarazin's rhetoric. Hands furtively scabbing at an itch at his crotch. Then eyes . . . shifting to Jarl.

Yes, Jarl worried him. The Regency feared assassins by night, riot by day. Coup, revolution, civil war. Thus any blade in Farfalla's fee was a threat. But a scholar . . . ? No. So it was safe to grant Elkin whatever was in her boon. Giving much to Elkin and little to Jarl would widen the gap between those two.

—But that's not my problem. I want Jarl left alive. I might have use of him in future.

Sarazin was concluding.

'. . . therefore ask you to grant what you can to these two who have been so loyal for so long with so little reward.'

Farfalla was decided, yet forced herself to make a show of hesitation. The less that Plovey saw of her ability the better. While she was thinking thus, Plovey caught her eye. Both, embarrassed, looked away. And Farfalla thought:

—He's not fooled for a moment. He knows just how good I am!

He must. Unless there was a fool behind his facade of razor-sharp intelligence and unlimited efficiency. As they customarily did business 'a step away from each other's steel', as the saying had it, she found it difficult to truly gauge his calibre.

Sarazin, disconcerted by Farfalla's evident indecision, cleared his throat, as if to speak. But she held up her hand for silence, then delivered her judgment.

'The scholar Epelthin Elkin is welcome in the city of Selzirk the Fair. I, as kingmaker, chosen from the common people by the Regency, ruling in accordance with the Constitution, welcome him.'

Thus Farfalla reminded her son of things he surely knew already: unless ambition had led him to discount what he had been taught. She continued:

'Certain appointments lie within the gift of the See of

37

the Sun. One such is the position of Archivist in—'

Horrors! She had forgotten the name of the place!

'—in the famous library of Libernek Square. This position carries a stipend of five sanarands a month. Accommodation for the Archivist is provided within the library itself; it is, if memory serves, at least adequate.'

Elkin bowed his head in gratitude, then said:

'My lady is as generous as she is beautiful.'

Farfalla smiled on Elkin, for, while she governed herself severely, she allowed herself this one luxury: to accept all compliments to her flesh at face value. She let her smile last to the limits of the allowable, then turned to Jarl.

'Truly,' said she, 'as a mother, I rejoice that my son has learnt the use of weapons. For the Constitution decrees that he serve with the army of the Harvest Plains. No other future lies open to him. His doom is written in the law, and rightly so.'

What could be more plain than that? Farfalla was telling Sarazin, and in public, exactly what he could expect. Though he must have known as much before.

'So,' said Farfalla, 'while Thodric Jarl has taught Sarazin in exile, now the army will provide his military education.'

She kept her voice cool, controlled. As a mother long deprived of her eldest child, she longed to sweep him into her arms, to hold him, to laugh, to weep. But she forbade herself such public display, thinking him safer if the Regency believed a breach to exist between mother and son.

Thus Farfalla, when saying 'my son', found it politic to use the neutral 'yo chorol', literally 'my child-male', instead of the words of love and passion: 'yo sovrol', 'my womb-male'. Her phraseology made her sound cold, remote, analytical.

Sarazin did not wonder at this, for his rudimentary grasp of Churl left him incapable of following the nuances of Farfalla's speech. In fact, as he saw no point in bending his brain without cause, he had stopped listening to Farfalla: he attended instead to the translator rendering her words into Galish.

Would this audience never end? He was finding the throne room too hot and too cold by turns, and once he felt quite dizzy and the whole world wavered before his eyes. Despite his saddle-chafed backside, he longed to sit down. He hoped, desperately, that he would not disgrace himself by fainting.

Meanwhile, Farfalla, having lectured on the sterling service rendered to the state by the sons of kingmakers who had entered the army, returned to the future of Thodric Jarl:

'. . . therefore, as my son's training is spoken for, he no longer needs a mentor such as Thodric Jarl. However, the Watch has lacked a properly qualified Master of Combat these last five years.'

She paused. Jarl, on hearing her words translated into Galish, said suspiciously:

'Why should a good job go begging for so long?'

'Because,' said Farfalla, offended by his ingratitude, 'by law a prerequisite for the job is military experience, but, thanks to an enmity between the Watch and the army which is as ancient as it is senseless, no soldier will take the job on retirement.'

'On retirement?' said Jarl. 'Is this an old man's job?'

'An experienced man's job,' said Farfalla, now close to losing patience with him. 'The pay is five ilavales a month.'

If Jarl ran true to form, he would now object, since Elkin's job would pay five pieces of gold, whereas Jarl would draw but five of silver. He did object. But not on account of the size of his reward.

'The ilavale,' said Jarl, 'is a coin of the Confederation of Wizards. I am of the Rovac, as you know. Is it any secret that there is a feud of long standing between wizards and Rovac? Why then name my pay in such coinage? Do you seek to insult me?'

Farfalla, ignorant of any such feud, wondered whether she was meant to smile at this extravagance. Then realised the man was serious. Gods! As if there weren't enough real problems to worry about . . .

39

'The honour of Rovac is legendary,' said Farfalla drily. 'Yet in recent years the inflation of Selzirk has been finding its own place in legend. The debasement of our coinage has worsened this inflation. Some nine years ago, the Regency in its wisdom decided to denominate all state salaries in hard coinage.'

'Wizard coinage,' said Jarl.

'The coinage of trade,' said Farfalla smoothly. 'Rest assured, however, that you need not take such into your hand. Triners, ilavales and sanarands do but measure official salaries, which are in fact paid in our local coinage at the prevailing rate of exchange.'

Jarl, already regretting his outburst, protested no further. The ancient enmity between wizards and Rovac was a matter unfit for public discussion. He apologised for his outburst with surprising graciousness, and, after a handful of spurious speeches from a variety of officials, Farfalla was able to bring the audience to an end. Plovey then insisted on taking Sarazin to meet certain key members of the Regency.

Farfalla, exhausted by the ordeal of the audience, sat back in her throne. Shortly, her translator came to her, looked around for eavesdroppers, then said:

'My lady.'

'Yes?' said Farfalla.

This had better be good. She was in no mood for idle gossip.

'I heard your Sarazin at word with the old man Elkin before Plovey bore him away. He questioned his future in the army. Did Elkin believe your claims true? That was what he said. Also—'

From the translator's tale, Farfalla knew her efforts had been in vain. She had laid it on the line for Sarazin. But it had gone in one ear and out of the other. And now her son was with that monstrous Plovey, alone and unprotected. What indiscretions would he commit before she could retrieve him?

—*Gods! We'll be lucky if he lasts ten days.*

CHAPTER FIVE

Bizzie: Farfalla's wench; wife of Hof-Gof the ostler; mother of Sarazin's half-brother Benthorn (sired by the farrier Fox). She is big-built, red-faced and bustling, and has (this is not idle slander but incontrovertible fact) an unfortunate taste for strong drink.

While Farfalla feared disaster, luck favoured Plovey's innocent companion with an attack of diarrhoea, soon followed by nausea and vomiting. Giddy, pale and sweating, Sarazin was returned to his mother, who put him in Bizzie's care.

'You have the river-fever, love,' said Bizzie, bustling him into a bed.

But Sarazin understood her not, for the first victim of his mounting delirium was his access to Churl. By dayfail, his body was fire, his sheets sodden with sweat, his world a babbling torment of gloating claws. In the torrids of fever, he oft spoke of Jaluba. When Farfalla joined Bizzie's bedside vigil late that night, Sarazin was troubling after his whore in speech rank with lust: coarse speech of the questing cock. Fortunately, the Rice Empire's Geltic was entirely unknown to Farfalla.

'My son,' said she. Or meant to say. For her tongue stumbled, and what she said was: 'Fox.'

'Shall I fetch him?' said Bizzie. ''Twould be a sin to let the boy die unseen by his father.'

'No,' said Farfalla, lighting another taper to supplement the single bedside candle. 'Fox is banned from the boy's presence. He knows it, too.'

While Fox still worked in her palace as a farrier, she had banished him from her life, her thoughts, her dreams. So why did his name still haunt her tongue?

'My lady,' ventured Bizzie, 'if someone is to be punished, may it not be me? For, to be sure, 'tis cruel to you and him alike to cut him away entirely.'

'Fox is banned as a matter of policy,' said Farfalla. 'Not as punishment. Flesh is what flesh is, and men are made as men are made. And women, too. It is his advice I must fear, and the boy also.'

'He means well,' said Bizzie.

'I know, I know,' said Farfalla. Then: 'It's too late at night to talk politics. It suffices to say the man is dangerous.'

Dangerous indeed, for his political passions were strong, to say the least. All too clearly he saw the wrongs of the world: and urged the world to action. Often in the past he had forced Farfalla to act. In the cause of justice, true. But by doing his will Farfalla had provoked the Regency into passing the unanimous vote necessary to take away most of her power. If she yielded to him again, she might lose her life.

—*And his. And my sons' lives. He talks as if life was well lost for a cause. But can a cause laugh or cry, breathe or feel?*

Sarazin moaned. For luck, Farfalla ran her hand through the flame of one of the candles, slowly enough to feel the heat yet too quickly for flesh to burn.

Then touched Sarazin's forehead. Felt the protest of his scorched flesh. Stooped, and kissed. Salt on her tongue. His skin hot, unyielding, tight against the skull. But the width of a blade separates life from bone. Unwashed from his journey, he still stank of sun and horses. And piss, shit and vomit.

—*Like a baby.*

Child born in the years of her hope, the years of her love, when Fox had outshone the very sun. She had been young, strong, perfect. Alive in a world where all things were possible for her. And now?

'Don't cry, my lady,' said Bizzie, touching her by way of comfort. 'Don't cry. I spoke of death but I doubt he'll die.'

42

'Don't worry about me,' said Farfalla. 'Worry about him. I wish we had healers of worth in this city.'

'There was a pox doctor at your gates but recent,' said Bizzie. 'He was turned away by the guards, but I saw him well. A handsome young man, oh yes. The strangest green eyes! I thought the guard cruel to chase him away without hearing.'

'Perhaps,' said Farfalla indifferently.

She knew of no virtue in pox doctors, who were for the most part failed wizards or quacks more useless yet. As for her guards, they had orders to be ruthless, for all the world saw fit to beg at her gates yet her resources were but slender.

'You sleep now,' said Bizzie. 'It's not good for you to be awake and worried when you've work to do on the morrow.'

'I've work to do before I sleep,' said Farfalla. 'Hunt out some help. We're going to wash this boy then sponge him down to cool the fever. Clean sheets would not go amiss, either.'

'Yes, my lady,' said Bizzie.

Then bobbed her head and exited, leaving Farfalla alone with her son Sarazin. Delicately, she reached out and pinched a mosquito which had settled on his cheek. Plump with blood, it broke to a smear beneath her fingers.

She was alone in the room. Very much alone. A hot summer night. Airless. Hot candles burning. Flames silent, shading from yellow to red. A puckering of purple, a thread of smoke ascending. And heat, yes, heat and weight, blood breaking. The white-hot stars shivering on the horizon as she gasped.

—*Fox.*

She knelt by the bed. And she wept.

Fever racked Sean Sarazin for five days and five nights. Then receded, leaving him weak, troubled by persistent diarrhoea and a painful wheeze, and by hack-cough attacks

43

which saw him gobbing up lumps of green and yellow phlegm. He was dismayed by his jellyfish limbs, his smoke-fogged vision. But even more dismayed to find his sword missing. It was valuable in itself, but all the more precious because it was the gift of Lord Regan. A royal gift.

'My sword!' he cried. 'It's stolen!'

'Hush,' said the red-faced middle-aged woman at his bedside. 'Your mother has your weapon in her keeping.'

'My mother? What wants she with a weapon of war?'

'I know not, young master, for I have not the keeping of her will.'

'Who are you then?' said Sarazin.

'My name is Bizzie. Once your mother's maid, but now yours.'

Sarazin turned away, feeling sick. Was this a joke? Bizzie was the mother of Benthorn, his half-brother. Why had Farfalla done this to him?

'Your mother has ventured a certain suggestion,' said Bizzie, laying her hand on Sarazin's brow.

'To hell with her suggestions!' said Sarazin. 'I want my sword! I want it now! Go and get it!'

But Farfalla kept the blade, not trusting him with anything so valuable. On revisiting his bedside she told him so explicitly:

'This city of sin owns many temptations. I'd not have you lose a great treasure to such.'

'You treat me as a child,' said Sarazin, all resentment. 'My father would not treat me thus.'

'Fox is not a party to this argument, and never will be. Fox is banned from your presence, and you from his.'

'You can't do that!' said Sarazin.

'I can,' said Farfalla. 'I do. I must. Fox almost lost his life through radical politics, and almost cost me mine. Because of the dangers of such politics you must never meet.'

As Celadon, Peguero and Jarnel accepted this ban, Farfalla did not believe Sarazin would do otherwise. Until now, Sarazin himself had never thought to seek out Fox, who was but a low-bred farrier. But, his curiosity piqued, he asked:

'What kind of man is he?'

'Fox? He's . . . his best is excellent. Strength, wisdom, humour. But then . . . he has his moods. Black moods of anger when he . . . he wrecks his own work.'

'Did he — did he take Bizzie in such a mood?' said Sarazin.

'You a man and you ask me that?' said Farfalla. 'He took her because she was available and I eight months pregnant with you. Oh, I remember. I won't forget. One of your feet must have been jammed beneath my ribs, because its reminder never left me. You were born in winter, I remember, and . . .'

On and on she went, detailing Sarazin's genesis. This he found intensely embarrassing. He could have discussed sexual intercourse easily, even with his mother, for there a man found power and pleasure both. But birth? No! To have been born: it was, really, demeaning. He was scarcely pleased to be reminded that he had been small and helpless, yolk-wet and toothless, a writhing bundle of hunger-bawling incontinence.

'. . . but I loved you, not least because you were my first. You cried when they took you, oh, you were so little, only four years old and you cried and cried, it near broke my heart, I cried myself for days . . .'

This was a different woman from the one Sarazin had seen so far. Not the cold, hard, efficient ruler of the See of the Sun, but his mother. Who wanted him, who needed him, who had longed for him, who was unutterably lonely. Who embarrassed him. With her talk. With what she was. Big bones in her hands and her coarse-featured face. A wrestler's neck, a washerwoman's forearms.

Had she no modesty?

Surely only a peasant would talk so frankly of a bond of blood and milk. He had dreamed of a mother elegant, sophisticated and, above all, powerful. And had found instead this near-desperate woman who, it seemed, had

45

nothing to give him. He was offended by the shapeless robes she wore, her unabashed physical strength, and her rude health — which was that of a well-fed peasant.

Farfalla talked long and late with Sarazin, who devoted his own efforts to concealing his shame. When at last she left him, he found his thoughts turning again to his father. Fox. He was intrigued by what he had heard. A man of dangerous politics.

—*He sought to make himself emperor, perhaps.*

Thus thought Sarazin, and resolved to seek out Fox as soon as he was fit to rise from his bed. Which, judging from the condition of his flesh, would be a little while yet.

While Farfalla won the day when Sarazin demanded the return of his blade of firelight steel, she could not always get her own way. For example: despite her objections, a team of army surgeons subjected her son to a medical. They listened to his chest and palpated his spleen without mercy; they thumped his knees with padded mallets and tweaked his ears with tuning forks; they smelt his urine, tasted his ordure, and drew a cup of his blood to weigh against an equal volume of water.

Having done all this and more they diagnosed, variously, malaria, consumption, hepatitis, pneumonia and Favlingskon's disease; their prescriptions included a tincture of squids' ink and basilisk gall, powdered unicorn horn to be taken with gold dust and deer velvet, carefully calculated doses of dwale and hemlock, tablets of chalk and oxidised iron, and disks of sun-baked kaolin (to be chewed slowly then swallowed).

'It is nonsense they talk,' said Bizzie, 'for this is but the river-fever, which cures itself if it heals at all.'

Then that illiterate washerwoman showed her total ignorance of the wonders of medical science by throwing out all the prescriptions — even the most rare and valuable unicorn horn. She fed Sarazin upon honey, boiled skimmed milk, omelettes, and fresh placenta fried up with garlic.

46

Slowly, he began to get better. So slowly, in fact, that the surgeons deferred his recruitment into the army indefinitely.

'Since science had failed your flesh,' said one, 'I suggest theology. Pray to your god for a cure.'

'But I have no god,' said Sarazin.

This comment was widely reported, and brought Farfalla hastening to her son's bedside. Once she had ensured their privacy she said, with unconcealed alarm:

'Are you an atheist?'

'Of course not,' said Sarazin.

Illness had made him irritable, and being accused of a foible as witless as atheism would have annoyed him even in days of health perfect.

'Yet you told the surgeons you were godless,' said Farfalla.

'I was passing an idle comment,' said Sarazin, 'not lecturing on theology. As it happens, Epelthin Elkin has taught me of half a hundred gods all worthy of belief.'

Indeed, Elkin had taught Sarazin many subtle truths about theology. For example, that the gods themselves are subject to evolutionary forces, and, like plants and animals, change down through the ages. This of course explains why deities worshipped in ancient times are so different from those holding sway today.

Where now is the Horn? Where now is Ameeshoth? They, the First Ones, are gone. They are as dead as the snow dragon, once the strongest, wisest and most beautiful of all the dragon breeds, but now gone and forgotten except where arcanely knowledged by a few of the world's greatest living scholars.

Sarazin, therefore, was immune to atheism, a distemper which afflicts only the smallest and narrowest of minds. However, thanks to his excellent education, he knew that the hierarchies of the World Beyond are so complex that anyone claiming absolute authority on religious matters is ignorant, deluded or bluffing. Thus it is difficult to be sure one has chosen the right god to worship, particularly since many low-grade demons can inspire visions, work miracles and so forth. Sarazin, wishing to prosper in the afterlife, was still shopping around.

He explained as much to Farfalla.

'Your concern for the afterlife must yield to temporal concerns,' said Farfalla. 'Selzirk looks with suspicion upon atheists proven or suspected. You must declare for the sungod today.'

The sungod? A safe, middle-of-the-road choice. An austere, reasonably competent, fairly tolerant god who offered a choice of five different heavens. The sungod's followers had to do something truly abominable to be sent to hell, and the sungod's hell was, in any case, less threatening than most — it was a rainy day which went on forever.

'Why hesitate?' said Farfalla, all brisk efficiency. 'This is a sure thing! The sungod is one of the Proven Deities, and a good-tempered deity at that. Cheap to worship, too. No need to burn incense, make sacrifices, chastise your flesh or cut off your nose. All you have to do is Declare yourself, then say a couple of prayers every time Midsummer's Day comes around.'

'Yes, but,' said Sarazin.

'But what?'

'You spoke of temporal considerations. It's precisely those which make me hesitate. You see, I want a god who will help me in the here and now. Everyone knows the sungod doesn't go in for miracles.'

'Well, and what self-respecting deity does?' said Farfalla. 'I'm sure Elkin's taught you that most of the miracle-working gods only concern themselves with the world of events because they are virtually powerless in the World Beyond.'

'That's so,' said Sarazin. 'But—'

'But nothing!' said Farfalla. 'You Declare for the sungod today. Let me explain . . .'

Then she detailed her long-standing struggle with the Regency, which, early in her reign, had produced the unanimous vote necessary to take away most of her executive powers. Since she now knew that her son was expert at forgetting things he did not care to remember, she made no apologies for telling him things he might well know already.

'. . . and ever more the Regency seeks excuse sufficient to impeach me. If impeached and convicted of crimes against the Constitution, then I will be executed, letting the Regency choose a more pliable puppet to be kingmaker.'

'How does my religion come into it?' said Sarazin, feeling it quite unfair that his mother's past should burden his own future.

'Everything about you comes into it,' said Farfalla. 'Not discounting the things you say in fever.'

'What things were they?' said Sarazin.

'I know not, for you spoke in a foreign tongue. But remember! From now on whatever you say, dreaming, drunk or in fever, may be used against you. And me! Say little, trust nobody, and steer clear of politics.'

'Will the sungod help mute me?' said Sarazin, bemused at the way his mother rattled on about politics when the question at hand was religion.

'If I conspire to establish a dynasty,' said she, as if he had not spoken, 'to set a son of mine upon the throne of Selzirk, then that will be a crime against the Constitution. Political ambition on your part might well be seen as evidence of such conspiracy.'

'But religion . . .?'

'All know the sungod approves of tradition, stability, the status quo. Once you Declare for the sungod, unlawful ambition on your part will immediately seem less likely, less believable.'

Under powerful pressure from Farfalla, Sarazin shortly converted to worship of the sungod. He felt cheated, feeling he deserved a god who could offer him more in the way of practical day-to-day power. This was his constant thought:

—*I was made for better things.*

Others suspected his strong sense of entitlement. One such was Plovey zar Plovey, a career bureaucrat, spokesman for the Regency and one of the most powerful players in Selzirk's politics. And one of the most dangerous.

'The young man looks to be a posturing fool,' said Plovey to his colleagues, 'but he could yet be a danger to us.'

'Then you will arrange his destruction,' answered the colleagues in question.

'It will be,' said Plovey, 'my pleasure.'

True. It would be a special pleasure if Plovey could destroy Fox and Farfalla along with their son. As his first move, Plovey took out the files which had provoked the unanimous vote by which the Regency had deprived the kingmaker Farfalla of most of her powers.

The files made it clear that both Fox and Farfalla had nearly been indicted on charges of high treason. However, three potential witnesses against them had committed suicide rather than submit to torture. The fact that Fox and Farfalla could command such loyalty made them very dangerous people indeed . . .

CHAPTER SIX

Name: Thodric Jarl.
Birthplace: the islands of Rovac.
Description: world-weary man of 45, brusque in speech and manner; grey eyes, hair and bulky beard; always clad in battle-leathers; infallibly armed.
Status: a wanted criminal in Chi'ash-lan; a general on the Reserve List of the Imperial Army of the Witchlord Onosh Gulkan, lord of Safrak; blood-sworn enemy of the better part of a hundred men; a civil servant in the pay of two hostile states.

Career: soldiered in places as far afield as the snows of the Cold West and Tameran's horselands. After many vicissitudes became combat instructor to the hostage Sarazin in Voice. This sinecure ended when the Rice Empire's ruler sent him north to spy in Selzirk, where he got a real job of work as Master of Combat for the Watch.

Shortly after Jarl started his new job, he was approached by one of the Watch, Qid by name. As Jarl had learnt as yet but little Churl, they conversed in Galish. Qid began by noting that Sean Sarazin was ill, but would join the army on recovery.

'You think he should do otherwise?' said Jarl.

'Let me speak frankly,' said Qid. 'Some of us in the Watch think the prince is meant for better things.'

The Galish Trading Tongue, a language fitted for commerce rather than courtly use, had no precise word for 'prince'. So the actual term Qid used was 'ral-gunth', literally 'power-born'.

Jarl, unversed in the intricacies of Selzirk's politics, knew but the bare outlines of the game of power and influence in which the principals were kingmaker, Regency, army, law courts, guilds and temples, the Watch, the Secret Service, the Diplomatic Corps and the treasury. But he knew enough to say:

'Ral-gunth? Such talk is unsound and unsafe. Sean Sarazin was not born to power but to service. His fate is to join the army like his brothers.'

'His brothers,' said Qid, 'might think their mother's son as worthy of service as any army. What say? Did they speak of power as all four rode together from Voice to Selzirk?'

'They spoke of beer, brothels, hounds, horse, dice and cards,' said Jarl. 'You are bold, Qid, but a fool. There's no conspiracy to be made in Selzirk. Certainly not between Sean Sarazin and his brothers!'

'You cannot know that of a certainty,' said Qid.

'Have you not heard? Such a conspiracy is now a physical impossibility, for the army has dispersed the brothers.'

'Where to?' said Qid.

'I don't know and don't care,' said Jarl brusquely.

In fact, he had paid good gold to get the details for the latest coded despatch he had sent to Lord Regan with a southbound Galish kafila. Celadon had gone to Shin as a military attaché, Peguero was posted to Kelebes to be aide-de-camp to the governor of that town and region, while Jarnel had been given the hopeless task of collecting taxes (unpaid for the last three hundred years) from anarchists dwelling in the marshlands of Tyte.

'Wherever they've gone,' said Qid, 'they'll be back.'

'But not for a while,' said Jarl. 'That gives all who think or talk treason time in which to come to their senses.'

With that, Jarl terminated the interview. What he wanted — or so he told himself — was a quiet life. More of the pasture time he had enjoyed for so long in Voice. Yet, when others of the Watch came to him in secret to say they would throw in their lot with Sarazin if he sought to rule in Selzirk, Jarl had to admit to himself that he was tempted.

Power! That would be his reward if he helped Sarazin win the throne. He had known power before. Had known victory, triumph, glory. However . . . while serving with the Rovac armies in the Cold West, Jarl had spent years in Chi'ash-lan, city of intrigues. There he had learnt habits of caution which now helped him frame his response to the conspirators:

'I am but a simple solider who is not paid to think. Sean Sarazin's fate is not in my keeping, since he is no longer my student. Whatever his future, I have no part in it. If you must conspire, then conspire with him direct.'

'His years are not those of discretion,' was the answer. 'We dare not approach him direct. Hence we seek his answer to an invitation to power through one of years more mature.'

'Well then,' said Jarl, suddenly in the best of all possible humours, 'I believe the scholar Epelthin Elkin tutors young Sarazin still. So speak to him if you wish. But, as for me: I have forgotten this meeting already. If need be, I will deny its history, even in the teeth of torture.'

Thus rebuffed, some members of the Watch followed Jarl's advice, and sought to approach Sarazin by means of the good offices of Epelthin Elkin. But the old scholar came to no harm through the warrior's malice, since he was every bit as cunning and cautious as the Rovac warrior. Thinking the conspirators to be, in all likelihood, agents in the pay of the Regency, he dismissed them, saying:

'Sarazin is too young for me to know what he is made of, but I doubt that treason has been bred in his bones.'

That, then, was the state of the Great Game in Selzirk in the dying days of the year Alliance 4324.

Farfalla and Plovey alike watched Sean Sarazin, both fearing that he might be tempted to violence by ambition.

Qid and others of the Watch met often in secret, and, slowly, more and more members of Selzirk's law-enforcement agency were drawn into conspiracy. The Brotherhood of the Watch — a secret society outlawed for over a hundred years, but flourishing still — discussed Sean Sarazin's potential in cities as far away as Androlmarphos and Kelebes.

Military intelligence, suspecting something untoward was afoot, tried (not for the first time) to infiltrate Watch and Brotherhood both.

The scholarly Epelthin Elkin sent long, detailed reports to Lord Regan on the economic strength of the Harvest Plains. Thodric Jarl, for his part, included a question in his next report:

'Does my lord intend Sean Sarazin to overthrow the ruling order in Selzirk? If so, what help does the south offer? Know this: if my lord commands it, I am ready.'

Finally, Midsummer's Day arrived: the start of the year Alliance 4325. As Sarazin, true to his religion, began the praise-prayers due to the sungod, some of the fiercer spirits in the Watch came to a decision. They would approach Sarazin on the morrow and speak to him. About power. Revolution. Empire. Qid, they decided, would be the man to make the approach.

When Sarazin satisfied his nagging curiosity by seeking out his father, Fox proved to be a heavyset man as old as Thodric Jarl and bearded likewise, though his beard was not grey but tawny. He was distant, reserved and cautious, preferring to listen rather than speak. Finally Sarazin asked a frank question:

'Farfalla says you sought power in Selzirk. Is that true?'

'I sought power through her, yes,' said Fox. 'We planned to end slavery in the Harvest Plains.'

Sarazin, thinking this was a joke, laughed heartily. A natural reaction — for the notion was, of course, absurd.

'Oh yes, you can laugh,' said Fox, misunderstanding the cause of Sarazin's mirth. 'We were fools in the thrall of hope. But we were young! We believed! We truly thought justice could conquer regardless of the odds.'

'You mean,' said Sarazin, incredulously, 'you — you really did mean to liberate the slaves?'

'Justice, as I said, was our motivator,' said Fox.

'But is not justice the rule of law? And are not property rights the foundation of law? And are not slaves property?'

'Slaves,' said Fox, with undisguised anger, 'are people.'

'Perhaps. But property first and foremost.'

'You think the lives of some worth more than the lives of others?' said Fox.

'Of course!' said Sarazin.

It would be tiresome to detail the convoluted political argument which then ensued. And pointless, since the wise will already be familiar with this perennial debate, while the unwise are unlikely to modify their prejudices in the light of reason. Let it simply be said, then, that neither combatant changed the opinions of the other by so much as an iota.

Fox was fierce and passionate — and a demagogue of considerable power. But Sarazin had law and convention on his side, and, thinking he would win easily, at first argued lightheartedly. Neither the wise nor the unwise will be surprised to learn that he himself became passionate as the debate proceeded, that the tempers of both participants shortened, and that they departed on bad terms, both thinking less of each other than they had before.

The next day, Farfalla summoned Sarazin to her throne room, which typified her palace: it was uncomfortable, inconvenient and built to an inhuman scale. To get there involved a weary climb to the top of the High Court, a tower so high that Farfalla's throne afforded her a view over all of Selzirk. There she confronted her son in private.

'You have met with Fox,' said Farfalla. 'I ordered you not to, yet you did.'

'Yes! But what right have you to deny me my father?'

'None. I see that now. I was wrong to try, and I apologise. You may meet Fox freely, whenever you see fit. If Fox makes you a madman like himself , well . . . we'll worry about that when it happens. Right now, I have more urgent concerns. Three days ago, you met a man.'

'Did I?' said Sarazin.

'Yes! In the Cat's Head, a brothel of the worst repute.'

'Men,' said Sarazin drily, 'are not to my taste.'

'Don't play innocent with me!' said Farfalla. 'The man's name was Qid. He serves in the Watch.'

'Well,' said Sarazin, 'and what of it? Thodric Jarl serves in the Watch. I see Jarl from time to time. Is that wrong?'

'This man Qid asked after your hopes and dreams.'

'Who told you this?' said Sarazin fiercely, shocked that his secrets had been exposed. 'Was it Lod?'

'Oho!' said Farfalla. 'Did Master Lod have a part in this?'

'He did set up my meeting with Qid,' admitted Sarazin.

'Then I will have a word or two with Master Lod before I'm done,' said Farfalla grimly. 'But rest assured, it was not Lod who betrayed you. I have other eyes and ears in the city. Furthermore, the Regency has spies who work as hard as mine. Exactly what treason were you plotting with Qid? Tell!'

'I'm no fool,' said Sarazin angrily. 'I let him do the talking.'

'So far so good. But will you shun him henceforth, or are you meeting again? Well? Are you?'

'I'm not saying,' said Sarazin, turning to go.

'Don't you walk out on me!' said Farfalla, catching him by the shoulder.

Which was too much to bear. She had chastised him like a little child, and now—

Sarazin turned in fury. His fist clenched, striking. Ump! Something hit him. And his legs were gone, kicked away, he was falling, going down towards the stone. He landed heavily and lay there with the breath knocked out of him. His mother looked down at him. She was utterly relaxed. Impassive. Watchful. And Sarazin, sore, bruised and shocked, thought:

—*She could have killed me!*

Farfalla resumed her throne.

Sarazin, shaken, picked himself up off the floor. He had never before been hit so hard, so fast, so suddenly. What was Farfalla? A witch? (She was in fact a master of Sunoya Dance, a mind/body training system perfected in Selzirk, and unknown to the world at large.)

'How did you do that?' said Sarazin.

But Farfalla, ignoring his question, continued thus:

'My spies tell me the Regency wants you dead. They will send agent provocateurs to tempt you into evil, then they will destroy you through the due process of the law, hoping to destroy or discredit me in the process. If Qid is not their man, they will have him under surveillance by now, for they have spies everywhere.'

'I won't meet him again,' said Sarazin sullenly, 'so don't worry. If you're quite through, I'm leaving. I'll send you Lod, since you're so keen to have a piece of him as well.'

'Wait about!' said Farfalla. 'I haven't finished yet!'

'What is it now?' said Sarazin, turning back to his mother.

'Who is Jaluba?' said Farfalla.

'Pardon?' said Sarazin.

'Jaluba,' said his mother impatiently. 'Is she a whore?'

'I don't know what you're talking about,' said he.

'Then read this,' said Farfalla, brandishing a letter, a translation of which had been made for her by her interpreter that very morning, 'and you'll know soon enough.'

One glance at the letter told Sarazin who it was from.

'You've been intercepting my mail!' he said, outraged.

'If I don't the Regency will,' retorted Farfalla.

Then sat back and watched him as he read.

'Well?' said Farfalla, once Sarazin had finished.

'How did you come by this?' he said.

'My agents intercept Galish kafilas from south and north some leagues before they reach Selzirk. Thus I get at least a few of my own letters before Plovey does. An expensive business — but the cheap alternative might well be an early death.'

'Then I'll tell Jaluba to write with less passion in future,' said Sarazin. 'I for my part will be circumspect in my reply.'

'You'll not write back to this whore,' said Farfalla in unsuppressed fury. 'If you're known to have contact with an agent in or of the Rice Empire, that alone may be evidence sufficient for the Regency to impeach—'

'Impeach! Impeach!' said Sarazin. Having made some concessions to his mother already that day, he was in no mood to surrender on this point also. 'Are our lives entire to be ruled by this mythical impeachment?'

'Politics is our life whether we like it or not.'

'Your life, you mean,' said Sarazin. 'You've got the fun of it, the command of secret agents, rights of release and pardon, powers over half the best jobs in Selzirk. You've got—'

'Responsibility,' said Farfalla, cutting him off. 'A responsibility to keep us alive. Both of us, if possible.'

'Then what have I got?'

A rhetorical question. But it earnt itself a straight answer nonetheless:

'You've got your education. Since you won't be fit to join the army for some time yet, concentrate on your studies with Elkin. Also, Thodric Jarl has consented to continue your combat training, so you've that to work on as well.'

The river-fever does no lasting damage — except when it kills — so by late summer in the year Alliance 4325 Sarazin was most definitely once more fighting fit.

'The army thinks your enlistment delayed indefinitely by disease,' said Farfalla. 'But you know yourself you've made a perfect recovery. I can see that for myself — as can others. It would be safer for all of us if you joined up now.'

'That would upset the army surgeons,' said Sarazin blandly, confident his mother would indulge him in this small matter. 'Their professional judgment would be called into question.'

'Don't give me that nonsense,' said Farfalla.

She spoke so curtly that Sarazin, hurt, felt momentarily

58

tearful. She had terminated his intrigues with Qid. She had cancelled his correspondence with Jaluba. Was he not going to be allowed any freedom whatsoever? He mastered his emotions then said:

'I won't be a soldier. I couldn't stand it. A lifetime of garrison routine with that drunken mob of foul-mouthed oafs? It would kill me.'

'What do you want then?' said Farfalla.

'To be what I feel I have the ability to be. To make the most of myself. To fulfil the purpose for which I was born.'

His mother would have wanted as much for him, had they lived in a time and a place where ambition did not promise death. As it was . . .

'You were born,' said Farfalla, 'as the natural consequence of an act of lust. That's all there is to it. You understand?'

It hurt her to talk of his birth so coldly. Sarazin, her firstborn. A child conceived in love. Worshipped at birth as something sacred. His hand so small, clutching her finger to tightly! Yet talk harshly she must, to try to make him see sense.

Sarazin did not answer. Farfalla had already betrayed herself to him in an earlier meeting when she had spoken of his foot jammed beneath her rib, of his birth, his first words, his first step, the agony of their parting when he was aged but four. Did she think he had forgotten already? She loved him. Wanted him. Needed him. Valued him above almost anything in the world. Surely he could secure her indulgence. Seeking to do that, he said:

'I believe I can have whatever I want. I can be whatever I want to be. I can win whatever I want to win. All I need is just a little help to tap my true potential.'

'I give up!' said Farfalla. 'You're as senseless as a teenager. It's Lord Regan's fault. The old fool indulged you in a game of princes. But you're not a prince. You're a farrier's bastard, that's all.'

She hoped to educate through shock where reason had failed. Her vehement outburst shocked herself. But made little impact on Sarazin, who proved as much by saying:

'You were consecrated as one of the Favoured Blood. In sacred ceremony, you joined your blood to that of the lineage of the rightful rulers of Argan. As all legend knows—'

'Legend! Legend!' said Farfalla. 'Do you want to be a legend-hero? Very well! Ride forth, my son, and kill yourself a dragon. Or dare the lands beyond Drangsturm and make a name for yourself as explorer. Or win yourself a princess, and make yourself lord of some kingdom through her inheritance.'

Thus raged Farfalla. Sarazin knew she was being sarcastic, but, even so, once he had escaped from her wrath he began considering her suggestions in earnest. Neither dragons nor Drangsturm appealed, but the idea of winning a princess recommended itself to his imagination.

The next day, Lod found Sarazin deep in research amidst heaps of books, scrolls, papers and maps.

'What are you doing?' said Lod.

'Researching my marriage to a princess,' answered Sarazin.

'Really! Have you found any candidates?'

'One or two. Things may have changed, but some of these reports claim that the kings of both Dybra and Chorst have daughters as yet unmarried. Slerma of Sung is also unmarried. Unfortunately, a traveller's tale alleges that she's slightly overweight. I must say I don't like fat.'

'Then you must see my sister Amantha,' said Lod, whose appetite for devilment was unconstrained by any thought of the probable consequences of such. 'She's thin as an eel. And, I'm sure, every bit as slippery when wet.'

He winked.

'I don't think you quite understand,' said Sarazin. 'I want a princess who comes with a kingdom. Slerma of Sung, for instance. She sounds nearly ideal. Her father rules from a mighty mountain city rich with the wealth of a thousand mines. Whereas Chenameg — well, it's a nice place, but Tarkal inherits, doesn't he?'

60

There was a pause. Then Lod said:

'Tarkal is not immortal.'

'Who . . . who is next in the line of succession?'

'Amantha, of course. Tarkal was the firstborn. Then there was Amantha. Then me. The succession is from the oldest to youngest, regardless of sex.'

'But Tarkal is young,' insisted Sarazin.

'And, as I said, he is not immortal.'

They eyed each other in silence. Then:

'Tell me then,' said Sarazin, choosing his words very, very carefully, 'what exactly do you want for yourself?'

'To live in my homeland, to start with. Only fear of my life sent me running to Selzirk. Tarkal thrice tried to kill me, I'm sure of it. He's three parts mad, I've seen it clear. But my father refuses to believe it.'

'This is all . . . very interesting,' said Sarazin. 'I'll have to think carefully about this.'

'Think quickly,' said Lod. 'For Tarkal and Amantha will both be here some ten days hence. They come as part of an embassy, and will lodge within the walls of your mother's castle. That will be your best chance, perhaps your only chance, if you seek opportunity for romance. Or for . . . for other things.'

Ten days! Yes, ten days for Sarazin to think things through. What did he have to lose? His life! But then, of course, he had a kingdom to win.

CHAPTER EIGHT

Sing me a song of love, my dear,
Once more before I perish —
Of love, the word that all men know,
Of nuzzling lips, of golls which gloat,

61

Of womanheat ready and waiting.
Sing me a song, and make it of love:
For my money for whores is exhausted.
    —Saba Yavendar, 'Lust Song'.

Fortune had indulged her with a royal name. She was Amantha of Chenameg, and she came to Selzirk of the Harvest Plains with the embassy which brought her brother Tarkal to the city. At an official reception, she met with Sean Kelebes Sarazin, a young man known to his mother as Sarazin Sky. He would, in the fulness of time, bear the name Watashi — which means, among other things, death.

They met beneath a sky of cerulean blue, when the world was at peace, for both had been born into the final years of the Golden Age. Then, the Swarms were kept safely south of Drangsturm, allowing the lands of Argan North to flourish in peace and prosperity. Sean Sarazin was then twenty-two years old. The fair lady Amantha was the same age, and carried herself with all the grace befitting a princess of the Chenameg Kingdom.

Sarazin fell in love with Amantha immediately. Just as he had expected to. Which was fortunate, since it would scarcely have been proper for him to pursue his princess unless he loved her. It is certain that love rules Sarazin's heart, not lust, for his princess was not made to excite the flesh.

She was tall.

She was thin.

She was pallid.

She had buck teeth.

Therefore why did he adore her?

Because she moved with the mystic grace immanent in the flesh of those of the Favoured Blood. Because she was of a line of kings, and therefore possessed a share of divinity. She was the woman of his dreams.

On introduction, he had no immediate chance to profess

his love, for three hundred others were waiting to kiss her hand. Afterwards, however, they dined alfresco, choosing food at liberty from the buffet spread beneath a marquee on the banks of the Velvet River at a spot some half a league east of Selzirk, and Sarazin shortly seized his chance to accost her.

'Amantha,' he said.

'I know my name,' she said tartly.

It was not an auspicious beginning. Already she was turning away from him.

'But you don't know mine,' he said. 'It's Sean. Sean Sarazin.'

'Oh yes, I've heard of you,' said Amantha. 'You're the washerwoman's bastard.'

'No, no,' said Sarazin, desperately. 'You're confusing me with someone else. That's Benthorn you're thinking of. Benthorn, my half-brother. I'm Farfalla's son.'

He was close enough to breathe the perfume from the silken sachet hanging at her neck.

'I was not mistaken, then,' said Amantha. 'You're the son of a farrier.'

'The kingmaker's son! Farfalla's son! And — and I love you!'

'You what!?' she said, half gasping, half laughing.

'I love you!'

'How can you?' she said. 'I am a princess and you a peasant.'

'I must die unless I can have you,' said Sarazin.

'Die, then,' she said, indifferent to his fate.

He seized her hand in his.

'Fair lady,' he said, 'I pray, hear me out.'

'Oh, what style it has!' said Amantha.

She pursed her lips for a kiss, raised Sarazin's hand to her lips — then bit it. Hard. Sarazin jerked his hand away. And Amantha, laughing, flirted away into the midst of a gaggle of hard-drinking cavalry officers.

She had a nice grasp of the political realities. While the Harvest Plains were more powerful than Chenameg,

Sarazin commanded none of that power in his own right, and never would. His prospects were zero.

A little later, Lod of Chenameg caught up with Sarazin, and asked how Sarazin had made out.

'Amantha,' said Sarazin, 'bit me.'

'Oh, doubtless she was in one of her little moods,' said Lod.

'Tell me about these little moods,' said Sarazin. 'How long do they last for?'

'A few days,' said Lod.

'How many is a few?'

'Any number less than twenty.'

'So she sulks, then,' said Sarazin. 'In a very professional way, by the sound of it. Has anyone tried using a whip on her?'

'Sarazin, my man!' cried Lod. 'What a delicious thought! You're a genius. But, alas — the world so seldom appreciates true talent. Indeed, I suspect your genius in action might get us both arrested. Come, there's no joy for us here. Let's be away.'

So the pair saddled up, quit the riverside buffet and set off for Selzirk.

'How did you find Tarkal?' said Sarazin.

Tarkal's health was of course a matter of intense interest, since only his death would let Amantha ascend the throne of Chenameg.

'Tarkal I found fiery,' said Lod. 'A dragon in his eye. Methinks my head was gripped in the jaws of that dragon.'

'Dragonising apart, how did he treat you?'

'In truth, we scarcely spoke two words. But the way he looked at me . . . it bodes ill for the future.'

'You still think he means to kill you?'

'Think!' said Lod. 'I know it! Murder is his middle name.'

On reaching Selzirk, they rode through the streets of Wake to Kesh, walked their horses through the crush of people shuffling through that gate-tower, won their way through to Santrim then rode through that elegant quarter to Farfalla's palace.

There they returned their horses (theirs to borrow, though technically the kingmaker's property) to the stables, then walked back to Kesh and then on to Lod's favourite watering hole, a smoke-sour tavern in Jone where the rough-brawling inhabitants of the city's dockside quarter came to gamble and get drunk.

In that maze of barracks, brothels, shipyards and bars, of tenement slumlands, thieves' dens and rat-rule warehouses, Sarazin was safer than when at home. In Farfalla's palace, he was ever watched by spies from the Regency — but few such would dare to follow him into Jone, most dangerous of the Four Worlds of Selzirk.

That, at least, was the theory advanced by Lod when the rascal first tempted Sarazin into the slum streets. Later, Sarazin had realised he was watched always and every-where, regardless of the dangers of his environment. Still, he had to admit he sometimes found the atmosphere in Farfalla's palace claustrophobic, and was glad to escape to the free and easy dockside life.

These excursions were not really reckless, for Sarazin was too poor to be mugged for his money, since Farfalla gave him only a trifling allowance. He was not pretty enough to be kidnapped for the sake of his flesh. He carried weapons from habit, and knew how to use them. And, most important of all: Lod had many friends in Jone. Heavymen, bouncers and gateguards would protect Sarazin, for Lod's sake, if the going ever got rough.

For a while Lod and Sarazin sat brooding over a couple of beers, playing a desultory game of cards. Sarazin won a few dorths off Lod.

'It's getting late,' said Lod at length. 'Shall we liven the evening?'

'How so?' said Sarazin.

'There's cock fighting at the Vampire's Stake tonight. Want to come along?'

'Not this evening,' said Sarazin. 'I've an appointment with a fortune teller.'

65

'The one to whom I introduced you?' said Lod. 'Madam Ix?'

'The same,' said Sarazin.

Idly, he wondered if Lod got a cut from the money he paid out to these palmists and shadow-thinkers. But Lod put his mind to rest by his very next words.

'You should beware,' said Lod. 'These people always overcharge. Never part with so much as a dorth if you're short of full satisfaction.'

'You're a fund of good advice,' said Sarazin.

'That,' said Lod, 'is the source of my pride.'

So Sarazin was certain Lod was honest. But even if Lod had been in the pay of the fortune tellers to whom he introduced Sarazin, it would still have been necessary for Sarazin to use their services. For how else could he find out why he was not succeeding in life?

There was so much he wanted so very very badly. Power. Fame. Prestige. Honour. Glory. And money money money. But none of it was coming his way. Indeed, wherever he turned his prospects seemed to be blocked by insuperable barriers. However, he knew there had to be a way to get what he wanted.

For, after all, since we have free will, all things are possible. Furthermore, possession of free will makes us entirely responsible for our lives. Everything happens to us by our own choice.

'All I want, then,' said Sarazin to himself, 'is a little advice on how to take responsibility for myself. That's not asking too much, is it now?'

Madam Ix did not dwell in the slumlands of Jone, but resided to the north, in Wake, hard up by Ol Unamon (the inner battle-wall of Selzirk). Her house was right next to the Seventh College of the Inner Circle of the Fish-Star Astrologers — just across the road from Wargol's Statue Hire and Thatcher's Slave Correction Services.

When Sarazin entered her chambers, joss sticks were

burning, scenting the air with mysterious perfumes. Candlelight stirred shadows in dusty corners. Quarles the owl — to whom Sarazin was introduced with a considerable degree of ceremony — sat on Madam Ix's shoulder. Blinking.

'Sit you down, young Sarazin,' said Madam Ix, patting her powdered wig, which was adorned with three dozen fishbones.

Sarazin sat.

'What is it you wish to know?' said Madam Ix.

'The future,' said Sarazin.

Then he crossed her palm with silver in the time-approved manner. It is often averred that Money, like Music, hath Powers; what is beyond dispute is that professional powers of prognosis can seldom be made to work without it.

There was a pause while Madam Ix tossed the yarrow sticks, consulted the Book, sacrificed a pinch of salt to the Sacred Goldfish, engaged in telepathic communion with Quarles the owl, then orientated her turtle-shell knife towards north.

'Now,' she said, breathing heavily, 'now I am ready to commune with the Beyond.'

Madam Ix stared for a while at nothing. Eyes vacant. Then began twitching. Shaking. Shivering. Voices muttered in the corners of the room. Sarazin had the fearful impression that something without was trying to break into the room. To get at them. To—

To what? He dared not think, but was relieved when life returned to the eyes of Madam Ix. Now she would speak. She had seen Beyond: now she would talk and reveal.

'I see war,' she said. 'I see, too, you yourself named for war. Watashi they will call you.'

'A strange name!' said Sarazin, perplexed by this. Then, keen to know how he would fare with Amantha, he said: 'What do you see of love?'

The fortune-teller looked at his face and saw there what

67

she took to be the hormone-hyped gleam of puppy love, though it was in fact the lust for power, fame, wealth and glamour. She told him what he wanted to hear.

'You love a lady,' she said. 'Through love, your destiny you'll find.'

'But how?' said Sarazin, in a voice close to despair.

'The how and the why are not in my keeping,' she said.

And, lacking the money to persuade her to say more, he had to depart unsatisfied.

That night, Sarazin lay dreaming of Amantha. He dreamed in particular of the pink flesh which lined her naos, the holy of holies which he wished to penetrate. By force, if there was no other way. Force? Yes! In his dreams, at least, that much was possible. He raped her: and woke pumping.

'Shtig!' said Sarazin, giving vent to sour obscenity.

Unable to sleep, he took to his sword and trained with the blade until the moth-shy light of morning began to unshadow the world. The sword in question was not, of course, the blade of firelight steel given to him by Lord Regan. It was a workaday weapon which Farfalla bade him keep with him always for protection.

At sunrise, Sarazin finally gave this sword a name.

'Onslaught be your name,' he said. 'Yes, you are Onslaught from now on.'

The name expressed Sarazin's own grim determination to renew his attack on Amantha, to press home the assault, to give no quarter, to strive, to win, to conquer. To make the woman his.

Sarazin, realising it was going to be difficult to persuade Amantha to yield to his charms, decided he needed to know more about her, particularly her likes and dislikes. Therefore early that morning he went looking for Lod, hoping for a long and productive talk with his friend from Chenameg.

However, Lod was not available for such a talk. The

young prince was closeted in conference with his brother Tarkal. So Sarazin, impatient to bring his campaign against Amantha to a successful conclusion, took his problem to Thodric Jarl, whom he found renewing the sharkskin grip on a favourite sword.

Now Jarl was Master of Combat for the Watch, he usually only saw Sarazin during their daily combat training sessions. But, knowing his young charge well, he had no trouble divining his problem.

'A woman, is it?' said Jarl.

His hard face unsympathetic. Gnarled by the weather of half a dozen wars.

'Not just a woman!' protested Sarazin. 'I'm in love!'

'Oh, love,' said Jarl, in a dismissive tone. 'A sorry sickness! Haven't you yet got a regular whore? Believe me, these fevers pass soon enough if properly treated.'

But Sarazin knew merely slaking his lust would not cure his passion. He wanted Amantha. Not just for a night, but for life. As his true love. His wife.

'This is a special woman,' said Sarazin. 'It has to be her. Nobody else will do.'

'Then knock her over the head and have your wicked way with her,' said Jarl. 'Have you anything else on your mind? If not, I've got work to do.'

Sarazin left Jarl, mind full of plots and plans. Could he seize Amantha by force? No! The very idea was absurd! Kidnapping would scarcely serve his purposes. He wanted a legal marriage which would see him in line for the throne of Chenamag.

Again he asked after Lod. On finding his friend was still in conference with Tarkal, Sarazin took his problem to his aged tutor, the venerable Epelthin Elkin.

'In love, are you?' said Elkin. 'Ah, love! I've not learnt much of love in my life of dusty scholarship.'

'But you must have some idea!' said Sarazin. 'How can I win the woman? Not just for a night, but for life.'

'You can never win a woman for life,' said Elkin, 'for all liaisons are but treaties which must nightly be renewed.'

'For a night, then! A night would be a start. How can I win her for a night?'

'Jewels, boy,' said Elkin. 'That's the answer. The scintillation of diamonds. The gleam of rubies, glowing like blood amidst yellow butter.'

'You suggest I give her gemstones in butter?' said Sarazin, who was always hoping to catch Elkin in open senility.

'Nay, boy. Jewels and gold.'

'But I'm broke!'

He was certainly impoverished, since whatever money came his way soon went on drink, cards and fortune tellers. And tips for Bizzie, his maid. Besides, he did not want to bribe Amantha. He wanted her to choose him out of love, lust, respect, admiration. Or any combination of those.

'So you've no gold,' said Elkin.

'None.'

'Any diamonds?'

'No.'

'Jade? Silver? Amber? Silk?'

'You know the answer already.'

Sarazin's one valuable possession was his blade of firelight steel. But his mother had taken away that weapon. Thodric Jarl had been given custody of it, and Sarazin only saw it during training sessions with the Rovac warrior.

'Then,' said Elkin, maliciously, 'all I can suggest is that you take your problem to Amantha's brother.'

'Lod can't help me,' said Sarazin.

'I didn't mean Lod. I meant Tarkal.'

'Tarkal?' said Sarazin, incredulously.

'Trust me,' said Elkin, sure that Tarkal would beat some sense into Sarazin — and sure, also, that this was the neatest way to deal with the problem.

Thus, on the advice of his tutor, Sarazin sought out Tarkal, who, having finished his business with Lod, was busy with his armourer in the guest quarters.

'I want to talk to you,' said Sarazin.

'Then wait,' said Tarkal brusquely.

Then resumed his conversation with his armourer. He

70

wanted the aventail of his helm modified. This subject was dear to his heart, and very technical. Sarazin, listening, was embarrassed to find the niceties of the matter completely beyond his comprehension.

'What do you want?' said Tarkal, when the armourer had left.

'A private audience with your sister.'

'Who are you?' said Tarkal.

'I am Sean Sarazin, a prince of the Harvest Plains.'

'You are no prince,' said Tarkal.

'My mother is Farfalla.'

'I've seen that fat sow for myself. If such spawned you, that makes you a piglet at best.'

Sarazin declined to be insulted. Deciding boldness would serve him best, he said:

'I wish to—'

'To what?'

'To marry your sister.'

'You are refused,' said Tarkal, not bothering to laugh since he had no audience to appreciate the laughter.

And, when Sarazin persisted, Tarkal booted him. Hard. Since the event happened in privacy, Sarazin chose to ignore it. He left the Chenameg princeling's presence, and went and sought out Lod.

CHAPTER NINE

Bizzie: a matronly woman who is wife of the ostler Hof-Gof, a past lover of Farfalla's sometime paramour Fox, and mother of Sarazin's half-brother Benthorn.

'You were with Tarkal for a long time,' said Sarazin.

'So I was,' said Lod.

71

'How did it go?'

'Badly,' said Lod. 'Tarkal claims my father demands my return to Chenamag. But he showed me no proof of this order, so I refused absolutely to obey. He then threatened me. But I've no fear of his threats, for he has no powers in Selzirk.'

'Still,' said Sarazin, 'it can't have been pleasant. Tell me — have you always been at odds with Tarkal?'

'No, not always,' said Lod. 'Only for twenty years.'

This was one of Lod's jokes, since Lod was, as Sarazin knew well, twenty years old — two years younger than Amantha and five years younger than Tarkal. But, as the joke was so weak, Sarazin did not waste time laughing. Instead he asked:

'How about Amantha?'

'Oh, we get on all right,' said Lod. 'I don't think she's much of a sister, but then I've nothing much to compare her with, have I?'

'No,' said Sarazin, 'I meant Amantha and Tarkal. How do they get on?'

'Oh, very well,' said Lod. 'Very well indeed. Friend Sarazin, you wouldn't believe how well they get on.'

Then Lod laughed aloud at some very private joke, which he declined to share with Sarazin even when asked to.

'Why do you ask anyway?' said Lod.

'I want to know as much about Amantha as I can,' said Sarazin. 'I want you to tell me everything you know about her.'

'Why,' said Lod, dismissively, 'she's a woman, is she not? That tells you everything you need to know.'

'But not how to make her love me!'

'Friend Sarazin, I'm no expert on love. What say we take your questions to a fortune-teller?'

'We've done that.'

'Ah, but so far you've only consulted the second-rate. Now it's time to seek help from the best. The woman I'm talking of is Madam Sosostris. Let me tell you about her . . .'

What Lod told Sarazin of the skill, power and ability of Madam Sosostris convinced him that she was worth a visit. So he allowed Lod to lead him to her premises. However, on arrival they found she was laid up with a bad cold.

'Nevertheless,' said Lod, 'she's known to be the wisest woman in Selzirk.'

'I believe you,' said Sarazin, who did. 'But, when do you think I can see her?'

'I'm no doctor,' said Lod, 'so I couldn't tell you. How about we try again tomorrow?'

'All right,' said Sarazin.

But when they called round early the next day they were told Madam Sosostris was still sick in bed. So Sarazin had to continue his campaign against Amantha without her advice.

Later that day, there was an official banquet at which Sarazin was one of the guests, Amantha another. Music tranced around them as they gorged themselves on delight. Clean napery and the sparkle of jewels. A night to remember.

Sarazin tried to catch Amantha's eye, yet her very gaze refused him.

Disgruntled, he quit the banquet early, pleading nausea, and retired to his own quarters, where he lay on his bed in something close to a sulk. Dreaming of taming Amantha with whips and chains, spurs and goads. Her pride wet-whimpering at his feet.

'What is the problem?' said Bizzie, his maid, on seeing that he was downcast.

'A woman,' he said gloomily.

He knew what she would suggest, and wanted nothing to do with it. While he had only recently begun taking advantage of her availability, he was already tired of her fat red face, her bloated body. There was something disgusting about her earthy intimacies: so different from the silken soft-voiced pleasures he had enjoyed with Jaluba in Voice.

'In lust again, ducks?' said Bizzie. 'Well, never mind.'

She laid herself down on his bed and pulled up her skirts, exposing her triangle. Hating himself for his weakness, Sarazin once again made good use of her flesh. It humiliated him, this traffic with a member of the lower orders. But he could not deny his animal.

'Cheer up,' said Bizzie. 'It can't be that bad.'

Then she licked, tickled and told rude jokes, but got not the whisper of a smile out of him.

'You'll feel better tomorrow,' she said, taking her accustomed silver.

'Tomorrow,' said Sarazin gloomily, 'never comes.'

But Bizzie was already gone, for she had work to do. Left alone, Sarazin lay staring up at the ceiling. Brooding. Degraded by tumbling with a common servant.

'Farfalla,' he muttered, a touch of hatred in his voice.

It was her fault. She it was who had bred him to his station. And who had, shortly after his recovery from the river-fever, encouraged him to make an arrangement with Bizzie. Lust will out somehow, Farfalla had said — pointing out that Selzirk's whores were rich with venereal diseases.

'Amantha,' said Sarazin, treasuring the name of his princess.

Was he really in love? He hoped so. After all, there was no other genuine princess on the horizon. So if he was not in love with this one, then he was in trouble.

He touched his limpness. Dank thing smelling, now, of woman.

'Why is it this?' he said, in a voice which was almost a moan. 'This which rules us?'

Love, thought Sarazin, *should not be so physical. So vulgar. Smells and slurpings. Stickiness of skin against skin. Wet exudate aftermath.*

—Music. I wish for a love like music.

Maybe he could make a poem out of that.

Attempting to do just that, Sarazin sat up late, trying to pen lines which would body forth his regret for his

74

possession of a body, and enshrine in deathless verse his wish to be made out of music. He was still hard at it towards midnight, when Bizzie came to him again.

'Still awake?' she said. 'I thought you might be.'

'It's no use,' he said. 'Apart from anything else, I've no more silver.'

'Goodwill's got a value of its own,' she said. 'And my husband's out late again with his darts team. Come on, love, shove over.'

She did her best, as ever. And his flesh, as always, could not deny its nature.

That night, Sarazin dreamed he possessed Amantha. His dream was so real, so intense, so certain, that, on waking, he was ready to dare her scorn again. His chance came when he was sent to escort the noble guests, who were going hawking for the day.

It was the very end of summer: hot, dry and dusty. Soon, autumn rains would cool the weather. But, for the moment, the heat and dust were almost unendurable. They were favoured with very little sport, for shooting birds was a standard child's pastime in the Harvest Plains, so little was left for royal hunters.

When far from Selzirk, Sarazin again tried Amantha's temper, riding up alongside his princess so he could proposition her.

'Sweetest charm,' he began.

'Forget it,' said Amantha.

'You haven't even heard me out!'

'I know what you want to talk about. About tupping.'

'About marriage!' protested Sarazin.

'The substance,' said Amantha, 'is the same.'

'What's your objection?' said Sarazin. 'Do you wish to be virgin forever?'

'You know my objection already,' said Amantha. 'You are not of the Favoured Blood, and never will be.'

Meaning he was not royal.

At which point Sarazin realised Tarkal had ridden up beside him.

'Are you troubling my sister?' said Tarkal.

While Sarazin was still trying to think of a diplomatic reply, Tarkal grabbed him by the collar then raked his horse with his spurs. The horse reared. Sarazin was hauled from the saddle and flung to the dust. He landed heavily. Looking up, he saw Tarkal staring down at him from horse-height.

'Peon!' said Tarkal. 'How dare you proposition my sister?'

Thus spoke Tarkal. Then spat. Accurately.

Sarazin wiped saliva from his face. Slowly. He hoisted himself from the ground. It hurt to move, but nothing was broken.

'Does it demand satisfaction?' asked Tarkal.

'I have gutted dung-eating pigs before,' said Sarazin. 'I already know the colour of their offal.'

'Now I demand satisfaction!' said Tarkal. 'You have the choice of weapons, of course.'

Sarazin hesitated.

'Do you deny me satisfaction?' said Tarkal.

'Are you a coward?' asked Amantha, her scorn denouncing him as exactly that.

They began riding round and round him, their horses kicking up dust which infiltrated his nose. Sarazin tried hard not to sneeze, because that would have been undignified. Some dust got in his eyes, which began watering furiously.

'He's crying!' said Tarkal.

'I am not!' shouted Sarazin.

'Of course you are,' jeered Tarkal. 'You're scared. You're a coward. Crying like a baby!'

'There's dust in my eyes,' protested Sarazin.

'Heroes fight and cowards run,' said Tarkal. 'Heroes fight and cowards run.'

He made a chant from the words, like a big child taunting a smaller. His companions joined him in the chant.

'I'll fight then!' shouted Sarazin.

Amantha laughed.

'Did I hear aright?' she said. 'I thought I heard it say it will fight.'

'I will fight!' said Sarazin.

'With what weapons?' said Tarkal.

'Swords, of course,' said Sarazin. 'Swords and shields.'

The reply came naturally, for these were the weapons he used when training with Thodric Jarl. Training for battle. Training for war.

'You mean to fight with shields?' said Tarkal, incredulously. 'What kind of daffing is this?'

'Swords and shields,' said Sarazin. 'I can bear the weight, even if you cannot.'

'He means it,' said someone.

And there was a titter of poorly suppressed laughter.

'Shields, then,' said Tarkal.

And grabbed the reins of Sarazin's horse, and galloped away.

'Hey!' shouted Sarazin. 'Hey! Hey! Come back!'

Laughing, they jaunted away with a jingle of sharps and spurs. Sarazin was left to walk back to Selzirk. Which he did. Counting the paces. With every step, he added details to Tarkal's death.

CHAPTER TEN

Come, daemon of war, enchant my sword,
That dead as daddock may my enemies fall,
Their uninhabited bodies sprawl
To fields where carrion crows
May glutton their blood as potage.
I will be a hero,
And wage to war forever in foreign fields:
For my mother-in-law guards the gates of my return.
                            —Saba Yavendar, 'Hero Talk'

When Thodric Jarl heard of the duel, he cursed Sarazin
for a fool. Jarl, the Rovac warrior who had taught Sarazin
weaponwork during his long captivity in Voice, knew full
well that Farfalla's son was unready for combat. Oh, he
had exchanged cuts in duels in Voice, for sure. But that
was mere sport undertaken for the sake of scars. This was
a matter of death.

'Still,' said Jarl, 'what's done is done.'

After making formal arrangements for the fight — which
would take place on the morrow's dawn on the palace
battlements — Jarl worked Sarazin hard, thinking fatigue
better than fear.

'I'll be wrecked by tomorrow,' said Sarazin at one stage,
drenched with sweat from sparring.

'You're young,' said Jarl. 'You'll live.'

Jarl, being the war-wise veteran that he was, thought it
best to deny Sarazin the leisure that would allow fear to
unman him. Wine and women he saw as equally dangerous
before a fight, for they comfort, pleasure and relax, mellow-
ing the world — whereas battle thrives on bone-cold hatred.

'We have but an evening,' said Jarl. 'That's no time at
all. Concentrate! Think combat!'

With Jarl setting the pace, they practised. Not with the
dance-light rapiers with which Sarazin had duelled in
Voice, but with war weapons of Stokos steel. Strong
blades, light enough to be wielded with one hand but heavy
enough to cleave through leather and bone. Swords built
for endurance in war, blade and tang forged from a single
piece of firelight steel, free from weak points such as welds
and rivets. While Sarazin's blade was a gift from Lord
Regan, Jarl had won his own on a battlefield.

'Likely your nobleman knows no shieldwork,' said Jarl.
'He won't be used to the weight, or trained for it.'

'Why?' said Sarazin. 'Surely Tarkal has his place in
Chenameg's army.'

'Chenameg has no army,' said Thodric Jarl. 'So Tarkal
has never trained for war. So how will he fight?'

'Duelling style. In and out. In and out.'

'Yes. Quick as a frog after flies. What will his feet be doing?'

'Quickwork also,' said Sarazin. 'In and out, in time with his blade.'

'Right! So watch. Wait. Brunt him with the shield. Let him exhaust himself. Then, when you get a good chance, strike. Hard! But not at his head, mind. Nor at his shield. Strike for his sword.'

'Why?'

'Likely as not, he'll bear a flimsy Chenameg duelling sword. I've seen no firelight steel with this embassy. Since they do no soldiering in Chenameg, all the stuff of local make is designed for fashion.'

'But sharp regardless,' said Sarazin.

'Sharp, yes, but weak. Likely blade will be riveted to the hilt. That's weakness. Sword against sword, you can likely break him.'

'If I'm going to try that,' said Sarazin. 'I don't think I'll use Lord Regan's gift. I'll use my second-best sword. It's strong enough, I think. I've given it a name: Onslaught.'

'A good name for a good weapon,' said Jarl. 'But second-best is not good enough for tomorrow. You'll use the weapon Lord Regan gave you.'

'But I might damage it! It's fearfully valuable!'

Jarl laughed, and clapped Sarazin on the shoulder. Feeling the young man's linen wet with sweat.

'It's your liver to worry about,' he said. 'Never your steel. That's war. Listen: here's a lesson for your life. Always take your best steel to war. Best sword, best horse, best boots, best men. Expense saved means nothing to a corpse.'

Lightly he spoke, yet his words brought home to Sarazin the reality of the doom which faced him. As Jarl took Sarazin through a series of stretching exercises, Sarazin realised that this time tomorrow he might be dead. He tried to imagine his death, but found it impossible. The world was but an extension of himself — so how could the world exist if he did not?

—Yet once, before I was born, the world existed without me. Or so it claims.

The thought was so improbable that Sarazin — not for the first time — doubted that the world really existed. Quite apart from its denial of the centrality of Sean Sarazin, there were other things about the world which struck him as unreal. Mortality, for instance.

—A world of people, all doomed to certain death. How could that be possible? If all flesh were truly mortal, how could there be laughter?

—If the world were a fact, and death universal a fact in that fact, surely the streets would run screaming from dawn to dusk. To be born, just to die? What kind of reality is that?

As he had done in the past, Sarazin conjured with the notion that perhaps he was really a god, dreaming. That he would wake, shortly, and resume his true life of power and creation.

Death?

A word beyond meaning.

'This ends our training,' said Jarl, for Sarazin had worked through the last of his stretching exercises while doing his thinking. 'I judge you tired enough to sleep by now. Mind you do! A warrior gets his head down and sleeps whenever the chance is given. That's one of the first lessons of war!'

But, though Jarl had thought Sarazin tired enough to sleep, Farfalla's son lay sleepless long, staring at the dark, conjuring with skulls and bloodclot disaster.

Throughout the night, Thodric Jarl slept soundly on a pallet outside Sarazin's door. If the young man had been fool enough to venture forth to search for card companions or other distractions, Jarl would have woken on the moment. As it was, his guard duty proved eventless.

Sarazin did in fact divert himself. With wine — yes, and with Amantha's flesh. And (lust cruel, direct and

80

shameless, like something done by the body of one insect to another) the very heat of his mother herself. But all this, of course, took place within dream's world of delusions.

Sarazin was still sleeping, still dreaming, when Jarl shook him awake. The young man who would be king startled awake. Smelt the roughwork sweat of the Rovac warrior.

'It's dark,' said Sarazin.

'Yes, but near dawn,' said Jarl. 'Rouse yourself. It's a great day for it.'

—A great day to die.

To his discomfort, Sarazin found he had diarrhoea. He refused breakfast, but accepted the cup of hot green tea which Bizzie brought him. Tea was drunk by few people in Selzirk, but Sarazin indulged himself in it daily. Every morning its savour conjured up memories of Voice, and he wished himself back in that city.

'Fighting, are we?' said Bizzie. 'Well, good luck to you.'

'Thanks,' said Sarazin.

Grateful, despite himself, for such good wishes, even though they came from the low-bred mother of his bastard brother Benthorn.

'Get this inside you,' said Jarl, offering Sarazin a tot of rum to follow the tea.

'I thought you told me never to drink and fight.'

'A smahan of rum will do you no harm. Drink!'

Sarazan drank. It was good. Heat in his belly. Warmth in his veins. He longed to linger to enjoy that heat. To rest. To sleep a little more — till noon perhaps. But Jarl was setting the pace and, all too soon, Sarazin was fastening his swordbelt.

'My shield?'

'I'll carry it,' said Jarl.

Then they were on their way to the battlements where Sarazin would confront Tarkal at dawn. The morning was cold, yet the last icechip stars were melting. Pink clouds swathed the eastern horizon.

Sarazin shivered.

'Are we late?' he said, seeing Tarkal and his courtiers

clustered on the battlements ahead. 'Let's not be late. They'd think me a coward.'

'No need to hurry,' said Jarl. 'They won't run away. Step loose. Step even.'

Jarl persuaded Sarazin to unstring his battle-tense muscles, making him take it slowly.

'Think now,' said Jarl. 'Think of a stone in water. Deepen your breathing. Deep and slow. Think of a stone steady amidst water. You are that stone. Deep and slow. Breathe in. And out. Deep and slow . . .'

The lull of Jarl's voice and the steady rhythm of walking calmed Sarazin. Then he looked up, and saw the opposition close ahead, a gaudy cabal of silks and smirks, ready, waiting. The morning light was stronger. Conjuring with colours.

His footsteps faltered.

'Take the shield, then,' said Jarl, loudly, to give the impression that Sarazin had halted to ask for that object.

Sarazin took the weight.

'Onward,' urged Jarl, low-voiced.

Sarazin closed the distance. Amantha, her hands buried deep in a wolverine muff, studied him with disdain. Her maids exchanged glances and giggles. A courtier indulged himself with a pinch of snuff. Yawned. As Tarkal stepped forward.

'So,' said Tarkal, beginning a devastatingly witty speech which he had carefully prepared the night before. 'Our young peasant friend has condescended to join us at last. I see he—'

Without warning, Jarl slapped Sarazin on the back and shouted:

'Draw!'

Sarazin drew. Sword lept from sheath. He shouted as he had been taught:

'Ah-hai!'

The battle-cry came from his gut, focusing energy on action. He quivered with warlike aggression. Which made Amantha laugh. Her laughter tinkled like fractured glass.

'It shivers,' she said. 'See? It is frightened.'

'That,' said Tarkal, no sword in his hands but no fear in his voice, 'reflects its breeding.'

'Draw, dog!' shouted Sarazin, enraged.

'No need for amateur theatricals,' said Tarkal, his voice as cool as bone beneath water. 'Shall we wait until the sun has warmed the world before we fight?'

'We wait for nothing,' said Jarl. 'We fight. Now!'

Sarazin, quick-breathing, was gladdened by Jarl's voice. He remembered to slow his breathing. The iron grip of the shield was warming beneath his fingers. He was ready.

'No games now,' said Jarl. 'Fight to kill.'

But Tarkal, with studied insolence, delayed while he cracked his knuckles one by one, donned leather gauntlets, accepted sword and shield from retainers, then paused to test the weight and balance of his equipment.

Then, finally — when Sarazin was tense enough to scream — Tarkal settled himself for combat. A sardonic smile on his face. And Sarazin found himself—

Paralysed.

Incapable of action.

Strange gnat-sized squiggles of darkness scrawled across his field of vision. His legs were shaking. And Tarkal, smiling, smiling, was leisuring towards him, sword on guard and—

'Strike!' screamed Jarl.

The word snapped Sarazin into action. His blade leapt for Tarkal's throat, as if of its own volition. Sword clashed with sword. Then the two broke apart. Panting.

Jarl shouted:

'Lunge!'

Tarkal moved to parry a lunge which never came. The unaccustomed shield-weight tricked his feet. Momentarily, Tarkal stumbled. Sarazin seized his chance. He charged. Shield smashed against shield. All Sarazin's bodyweight was behind the charge. Tarkal staggered backwards, went down.

'No!' screamed Amantha.

But already Tarkal was getting to his feet. He scrabbled for shield and sword, found sword alone, brought the blade to the challenge — and saw Sarazin's shield flying through the air towards him. Thrown full force. No time to dodge. No time to duck. Steel must avail. Tarkal met shield with sword.

'Ha!' screamed Jarl, expecting the sword to break.

But sword deflected shield.

'Take him as I've taught you!' shouted Jarl.

Sarazin advanced upon Tarkal. Breathing harshly. Both hands on the hilt of his sword. As both combatants had lost their shields, it was bare blades now. To the death.

'Ska!' screamed Tarkal.

Striking with all his force.

'Ha!' screamed Sarazin.

Striking full-force at Tarkal's oncoming blade.

The blades met. The full strength of two men was devoted to their meeting. And one blade broke. Steel went flying, somersaulting, sun-spangling. Tarkal dared a thrust — then realised his fist held nothing but a swordhilt. The Chenameg princeling gaped at the hilt of the sword. The blade had been torn clean away from the hilt.

'Kill!' yelled Jarl.

But before Sarazin could lunge, Tarkal was running. He fled slap-bang into the arms of his startled supporters.

'Now!' screamed Jarl.

Sarazin lunged. And spiked Tarkal's left buttock.

'The spine!' roared Jarl. 'Stab him in the spine!'

But Tarkal dropped to his hands and knees and rabbited away between the legs of his courtiers. Two of those worthies drew swords and advanced on Sarazin, meaning to kill him.

'None of that,' said Jarl, interposing his death-blade between the would-be murderers and their intended victim. The courtiers, who were but overgrown boys, stepped back smartly, unwilling to fight such a hard-bitten veteran. 'All

84

right,' said Jarl. 'Clean the rat's blood from your blade and we'll be going.'

So saying, he gave Sarazin a rag with which to clean his blade. Meanwhile, Amantha had gone to the aid of her wounded brother.

'Tarkal!' she cried.

'It is nothing,' he said, waving her away.

'My darling,' she said, dabbing at the blood with her handkerchief.

While his sister tended his wound, Tarkal said to Sarazin:

'You have ended my quest. You have ruined my hopes of glory. Does that give your warped peasant brain some grain of satisfaction?'

'What quest is that?' said Sarazin.

And heard one of the retainers whisper to another, in shocked delight:

'He doesn't know!'

'What have I done?' said Sarazin, bewildered and distressed.

But they gave him no answer.

'Come,' said Jarl to Sarazin. 'Let's be going.'

Once they were decently removed from the courtiers, Sarazin asked:

'How did I do?'

'Better than I expected,' said Jarl. 'After all, you're alive.'

'But — but I did something wrong, didn't I? Because they were so upset — about the quest, I mean. What was that all about?'

'Their own business,' said Jarl, 'which is no concern of ours. Tarkal was on the quest which is traditional for the oldest son of the king of Chenameg.'

'What quest is that?' said Sarazin.

'To search for the tectonic lever and set the same in action.'

'Tectonic lever?'

'A war machine from the days of the Technic Renaissance. Legend sets it in the terror-lands of the Deep South,

85

far beyond Drangsturm. It is said to have the power to sink Argan.'

'To sink . . . ?'

'To plunge the continent beneath the waves.'

'A weapon indeed!' said Sarazin. 'But how would Chenameg profit if Argan sank? Chenameg is itself but a part of Argan.'

'Ah!' said Jarl. 'But legend holds that Argan North would not entirely be swallowed by the sea. While waves would swamp the Harvest Plains entire, the rising seas would leave Chenameg with a border with the ocean.'

'I see! The Harvest Plains would drown, and Chenameg—'

'Chenameg would become a great seapower,' said Jarl, 'lording its power over the ruins of a sunken world.'

'And we — we allow these princes thus to try to encompass our doom?'

Jarl laughed.

'By tradition, each questing hero turns back on getting his first wound. You gave Tarkal a scratch, so he goes home a hero.'

'That's not much of a quest!' said Sarazin, with a touch of outrage in his voice.

'Ah,' said Jarl, 'but it's the best kind of quest for one in line for wealth and power. A survivable quest, quickly undertaken near to home. No prince in the last five generations has needed to quest beyond the borders of the Harvest Plains to get the scratch which sent him home.'

'If I were a prince of Chenameg—'

'Yes,' said Jarl, 'yes, I know. You'd feel yourself honour-bound to quest through danger until you came to this tectonic lever, yea, though you had to fight through fifty thousand dragons to reach its doorstep.'

Sarazin, chagrined to be so easily read, blushed. To cover his confusion, he went on the attack:

'How come you never told me this in Voice? Surely I should have been told!'

'Why?' said Jarl. 'I taught you weapons. That was my responsibility. Nothing more, nothing less. Anyway, I never knew much of Chenameg till I came to Selzirk. But since then, I've found out much.'

As members of the Watch were still trying to persuade Jarl to mastermind a coup and put Sarazin on the throne of the Harvest Plains, Jarl was doing his very best to learn all he could of both the internal and external politics of the nation.

'I've never asked you this before,' said Sarazin, 'but — why did you come back with me? From Voice, I mean.'

'I like to finish what I start,' said Jarl.

Which reminded him: it was about time for him to complete his latest report and send it off to Lord Regan of the Rice Empire. Master of Combat, conspirator, spy and tutor to Sarazin to boot: Thodric Jarl was a busy man indeed.

'I've another question,' said Sarazin.

'What?'

'At the end of the fight, why did Amantha go to Tarkal, not to me?'

'What a senseless question!' said Jarl. 'He's her brother, hence owns her allegiance. What did you expect?'

'But it was for love of her that I got myself into all this trouble!'

'Then the more fool you,' said Jarl, 'for she's a nasty piece of work, if I'm any judge of womanflesh.'

Perhaps. But she was the woman Sarazin wanted. And he was still determined to make her his before the embassy left Selzirk to return to Chenameg.

CHAPTER ELEVEN

Lod: gambler, layabout and professional debtor who also happens to be the youngest son of King Lyra of Chenameg and guest of Farfalla of the Harvest Plains.

Description: a slim, graceful man of twenty who has athlete's foot and (alas!) syphilis, and a wary eye alert for approaching creditors.

Residence: guest quarters (by the Hall of Wine), palace of the kingmaker, Selzirk.

Once Sarazin was back in his quarters the full import of what had happened began to sink in. He was alive! Alive and — blessed be the gods! — unhurt. He was ebullient. He danced up and down on the spot for the sheer joy of being alive.

Abruptly his mood changed. Realising how completely he had failed, he threw himself down on his bed. He was disgusted with himself. The duel had been his big chance: but he had bungled it. He could have killed Tarkal three times over if his heart had really been in the fight. But his enemy had escaped with little more than a scratch.

—*What could I have been thinking of?*

Unfortunately, he knew exactly what he had been thinking of: chiefly his own mortality. He had been scared. Shit scared. (Literally, since fear was the source of that morning's diarrhoea.) And he had let Tarkal escape. A bad mistake indeed, since he must kill Tarkal sooner or later, otherwise there was very little point pursuing Amantha.

—*What now?*

Self-disgust was already giving way to fatigue. He was very, very weary. He closed his eyes, intending to take just a little nap, and when he woke it was afternoon. A meal was sitting on a chair by his bed, the plate covered by muslin to protect it against the summer flies. Lunch, doubtless. He wished Bizzie had woken him when she brought the meal, for he had work to do.

He had to arrange another meeting with Amantha so he could once more declare his love to her.

When Sarazin found the embassy was returning to the

Chenameg Kingdom the very next day, he looked for Lod, since he wanted advice urgently. He had decided to pen some lines in praise of Amantha and wanted Lod to tell him what would appeal to his sister. But Lod was nowhere to be found. Accordingly, Sarazin did the best he could unaided.

The next day, Sarazin was on hand when the visitors assembled at noon to take their departure. They faced a long journey eastward from Selzirk to Chenameg's borders, then through the forests to Shin, which was King Lyra's capital.

Farfalla herself was not there to farewell the embassy. Word had come from Androlmarphos to say the governor of the place had died, so she had departed for that city, where she would officiate at the funeral.

She would not, however, appoint another governor. Not today, not tomorrow. The privilege of appointing such 'kings' was one of the few powers the Regency had been unable to alienate from her. Such positions were eagerly sought after, and competition would be fierce.

For once, Farfalla would have real power, real influence. Of course, while she toyed with those who sought to become king of Androlmarphos, the city's administration would suffer. But — what of it? Once she appointed a king, another vacancy might not occur for twenty years. Or thirty. By which time she might be long dead.

—*This is not the game I would have chosen.*

Thus thought Farfalla.

But it was the only game in town.

Farfalla's downstream journey westward from Selzirk to Androlmarphos would be swift. But the embassy travelling east would have a slow journey, for the riders had but one horse apiece. Furthermore, three baggage wagons were going with them, heavily laden with goods usually unobtainable in Chenameg, plus gifts from Farfalla and from the Regency.

None of the travellers condescended to notice Sarazin's existence — least of all Tarkal, who was sitting bravely in his saddle with a plump swansdown pillow between his injured buttock and the unforgiving leather.

In a few moments they would leave and Sarazin's chance would be gone. So:

'In honour of the Princess Amantha,' said Sarazin loudly, 'I wish to read a poem.'

'So it can read,' said Tarkal.

'Hush,' said Amantha. 'Let it read. That can do no harm.'

Amantha, despite herself, could not help being interested in a poem which promised to honour her. Sarazin produced his manuscript with a flourish, and cleared his throat.

He had been trained in oratory, and had read his poems in public in Voice often enough, to generous applause — but, even so, could not help but feel nervous.

'Well,' said Tarkal. 'Get on with it. We haven't got all day.'

So Sarazin began to read his poem:

'Though even phoenix must in time renew—'

Tarkal sneezed, and his horse suddenly began to sidestep with a clatter of hooves on cobblestones. As if by black magic, an epidemic of coughing and sneezing broke out amongst the courtiers; their horses became restless; their hound-dogs howled—

But Sarazin, raising his voice, continued his lines about petal-scented wonder, the worship of shadows, the adoration of hearts, the difficulties which must lovers sunder, and that fine renaissance of feeling which will in time splendour love anew.

Concluding, he offered his manuscript to Amantha, saying:

'Fair flower of inspiration, please accept this humble token of my esteem.'

This kind of flowery phraseology had been all the fashion in Voice (though there, of course, Sarazin had couched his phrases in the Geltic of the Rice Empire, instead of the City Churl which he spoke in Selzirk).

Amantha did not accept his offering.

'Ah, so it is in love,' said she. 'Poor thing! Like a pig-dog in lust with the moon.'

And all the retinue laughed.

'You know how to brawl,' said Tarkal, 'if not how to duel, but you'll never make a poet in a million years.'

'How dare you sneer at me?' said Sarazin. 'I beat you in fair combat!'

'You came armed as if for a gutter fight,' said Tarkal, 'armed with a common brawler's weapon. How was I to know you would stoop so low?'

'I came with a weapon of war!' said Sarazin.

'Oh, indeed!' said Amantha. 'A weapon of war! Do you expect me to hold you in great wish when you try for your honour with a common soldier's bludgeon?'

'My blade's no bludgeon!' protested Sarazin. 'It's a weapon-sword true, a tooth of Stokos steel, the world's most expensive bladework!'

'Money,' said Amantha, 'never yet bought class.'

And, as Sarazin stood there, dismayed, his mouth agape, she flicked the reins of her horse and rode away.

Sarazin was devastated by Amantha's rejection of his poem. He had laboured on it long and hard, first writing it in Geltic, then translating it into Churl, then trying it out on Bizzie (no other critic being available).

Still, he could survive the rejection of his art. He knew genius creates the taste by which it is appreciated; this takes time, a commodity Amantha was not prepared to afford him. But the insult to his weapon was a more serious matter.

Sarazin took his woes to his swordmaster.

'What's the problem?' said Thodric Jarl.

'They say my blade is that of a common soldier.'

'Who says?'

'The people from Chenameg.'

'Who heeds the defeated?' said Jarl, scornfully. 'This much I've learnt from a lifetime's campaigning: no loser was ever outclassed or outfought. The victor always bluffed, cheated or was aided by the weather. Thus speak the defeated.'

'But they—'

'They play at battle as if it was a game,' said Jarl.

'Duelling,' said Sarazin, with more than a touch of pomposity, 'has ever been a feature of the noble life.'

'Games,' repeated Jarl. 'Well, that's not what I was hired to teach you.'

'What have you taught me, then?' said Sarazin, unwisely.

'Death, not dancing. Survival, not style. If princes and such wish to charade with steel and call it combat — well, that's no business of mine. But — mark well! — you'll meet with no fighting for fashion's sake in a brothel brawl or a battlefield bloodbath.'

Sarazin had the impression he had heard all this before. As indeed he had. Six or seven times at least.

'So I was right to fight with my Stokos steel?' said Sarazin.

'To stay alive? Of course! Whatever weapon serves, that's the one to use. Over the years, I've defended my life with everything from a dead cat to a full-charged chamber pot.'

'But I wasn't being fair to Tarkal, was I?' said Sarazin. 'I knew he wouldn't know the tricks of shieldwork. I knew my blade would likely break his.'

'You were right to fight on your terms, not his,' said Jarl. 'After all, he started it. Anyway, that's one of the greater parts of the art of war: forcing the enemy to fight on ground of your choosing.'

'But they laughed at me!'

'They laughed, you lived,' said Jarl. 'I wouldn't complain too much about that.'

'What about my poem?' said Sarazin. 'They laughed at that, too. Amantha in particular.'

'That does you no lasting harm either,' said Jarl.

'But why did she laugh at my poem?'

'Ask the sun, the moon or the fish in the sea, but don't ask me. Poems are pretty enough, if you like that kind of thing, but one sounds much like another to me.'

Then, since Sarazin was on hand, Jarl launched him upon a session of sword-training.

One sweaty training session later, Sarazin surrendered his blade of firelight steel to Thodric Jarl and went hunting for Lod. Who was nowhere to be found. It was scarcely practical to quarter Selzirk entire in the hope of finding him by chance, so, after some thought, Sarazin went to ask Madam Ix for news of Lod.

Since Sarazin sometimes had his doubts about the efficacy of fortune telling he had often wanted to test the skills of the mystery workers on some practical problem. This looked to be the ideal opportunity.

'I'm hunting for Lod,' said Sarazin, when he was admitted to the presence of Ix of the Mystery.

'Does this look like a brothel?' said Madam Ix. 'Or a booze barn? Or a gambling den? You'll not find him here. But just for interest's sake — how much money does he owe you?'

'None,' said Sarazin, promptly.

On a little reflection, he was surprised to realise it was true. Jarl's lecturing must have taught Sarazin some wisdom, because he had never let Lod borrow money from him. Mind you: he had never really had money spare to lend.

'Then,' said Madam Ix, 'if he owes you no money, what do you want him for? Have you decided you love him?'

'Nay,' said Sarazin. 'We exhausted love in our last incarnations when we were dogs in the street together. He's missing. I'm worried about him. If he's not here, can your Art find him?'

'Of course,' said Madam Ix, 'for the Art knows no limits.'

But the price she named was very, very high. Sarazin, entirely unable to meet such a price, asked:

'Pray tell, why is this service priced so high? Do you seek to avoid a true test of your Art by setting such a price?'

'Selzirk is a sewer,' said Madam Ix, 'and Lod a clod lost

93

somewhere in that sewer. The price I set is the price for delving in unclean things. If you must use the Art for improper purposes you must pay the penalty.'

'What, then, is the proper purpose of the Art?' said Sarazin.

'To read character,' said Madam Ix, 'to commune with the spirits, to speak with the dead, to tell the past and future both. To deal with the higher things and the greater purposes. Not to find lost boys, lost dogs or wayward debtors.'

'I tell you,' said Sarazin, 'Lod owes me no money.'

'So you have said already,' said Madam Ix. 'But he owes others. If he's missing I have no doubt he's missing from choice. I vum he's lying low while his creditors hunt him. Now tell me, young Sarazin, before you go — have you seen Madam Sosostris yet?'

'No,' said Sarazin. 'I went there with Lod, but she was sick so we couldn't get in.'

'You must go again,' said Madam Ix, 'for I hear my colleague Sosostris has discovered a new book of prophecy.'

'I've no interest in prophecy,' said Sarazin.

'This book concerns a prince. A prince by name of Watashi.'

'Watashi?' said Sarazin. 'That is an ill name!' Indeed it was, for it meant, amongst other things, fear. Blood. And death. It was, for some reason, strangely familiar. Why? After a moment's thought Sarazin said: 'An ill name, yes, and the one you claimed that I myself would bear.'

'So I did!' said Madam Ix, as if the thought had just occurred to her. 'I saw war, and saw you yourself named for war. Why, this is a strange coincidence!'

'I hope this book's no forgery cooked up by grasping fortune tellers to gull a client,' said Sarazin, who also thought the coincidence strange.

'No, no, it's no forgery,' said Ix. 'You'd see that in a moment. This is a text of great antiquity. Madam Sosostris claims the book most interesting. She thinks it may have

94

a bearing on . . . on the life of a certain person whom politics makes it dangerous to name.'

Ancient books, prophecies, a promise of politics — it made a most enticing mix.

'Once I've found Lod, I'll look into it,' said Sarazin. 'But I don't have the time right now.'

'There's one more thing you should know,' said Ix. 'Madam Sosostris has a new assistant. A female beauty from the Rice Empire. Her name is Jaluba.'

Electrifying news!

But Sarazin, fearing interest on his part would be communicated from Ix to Sosostris and would raise the price of admission, pretended a complete lack of interest.

'Well,' said he, working so hard on the business of acting casual that his hands trembled, 'I'll look into that, too, in due course. But for now, I have to go hunting for Lod.'

However, on escaping into the street Sarazin went directly to the Sosostris lair. The hunt for Lod could wait. Jaluba was in town! Melon-fleshed Jaluba, she of the scented omphalos, the ticklish armpits. Mistress of the raptures, the joys, the delights.

On his way to see Sosostris (and Jaluba) Sarazin dreamt dreams and saw visions. But his prospects for converting these dreams and visions to reality fell sharply when the gateman guarding the Sosostris lair asked him a ridiculous price for admission alone.

'Once you get the price down to something reasonable,' said Sarazin, 'I'll think about it.'

But the gateman proved reluctant to bargain.

'I'll wait for you to see reason,' said Sarazin, 'I'm in no hurry.'

And wait he did, drawing his good sword Onslaught to practise his weapon-work. Though the sky was clouding over, it was still hot; in fact, though the weather promised rain, this was the hottest day Sarazin had endured in Selzirk. He was soon sweating profusely.

A small boy challenged him with a stick, and Sarazin indulged him by engaging in a slow-motion duel. While he was amusing himself thus, a palankeen came by. It halted, and a woman dismounted.

Sarazin paid her no attention till she spoke to him.

'Do you think it will rain?' she said.

Sarazin turned to examine the body which went with the voice, and found himself face to face with a veiled matron awash with scent. The child who had been duelling with Sarazin poked him in the gut with his stick and said 'Die!' Sarazin brushed the stick away, said 'Vanish!' in a tone which commanded instant obedience, then said: 'Madam Sosostris?'

'Oh no, oh no,' said the perfume-drenched matron, with a girlish giggle which ill befitted her years. 'I am Mistress Turbothot. I have an audience with Sosostris, though. And you?'

'I'm just leaving,' said Sarazin.

The Turbothot woman was obviously rich. Her silks, her rings and her gold-braided shoes told him that. The waiting palankeen, of course, also spoke of wealth. Whatever plans Madam Sosostris might have for Sean Sarazin, he was unlikely to command her attention when she had a client so wealthy waiting for her services.

'Wait, wait, don't go!' said Mistress Turbothot, as Sarazin turned to go. 'Or, if you must, tell me at least this — who are you, darling boy?'

'I am no boy but a warrior,' said he. 'I am Sean Kelebes Sarazin, son of the kingmaker Farfalla.'

'Oh, a prince!' she said, in tones of unabashed admiration.

While Sarazin liked the title, he saw no point in smallchat with a woman older than his mother and twice the weight, so without further ado he departed for Jone to search for Lod amongst the streets of the poor and the ruthless.

Now that the prospect of an immediate interview with Jaluba had vanished, Sarazin finally began to think. And realised he had indeed a lot to think about. Obviously, Ix and Sosostris already knew of his lust for Jaluba. The wench must have told them her past. But this was a strange coincidence, was it not?

—Too much of a coincidence.

—It must be conspiracy!

Madam Ix and Madam Sosostris must have learnt Sarazin's past from Lod — who had, after all, introduced Sarazin to these practitioners of the Art. They must have sent all the way to Voice for Jaluba. Hoping for — for what? Money?

—Perhaps Lod told them I'm rich. Perhaps he gulled them completely. As a joke, perhaps.

—Or it could be that this is political. Perhaps they think I've influence over my mother.

Either way, the really intelligent thing would be for Sarazin to forget about Jaluba. Because, one way or another, he would surely be made to pay heavily for the privilege of bedding the woman. Sarazin knew this. But could not help himself.

—The world would be well lost for such a woman.

Then Sarazin reminded himself that he was wrong to be thinking thus, for he was in love with a princess. Yes, his true love was Amantha of Chenameg, who came complete with a kingdom, whereas Jaluba owned little more than a giggle.

Sarazin diligently conjured with visions of Amantha (and of power, of fame, of fortune) as he strode on towards Jone.

CHAPTER TWELVE

Benthorn: Sarazin's half-brother, son of Fox and Bizzie. The owner-operator of a dung cart who has an uncommonly keen interest in the Constitution and other matters political.

* * *

In Jone's bars and taverns, in brothels and wharfside gambling pits, Sarazin saw no sign of Lod. But he did meet several people whom Lod would usually have seen on a typical visit to the quarter. All averred that Lod had certainly not been in Jone that day. By evening, Sarazin was thoroughly frustrated. Lod was the key to his life. Lod alone would know how he should pursue Amantha now that the lady had left Selzirk. Should he write her letters, send her poems? Or saddle a horse and ride to Chenameg in person?

Sarazin also believed Lod might also be able to help him work out a strategy for securing admission to Jaluba's charms without paying exorbitant amounts of money to Madam Sosostris. Yet he had no idea where he should look next.

On his way home, Sarazin had to pass through Libernek Square, the site of the Voat Library where the old man Elkin worked as Archivist. Sarazin wondered if his tutor could help him. Epelthin Elkin had a very organised intellect. Any problem discussed with him automatically became clearer, even if it did not necessarily become soluble.

Without further ado, Sarazin invited himself into the library and was shortly discussing his woes with the elderly scholar. Who told him, of course, what he would have been told by Thodric Jarl, or Bizzie, or his father or mother. Namely: to go home, get to bed, and forget Amantha and Jaluba both. And not to waste so much as another dorth on fortune-tellers!

'Fine advice!' said Sarazin, unimpressed by Elkin's little homily. 'But it hardly helps me find Lod.'

'You want Lod, do you?' said Elkin, rummaging around for a map. 'Very well,' he said, one map-stabbing finger striking. 'This is Selzirk. And this?'

'The Velvet River, of course,' said Sarazin.

'Where, no doubt, you'll find young Lod,' said Elkin maliciously. 'Floating downstream with his throat cut.'

'Some help you've been!' said Sarazin, rising to go.

Elkin showed him to the door. The night was dark and

clouded, and Sarazin would not be surprised if the weather broke on the morrow. He was weary, and could smell his own body. He wanted a wash. Then bed. Sleep. Dreams. It had been a long, long day.

'Well,' said Sarazin, 'I'll tell you this, I wouldn't pay much for your advice.'

'You're not being asked to,' said Elkin. 'But—' He broke off. Peered into the dark, suddenly intent. Then said, in a loud voice: 'You! Yes, you! Come here!'

Someone came forward into the lamplight spilling from the library's open door. It was Benthorn.

'What were you doing lurking around out there?' said Elkin.

'Just waiting for Sarazin,' said Benthorn. 'I didn't want to disturb you.'

'You waited all this time?' said Elkin. 'Why?'

'Oh, it's nothing, nothing, just a personal thing.'

'Come inside,' said Elkin.

'Sorry,' said Benthorn, 'but I don't have time.'

'All night to play shadows but not a moment to spare for me? Don't give me that nonsense. Inside!'

Reluctantly, Benthorn came into the library, bringing with him a pervasive smell of dung. Out in the streets his condition could pass without notice, since there were so many stinks and smells in Selzirk. But in enclosed spaces he was positively offensive.

'Did you know Benthorn was waiting for you?' said Elkin.

'No,' said Sarazin.

'So how did he know you were here?' said Elkin.

'Why, he . . . I . . . I don't know . . .'

'Is he psychic?' said Elkin.

'My best beloved Benthorn?' said Sarazin, looking his half-brother in the face. 'Why, no, I don't think so.'

'Therefore what follows?'

'He . . . why . . . perhaps he was following me.'

'Perhaps? Of course! What do you want with Sean Sarazin, boy? Why were you following him? Speak!'

Benthorn said:

'I haven't been following Sarazin, but I have been looking for him. I've been hunting for him all over Selzirk. At last I thought of the library here. A servant departing told me he was within. I did not care to disturb him, for my news is for his ears, not all ears.'

'Speak!' said Elkin.

Benthorn was silent.

'I've had a long day,' said Sarazin. 'I'm tired, I want to go to bed. I've no time for plots, plans, conspiracies or revelations. If my best beloved Benthorn wishes to say something unfit for Elkin's ears them I'm in no mood to hear it.'

Whereupon Benthorn blurted out the truth. Tarkal had kidnapped Lod. Servants had seen Lod — drugged and unconscious — being bundled on to one of the baggage wagons which were going east to Chenameg with the embassy.

'He'll likely be killed!' said Sarazin in alarm. 'He told me often that Tarkal meant to kill him.'

'Now, now,' said Elkin, 'don't over-react. I've heard myself that King Lyra wants Lod back in Chenameg. This is a small city, you know. News travels. Doubtless Tarkal's used methods somewhat underhand simply to get the young scallyway to conform to his father's wishes. We've no proof that murder comes into it.'

'No proof!' said Sarazin. 'What then is proof? A corpse? Lod's been kidnapped! We must turn out the Watch!'

'You cannot,' said Elkin. 'There is such a thing as diplomatic immunity. Have you never heard of that?'

'It gives no licence for kidnapping,' said Sarazin. 'We can still rescue Lod, even if we cannot prosecute Tarkal.'

'We can do neither legally,' said Benthorn, 'for the law of Selzirk is specific. No person can move against an embassy on any provocation without prior written permission from the kingmaker.'

'But that's absurd!' cried Sarazin. 'My mother's gone to Androlmarphos. Tarkal goes east, she goes west — the thing's impossible.'

'By law, yes,' said Benthorn. 'But there is another way. I've mustered some friends, good people who owe all manner of debts. We're ready to ride in pursuit. Do you join us?'

'Of course he won't!' said Elkin.

But Sarazin said:

'They left at noon. Could we possibly catch them?'

'My informants say the embassy will have halted for the night at the village of Smork,' said Benthorn. 'We can be there long before dawn. We can win Lod's freedom tonight. With swords.'

'Good,' said Sarazin, rising to leave. 'Then let's be gone.'

Elkin caught hold of him.

'Are you both mad?' said Elkin. 'You're not going anywhere!'

'Are you threatening us?' said Sarazin.

'There are ways of handling this old man if he's a danger to us,' said Benthorn.

'In the company of youths so reckless and ruthless,' said Elkin, 'I feel like a man environed with dragons. Yet speak I must, regardless of fear. To rush off blindly—'

'This has nothing to do with you!' said Sarazin, giving way to his anger. 'Stay out of it, or you'll get hurt. Badly!'

No sooner had he spoken than his body began to grow heavy. He could not see properly. Mists of darkness veiled his eyes, as if the world had become a dream. A millstone was crushing his chest. In panic he kicked and flailed. But his limbs refused him obedience. Then, slowly, the darkness cleared.

'How do you feel?' said Elkin.

'I don't know,' said Sarazin, surprised to find himself on the floor. He got up, slowly. 'I had — I had some kind of turn. I almost felt as if I was going to pass out.'

'You did,' said Elkin. 'You were unconscious long enough for me to have boiled an egg, had I been so inclined.'

'The epilepsy!' said Benthorn, in dread. 'That's what it is! The epilepsy!'

'Don't look so scared,' said Elkin. 'If he did have a touch

101

of the epilepsy, that's nothing to worry about. It's not contagious.'

'But it is!' said Benthorn. 'Fearfully so!'

Benthorn, like most people in Selzirk, believed the epilepsy to be a disease akin to that which sets mad dogs on the growl in the streets with jaws foaming. But Elkin knew better, and managed to assuage Benthorn's fears. Slightly.

'I hope it wasn't the epilepsy,' said Sarazin, not one jot reassured himself. Seeking a more favourable verdict, he said: 'Perhaps it was a stroke. Or a heart attack.'

'You're too young for strokes or heart attacks,' said Elkin. 'Maybe it's just something you ate. I wouldn't bother about it. Off you go!'

Then — for Sarazin, at least — the world dimmed again. And when it cleared he found himself leaning against the wall. Legs weak, ears ringing, chest tight.

'Perhaps I'd better sit down for a bit,' said Sarazin, for he was trembling, his heart was tottering, and there was sweat cold on his brow. He was afraid he was truly having a heart attack. It no longer seemed so preferable to epilepsy.

'On your bike!' said Elkin.

Or, to quote him in the Galish he used: 'Sam tam jertotham.' Meaning, literally, 'ride quick this stolen camel'.

'Where's Benthorn?' said Sarazin.

'Your brother's waiting for you out in the street.'

'How did he get out there? He was standing here just a moment ago. Did I — did I pass out again?'

'You did,' said Elkin. 'If you have another such turn it may be the death of you, particularly if you're riding a horse at the time. But that's your problem, not mine.'

With that, Elkin showed Sarazin out to the street, where Benthorn was indeed waiting.

'Are you all right?' said Benthorn.

'I think so,' said Sarazin.

'Then let's be going,' said his brother.

And off they went. Sarazin, though unsteady on his feet, durst not complain, lest complaint be taken as proof positive of cowardice.

At Farfalla's palace, half a dozen of Benthorn's friends were waiting, already armed, saddled up and ready to go. It was dark, and Sarazin was introduced to none of them. Yet one betrayed himself by his voice. Qid! Yes, Qid, the man of the Watch who had earlier tried to tangle Sarazin in conspiracy.

A horse was brought for Sarazin and he mounted up. Then they were challenged by a voice from the dark:

'What's going on here?'

At first, Sarazin thought the voice belonged to Bizzie's husband, Hof-Gof. Then, startled, realised it was Fox who was speaking. Already, Benthorn was explaining. About Tarkal, Lod, Smork. Fox heard him out, then said:

'You can't do this! It's lunacy! Sarazin! Where are you?'

'Here,' said Sarazin.

'Get off that horse!' said Fox.

'I ride for my friend and my honour,' said Sarazin. 'I'll not be turned from this venture.'

Then Fox tried to use force, but some of Benthorn's men overpowered him before he could grapple with Sarazin.

'What shall we do with him?' said Qid.

'Kill him,' said Benthorn, curtly.

'No!' cried Sarazin.

He spoke without thought. Fox was a peasant, true, a breeder of bastards, a political madman and a fool to boot. But Fox was still his father.

'Sarazin, be reasonable,' said Benthorn. 'He's a danger to us. There's nine of us here and he's but one. What if he betrays us to the law?'

'Let him ride with us,' said Sarazin. 'That then makes him as guilty as us.'

'A pretty thought but a foolish one,' said Benthorn. 'He needs but shout once as we exit the gates to doom us all dead.'

'His word will bind him,' said Sarazin. 'Let him swear himself to our cause. If he won't, why, then kill away. But if you'll not give him the chance then my sword will claim you before yours claims his.'

So saying, Sarazin drew his stout blade Onslaught, hoping he would be able to tell Benthorn from his comrades in the dark if it came to a matter of killing.

'I don't know about this,' said Benthorn. 'Can we trust Fox if he gives his word?'

'Fox,' said Qid, impatiently, 'what say you?'

'I still say you're all mad,' said Fox. Then, to Sarazin's surprise, his father laughed, and said: 'But something in your madness makes me glad. As a sword against princes — yes, if I must die, that's a good way to go. I'll ride with you tonight, aye, ride hard, then fight by your side when we get to Smork.'

'Fox has a reputation for honour,' said Qid. 'I trust him to live to his word. Get him a horse. Have we spare weapons? Good! Give him one . . .'

Shortly, Fox himself was armed and saddled up, and they were off.

Sarazin, Benthorn, Fox, Qid and the others quit Selzirk then rode for the east. A long ride it was, too. As the leagues slipped by, fatigue conquered tension, and Sarazin found it hard to stay awake. Once or twice he woke with a start, realising he had been asleep in the saddle. He remembered stories Thodric Jarl had told him about brutal marches in the Cold West when men roped themselves together so they would not be left behind, then stumbled through the night asleep on their feet.

He wished Jarl was with them.

'Got any water?' said Qid. 'Anyone got any water?'

Sarazin's exploring fingers found a leather waterbottle tied to his saddle. He loosened it, felt the weight of it, judged it half full. Uncorked it, took a swig himself.

'Has nobody any water?' said Qid.

'I have,' said Sarazin, 'Here. Catch.'

He tossed the waterbottle to Qid. Who saw the shadowy object as it was lobbed towards him. Grabbed for it. But unaccountably missed.

'Gah!' he said.

'You missed?' said Sarazin. 'Butterfingers!'

'Stop, stop,' said Qid, 'I have to look for the water.'

'No time to stop,' said Benthorn. 'Onward!'

And on they rode, a band of shadows striving through the night. Sarazin once more fell asleep, waking to hear a cock scream, a dog bark. They were at the village of Smork. And already more dogs were waking, rousing the night to fury.

'Wagons!' shouted Sarazin, as villagers began to spill into the streets. 'Look for wagons, they had him in a wagon.'

Even as he shouted, his voice began to fail. Strength drained from his limbs. He could not see properly. As his hands loosened on the reins he slid from the saddle. He was sliding, was falling, was helpless to save himself. He hit the ground, but found it soft. Heard Fox screaming a slaughter-shout. But the scream was distant. Fading. To a whisper, then to nothing.

When Sarazin regained consciousness, buildings all around were burning. Dead men and dead horses lay in the street. Above the uproar of flames he could hear sounds of distant fighting, women wailing, dogs howling.

Unsteadily, he got to his feet, remembering what Jarl had often told him:

'Look first to your weapon.'

The brave blade Onslaught was still at his side. Sarazin unsheathed it. Flamelight ran blood red down the steel. Fearfully, he looked around. Saw a man coming down the street, a sword in his hand. Who? The man came closer, and Sarazin saw it was Tarkal.

Tarkal recognised Sarazin. Smiled. Said nothing, but advanced with his blade at the ready. A burning building collapsed with a crash, spewing burning beams across the street between the two would-be fighters. Fire-fumes wraithed across Sarazin's face, yet he smelt them not. He saw Tarkal dare himself forward, leap the burning beams.

'Where is Lod?' said Sarazin.

His voice to his own ears sounded flat. Distant. Distorted. Yet Tarkal heard it clearly enough.

'Dead,' said Tarkal.

Then coughed on smoke, shook his head, and, blinking to squeeze tears from his smoke-watering eyes, abandoned speech for action. As Tarkal strode forward, murder his intent, Sarazin scuffed his feet on the street as he had been taught to do, testing the surface for purchase without taking his eyes off his opponent.

—*My feet. What's with my feet?*

His feet were numb. But Tarkal was almost upon him, and there was no time left for worry.

Tarkal closed for the kill. Reflected fire blazed in his eyes. Sarazin feinted, sidestepped, feinted again. Then Tarkal stumbled, fell.

'Ah-hai!' screamed Sarazin, striking at his fallen opponent.

His sword sliced through Tarkal's flesh, meeting no resistance. As if Tarkal was made out of smoke. Tarkal scrambled to his feet. Unwounded, unmarked. Sarazin stared at him in horror.

'Are you a ghost?' said Sarazin.

In reply, Tarkal merely coughed, grimaced — then stabbed. Sarazin, caught off-guard by the sudden blow, backstepped to avoid it. And stepped so far back that he fell into darkness. He fell for a long time, screaming, finishing in a pit of snake-twisting dreams and incontrovertible delusions.

CHAPTER THIRTEEN

Plovey zar Plovey: spokesman for the Regency of Selzirk and mortal enemy of the kingmaker Farfalla.

Selzirk's first news from Smork was panic-garbled,

contradictory and fragmentary. But by noon a supposedly reliable version of the night's events had been compiled. Terrorists, Fox and Sean Sarazin among them, had struck at Smork during the night, attacking Chenameg's embassy and liberating three score chaingang slaves who had then run amok, killing, raping, looting and burning. When presented to a meeting of the Regency, this news was greeted with uproar.

'Where then,' said one bureaucrat, 'is Sean Sarazin?'

'He has fled,' came the reply. 'Tarkal of Chenameg wounded him sorely in combat, but was then overcome by smoke and was unable to pursue him.'

'Then,' said another bureaucrat, 'let us have warrants sworn out for the arrest of Sean Sarazin on charges of assault, hooliganism, conspiracy and high treason, liberating slaves and wanton arson.'

'And cruelty to animals, too,' said another. 'Doubtless the terrorists rode their horses harder than the law permits.'

'Do we have witnesses?' said yet another bureaucrat. 'Witnesses who will swear to Sean Sarazin's complicity? After all, Tarkal is a foreigner. His word might not hold good against Sarazin's in a court of law.'

'We have two reliable witnesses,' came the reply. 'They have turned state's evidence to save their own skins. They are Fox's son Benthorn and a man of the Watch called Qid. Both will testify to the guilt of Sean Sarazin and Fox.'

Several voices spoke at once, but one query was clearly heard:

'Where is Fox?'

'Missing,' came the reply. 'Fled with Sean Sarazin.'

Plovey zar Plovey, who had listened to this impassively, then called for silence. Granted silence, he asked for wine to be served. The delay allowed the hysterical excitement to die down. Then Plovey, emphasising that he wished to be heard in silence, unfolded his tale.

'Most cherished colleagues,' said he, 'young Benthorn is a most useful agent whom I hold in the highest regard. Yet he and his witnesses must on this occasion be mistaken.

'You see, dearest friends, last night I was summoned by Sarazin's tutor. Not his weapon master, Thodric Jarl, but Epelthin Elkin, who learns him in scholarship. It seems Sarazin was studying with Elkin when he collapsed, seized by a fit.

'Sarazin could not be roused, and Elkin feared him dying — perhaps from the epilepsy. He summoned army surgeons to his assistance, and, that the death might be well-witnessed, called on certain people to mount a death watch. One of those people, dear friends, was me.'

Incredulity greeted his words: but his tale proved true. In all, a dozen people had stood watch at Sarazin's side throughout the night; he was unconscious still, scarce breathing, and obviously close to death. The Regency therefore had Benthorn and Qid interrogated under torture: an acknowledged road to the truth. Before the torturers could draw blood, both Benthorn and Qid had confessed that:

1. Fox had planned the raid on Smork, and had coerced them into joining him by extracting oaths of obedience from them under threat of death.

2. Amongst the raiding party's riders had been a masked man whom Fox had named as his son Sean Sarazin; neither Qid nor Benthorn had actually seen his face.

3. Fox had personally freed the slaves then incited them to torch the buildings and commit all manner of atrocities.

This confession fitted the circumstances fairly well, so it was accepted as truth. Warrants were sent out for the arrest of Fox and troops began to quarter the countryside, hunting for him. And Plovey of the Regency had an angry interview with both Qid and Benthorn, at which he chastised them severely for being so unreliable.

This, then, was the situation to which Sean Sarazin awoke after being unconscious for a night, a day and a night. But he, of course, found the publicly accepted explanation entirely unacceptable, and very soon reached his own conclusions.

*   *   *

108

Farfalla was still officiating at the protracted funeral rites for the dead king of Androlmarphos when the news reached her. Fox missing, outlawed, on the run. Sarazin bedridden following a life-threatening collapse. The village of Smork burnt to the ground by runaway chaingang slaves now pillaging their way across the countryside while soldiers hunted them.

To abort the funeral rites and return to Selzirk would have been an unthinkable insult to the dead king. Besides, Farfalla had work to do in 'Marphos, for she was already negotiating with some of those who wished to become king in that city.

These powerful yet power-hungry men included two generals, three bankers, and the master of one of the guilds. To remain in contention they would have to glut Farfalla's greed with money, information, and political favours. Farfalla had few chances to exercise such power, so wanted to make the most of this one.

As Farfalla was therefore unable to interrogate personally those involved in the latest scandal, she could only guess at the truth. However, even at a distance she divined — rightly — that there was more to this affair than met the eye.

Why had Benthorn and Qid turned state's evidence so promptly? From what she knew of them — and her spies kept her well-informed about those whose lives were entangled with Sarazin's — she did not think them cowards. Logic suggested they had not been terrorists at all, but agents of the Regency sent to tangle Fox (and, perhaps, Sarazin as well) in treason.

Ten days later, with the rites at an end, Farfalla was aboard a slave-powered galley slowly making its way upstream against the flow of the Velvet River. The slaves worked like brute animals, like animated corpses. Yet Farfalla was sure their minds were active, imagining the dance of power bringing them the rule of empire, the possession of silken women, the fame of forever.

From thinking of the slaves Farfalla went on to think of Benthorn and Qid. Why should they conspire to evil at the behest of the Regency? Unlike chained galley slaves, both had reasonable jobs, reasonable lives. But they wanted more. Everyone wanted more.

That was her opinion: and it was founded on experience. Take her own case, for example. She had a palace of her own (an architectural monstrosity, admittedly, but nevertheless a palace), had comfortable clothes, had three meals a day (four or five if she wished), yet was not satisfied.

It was not enough.

—*Nobody is ever satisfied.*

Watching the slaves at labour on the oars, Farfalla knew all they wanted for the moment was release from pain and effort. But, set free, if given palaces, clothes and food, they would soon be wanting more. Focusing on one young man in particular, she wondered how he would look dressed in silks. Or undressed. A notion occurred to her. She suppressed it. Then thought, defiantly:

—*But I could.*

It was one privilege of her position. Selzirk's Constitution forbid the kingmaker to marry, but did not forbid mating or breeding. Nobody cared who she mated with, as long as she did not take that person too seriously. She had made her first mistake with Fox. Her only mistake. Her worst mistake.

In the first year of her reign, the young and lovely Farfalla had fallen heavily for the apprentice farrier Fox, and their love had been both tender and passionate. If content with the possession of her body, he would have done her no harm. But this ambitious young man had sought to convert her to his own political beliefs. Which had been wild. Naive. Fantastical.

For Fox, believing in the equality of all, had campaigned for the abolition of slavery, very soon converting Farfalla to his own cause. She herself had been cautious, knowing such radicalism would wrath the established order.

But, soon enough, her commitment to the cause of the

110

slaves had been suspected, and suspicion alone had been sufficient to unite the Regency in the unanimous vote which had so early in her career taken away nearly all of her executive powers. Since then, kingmaker and Regency had been forever at odds, their best energies devoted to power politics while the practical issues of the day were ignored.

Issues such as inflation, now painfully high; poverty; unemployment; military indiscipline; the growth of the criminal classes; and the (possibly insoluble) problem of slowly but steadily declining crop yields. Long years of irrigation had led to ever-increasing amounts of salt in the soil of the Harvest Plains, threatening to doom Argan's greatest civilization within a few short generations.

Salt?

Yes, salt alone could overthrow an empire.

In idle fantasy, Farfalla imagined herself as an all-powerful ruler mastering the practical tasks of empire: salt, water, work, crime, inflation, law, trade, language, literacy, treaties, diplomacy, matters of war and peace. All that and more. But her actual life was dominated by political intrigue, much of it devoted to the business of simply staying alive. Her war with the Regency was the tragedy of her life. She exhausted herself simply struggling to stay alive. As for the slaves, why, they were no better off.

What if she had never met Fox, had never fallen under his spell, had never been intoxicated by his radical rhetoric? Then, doubtless she would never have taken it into her head to worry about the slaves. By ignoring their suffering, she would have achieved far more both for herself and for her country. As it was, history would record her reign as one long exercise in procrastination.

Still, she had loved Fox dearly, thinking him ever faithful in a world of uncertainty. Her only lover, her only friend. Her emotional investment in the man had been enormous. She had even forgiven him when he had betrayed her love, siring his bastard son Benthorn upon the varletess Bizzie.

But one can only forgive so much . . .

Recently, there had been days of rain as summer gave

way to autumn. But today the sun shone, it was hot, and, stirred by the heat of old memories, Farfalla at length summoned the slavemaster. He stood there silent while she hesitated still. Was this what she really wanted? At last she said:

'I want . . .'

'The one with the dragon tattoo?'

'Yes,' said Farfalla.

Though she had meant to say 'no'. And the slavemaster was gone before she could cancel her order. Well, time enough to do that when the boy had been brought to her. She could send him back easily enough, no harm done, though it would be courteous to offer him some wine first.

Farfalla retired to her cabin to wait. At length the dragon-adorned slave was brought to her. He had been washed, cleansed, scrubbed. His hair was still wet. And, watching the grace with which he seated himself, she was no longer so certain she had made a mistake . . .

CHAPTER FOURTEEN

Sean Sarazin: oldest son of kingmaker Farfalla. Is doomed by Constitution to spend his life in the armed forces of the Harvest Plains, but is most reluctant to accept that fate.

Sarazin was in no hurry to rise from his sickbed. Indeed, having much to gain from illness, he did his best to stay there. When the army surgeons visited, he took care to answer their questions in a slow and stumbling voice. He complained of joint pains, dizziness, inexplicable echoes and shadows which spoke to him. Thus they decided to defer his enlistment into the armed forces for a full three years, 'that time may determine whether he is possessed by the demons of epilepsy'.

In secret, Sarazin smiled, for this was the outcome he had been seeking. But still he lay abed, busy with brain-work: brooding, planning and plotting. It was very pleasant to lie there warm and comfortable while autumn rains drummed against the shutters. However, on Farfalla's return his holiday ended. She listened to his recital of symptoms with every appearance of sympathy — then ordered him out of bed.

'Get fit!' she said. 'And fast! For you're joining the army in spring whatever the surgeons say.'

Next, a petition from Lod came to Selzirk by diplomatic courier. Unlike a certain notorious group of chaingang slaves, Lod had not had the good luck to be freed during the battle at Smork, but had been carried all the way back to Chenameg as a prisoner of his kidnappers. On reaching Shin, he had been imprisoned by his father on a charge of being a wastrel, a crime carrying a penalty of thirty years' penal servitude. Lod begged Farfalla to send Sarazin to Shin to be a character witness at his trial.

'I must go!' said Sarazin, when he learnt of this. 'Lod needs my help.'

'No,' said Farfalla.

'But he's my friend,' protested Sarazin.

True. Also, Amantha had returned to Shin, and Sarazin needed to follow to pursue his destiny.

'You are not going to Chenameg,' said Farfalla. 'The very thought is lunatic.'

'But Lod needs my help.'

'What do you know of Lod?' said Farfalla.

'Why,' said Sarazin, 'that he's a fine fellow with a spritely wit. I'd not want him dead.'

'Nobody wants him dead, but his father obviously wants him chastised. Who are we to argue with that? I got the boy's measure while he was here. Lod's an idle wit, a reckless gambler, a profligate whoremaster — in a word, the wastrel he's alleged to be.'

113

'You condemn him?' said Sarazin.

'I leave that to Chenameg's courts. But surely if you evidenced in Shin, you yourself would condemn him. For you know yourself of his idleness, his debts, his drinking, his debauchery.'

'Lod wants me,' said Sarazin stubbornly.

'Then Lod,' said Farfalla, 'is a fool.'

And she sent a message back to Shin saying the petition was denied.

A day after this disappointment, Sarazin received a letter from Madam Sosostris inviting him to inspect the new book of prophecy which she had discovered. From Madam Ix, he already knew this book concerned a prince called Watashi; he could not deny that he was curious.

However, he suspected curiosity might cost him dear, and he was saving his dorths to finance a projected journey east to Shin. Despite Farfalla's interdict, he yet hoped to attend Lod's trial, save his friend, win Amantha's hand — and kill Tarkal, thus clearing the way to the throne of Chenameg.

The next evening, another letter arrived from Madam Sosostris. With it was a note written in the Rice Empire's Geltic in a familiar hand. All it said was:

'I will be there.'

This Sarazin could not resist. However, he could not hurry to Jaluba's charms immediately, for Farfalla required him to banquet that night with certain candidates for the kingship of Androlmarphos. Sarazin was abstracted throughout the feast, to his mother's great annoyance. She took him aside to say:

'Those here tonight are all powerful people well worth cultivating. Charm them. Delight them. Impress them. Win their confidence. It may be worth your while.'

'I thought you didn't want me to play politics,' said Sarazin.

'It never hurts to make friends,' said Farfalla. 'You won't

114

play politics with these people, but their friendship, if you can win it, may yet save your life.'

But Sarazin was too deeply engrossed with thoughts of Jaluba to pay much attention. He slept poorly that night, woke at dawn, and was soon off and away.

'Jaluba,' he murmured. 'Heart of my heart. Dream of my dreams. Shortly, my darling, shortly. Soon . . .'

Thus murmuring, he hurried to the Sosostris lair. He was allowed in through the door without charge, but his attempts to see Jaluba were rebuffed.

'She has a headache,' he was told by Madam Sosostris herself, a much-scented heavily ornamented woman who shrouded her face with an inscrutable veil.

'I see,' said Sarazin, 'so this is a con! You've tempted me here on false pretences. Well, you're out of luck. You'll not gouge money out of me today, no, not so much as a dorth. I'm leaving.'

'You misjudge us!' said Madam Sosostris. 'Is it my fault that Jaluba is ill? Her beauty is tender, like that of a flower. It bruises easily. You must have patience, patience. She will recover shortly, if not today then tomorrow. Meantime . . . surely you wish to see this marvellous book which speaks of power and princes.'

'I cannot afford such marvels,' said Sarazin.

'But this is free,' said Madam Sosostris.

'Free?' said Sarazin. 'What do you mean by free?'

'I mean, there's no charge for it.'

'Then what are you demanding by way of donation?'

'I demand no donation.'

Colloquy continued further along these lines, for Sarazin was sure there had to be a catch. Somewhere. But, at length, he allowed the seer to usher him into a small uncarpeted upstairs room where an immense volume with a cracked leather binding lay on a reading desk. Open shutters showed the morning bluesky bright. Perhaps the autumn rains would resume on the morrow, but today was perfect. Sarazin took this as a good omen.

Now . . . why were there bars on the windows?

'What's with the bars?' said Sarazin.

'This was built as a strongroom,' said Madam Sosostris, settling herself into a chair.

'You're staying?' said Sarazin, still standing.

'It is a valuable book,' said Madam Sosostris.

Sarazin hesitated, then drew up a chair and sat down at the reading desk. Touched the cracked leather. Opened the book, carefully. Breathed antiquity's dust. Gazed upon the ornate illuminated text, and knew at once that this could not possibly be a forgery worked up for his benefit.

A book of this quality, so painstakingly illuminated, took immense labour to create. Its colours glowed. The gold of gold, the silver of silver. Sky, leaf, river, sea. The orange of a dusty sunset, the purple of aubergine. The capital letters were works of art in themselves, each evolving itself into a plant, an animal or an element.

In wide white margins other fantasies ran amok. Trailing vines grew leaves, grew flames. Fish metamorphosed to dragons. Eagle-winged cats chased yelping dogs beneath trees from which skulls hung as fruit. A basilisk peered from beneath a rock, eyes smouldering. An armed and armoured warrior, mounted on a gryphon, assailed a gigantic wasp with a flaming spear. A huntsman with a vulture's head rode an oliphant, urging a pack of carrion-eaters to close with their helpless human prey.

Fascinating.

Now Sarazin knew why his hostess was sitting there watching him. And why there were bars on the windows. This was a priceless treasure, whatever the text might say. And what might that be?

Turning his attention from art to content, he was dismayed to see that the elaborately decorated text was written in Churl in the antiquated Spiral Style. He could decipher it, but only with great difficulty.

'I don't speak Churl that well,' said Sarazin. 'Could you translate this into Galish for me?'

'Why, no,' said Madam Sosostris, 'for I know not what it says.'

116

'But you must,' said Sarazin. 'for Madam Ix had knowledge of its contents. It's about princes and prophecy and such. How did she come by such knowledge except through you?'

'I bought this book from a travelling pox doctor,' said Madam Sosostris. 'He himself told me what was in it. But it was only the outline he gave me. I know no more than the outline.'

'I don't suppose I could take this book away,' said Sarazin.

'Impossible,' said Madam Sosostris. Then: 'Why do you ask?'

'There's someone who could help me with it. Epelthin Elkin.'

Ever since his collapse in the Voat Library, Sarazin had steered well clear of Elkin, believing the old scholar to have previously unsuspected powers. Powers that were potentially very dangerous. But he would rather risk further acquaintance with Elkin than grapple with the complexities of Spiral Style.

'Oh, Elkin,' said Madam Sosostris. 'The Archivist. No, I couldn't let you take it to him. Nor could I let you bring him here. If he saw a text so valuable he'd likely commandeer it for his own library.'

So Sarazin, this help denied him, went to work, while Madam Sosostris got on with her knitting. After much painful labour, Sarazin's version of the book's opening lines ran as follows:

'To feed four you will need half a basket of mushrooms, a cup of pork pieces, one bundle of vermicelli, some dragon-tongue sauce, some fresh asparagus and a hedgehog. First wrap the hedgehog in clay and put it amidst coals to bake. Then take a pan of cast iron and—'

Sarazin, after racking his brain to extract some mystic meaning from this, closed the book angrily.

'This is a joke,' he said. 'And a very poor joke. This is a cookery book!'

''Tis a wondrous book rich in things both rare and

strange,' said Madam Sosostris, looking up from her knitting. 'The part of interest to you is near the end. It's marked by a wafer.'

'You could have told me that to start with!' said Sarazin.

'I was testing you,' said Madam Sosostris, 'to see whether you command any of the Art in your own right.'

'An idiot thing to do,' said Sarazin.

'Perhaps, perhaps not. For there are those in Selzirk who swear still that Sean Sarazin rode to Smork. That they were there. That they saw him, heard him, touched him, smelt him. Yet others of equal reputation swear he lay lifeless in Selzirk all the while. I do not believe the contradiction of stories suggests untruth. No: I believe it suggestive of magic at work.'

'Then look elsewhere for that magic,' said Sarazin, 'for I've none of my own. Anyway, now you've tested me, how about translating this for me? You obviously know what it says.'

'Not at all. As I told you, I bought it from a pox doctor. 'Twas he who placed the wafer for me. I myself can read but little, and that weird script — why, that is known only to scholars like yourself.'

So Sarazin turned to the place marked by the wafer and began work in earnest. A bitter struggle he had, too, for it was hard to make sense of the tangled syntax of the complex Churl. He did not finish his translation till early evening. But he did not regret investing so much energy, for it made fascinating reading.

The book contained a prophecy which could be summarised thus:

—*A prince of the Favoured Blood would be exiled from Selzirk in his youth, but would later return to the city.*

—*Wicked and witless men would unleash great dangers threatening the very survival of the city.*

—*The prince would see how to save Selzirk, but would be scorned and reviled by the city when he revealed the solution to Selzirk's dangers.*

—*He would endure great hardship and greater danger,*

earn himself the name Watashi, marry the princess of an ancient kingdom and wage a war against his own father, whom he would kill.

—His father's death would bring the prince the power he needed to save Selzirk. He would rescue the city from danger; the people would praise him with great praises, and his name would endure forever in glory.

Sarazin thought things through. Carefully. While Selzirk's law did not recognise him as a prince of the Favoured Blood, he truly thought of himself as such. His mother, Farfalla, had been consecrated as one of the Blood on becoming kingmaker. Prophecy might well accord her sons with rights, titles and prerogatives which the Constitution of the Harvest Plains denied them.

Certainly Sarazin had been exiled from Selzirk in his youth. Also, in a sense, he could be said to have killed his father. After all, if Sarazin had not agreed to go with Benthorn to attack the embassy at Smork, Fox would not be an outlaw. As an outlaw, he could not hope to live long.

So who were the wicked and the witless against whom Selzirk must be defended? Undoubtedly, the men of the Regency. The bureaucrats like Plovey.

What about the prophecy's other points?

The prophecy spoke of hardship. Of great danger. That fitted. After all, Sarazin had endured poverty, scorn and fever in Selzirk. Had dared his life, blade against blade, with a genuine questing hero, Tarkal of Chenameg. That much had come to pass.

The name, though. That was a bit of a problem. Watashi? An odd word to conjure into a name. Perhaps that was why the fates had willed that he should see the prophecy now: so he could fulfil it by changing his name. Easily done!

But what about the next point? Marriage to the princess of an ancient kingdom? Chenameg was doubtless that kingdom, and Amantha that princess. But how could he woo her when his mother forbade him to leave Selzirk? Did he dare disobey her? She'd be fearfully angry. And he feared her dragon-wrath rages.

119

Before running such risks, he'd like some assurances as to the validity of the prophecy. He should talk it through with . . . well, someone like Elkin.

Though, if truth be told, in his heart of hearts he believed the prophecy already. He was already prince. Some day he would be king. Emperor. Lord of Selzirk! Master of the Harvest Plains! The prophecy did but confirm his own vision of the radiant future.

— *Hallelujah!*

Thus thought Sean Sarazin. Staring hard at a flyspeck on the wall in an effort to control his face and betray nothing.

'Finished?' said Madam Sosostris, on seeing his blank, vacuous stare.

'No,' said Sarazin, thinking that the safest answer. 'The script is near impossible to read, the grammar worse, the words rare beyond my understanding. I am defeated.'

'Then you must come again,' said Madam Sosostris, 'and study the book further.'

And with that she showed him out into the street.

Sarazin did not ask if he could see Jaluba on his next visit, since such a display of interest could only tend to raise the price Sosostris surely intended to place on that delightful damsel. There had to be some pay-off for Sosostris in all this, there just had to. And how else could she make money out of Sarazin except by selling him Jaluba?

CHAPTER FIFTEEN

Theodora Turbothot (nèe Thrug): wife of Troldot 'Heavy Fist' Turbothot.

Although she is an alumnus of the Santrim Institute for Feminine Arts, Theodora is not one of Selzirk's chaste and respectable matrons, but is instead a wanton foreigner, an import from far-distant Untunchilamon.

In truth, in terms of appetite, there are few women in the upper echelons of Selzirk's society who could compete with Theodora. With the exception, of course, of Farfalla, whose approach to the flesh is equally direct and vigorous.

Once out in the streets, Sarazin had the uneasy feeling he was being followed. However, there were so many people out and about in the early evening that it was impossible to tell for sure.

'Follow me, then,' muttered Sarazin, to whoever it was who might be tracking him.

And made his way to Jone, where he shortly entered his favourite tavern and called for a tankard of the best ale in town. At first he drank alone, wishing Lod was there to help celebrate the prophecy which promised Sarazin such a spectacular future. Then some of Lod's friends turned up, and, remembering Sarazin's earlier enquiries, asked if he had any news of their mutual acquaintance.

'I have,' said Sarazin. 'He rots in jail in Shin, in Chenameg, waiting to come up on trial.'

'On what charge?' said one of Lod's friends.

'It is claimed he is a wastrel,' said Sarazin.

'A wastrel? Nay! He's a philosopher, man. Truth is his pursuit, and ever he seeks it in wine and in women. Have they no knowledge of things academic in Shin?'

'None,' said Sarazin, 'for they are but peasants. Come — may I buy you a beer?'

'You could,' said one of his interlocutors, 'but only if you let us buy you three. We're in luck, see. The cards have been running our way. It's a night for celebration.'

'Yes,' said Sarazin, with a sudden grin. He was thinking of his prophecy. 'It must be an omen. A good omen. We'll celebrate sure. But let's not forget our friend. Let our first toast be in honour of Lod.'

The first toast was indeed in honour of Lod. So was the third — and the seventh. Sarazin did not usually drink very much, but tonight was a special occasion, and Lod had

121

been long and deeply honoured by the time Sarazin and his drinking companions stumbled from the tavern.

Arm in arm, they staggered through the streets, singing:

> 'I took a little magic pill
> Which made my dragon scream;
> I raped a golden daffodil
> In a pool of curdled cream.'

While they were singing thus, a palankeen drew up beside them. The chairmen halted, and a voice from behind the palankeen's screen said (with a whisper of perfume):

'Are you Sarazin Sky?'

Sarazin, leaning heavily on one of his comrades, said:

'Who is it who wants to know?'

'Theodora,' came the answer. 'The ruling goddess of love.'

Sarazin untangled himself from his comrade, who slid helplessly to the ground.

'Let me see your face,' said Sarazin to the palankeen.

'Get in,' said the perfume-whispering voice, 'and you shall see all that and more. Yes, you shall see all.'

The palankeen lurched as Sarazin got in. Within a bafflement of shadows he found what seemed to be a veiled woman. She giggled as he grappled with her perfumed flesh.

'Not so fast,' she said. 'Only goats and peasants lech in haste.'

'Oh,' said Sarazin.

Even drunk he did not want to behave like a peasant. He tried his drunken best to behave himself: and succeeded so well that he fell asleep. He woke to find muscular doormen carrying him into a house. They dumped him into an enormous bed where he wallowed, dazed by drink and fatigue, while his new-found mistress stripped herself by the light of a lamp so dim it was scarcely more than a living shadow.

He submerged himself in her heat as she fondled herself to his flesh, fold by fold and crease by crease. He was drowning, billowing, lumbered, laden. Lost amidst flesh

122

enfolding. He was failing. Then, urging him, she cried:

'My stallion! Most Favoured Blood, most noble prince!'

Prince. Yes. Lordly in conquest. The thought excited him.

'Govern me,' she whispered, her voice husky. 'Govern me, rule me, beloved.'

Urged by that voice, nourished by an ooze of lips, teased by fingers sly and well-practised, Sarazin found himself hard as a hero. Thrusting and striving, he abandoned himself to his lust. Then finished, subsided and slept.

He floundered long through hippopotamus dreams, clagged and digested, rolled up with lard then toasted by fatlight. Woke bleary by darkness to find hands and lips at work, breasts jiggling, a voice giggling, teasing his manhood, flattering his thighs.

'My prince . . .'

He managed. Then, weary beyond dreams, he slept.

At dawn, Sarazin woke to find himself in bed with an elephant-rivalling woman on the wrong side of fifty. She was big and fat and grey and frowsty. Teeth brown, except where they were black. A nose like a potato, stubbed with purple warts.

As he cringed from her rolls of lard-soft skin, she burped, farted, then seized him. Her strength was enormous. He held his breath as she slobbered him.

'Wonderful,' she crooned. 'You were wonderful, beautiful, sweet. A frabjous night.'

'Who are you?' said Sarazin.

'Theodora, as I told you,' she said.

After a little hard questioning, he learnt that she was Theodora Turbothot. Mistress Turbothot, in fact, patron of the Seventh College of the Inner Circle of the Fish-Star Astrologers. That rang a bell! Yes: the Fish-Star sect was quartered not far from Madam Ix's premises. Ix was a friend of Sosostris. Who had let Sarazin see her precious book of prophecy for nothing.

'Someone followed me when I left Madam Sosostris last night,' said Sarazin.

'Did they?' said Theodora. 'How very strange!'

123

Then she giggled.

That giggle made Sarazin — at last! — remember their first meeting. He had gone to see Sosostris some days ago, but the gateman had demanded an outrageous fee just to let him inside. He had hung around outside. And this dreadful overaged creature, her face then masked by a veil, had called him 'darling boy' and had begged his name.

Which he, thinking nothing of it, had given.

Sarazin could see the dreadful truth now — or part of it, at least. Madam Sosostris had procured him for this dreadful creature. He had been watched, spied on, manoeuvred, trapped, tricked, used, abused. Raped, in a word!

He threw back the bedclothes, intending to make his escape. But Theodora grabbed him by the neck. They wrestled, and, to his shame, she got the better of him.

'Ease up!' cried Sarazin, panting. 'You'll break my arm.'

She relaxed her grip. All she kept in her possession was the smallest finger of his left hand. But the sly pressure she put on the digit warned him not to struggle.

'Darling,' she said. 'Do it to me again.'

'Who are you to command me?' said Sarazin.

'Well, once,' she said, slyly, 'I was a princess. The sister of an empress.'

Sarazin tried to persuade himself that Mistress Turbothot was indeed a princess. He tried to rouse his flesh to its duty. He tried: but failed. But she giggled, and let him go. Hurriedly, he dressed, and tried to make his escape. But found the front door blocked by a stocky little man who said:

'I am Troldot Turbothot. Who the hell are you?'

'Never mind,' said Sarazin. 'I'm just leaving.'

He tried to barge past the man. But Troldot 'Heavy Fist' Turbothot was a formidable wrestler, and Sarazin ended up flat on his back.

'Guards!' shouted Turbothot. 'Help me with this rubbish!' Then, as guards came rushing to his assistance, he raised his voice and shouted: 'Theodora, you shameless hussy! You've gone too far this time!'

124

The only answer he got was a giggle.

Sarazin was held by Troldot Turbothot's guards until the Watch could be summoned. Then he was dragged away and thrown into prison. The charge: debauching another man's wife. The maximum penalty: death.

At the time of Sarazin's arrest, Selzirk's judicial system was in such a mess that he could easily have languished in a rat-ridden dungeon for three to four years before his case came to trial. Then his chances of dying before trial would have been high, for tuberculosis and other diseases equally as lethal flourished in the crowded cells.

Fortunately, since a number of judges were among those hoping to be made king of Androlmarphos, Farfalla was able to pull strings, with spectacular results: Sarazin's case came to trial after he had been in jail for only twenty-three days.

Plovey of the Regency attended the trial as a spectator. Farfalla, also in attendance, wondered if that murderous master of conspiracy had arranged for the Turbothot woman to ensnare her son. She would not have put it past him.

Then, as Sarazin's lawyer arrived in court, Farfalla saw Plovey's face fall. Immediately she felt better about the extravagant amounts of money she was paying to retain Childermass Imbleprig to defend her son. Imbleprig was the best — which was what Sean Sarazin needed! Bribery had bought Farfalla details of the prosecution's evidence. Thus she knew that Mistress Turbothot was prepared to swear that Sarazin had indeed debauched her.

Imbleprig had prepared an elaborate defence. Medical evidence to prove Sarazin an invalid, a victim of fevers and epilepsy, and likely so debilitated as to be impotent. A publican who would happily testify that Sarazin had been incapably drunk on the night of the alleged crime. Experts willing to testify that alcohol in quantity was incompatible with lust. And Sarazin's drinking companions

125

had been found, and, suitably bribed, were ready to say on oath that they had left him unconscious in the gutters of Jone.

The defence would claim, then, that Sarazin had been medically incapable of performing when Mistress Turbothot picked him up off the street, and that she must therefore be fantasising. If that failed, and Sarazin was found guilty, then Imbleprig would appeal on grounds of temporary insanity.

But first Imbleprig tried a simple move which might just work. Once the charges had been read, he had Mistress Turbothot brought forth, then said to the judge:

'It is alleged that somewhere in this bloated cow there is a woman. We'd need an autopsy to get to the truth of that — but clearly nothing less like an aphrodisiac has ever before walked the earth on two legs. My client is charged with debauching this thing. Absurd! Patently absurd! What man would touch it, let alone couple with it, except under the pain of instant death? I ask that the charge be struck out on grounds of its patent absurdity.'

The judge looked from Mistress Turbothot to the slim Sean Sarazin.

Said 'hm', said 'hum', then said:

'Agreed. Your charge is so struck out.'

Farfalla watched Plovey trying to make his face an inscrutable mask — and making quite a good job of it. Then looked to Mistress Turbothot. Nothing inscrutable there! Wrath incarnate. Pity help Childermass Imbleprig if the Turbothot woman ever got hold of him. For that matter, pity help Sean Sarazin when Farfalla got hold of him . . .

Pity did not help Sean Sarazin. Alone and unaided he had to endure an exquisitely painful interview with Farfalla on their return to the palace.

'You,' she said, 'will be the death of yourself, if not the death of me. What a lunatic thing to do! What will you do next? Rape a pig? Or what?'

Sarazin knew exactly what he would do next, but kept it a secret. While enduring the horror of Selzirk's dungeons for twenty-three days, he had sworn a sacred oath to himself. The burden of that oath was this: if he got out of prison alive then he would ride to Shin to give whatever help he could to Lod.

His determination to do just that was reinforced when a second petition arrived from Lod, once more entreating Farfalla to send her eldest son to Chenameg to be a witness at Lod's trial.

'. . . for the charge,' said Lod's petition, 'carries a penalty of death, and Sarazin alone can save me.'

CHAPTER SIXTEEN

Ebber: an order of wizards with powers over human minds. Has bad reputation in the Harvest Plains, once ruled by the evil Ebonair of that order.

When approached by Sarazin, Thodric Jarl refused to dare go to Shin in the face of Farfalla's displeasure.

'My duty forbids such madcap adventures,' said Jarl.

'Not if you make the trip a part of your duty,' said Sarazin.

'Impossible!'

'But no. I disappear. Terrorists from Chenamag claim responsibility. You volunteer to pursue the villains. Thus job and duty take you to Chenameg.'

'Dream on,' said Jarl.

'It's a good scheme,' protested Sarazin. 'We'd meet on Chenameg's border then ride to Shin. I'd attend Lod's trial as a character witness then home we'd come, with you as a hero. We'd spin a wonderful story about you fighting hundreds of Chenameg terrorists to rescue me.'

So Sarazin spoke, though he actually planned to stay in Shin after Lod's trial, to win the hand of his true love Amantha and encompass the death of his arch-enemy Tarkal.

'Chasing terrorists is the army's job,' said Jarl. 'I work for the Watch, which only works within the cities.'

'What matters that?' said Sarazin. 'Surely the army would welcome help from the Watch.'

'What a witless thing to say!' said Jarl. 'Armies lust for war because wars make careers. Failing war, manhunts, bandit-fighting and such are the next best thing.'

'You sound very sure of yourself.'

'With near half a century of war behind me I should be sure. Now get out! Before I lose patience and kick you out!'

'Just one thing.'

'Out!'

'One moment! If I got you sent to Chenameg to hunt me, would you—'

'Away with your nonsense!'

'Very well then,' said Sarazin. 'But I leave you this.'

So saying, he gave Jarl a large-scale map of Chenameg's western border plus a note giving details of when and where the pair could meet after Sarazin faked his own kidnapping.

'You're mad!' said Jarl. 'This note alone could be the death of you.'

'But I trust you,' said Sarazin.

'Don't!' said Jarl. 'Trust nobody.'

'But you've proved your loyalty by leaving a rich living in Voice to follow me here. Thus I trust you with my life.'

'Then trust less,' said Jarl. 'for if you linger here longer I'll gut you.'

All this left Sarazin undismayed, for he had expected something of the sort. He had already planned his next move: to blackmail Epelthin Elkin. After a stiff drink to help nerve himself to the task, he took himself off to the

Voat Library in Libernek Square, and there bearded the elderly Archivist in his private office.

Sean Kelebes Sarazin, though not one of the wise, had nevertheless drawn the logical conclusions from his experiences. It was thanks to Elkin, surely, that he had imagined himself riding with Benthorn to Smork while he actually lay unconscious in Selzirk. Elkin must be a wizard of Ebber, the dark order, with powers over human minds.

In Selzirk, wizards of Ebber were feared and hated on account of the tyrannical rule once exercised by a member of that order. Consequently, Elkin would be in great danger if he were to be denounced as such a wizard. Sarazin therefore thought it would be easy enough to persuade Elkin to do him just one small favour.

When Sarazin was admitted into Elkin's presence, the old scholar immediately saw his fear, tension and excitement.

'Welcome, Sean Sarazin,' said Elkin, in tones distinctly unwelcoming. 'What can I do for you? Well? What is it? Insects eating your brain? Or what? Out with it, boy!'

'There's something — something I have to do,' said Sarazin, stumbling over his words as his courage began to fail him. 'And I need some help. There's this prophecy, see, and—'

'Oh no,' groaned Elkin. 'Not that. Not prophecy. Let me guess. You've met a fortune teller. An old hag with dirty claws who says—'

'You haven't heard what it's all about yet!' protested Sarazin.

'I can guess,' said Elkin.

But, nevertheless, let Sarazin tell him all about the prophetic book stashed in the Sosostris lair.

'. . . so,' said Sarazin, in conclusion, 'the prophecy makes everthing clear, doesn't it? I'm back from exile, my father's doomed to an outlaw's death, it's all set to happen. I'm the one! The prince fated to rise to power. To rule. To conquer.'

'Trash,' said Elkin.

'I beg your pardon?' said Sarazin.

129

'Trash. Nonsense. Rubbish. Piffle. Suloshamaniqik.'

'You mean,' said Sarazin, 'you're not yet quite convinced by this prophecy.'

'Not yet?' said Elkin. 'I never will be! I know these fortune tellers. Their whole business is telling people exactly what they want to hear.'

'But this prophecy wasn't invented on the spot for my benefit,' said Sarazin. 'It's an old, old book, old as—'

'Old as the story of human sin. Are you the first boy in your situation? Hardly! An old king rules. His son longs to kill his father, to seize power. So a prophecy conveniently—'

'But Fox doesn't rule! The prophecy—'

'Bollocks,' said Elkin.

While Elkin was capable of elegant eloquence on occasion a trifling bit of nonsense like Sarazin's prophecy failed to inspire him with forensic genius.

'You must admit,' said Sarazin, 'I fit the prophecy neatly. For a start, I'm Farfalla's son, so I'm of the Favoured Blood.'

'Oh, come on!' said Elkin. 'You don't believe that nonsense, do you?'

'The Noble Families of the Favoured Blood saved Argan from the tyranny of the Empire of Wizards,' said Sarazin coldly. 'All know their line must rule lest chaos come upon Argan.'

'Twaddle!' said Elkin. 'The Empire of Wizards fell to pieces because of internal power struggles. All scholars know that.'

'You, doubtless,' said Sarazin, 'have cause to know.'

'Because I am a scholar, yes,' said Elkin.

'Because you were there!' said Sarazin.

Elkin's response was silence. Sarazin realised he was frightened of Elkin. Very frightened. Yet he pushed on regardless.

'You were there,' said Sarazin. 'Because you — you're more than you seem. So you'll help me. Or else. Or else I'll — I'll—'

Sarazin's lips were trembling. His throat was dry. He

130

wished he had never started this. The room had darkened while he spoke. Elkin, a malign and ominous Force, loomed huge in that darkness.

Sarazin tried to run, but his legs failed, flesh quivering uselessly. He fell. The last light fled. Through the dark, Elkin swaggered towards Sean Sarazin with gigantic footsteps, oncoming like an idol of earth-crushing basalt animated by a blood-dread Power from the Unseen Realm. His breathing harsh, rasping, rising to a roar.

His hand gripped Sarazin's head.

Sarazin felt as if his skull were being squeezed in a vice. He tried to scream. Could not. Tried to breathe. Could not. Tried to move. Could not. Felt his heart trip, stumble, stall. Knew he was dying. And fainted.

Endured a long dark . . .

But surfaced, at length, to find himself lying on a bed in a room crowded with books, scrolls, papers and parchments. He guessed it was Elkin's private bedroom. And there was Elkin himself, sitting in a chair, reading. Looking much as he always did. A sharp-eyed, grey-bearded old man with mahogany skin, his hair drawn back and plaited into a pigtail.

'Some wine?' said Elkin, in a pleasant voice.

'Please,' said Sarazin.

'I'm no fortune-teller,' said Elkin, handing him some wine, 'but I'll give you this prophecy for free: your lunatic foray to Chenameg will see you killed. But I'll do what you want. This once. But don't try to blackmail me again!'

'Thank you,' said Sarazin, who at that moment truly only wished to escape from there, to get away from the wizard, to get out to the sunlight.

'Now,' said Elkin, 'let's get down to details . . .'

And, together, they began to plan.

Thus it came to pass that in the autumn of the year Alliance 4325 Sean Kelebes Sarazin was kidnapped by terrorists. There were a dozen eyewitnesses to the kidnapping: that was Epelthin Elkin's first contribution to Sarazin's schemes.

131

Shortly, the city learnt that terrorists had dragged Sean Sarazin away to Chenameg, and were threatening to kill him unless all slaves in Selzirk were released. Then Elkin exercised his occult powers again: and the army devolved the responsibility for rescuing Sean Sarazin upon the Rovac warrior Thodric Jarl, Master of Combat for the Watch.

This move was legally permissible. Indeed, the fact that any army officer could command any officer of the Watch was a sore point indeed with the Watch. Nevertheless, for the Watch to be dragged into the chase was, to say the least, unusual. Jarl did not see how Sarazin could have arranged it. Unless . . .

As it happened, Thodric Jarl had entertained certain suspicions about Epelthin Elkin for some considerable time. So, making sure he was wearing a certain amulet which he believed would protect him against all magic, he dared a confrontation with the old scholar he thought might possibly be a wizard.

'I am to be sent hunting after Sarazin,' said Jarl, with his hand on the hilt of his sword. 'How came that to pass?'

'Why,' said Elkin, 'set a thief to catch a thief, or so they say. Friend Thodric, you look a very terrorist yourself, standing there so stalwart with death in your hand and blood in your eye.'

'There are no terrorists,' said Jarl, 'as you know well.'

'Tell me what I know,' said Elkin.

'That Sarazin has stage-managed his own kidnapping,' said Jarl. 'That he wishes to ride to Shin, and for me to ride with him. That he plans to rendezvous with me some eight days from now. Do you deny that you know it?'

'Why,' said Elkin, 'how can I deny knowing what you have just told me?'

'There's more,' said Jarl. 'I suspect that Sarazin made the army put me in charge of rescuing him. How did he manage that?'

'I know not,' said Elkin, 'but suspect bribery. Anyone can be bought, or so they say.'

'Do they now?' said Jarl. 'But I hear this: that Sarazin has not money enough to buy himself a whore, far less to bribe the army's high command. Here, methinks, is a mystery.'

'You think I have the answer?' said Elkin.

'I think,' said Jarl, 'you know more than the world believes.'

'Of course I do,' said Elkin impatiently. 'I know myself, for example, to be one of Lord Regan's spies, just as you are. Do you think Lord Regan has but the two of us in this city? Likely there's a third agent, if not a fourth, a fifth and a fiftieth. Perhaps the fourth or the fiftieth is a source of funds for Sean Sarazin.'

This was such a logical, reasonable explanation that Jarl chastised himself for not thinking of it, and realised he must be more than a little bit paranoid to think such a harmless old scholar a possible wizard, and hence one of the traditional enemies of Rovac . . .

That very same day, Thodric Jarl left Selzirk with a posse of 30 men of the Watch. Their mission was, very simply, to ride to Chenameg, to seek out the terrorists who had kidnapped Sean Sarazin, to kill the terrorists and liberate Farfalla's son.

As any attempt to liberate slaves was always taken very seriously in Selzirk, no expense had been spared in equipping Jarl's expedition. Every man was well-armed and had a horse for himself and a spare mount besides. In addition, the posse had 20 baggage animals carrying food enough for 60 days, plus a thousand sanarands to be used for bribing informants once they got to Chenameg.

Jarl kept his plans to himself as his posse travelled eastward along the northern bank of the Velvet River. He planned to cross the most easterly dam to the southern side of the river, then head to the South Road for a rendezvous with Sarazin.

However, on the long journey to the east, Jarl's paranoia had plenty of time to go to work. He began to suspect that this was all part of a devious plot for the disposal of

Thodric Jarl, and that soldiers from Selzirk would be waiting at the rendezvous to arrest him.

In his madness, Jarl considered all kinds of people possibly guilty of such a plot. Maybe Plovey of the Regency, suspecting Jarl to be a spy from the Rice Empire, had enlisted Sarazin's help to prove Jarl's guilt. Or perhaps Farfalla was behind it all. Or someone who hoped to succeed Jarl as Master of Combat for the Watch.

Jarl knew the road to the north of the Velvet River was his logical route to Shin, which in turn was the logical place for him to start his operations in Chenameg. He had no good excuse to take the road lying south of the river.

—*Leading my men to the South Road might in itself be proof sufficient to see me condemned for conspiracy. But if I keep to the North Road, nothing can be proved against me. No harm will come to Sarazin, since there will surely be soldiers at the rendezvous point already, waiting to arrest me.*

—*On the other hand, what if there is no conspiracy? Sarazin will wait at the rendezvous point. And wait. And wait. And then? Why, that's over to him. After all, a ride of but a few days will take him from the border to Shin.*

—*Surely Sarazin can manage that on his own.*

Shortly after so thinking, Jarl revealed his strategy to his men:

'We ride first to Shin, King Lyra's capital, the greatest city in Chenameg. There we stay for thirty days, gathering intelligence. By then, I trust, we will know where to strike to destroy the terrorists and liberate Sean Sarazin . . .'

CHAPTER SEVENTEEN

The South Road: a road to the south of the Velvet River. Every map of Chenameg extant in Selzirk confidently shows it running east from Chenameg's western border through

134

the forests to Shin. But, as Sarazin is beginning to realise, it is long indeed since such maps were updated . . .

The dark and gloomy forest stretching away to the east was most certainly that which marked Chenameg's western border. And Sarazin knew he was at the start of the South Road, for he had found the vital landmarks which all the maps agreed on: a burial mound one league west of the forest and two gigantic time-disfigured heads of black stone squatting at the forest's edge.

The maps claimed the South Road started between the two heads. Well, the mound was there, the heads were there . . . but the road was but a senile track strangled by waspthorn and brambles.

None lived thereabouts for it was cursed, and any settlers would find their every child stillborn. It was an uncanny place to camp alone. Often Sarazin lay awake in the darkness while uncouth things crashed through the forest. Bears? Monsters? Ghouls? Who knows?

Worse things stalked his dreams, and more than once he woke from nightmares with a scream, his hand snatching for the hilt of the doughty blade Onslaught. At the end of his twelfth day of futile waiting he had his most terrible nightmare yet, in which he saw Thodric Jarl die a death too terrible to relate. He woke shaking, terror-stricken.

Was the dream an omen? Or what? It certainly helped him come to a decision. Jarl might have died, or met with an accident, or might have refused to leave Selzirk to search for Sarazin. Anything could have happened. Meanwhile, Sarazin's rations were getting lower. And his noble steed was not proving much of a conversationalist.

'We ride,' said Sarazin. 'We ride for Shin. Today.'

Thus decided, he mounted his horse (well, technically a pony — but, as a poet, he was surely entitled to a little poetic licence) and, with his vorpal blade at his side, set forth.

The gloomy overcast weather worsened the dooming

darkness of the moss-choked forest through which roughed his road, often forking and rejoining as it outflanked fallen trees, bog holes and mud spills. Towards noon, Sarazin passed a gross grey skull, so huge that half a dozen trees sprouted from holes in its dome. It gave him such a shock that he thereafter suspected the forest of evil intent, and scanned each thicket for ambush by werewolf or worse.

Fairly late in the afternoon, he finally realised he had been so intent on the trees that he had lost sight of the woods. Failing to keep track of his progress through the forest, he had become disorientated. Geographically embarrassed, in fact.

—But surely I could find my way back if I wanted to. Couldn't I? Or else follow my own tracks back . . .

To reassure himself, Sarazin tried retracing his steps. But the path forked and branched wildly, and nothing he saw looked familiar. He searched the mud for his own tracks — and found those of people, horses, wild cattle, pig, deer. Some fresh, others not. He was baffled by the confusion of signs.

'East, then,' said he, trying to persuade himself he felt bold and brave. 'East, to King Lyra's palace. To Shin.'

Shin was to the east, was it not? All the maps said so. If only he had some sun, so he could check his direction. The sky was swamped with clouds as dirty as dag-end wool. Mud and wet weather. Soon, doubtless, it would rain.

On rode Sarazin, his spirits steadily declining. Then he was startled by coarse shouts ahead. Festivities? Or a fight? Should he turn back? No! Was he not a hero? Whatever he was, best to seize this chance of intelligence.

So thinking, he spurred his horse, and shortly cantered into a muddy clearing where half a dozen cackling yokels were sitting around gnawing hunks of bread and quaffing strong ale. Tied to a tree was an old, old grey-bearded man with brushwood piled around his feet.

'What do you here?' demanded Sarazin, lapsing into Geltic.

'Gorp?' said a yokel.

'What,' said Sarazin, switching to the Galish Trading Tongue and speaking very slowly, 'are you doing here?'

When that got no intelligent response, he tried the question in Churl, and ohe toothless rascal answered with a cackle:

'Why, we be burning this druid.'

'Druid?' said Sarazin.

'The old fellow,' said a broad-shouldered black-bearded thug, indicating the ancient who was tied to the tree.

'I forbid it!' said Sarazin, without thinking.

'Who be you to forbid anything?' demanded the brute.

'A prince! A son of the dynast of Selzirk!'

'We've no truck with princes here,' said an unshaven gangster.

'I will cut free that oldster,' said Sarazin, dismounting. 'Stand aside if you know what's good for you.'

Whereupon one of the hooligans unsheathed a rusty cutlass. Sarazin drew steel with a scream, a battlecry from his dreams:

'Wa — wa — watashi!'

They clashed. Sword met cutlass, once, twice — then Sarazin booted his man in the crotch. The thug doubled over. Sarazin pumped knee to face, then turned to menace a man advancing with a hatchet.

'Stand back, you naughty artist!' quoth Sarazin.

The gangster threw the hatchet — which missed — then fled. As did the others. Admittedly, the man who had been kicked in the balls fled rather slowly, but vanished soon enough for all that.

'We'll kill you, Watashi!' screamed one.

But his voice was distant. Retreating still.

Sarazin, feeling rather pleased with himself, checked the bold blade Onslaught for damage then cut down the old man, who collapsed into his arms as if life had already left him. In time, helped by a little ale, the ancient revived. His first question made Sarazin start:

'What means this name, Watashi?'

137

His name! Watashi! He had earnt the name, just as prophecy said he would!

'It means death,' said Sarazin, voice shaking with excitement. 'It means fear. It means blood.'

'How did you come by it?' said the old man.

'Through combat,' said Sarazin, which was true enough, since it was the fight just gone which had first seen him called by that sobriquet. Then, thinking it was his turn to ask the questions, he said: 'Who are you?'

'We ourselves are Upical, druid of the Ifrael Forest, which is this wilderness in which you stand. Since you have saved our life we must reward you. Three parts has our reward, three parts of magic.'

That said, Upical delved into a little sleeve-pocket and, with great ceremony, produced what looked like a lump of mud. Sarazin took it gingerly.

'What is this?' he asked.

'She's a magic mudstone,' said the druid Upical. 'If you be ever in dire need, place her in water. Then the legions of the Dreaded Ones will come to your aid.'

'The Dreaded Ones?' said Sarazin, pocketing the magic mudstone. 'Who are they?'

'Oh, don't worry about that. You'll find out soon enough if you ever have need to use her. Now this—'

'What's that?'

'We be telling you, aren't we?' said Upical, twirling a silver chain between his fingers. On the silver chain was a silver ring. 'This is a ring of invisibility. Wear her close around your neck till great need takes her. Then put her on. But not for idle curiosity, mind! For sometimes she has her tempers.'

'Tempers?' said Sarazin.

'Oh, you'll find out the hard way, if you idle her at curiosity,' said Upical, with a disconcerting giggle, hanging the chain around Sarazin's neck.

Sarazin examined the ring and found it was in fact a close-wound spiral of metal which could, with a little manipulation, be unthreaded from the chain. He longed

138

to test it, but, at the same time, was rather fearful of doing so. In the end, he tucked the ring-bearing chain under his clothing so the silver lay cold against his skin.

'Ah!' said Upical. 'What do you think this is?'

So saying, he produced a small leaf-green bottle which, if Sarazin was any judge, was made of jade. It looked like the kind of bottle in which one would keep snuff.

'That,' said Sarazin, 'is a small bottle.'

'Ah! So far, so good. What be within her?'

'I've no idea,' said Sarazin.

'Guess. Guess! Or you don't get her.'

'Liquor,' guessed Sarazin. 'No? Water? Ghosts? I know, I know! Blood of a virgin. Wrong? How about perfume? Is it perfume? Or a philtre? That would be handy — I'm meeting a woman in Shin.'

'Philtres!' said Upical, with utter contempt. 'Oh no, she don't hold something so stupid. She holds dragons.'

'Dragons?' said Sarazin.

'She holds nine,' said the druid. 'Nine dragons. Their dux be the greatest of all the world's dragons. Untunchilamon he be called. Remember his name.'

'Untunchilamon,' said Sarazin, taking the bottle, which proved surprisingly heavy.

The leaf-green jade of the bottle was, he saw, carved in the shapes of dragons. He counted them. There were nine.

'That one there,' said the druid, fingering the largest, 'she be Untunchilamon.'

'You called it a he, now you call it a she,' said Sarazin who had picked up a touch of pedantry from Epelthin Elkin. A very small touch, admittedly — but nevetheless regrettable. 'Which is it?'

'Oh, his sex is a spike, for certain,' said Upical, 'but sometimes he has his moods so sometimes he's she as like as be, at least to me. Weigh the care of this bottle careful. Dragons such as these live but briefly, so she's not to be used till the time of greatest need. But when used they'll obey you. So there is your reward. Magic times thrice. This last thing I give you.'

139

'Wait a moment,' said Sarazin. 'You say dragons live briefly. How briefly is brief?'

'Oh, you'd die if you held your breath while you watched,' said the druid. 'But you couldn't cook a steak while they did their work. Not properly, any like. But dragons, young sir — ah, they don't need much time to be the alteration of history, do they now?'

So saying, Upical produced a little green candle. Like the magic bottle, it was heavy.

'This is my last gift,' he said.

'Tell me about this,' said Sarazin, smoothing his fingers over the candle. 'What does it do? What's it good for?'

'That we know not,' said Upical. 'But the wizard we garrotted to get her, ah, she valued her right enough. So she be worth something, we warrant.'

Sarazin wished he had Epelthin Elkin on hand to advise him about the correct use and care of all this magic he had suddenly obtained. He stashed the stump of candle away.

'Your horse,' said Upical. 'Can she carry two? Can you give us escort to our cave?'

'I can do no less,' said Sarazin.

At the druid's cave there would, surely, be something to eat and drink. Then he could ask for directions out of this bewildering wilderness.

The pony laboured through the forest under the double weight, bringing them at length to Upical's cave. Inside, the stench was so bad that the air was nearly unbreathable. Part of the problem was the corpses of a dozen children which hung by their heels from a clothesline which ran the length of the cave.

'How came they here?' said Sarazin, shocked.

The druid laughed.

'Oh, through trade,' he said. 'Through trade. We need but a few a year, yet buy in quantity for such gives bargains. We keep the live ones in the back here. Would you like to amuse yourself with one or two for the evening?'

'Where are they?' said Sarazin, trying to conceal his horror.

The druid led him deeper and deeper into the cave to a crack-lit chamber where lay half a dozen children, gagged, and tied hand and foot. They were alive. Kicking. Straining at their bonds. Making muffled sounds of horror and protest.

Sarazin waited to see no more. He drew his sword and stabbed Upical in the guts.

'Guh—' said Upical.

Sarazin, shaking, withdrew his sword. The druid writhed in agony. Said:

'I was . . . but . . . joking . . .'

'Joking!' roared Sarazin.

And, in fury, hacked off the druid's head. Then, blade filthy with gore, he advanced on the children.

'Don't be afraid, little ones,' he said. 'I'll do you no harm.'

But the children did not seem to understand, for, when he cut free their gags, they writhed, spat, and screamed in unearthly voices. Sarazin sliced away their bonds.

'Go to your homes,' he said. Then, as they seemed slow in understanding, he said again: 'Go!'

He whacked a child on the buttocks with the flat of his sword. Whereupon all the children turned into rats and scuttled away into the forest, leaving their rags on the ground behind them. Sarazin, startled, could but stand and gape.

Cold water dripped on his neck. The cave was not made of stone at all, but of black ice — which was melting. The druid's body was already decomposing. Maggots swarmed in the flesh, which blackened, stenched, then fell away, leaving only bones. Which creaked, and arose. Clothed in a writhing red mist.

'Gaark,' said the bones.

At which Sarazin fled the cave, vaulted into the saddle, spurred his horse and galloped away pell-mell until his mount was sweating and lathered. Thereafter he kept the beast on the trot until the day's last birdsong failed in the gathering dark.

In the gloaming, he came upon a gigantic leather boot lying on its side. Sword in hand, he tested the musty shadows within. Finding nothing.

'This,' said Sarazin, settling himself for the night, 'will have to do.'

He earnestly hoped the owner of the gigantic boot would not reclaim it before dawn.

CHAPTER EIGHTEEN

Ifrael Forest: an almost uninhabited area of Chenameg rumoured to be the haunt of wolves, witches, werewolves, vampires and worse. Sean Kelebes Sarazin, aka Watashi, has blundered into the deepest, darkest, most dangerous part of this shadow-doomed wasteland.

In the cold dawn Sarazin breakfasted upon broken biscuits and leather-tough jerked meat while the sullen rain fell with a noise like fifty million rats scuttling through the undergrowth. Then he pushed on, hoping he was going in the right direction, but fearing he was hopelessly lost.

At mid-morning, he was riding at walking pace in a (possibly) easterly direction when he heard a woman screaming. He spurred his horse, and shortly came upon a frightening scene. In a muddy clearing were two people tied to posts. One a fair damsel; the other, a dwarf.

Both were being menaced by a gore-clawed monster which had the head of a rat (swollen to gigantic size), the body of a bull and the tail of a lizard. This apparition so disconcerted Sarazin's mount that it reared, throwing its rider. Sarazin, flung to the earth, scrabbled for his sword as the monster loomed over him. Finding his steel, he slashed at the brute, missed, drew back his blade and

142

saw the horrifying creature turn to mist then vanish.

'What's this?' said Sarazin, in bewilderment.

'Fewer questions and more action,' growled the dwarf. Then began making grotesque faces at Sarazin.

'Yes, cut us loose, for pity's sake,' said the damsel fair, in excellent Galish.

Sarazin advanced, awkwardly. He felt ashamed of the state he was in. He had not bathed for days. His clothes were befouled with mud and with worse.

Feeling gauche and uncomfortable, he cut free the lady. Her hair was fine-spun gold, her eyes chatoyant. Her silks — this was strange! — bore no spot of water. There was mud underfoot, but it had stopped raining.

'Now that,' she said, pointing at the dwarf. 'Loose that.'

'Yes, loose me, loose me!' said the dwarf frantically.

'I'll not set free that evil mannikin,' said Sarazin, who did not like the look of the dwarf at all.

'He'll swear to obey you,' said the damsel he had rescued.

'I'll do no such thing,' said the dwarf, promptly.

Her eyes flared. Momentarily, their captivating iridescence was gone — replaced by a baleful red.

'Naj aji jin inz n'zoor,' she said, her voice axe-hard.

The dwarf flinched. Like a spider cringing from flame.

'Glambrax will swear himself to your service,' she said. 'For my part, I will bind him to what he swears. Glambrax! Your oath!'

Reluctantly, the dwarf spoke, saying many things in a strange, hissing language Sarazin had never heard before. Then the woman spoke also in a similar tongue. Reverting to Galish she declared:

'He is yours. For life. His name is Glambrax.'

'Might I know your name, fair lady?' said Sarazin.

'I am Zelafona, a princess of the elven folk. Immortal is my health, yet insult sufficient can rend apart the spirit from the flesh.'

'That — that monster,' said Sarazin. 'Was that sent by someone to — what? Kill you? With claws? Or with terror?

What kind of monster was it? How come it vanished at a sword-slash?'

'I know not,' said Zelafona, 'for not all is given to me to know. Let us retire to my home.'

'I trust it is not far,' said Sarazin, 'for, as you see, my horse has fled.'

Upon which Zelafona put two fingers in her mouth and whistled. High, pure and clear sang the note, and forth from the forest came Sarazin's horse in company with a milk-white mare richly caparisoned with gold and velvet.

'Come, Sarazin,' said Zelafona. 'Mount. Ride!'

'How did . . . how did you know my name?'

'I have my arts,' said the damsel.

'Not art sufficient to protect against your enemies, though. Who was it who bound you to that post? Who conjured that monster?'

'My mind is clouded,' said Zelafona. 'You ask many questions to which I have no answers.'

With that, Sarazin had to be content. He mounted his horse. Glambrax scrambled up behind him, and they were off, with Zelafona leading.

'We are here,' she said, shortly.

The gloomy forest gave way to verdant lawns sweeping up to a house. A house? A four-storey mansion set amidst noble trees and groves of ornamental bamboo. A buttermilk sun shone down from a blue sky as soft as a baby's bum. The sun illuminated carp pools and soft-playing fountains of waters coloured variously green, blue and yellow. But Sarazin's eyes were all for the house, which offered them a frontage in which a hundred windows glittered.

'What . . . what are those windows made of?' said Sarazin. 'Of glass?'

'But of course,' said Zelafona, with a smile.

Sarazin had seen much built in stone, but had never in his life seen such a wealth of glass. He was impressed.

'What happened to the rain?' said Sarazin.

'Was there rain?' asked Zelafona, her voice dreamy, a slim smile dancing delicate on her lips.

144

'Yes. A downpour which seemed forever.'

'Elven folk live sideways from the rest of the world,' said Zelafona.

'You are . . . of the elven folk?'

'I told you so at first acquaintance,' said she.

Was that true? Possibly, for the elven folk were known to be most wondrous fair. Or, alternatively, the woman might be a princess of human breed, the daughter of some kingdom far greater than Chenameg, living exiled here in splendour. Either way, she was something special, that was for certain.

'You look distant,' said Zelafona, 'Are you all right?'

'The monster,' said Sarazin, 'it gave me a shock. Forgive me. My nerves—'

'I understand,' she said. 'You have my name, then. Zelafona. Our time together will be but brief, but you will have Glambrax with you for a lifetime. Thus you will remember me.'

'I don't want to sound ungrateful,' said Sarazin, 'but I'd have to think very carefully before taking Glambrax into my service.'

'But he's sworn his loyalty to you already!' said Zelafona. 'You heard him yourself.'

'Yes,' said Sarazin, 'but I — I'm not sure I want a dwarf as a servant.'

'But you will take him,' said she. 'As a courtesy. To me. You will swear as much.'

Such was her charm that Sarazin could not deny her this trifle. After all, he did not want to upset his princess. Whether she was a human or an elven daughter, she must surely be the one the prophecy spoke of, the one he would win. She was beautiful, voluptuous — she rivalled even Jaluba's charms. Therefore he gave his oath on the matter.

Inside the mansion, grey-masked servants showed Sarazin to his room. He tried to prevail on them to stay, for he had questions to ask. But they smiled and left. Vanished, almost. Grey cloaks swirling away. Soundlessly. Were they ghosts? Perhaps.

Still — the bath was real enough. It had limitless hot water pouring from a faucet of a kind Sarazin had once seen illustrated in a very ancient text preserved in a library in Voice. Sarazin soaked in the hot water, luxuriating in the warmth. Cleansed himself with sponges and strange perfumed soaps. Dressed himself in clean linen which had been laid out in his chambers. Then, overcome by weariness, he sank to his bed and slept.

He woke at dusk, and was delighted to find it was dinner-time. He ate with Zelafona at a table lit by a thousand candles gleaming in chandeliers. They had lamb, venison, beef, and three different kinds of fish. Then, for dessert, bananas topped with zabaglione.

'This is wondrous rare,' said Sarazin.

'What? The custard? My chef makes it from sugar, marsala and egg yolks.'

'No, I meant the bananas. I've seen them but twice before in my life.'

The bananas eaten in Selzirk came from Hexagon, one of the Scattered Islands far out in the Central Ocean.

'Think nothing of it,' said Zelafona.

Sarazin obeyed. He thought of her instead as he ate fruit salad, swilled red wine and slowly became tipsy.

He was not at all surprised when, after their meal, she led him to her private chambers, and there allowed him to seduce her. When he took her glimmering flesh he experienced a strange, unearthly ecstasy which he had never before experienced with a woman. She rode him until he was lathered. Yet still his lust did not diminish. Feverishly, he matched his man to her woman. Until, at last, dawn glimmered through the windows, and at last he slept.

Much later, Sarazin woke.

'Zelafona?' he murmured.

Opening his eyes. To a horror-shock insult to soul and sensibility. He was lying beside a dead woman on a frowsty truckle-bed in a filthy cottage, a place of whispering dust and creaking spiders, of rustling shadows and grey-masked rats.

'Zelafona?' he cried.

Nobody answered his call. The haggard flesh of the crone beside him looked like old leather cracked by a thousand seasons of relentless weather. Her slack jaw gaped down revealing a jumble of decayed teeth. A swollen purple tongue furred with green and yellow.

She stank of cat's piss.

Sarazin stumbled naked from the bed. He grabbed his mud-wet trousers, shuddering. Boots, where were his boots? In the corner, in a heap with the rest of his clothes, plus sword belt and sword. He dressed in haste, as if summoned to a battle. Then checked his pockets — and found his magic missing.

All his gifts from the druid Upical were gone. The silver ring of invisibility on its silver chain. The magic mudstone. The small bottle in which lurked the dragon Untunchilamon and eight other beasts almost as mighty. The green candle which was worth killing for.

All stolen!

Floorboards creaked as he strode to the door. Which fell off its hinges as he yanked it open. He strode out into the mud, the drizzling rain, the dismal grey, looking around as if hunting for a murderer.

The cottage, which had a thatched roof, stood beside a ramshackle barn in a wasteland of waterlogged mud in which lay a dead dog and the corpse of a bullock. A paling of sorts ran round that field of mud, and on the fenceposts were some lumpy things which Sarazin realised were the heads of assorted men and animals.

Beyond the fence was the dark, brooding forest. Overhead, a louring sky. Sarazin trudged through the drizzle to the barn, where he found his pony, looking thoroughly miserable. Something stirred in a heap of decaying straw, then sat up. It was the dwarf, Glambrax, grinning like an open wound.

'How did you like your night of passion?' said Glambrax in a sly, insinuating voice.

'Where is Zelafona?' said Sarazin, with murder in his voice.

'She's in bed, where you left her.'

'There's nothing in bed but a . . . a . . .'

'That's her,' said Glambrax, grinning still. 'She knew she was going, so she wanted to go out in style.'

'You mean . . . you . . . but . . . gods, this can't be true! She — she was a princess. She said so. An elven princess. That's what she said she was. She said she was a princess of the elven folk.'

'And you believed her!' said Glambrax scornfully. 'Aren't you a little old for fairy tales? She was no elf. There's no such thing as elves.'

'Then what was she?'

'A witch, of course,' said Glambrax. 'A death-hag. A nightwalker. You're lucky, oho, lucky you met her near death, my child.'

'Lucky! She — that—'

Sarazin thumped his head against the wall of the barn. This was intolerable!

'Doubtless you got a bit of a shock this morning,' said Glambrax. 'But, face it — any woman you have will end up that way. There's no such thing as immortal youth. Only difference is, most decay so slowly you've got time to get used to it.'

'I don't understand this,' said Sarazin. 'How come she knew my name? How come the monster — was that part of her game?'

'Oh, she saw you coming, you might say,' said Glambrax. 'Oh yes, she saw you coming.'

Then, whistling in a cheerful way, he quit the stable. Sarazin slumped down on the straw, cold, hungry, depressed, humiliated and disgusted with himself, with mortal flesh, with life, the world and the universe. He indulged himself in self-pity and despair until he was roused by the smell of smoke. Fire? Was something burning?

148

He quit the barn — and found the house aflame, with Glambrax capering up and down in front of it.

The house went up with a roar, vomiting smoke and spitting flame. A flight of blood-red bats burst from beneath the eaves, screaming in shrill, demented voices as they fled. Rats scarpered across the mud, making for the forest.

Sarazin ran towards the cottage, half-imagining he could extinguish the fire. He plunged into the billowing smoke. Its stench sent him staggering backwards, retching. Eyes bleared by smoke, he looked round wildly and saw Glambrax laughing.

'You!' said Sarazin, in fury. 'Tell! How did the house catch fire?'

'I set it alight,' said Glambrax.

'I never told you to!'

'You never told me not to.'

'There were things of mine lost somewhere within,' said Sarazin.

'What kind of things?' said Glambrax.

'There was — oh never mind.'

'A ring, perhaps?' said Glambrax.

There was — suddenly! — a silver ring on a silver chain dangling from his fingers.

'Give me that!' said Sarazin, grabbing for it.

Glambrax jerked his hand away.

'First you have to promise,' said Glambrax.

'Promise? Promise what? Give me my property, mannikin!'

'Ah,' said Glambrax, darting away. 'Promise first. To honour your oath.'

'What oath?'

'See!' said Glambrax. 'You've forgotten already!'

Belatedly, Sarazin remembered. He had sworn to keep Glambrax with him as his servant. For life. A disastrous mistake! For, as he saw all too clearly, the dwarf was unlikely to be an asset to his lifestyle.

'I have given my oath on the matter already,' said Sarazin. 'If you trust not my oath, what good is a promise?'

'So it remembers,' said Glambrax, cackling. 'It remembers!'

'Yes,' said Sarazin, bitterly, 'and I remember this, too. My oath was extracted from me under false pretences.'

'Was it?' said Glambrax. 'Oh no, I don't think so. I heard the lady say herself her time with you would be but brief. Your authority to think otherwise was but that of your own ego.'

Sarazin thought back to the day before and remembered.

'Yes,' he said. 'You're right. But I — I — oh, never mind. Give me my valuables.'

Satisfied, Glambrax handed over the ring of invisibility. And the magic mudstone. And the bottle.

'The candle!' said Sarazin. 'Give me the candle!'

'What do you want with a stub of old candle?' said Glambrax.

'Never you mind about that. Give it!'

The dwarf rummaged in his pockets and yielded up the green candle which Sarazin treasured away. Then Sarazin asked:

'Why did Zelafona make you mine?'

'Oh,' said Glambrax, 'she wouldn't want me alone in the world. I'm her son, you see. Her first born. Her only born.'

'A likely story!' said Sarazin.

'But true,' said Glambrax. 'But true!'

'Well,' said Sarazin, 'if you're to be my servant, then start making yourself useful. Make ready my horse.'

With that said, Sarazin sploshed away through the mud to the forest where he relieved his bowels and his bladder. When he returned, he found Glambrax standing atop the barn, looking around in all directions.

'What are you doing up there, clown?' said Sarazin.

'Searching for your horse, master,' said Glambrax.

'It's in the barn, half-wit!' said Sarazin.

'Nay, master. There's no horse within.'

Startled by this intelligence, Sarazin panicked into the barn. He found his noble steed within and led it outside. Glambrax was still on the roof.

150

'What do you think this is?' demanded Sarazin.

'That?' said Glambrax. 'That is a pony, unless I'm mistaken.'

'It's my horse!' said Sarazin. 'Get down from there so I can kick you.'

'Oho!' said Glambrax. 'A tyrant, is it? Will it kick me for not finding cat when it sends me for dog? Will it boot me for not bringing water when it asks after wine? That is no horse you have there. That is but a pony, ill-fed, ill-bred, ill-broken, aye, and dying of the glanders unless I'm mistaken.'

'You claim your mother a witch but I think her more likely a lawyer,' said Sarazin in disgust. 'Either that, or you were fathered by a passing solicitor. Come down here this instant!'

So saying, Sarazin pointed at the mud at his feet. Without a moment's hesitation Glambrax jumped. Landing feet together on the precise spot indicated. Sending mud flying in all directions. One of those directions was Sarazin's.

Then Sarazin finally realised, with dismay, that he had acquired the worst kind of servant imaginable: that is, one who will do exactly what he is told.

'You and me,' said Sarazin, breathing heavily, 'are going to have to go a long way together. So don't give me any trouble or I'll throttle you.'

'Yes, master,' said Glambrax, meekly.

Then grinned.

Then giggled.

Until Sarazin, provoked beyond endurance, kicked him to obtain his silence.

Shortly, with Glambrax saddled up behind him, Sarazin was on his way again. Hoping he could somehow find his way to Shin and to King Lyra's palace. Hoping his long-suffering pony could make the distance before it collapsed and died. He had stolen the horse for this journey; he now made a vow that, next time he played horse thief, he would get himself something more worth the stealing.

'Where are we making for?' said Glambrax.

'Shin,' said Sarazin. 'That's somewhere to the east, I think.'

'Whether it is or isn't,' said Glambrax, 'you'll never find it this way. East is a vague direction, is it not? Vague as a quarter of the sky. An unknown city is but a lightless star in that quarter.'

'I don't need your pessimism,' said Sarazin, who found Glambrax's comments uncomfortably accurate.

'I talk not pessimism but sense,' said Glambrax. 'Head north till you pick up the Velvet River, then follow the river upstream to Shin. Shin is by the river, is it not? So that way we can't get lost, can we?'

This advice was so sound that Sarazin was sure there must be something seriously wrong with it. But, in the end, he turned his horse to the north, thinking it worth a try.

CHAPTER NINETEEN

Place: Shin, capital of Chenameg. Stands on southern bank of Velvet River. Eastern end of North Road lies directly across river; a ferry runs between city and road.

Most notable features: King Lyra's palace (known as the Great House); associated Great Hall; Phoenix Temple; four lumber yards; sawmill; ferry house.

Population: 2,467 on the day of Sarazin's arrival in the autumn of Alliance 4325.

When Sarazin reached Shin, Thodric Jarl was there waiting for him. By then, Sarazin had worked up the most marvellous story about his heroic defiance of the terrorists who had kidnapped him, and his escape from the same. Glambrax corroborated the tale, which was well received by almost everyone in the city.

Only Lod had his doubts.

'I don't believe such dog-snot nonsense,' said Lod, when Sarazin was admitted to the dung-smelling jail where his friend was incarcerated, awaiting trial on charges of being a wastrel.

'But it's true,' protested Sarazin, 'all true.'

'No,' said Lod, bitterly, 'it's but part of a ploy to free yourself from Selzirk. Why did you do it? Do you hate me? Or what?'

'I don't understand!' said Sarazin, dismayed. 'You called, I came. You petitioned Farfalla, you—'

'Dolt!' said Lod. 'No trial in Chenameg can start until every witness sought by the defence is on hand. Hence my petition. By demanding a witness forever unavailable I delayed my trial forever, my conviction forever, my execution forever. I made myself immortal! Till you damned me to trial then death.'

With that said, Lod began to weep. Helplessly. As tears ran down his jail-grimed face, Sarazin, dismayed, said:

'But I — how was I — I mean . . .'

'You stupid sod,' said Lod. 'You stupid stupid sod. If you don't know the law, why not ask a lawyer? You suck-face fool! You've killed me!'

Sarazin's first thought was to flee from Shin to save Lod's life. So he sought an audience with King Lyra at which he said:

'My lord, it is not meet that I should dally here in Shin. Now that I have escaped the terrorists, duty compels me to Selzirk. There must I enlist with the army, for such is my doom, as all who know the Constitution of the Harvest Plains know well.'

'Nonsense, boy,' said King Lyra. 'You must stay for Lod's trial, for he wants you as a witness. We've scheduled it for after the Phoenix Festival.'

'The Phoenix Festival?' said Sarazin.

'Ten days of song, dance, feasting and poetry,' said King

153

Lyra. 'It starts on Midwinter's Day. We have hunting, too. Excellent hunting.'

'If it's going to be so long before the trial starts,' said Sarazin, 'surely I could go to Selzirk now then return after Midwinter's Day.'

'Oh no,' said King Lyra, shaking his head. 'Lod's lawyers will want you on hand from now till then to help prepare your testimony. No, I forbid it. You must stay here.'

'But,' said Sarazin, 'what if those in Selzirk think me lingering here in deliberate dereliction of my military duty?'

'Your brother Celadon is here as military attaché to the embassy your countrymen maintain in our fair city. I'll send him home with tidings of your fate. Thus Selzirk will know you are held here by my decree, not by your own choice.'

'May I speak with the ambassador himself?' said Sarazin.

'Impossible,' said King Lyra, 'for the ambassador is dead of a fever. Relax, young man, relax. No harm will come to you from this adventure.'

'I fear,' said Sarazin, trying one last move, 'that the terrorists who plucked me from Selzirk will seize me here in Shin. I was lucky to escape from them the first time. I doubt I'd manage it twice.'

'I've thought of that already,' said King Lyra. 'By my command, Thodric Jarl remains in Shin as your bodyguard. With thirty of the finest fighters of Selzirk's Watch to guard you he'll keep you safe enough.'

Well! Sean Sarazin had certainly tried. On realising his presence doomed Lod to defeat and death, he'd done his level best to quit Shin. But King Lyra had made that impossible. So what could he do but make the best of a bad thing?

He resolved to get on with the business which had really inspired him to come to Shin in the first place. To seduce Amantha (and marry her), to kill Tarkal (and perhaps King Lyra as well) and set himself up as king of Chenameg.

He would strike at Lod's trial, after midwinter. The

trial would bring all Chenameg's dignitaries together, so
Sarazin could capture all in a coup. King Lyra had but two
dozen men of arms serving under him, and those were of
dubious quality. Since Sarazin commanded (or thought he
commanded) the loyalty of Thodric Jarl and the men of
the Watch, the weight of numbers appeared to be on his
side already.

He would also, of course, have the advantage of surprise.

King Sarazin. It had such a nice ring to it that he could
hardly wait. King Sarazin? Perhaps he should use his new
name and style himself King Watashi. That sounded even
better!

CHAPTER TWENTY

> With literacy hath no trivia its termination
> For print preserves all paltriness forever;
> With literacy can no man recall his paradiso
> Or conjure forth the glories with his tongue.
> Thus Talaman said of the librarians:
> 'Kill them, lest they mute us.'
> Quite rightly.
>
> —Arez Stone, 'With Literacy'

'He's coarse,' said Flanny, peering at Sarazin through one
of the spyholes cut in her fan.

'He's incredibly conceited,' said Jilth, giggling.

'He amuses me,' said Amantha, fanning herself lightly.
'For the moment.'

'He has no breeding whatsoever!' said Flanny.

'Neither,' said Amantha, 'has my parrot. Yet both amuse.'

Sarazin was a novelty, hence — for the moment —
fashionable. Novelty was in season, for it was Midwinter's

155

Day, the start of the Phoenix Festival. To the delight of all, the winter rains had taken a rest, and the day was graced with sunshine. Everyone consented to ignore the mud.

By way of preliminary entertainment, they listened to the famous Arez Stone, a wild-eyed ancient with flowing beard and glittering eye, who held that literacy was the cause of all social evils.

To prove his point, Stone had elaborated his thesis in some 5,037 cantos in 473 different languages (some dead, some living, some three-parts missing), and planned to write a further 4,761 cantos before he dropped dead. Unfortunately, Stone's wisdom would inevitably die with him, since he refused to allow his productions to be written down, and nobody but himself could master the memorising of his epic productions.

After Stone had finished (he had been restricted to a recital of a mere two of his cantos) two minor poets performed. Then all gathered in the grounds of the Phoenix Temple where they were to watch the arrival of the phoenix itself, which was due at noon.

Once the phoenix used to arrive in Chenameg on Midsummer's Day. But, thanks to a curse put upon the land during the War of the Witches, it now arrived on the coldest, shortest day of the year, which of course considerably reduced the potential of the occasion as a tourist attraction.

The audience awaiting that arrival first had to listen to a scholarly dissertation by King Lyra, who was endeavouring to prove that the phoenix is in fact a reptile (though every reputable treatise available names it as a bird).

Sarazin was troubled to find himself profoundly bored by the king's dissertation. Maybe there was some ineluctable flaw in his character which prevented him from appreciating truly aristocratic intellectual pursuits.

At last, the king finished. Sarazin breathed a sigh of relief — then felt ashamed of himself. As it was noon, they all looked around for the phoenix.

'Why hasn't it come?' said Sarazin.

'It only does this once in every half a thousand years,' said Amantha, 'so maybe it's having trouble remembering the way.'

Sarazin wondered whether Phoenix Day was going to be another crushing disappointment — like the city of Shin, which had proved to be a dismal lumber town with unpaved streets and gloomy high-gabled wooden buildings. However, at last the bird of wonder came flying in from the east. It looked very much like a stork, except its feathers were every colour of the rainbow.

'Where does it live?' asked Sarazin.

'Somewhere in the dragonlands,' said Amantha, 'Ssh! Watch!'

She had spoken too late. People were already staring at them. Sarazin realised he had made a faux pas. He was acutely embarrassed. What he really needed in this place was a reliable guide to courtly behaviour whom he could consult in private. In that respect, Thodric Jarl had proved a total disappointment.

What was the phoenix doing? Circling overhead. Was it supposed to go round in circles? Maybe it had heard him speak. Maybe he had scared it off. Then what would happen to him?

To Sarazin's relief, after another half-dozen circles the phoenix landed on the altar of the Temple. There was a glitter like water on diamonds as it burst into flames. Incandescent, it writhed in an uproarious conflagration.

To the audience came an appalling stench of burnt feathers and charred flesh. Sarazin thought for a moment that something had gone wrong. Then the phoenix started to ascend. The bird of wonder rose sheathed with incandescent fire, which fell away to reveal brilliant new plumage.

As the phoenix climbed in glory, everyone clapped.

'Wasn't that marvellous?' said Amantha.

'Wonderful,' agreed Sarazin, out of duty.

He felt somehow cheated. The fact that the burning bird had stunk had spoilt the whole thing.

However, he cheered up soon enough when the poetry

157

competition began, for he had high hopes for his own composition. The ruling fashion at the moment was the poetry of extravagance, which had lately ousted the poetry of horror — which in turn had conquered the poetry of lust.

Sarazin's competition poem was entitled 'A One-winged Treacle-Bat Dares Its Dragon's Tongue To Make Some Observations'. He had written it in the Geltic of the Rice Empire before translating it into Churl. Since none other than Arez Stone had helped with the translation (flattery works wonders, and Sarazin knew its use well) it should be good.

When his turn came, Sarazin cleared his throat then began:

> 'The earthworms coagulate. The fish
> Throttles the politics of the mayfly.
> My love is red. Gashed. Wounded.
> Her vampire teeth a parrot, her nose a comb,
> No breadcrumbs but a nipple!
> Yea, leavened with lead and gold I mount
> (As dogs mount goats and diamonds,
> As fish mount quartz-dove rings)
> Past rhetorics of menstruating heavens,
> Past cloves of coal and petal-folds of cream,
> Then close — ah, say it, love! — with adoration.
> Fraught with revolutions then the moon
> Observes my buttermilk shock, my stirruped deed
> Drive to her grease and annul
> All pleasures in the heartlands of a rose.
> Her savour licks one pearl from my rampole strength,
> Splices with lead my gold, then sets my steel
> Quivering to the perfumes of her naos.'

His admiring auditors applauded his daring, for he had cunningly blended the poetries of lust and horror with the current style of extravagance, and with the poetry of nonsense which looked set to replace it. His art was a triumph of fashion.

158

'The winner,' said the herald, shortly, 'the winner is
. . . Sean Kelebes Sarazin, lately of Selzirk.'

Everyone cheered. And Sarazin, flushed and triumphant,
exulted. He was a leader of fashion, and intensely proud
of himself on that account. His pride only increased when
King Lyra handed over the poetry prize, which was an
ornate porcelain chamber-pot painted with pictures of
bluebirds and daffodils.

The day would not have been complete without a feast.
Thus, that evening, they were indulged with precisely that.
They dined upon roast dziggetai, upon mountain trout,
sparrows stuffed with raspberry jam, upon pickled pigs'
eyes and truffle delight, all washed down with draughts
of ale, skull and dandelion wine.

After eating: dancing. Whirling music. Laughter by
lantern light. Sarazin inveigled Amantha outside, and they
stood for a while together in a doorway in a romantic
silence. They could not wander beneath the stars because,
had they attempted anything so foolish, they would swiftly
have found themselves ankle-deep in mud.

'I'm cold,' said Amantha.

'I could warm you up,' said Sarazin.

And kissed her.

'Really!' said Amantha. 'I think we had better go back inside. And you, Sean Sarazin, had better remember yourself.'

CHAPTER TWENTY-ONE

King Lyra: portly widower who rules the Chenameg
Kingdom from his palace in Shin. Father of Tarkal (his
eldest child), Amantha (who will attain the throne if Tarkal
dies) and Lod (his youngest, currently in jail awaiting trial
on a charge of being a wastrel).

*   *   *

159

The next day, there was to be a royal hunt. When invited to participate, Sarazin had at first begged off, saying his pony was lame. In fact, he was too embarrassed to ride such a meagre beast in such elevated company. However, King Lyra discerned the true cause of Sarazin's discomfort, and forced Tarkal to lend him a beautiful caparisoned charger, a gallant grey looking ready to challenge the wind itself. He also ordered 'the best royal hunting garb' to be delivered to Sarazin in the morning.

Thus Sarazin went to sleep content, waking at dawn, rejoicing in his (temporary) possession of one of Tarkal's horses — not least because it was a mark of the monarch's favour. It seemed King Lyra (like Lord Regan of the Rice Empire) recognised Sarazin's princely qualities. The king, then, must truly be an excellent judge of character.

Sarazin's high spirits were, however, somewhat dampened when a set of hunting clothes was delivered to his quarters. He had imagined himself hunting in silks, but received instead some incredibly thick, virtually indestructible padded trousers of a very coarse wool which scratched his thighs, and a woollen jacket of similar strength and thickness, its exterior armoured by plates of lacquered wood stitched to the wool by means of threads passed through hundreds of awl-holes.

Sarazin was half-convinced this vile rigout was someone's idea of a practical joke. However, he dressed, put on his trusty boots, buckled on his swordbelt, checked his weapon for rust, popped a jaunty blue bycoket on his head, then went forth to the stables where he collected his noble grey.

Then he joined the riders of the hunt, who were congregating in a mudfield on the outskirts of Shin, hard up against the forest. Sarazin was glad to see his companions of the day were similarly accoutred. A light rain was falling, but it quite failed to dampen their spirits. As a cold wind began to urge the rain across the mudfield, Sarazin began to see the sense of being so warmly dressed.

He wished they could have been hunting in autumn, for autumn's treasury forest, with its hoard of bronze, copper, gold and unblemished silver, would have offered so many more opportunites for poetry. Still, even a winter hunt should be good for a few lines or so.

'Well, youngling,' said King Lyra genially, riding up beside him, 'they're bringing out the quarry. Are you ready?'

'With cock and sword!' said Sarazin.

'Ah, would that I were young!' said King Lyra. 'Still, I'll show you young dogs a thing or two before the day is over.'

'Do you ride with us?' said Sarazin.

'But of course, man, of course!'

Frankly Sarazin thought the gouty old gentleman unfit for such vigorous sport. But he thought no more on it, for his interest was now focused on the quarry, a slim young peasant woman. He watched as she was unchained and released.

At first, despairing of escape, she would not consent to run. But whips got her going. Her naked body flitted away between the trees. Silent as a dream-wraith.

'Now that,' said Lyra, nodding in the direction of the departing woman, 'that is a virgin. I checked her myself. Fresh meat for the victor!'

'Sire,' said Sarazin, 'you are a most generous host.'

For a while, the riders milled around, drinking from gilded cows' horns. Sarazin wondered aloud how they would find the woman in the forest.

'For,' he said, 'we have no dogs.'

'No need for them,' said King Lyra. 'See those fellows over there? Those ugly-looking brutes on the black horses? Those are our trackers. Capital men, capital. Here, get some of this inside you.'

So saying, the king passed Sarazin a drinking horn. Flames of a startling green danced the surface of the liquor within.

'Firewater,' said King Lyra, by way of explanation. 'From the Ebrell Islands, you know.'

Sarazin, having heard something of firewater, doubted it was really the thing to drink before a fast-paced ride through a dangerous forest. However, he durst not decline the offer.

'Sire,' he said, 'you honour me.'

'You honour us, man,' said King Lyra. 'Not often we get visitors from Selzirk, you know. Liked your poem. Don't say I understood it, but that's not what it's for, is it? Had some arse in it, eh? Arse! That's the stuff!'

And the king slapped Sarazin on the back, and laughed heartily.

What did he mean with his talk about arse? Was he making some sort of invitation? If so, how could Sarazin decline it? To cover his confusion, Sarazin sipped at the green-burning liquor in the horn, which fired his blood with summer warmth and made his head swim.

He handed the horn back to the king, who drained it. Then, swaying slightly in the saddle, began to sing a song of some considerable obscenity. Other hunters took up the tune. As it was, obviously, a tradition — and a royal tradition at that — Sarazin, after some hesitation, began to sing himself.

King Lyra's drinking horn was refilled, then emptied again. Not once, but twice. And not by the king alone — he had generous help from Sarazin. Who began to feel positively buoyant. There was strength in his chest, fire in his loins, a splendour in the weather. He looked around for Amantha, thinking to demand a kiss. But there were no women evident, for this was a strictly masculine assembly.

He began to get impatient. Surely their quarry would be leagues away by now! What if they lost her? What if she got away? That would put everyone in a bad humour, doubtless. Which Sarazin could not afford, since he wanted the king in the best of moods that evening.

Sarazin — even when under the influence of firewater — was not so foolish as to think he could ask the king for his daughter's hand in marriage on such short acquaintance. However, he thought he might, with some effect, be able to ask the king to show mercy to Lod.

By rescuing Lod he would win another ally in his

162

campaign for the throne of Chenameg. Doubtless Lod would be suitably grateful if Sarazin could pull it off — for otherwise he would surely be adjudged a wastrel and be put to death on that account.

'Sean Kelebes!' cried King Lyra, already some ways distant. 'Are you woolgathering? Come on, man — we're off!'

Sarazin sat up with a start. It was true! Horsemen were already thundering out of the mudfield. Sarazin spurred his steed and joined them, his eyes slit-gritted against the mud spraying in all directions from the hooves of the horses.

While Sarazin was one of the last of the riders to leave, he made up for it as they plunged through the bare-boughed forests of winter. Trees flashed past as he rode pell-mell, daring life and limb for glory. He was excited, exulted, exhilarated.

Swiftly he gained on the trackers, who rode with abandon, for they were drunk on firewater. Drunk as well was King Lyra, who rode whooping on the heels of the trackers, his son Tarkal close behind him. Sarazin, ardent in the pursuit of honour, strove to draw level with them.

In among the forest were tumbled piles of stone, the remnants of a settlement long since overthrown and overgrown. Here were thorny hedges, their winter-proof blue-black leaves rising in ramparts. And one lay directly across their path. In the base of the hedge was a scuffling hole through which, it seemed, the quarry had fled — for the trackers put their horses to the hedge.

King Lyra followed, as did Tarkal. So Sarazin, nothing daunted — a little firewater goes a long way — spurred his mount. Urged it to flight. And crashed to the ground when his horse fell heavily on the far side.

Bruised, dazed and dizzy, Sarazin struggled up from the ground. Tripped over something. What? A tracker, lying like a rag doll, neck broken. He heard swearing on the far side of the hedge where riders not reckless enough for the jump were deliberating a detour.

Sarazin's horse? The brute was getting to its feet. Sarazin stumbled towards it, to the tune of the click-clacking of a dozen free-swinging wooden plates which had been loosened by the shock of his fall to earth. He mounted up.

'Gah!' he said, urging his steed with a word expressive of disgust.

The horse allowed itself to be persuaded to walk, but would go no faster. Which way now?

In the winter mud, Sarazin had no trouble whatsoever in following the tracks of three horses — the steeds of the leading tracker, of King Lyra and of Tarkal. And — where they had not been overlaid by footprints — the impressions of someone's feet.

—*She must be close.*

Indeed. The woman could hardly be running still. She must have slowed to a walk. The horse would outpace her. But King Lyra and Tarkal would have her first.

Or would they?

Through the trees, Sarazin saw a glitter of water. Saw the surviving tracker floundering neck-deep in bog-mud, his arm wrapped around the neck of his struggling horse. Amidst mud and sedge, King Lyra himself. The king and his tracker, both intoxicated by firewater, had ridden straight into a swamp. But the king was only in it up to his waist, and Tarkal was nearby. Had dismounted. Had a long branch in his hands.

—*What now?*

Help with the rescue? No need. The king was in no danger. The tracker? Perhaps. But since the drunken loon had led his royal master into danger — why, he deserved death.

With all due care and caution — the effects of the firewater were wearing off — Sarazin skirted round the swamp, taking a wide swing through the forest. Picked up the stumbling trail of the woman's footprints. And rode on, his unsprung armour clock-clacking, the forest creaking around him in a gathering wind, the topmost branches of the skeletal trees clawing at the sky.

164

Ahead, Sarazin saw the naked woman, who had fallen exhausted to the muck beneath an oak tree. She was panting, her flanks heaving. Her wild eyes upstaring as his horse at leisure rode up alongside her.

Sarazin dismounted. He drew his sword in case she resisted him, but she quailed away, hiding her face in her hands. So he planted the brave blade Onslaught in the turf and, with masterful leisure, divested himself of his trousers and boots.

He felt a sensation of, above all else, power. But all was not perfect, for he was irked by his itchy-scratchy hunting coat with its click-clacking armour. So he shrugged it off and draped it over the saddle of his horse. He was so hot with lust, with the excitement of the chase, with the aftermath of indulgence in firewater, that he felt warm even once naked.

Looking down on the woman, Sarazin laughed for sheer delight at his own triumph. He touched himself. He was ready.

He was about to fall upon his prize and claim her with his swollen pride when he heard a branch break. Turning, he saw a black horse bearing a black-clad man who carried a blood-sharp spear. Saw the man's steady gaze. His orange-red beard. He looked remarkably like . . . like Fox.

He was Fox!

'Fox!' said Sarazin.

Fox made no reply, but gestured to the woman. With some handhold help from a nearby tree, she scrambled up behind him, then put her arms around him and laid her cheek against his black leathers.

'You can't take that woman!' said Sarazin, outraged. 'She's the king's meat. She's . . .'

His voice trailed away. He felt — what? Ashamed? Impossible! He'd done nothing wrong. Yet there was something in Fox's expression which he found hard to bear. He felt diminished. Dirtied. Soiled. And stupid, standing there bare-arse naked with winter's elements chilling his flesh.

165

A single acorn fell — ithlop! — to the mud. It was, perhaps, the very last acorn left over from the autumn. There was no sound louder. Then Fox urged his horse forward. The bare steel of his spearblade was pointed straight at Sarazin's chest. Sarazin stepped back, stumbled, fell, recovered himself, ran. He ducked between trees too close-grown for a horse to follow. Then turned at bay.

Fox leaned down from the saddle to pluck Sarazin's sword from the mud. He spiked Sarazin's trousers on the point of his spear. Took Sarazin's coat and passed it to the woman. Then grabbed the halter of Sarazin's horse and rode off at a leisurely pace.

'Hey!' said Sarazin. 'You can't — I mean — hey — stop! Whoa!'

Fox rode on, without looking back.

'I say,' said Sarazin. 'That's not — that's not my horse. Not mine to lose, I mean.'

Fox, by this time, was almost lost amidst the trees.

Sarazin began to patter along after his father. But ran into stinging nettles which brought him to a halt promptly. Feet smarting, he beat a retreat.

'Fox!' he cried. Then, in a moment of anguish: 'Father!'

But Fox was gone, and Sarazin was left with no horse, no sword, no trousers — and, worse, an unaccountable sense of shame which he could not for the life of him explain.

'Boots,' he said.

Yes, he still had his boots. He ran back to the clearing, rammed his feet into the boots, then raced after Fox. He pelted through the forest. Ducked beneath eye-claw branches. Sprinted up a bank and saw his father ahead, riding his woman-burdened horse through the trees.

'Fox!' bawled Sarazin.

Getting no response.

A bog lay between them. Fox had skirted it on his horse, but Sarazin plunged straight in. Desperate to catch up with his father. But the bog was deep, glutinous, clutching. He lost his boots to its suck and swallow. Found himself waist-deep, chest deep. Braved on, desperately. Stepped in a hole, went under. Clutched, grasped, rose gasping.

'Gluur!'

Thus screamed Sarazin, incoherent as an animal.

He was in desperate trouble. He was clinging to a rotten branch in the middle of a bottomless slough which was already slubbering at his lower lip.

'Fox!' he screamed. 'Come back! Come back! Help me! Help! I'm drowning!'

Then he clutched, clung, and listened. No reply.

The wind gusted in the swampside trees, then faded to silence. A single time-burnt leaf dwindled down to the swamp. Landing lightly, lightly, on its surface of curdled mud. Sarazin felt his lower lip quivering uncontrollably. He bit it. Hard. Tasted mud. Then tasted the salt of his hot, trickling tears.

Then realised he was getting cold.

Very cold.

He would have to get out of this bog, and soon, or he would be dead. He thrust around with his feet, questing for footing. Finding slurry-soft gulfs in all directions.

—*But the branch?*

He was holding the end of a branch. A rotten branch, lying just beneath the surface of the mud. Why didn't it sink? Because it was, presumably, attached to something.

—*It goes somewhere.*

Sarazin hauled on the branch. It held. So he dragged himself along through the swamp. Nearer the centre of the slough, the mud softened to grease, ooze, slime. Cold almost beyond endurance. And the branch was curving away into the depths. Too deep to reach with his hands. If he wanted to keep his head above mud, he must stand on it.

Sarazin stood on the branch, which he presumed to be attached to a dead tree somewhere far beneath the surface.

The branch broke.

He screamed.

'Ga—!'

Then screamed no more, for he had sundered under.

Flailing desperately, Sarazin struggled in the slime. And found himself on the surface, in what was, he realised, more like muddy water than watery mud.

He was swimming!

But now he faced a pretty dilemma. If he stayed in the muddy-water centre of the swamp he could keep himself afloat by swimming, but would shortly die from exposure. On the other hand, if he swam for the shore he would drown amidst clutching mud where swimming was impossible.

'Help!' wailed Sarazin.

But no help came.

So he floundered towards the nearest bank, hoping. The water gave way to a vile custard of mud and slime. He struggled through this as best he could, but found himself sinking. In a frenzy, he thrashed and struggled. And grabbed hold of something.

A snake!

'Aaaah!' screamed Sarazin.

But kept hold of the snake regardless, because it was keeping him afloat. A strong brute, then. But . . . passive.

Dead?

Then he realised he was not clutching a snake at all, but a tree root. He was too far gone to smile, but, slowly, began to drag himself along the tree root towards the shore.

Exhausted, stinking, shuddering, filthy, Sean Kelebes Sarazin trudged barefoot through the forest, arms wrapped round his body in a vain attempt to preserve some of his warmth against the mounting wind. He was utterly lost.

Then, at last, he saw some dark-shadowed huts which, on the basis of some softly-smoking earth-heaped mounds nearby, he identified as the habitation of some charcoal burners.

He staggered to the nearest doorway and fainted.

*   *   *

When Sarazin came to, Thodric Jarl was leaning over him, about to drape his nudity with a horseblanket.

'Awake?' said Jarl.

Sarazin simply stared at him.

He was lying in a dark, filthy hole of a hut, the lair of a charcoal burner. From outside, he heard Amantha's voice raised in outrage:

'Don't you dare!'

Then a laugh which, he knew very well, belonged to Glambrax.

'Come,' said Jarl. 'Can you stand?'

Sarazin did not think so, but on making the attempt found that he could. Jarl led him outside, where there were a full forty or fifty people mounted on horseback. Some were armed soldiers — mostly men Jarl had brought with him from Selzirk. Then there were stable boys, servants, and a scattering of high-born ladies, Amantha among them.

There was Glambrax, too, mounted on a mule.

Three of the horses had dead men lying across the saddles. Sarazin walked over to one of them, looked at his face.

'One of ours,' he said, recognising the corpse as a member of the Watch.

'We did not care to leave our dead in Shin,' said Jarl.

A spare horse was brought up for Sarazin. Jarl sliced a headhole in Sarazin's blanket so he could wear it like a poncho, the slack hauled in to his waist with a bit of rope. Then they set off.

Sarazin did not know what had happened, or where they were going, but he was too tired to ask.

CHAPTER TWENTY-TWO

Tarkal: eldest son of King Lyra, and hence heir to the Chenameg Kingdom. Deadly enemy of Sean Kelebes Sarazin, who defeated him in single combat in Selzirk. Brother of Amantha (with whom Sarazin is in love) and of Sarazin's friend Lod.

In due course they came to a derelict building which had once been the slave pen of a mine long since worked out and abandoned. There they took shelter and Sarazin began to learn of the disaster which had befallen Shin.

'King Lyra is dead,' said Jarl.

'How so?' said Sarazin, staring into the plattering rain.

'He fell from his horse,' said Glambrax, who paid close attention to whatever gossip was going. 'He was trapped beneath the brute. Thus a ditch drowned him.'

'Ditch?' said Sarazin.

'Some say ditch, some say swamp,' said Glambrax. 'But that he drowned there's no doubt. I saw the body myself. They brought it back to Shin.'

So Tarkal killed his father. There could be no doubt about that.

'What happened then?' said Sarazin.

Bit by bit, the story came out. Everyone had a different version of exactly what happened, but the outline was clear enough. On arriving in the capital with his father's corpse, Tarkal had declared himself king.

Without further ado, Tarkal had ordered that Lod be brought from his jail cell for instant execution. Men had gone away as if meaning to do just that — but had instead mutinied and placed themselves under Lod's command.

Why did that happen?

'Nobody knows,' said Jarl, 'but methinks them long in conspiracy with Lod. Either that, or they had a fear longstanding of Tarkal. In any event, there is now civil war in Shin, so I have come away from the place, meaning to leave the two brothers to fight it out for themselves.'

'Tarkal will win,' said Amantha, with confidence. 'When we return to Shin tomorrow we'll find my brother lord of the Great House with Lod's headless corpse kneeling in obeisance at his feet.'

There was something obscene about her obvious enthusiasm for the idea.

'We'll not return to Shin tomorrow,' said Jarl. 'We'll send scouts instead, and we'll not move from here until it's safe to.'

'Does a coward speak?' said Amantha.

Jarl laughed away the insult.

'A survivor speaks,' said he. 'A survivor with a warm regard for his own hide. If any hero wishes to ride back to Shin to get himself killed in this brawl between brothers then let him do so. But I'll not see myself dead for a cause so trivial.'

Sarazin did not think the cause trivial at all, for Sean Sarazin's future and that of the throne of Chenameg both depended on the outcome of this 'brawl'. However, a brief audit of his own condition convinced him he was in no condition to go anywhere, far less to go to war, so he could but go along with Jarl's plan.

The next morning, Jarl's scouts found Shin depopulated, abandoned by the populace and by both parties to Chenameg's civil war. Accordingly, Jarl led his people back to the capital. They entered the city towards noon.

There were signs of fighting — a few dog-worried corpses and a couple of burnt-out buildings — but few signs of looting. The stables were empty, but little appeared to be missing elsewhere.

'When they left,' said Jarl, 'they left in a hurry.'

'Yes,' said Sarazin, wishing he had been the one to say it, even though Jarl's comment was so obvious it was hardly worth making.

Jarl ordered everyone to lodge in the Great House, and, under his supervision, they attended to the fortification of the same. There was a great deal of sawing and hammering as windows were reduced to arrowslits and arrowslits cut in blind walls which would otherwise have allowed attackers to approach unhindered. Under Jarl's supervision, Shin was looted in earnest, and all of value was stockpiled within the Great House.

This work took seven days.

Meantime, scouts scoured the surrounds. Sarazin led one scouting party, and often sighted furtive groups of ragged men. Peasants? Escaped slaves? Bandits? Whoever they were, they ran when approached, and Sarazin — obedient to the strict guidelines issued by Thodric Jarl — did not pursue lest he be led into an ambush.

It was eerie and unsettling to live and work thus in ignorance of what had happened and what was yet to happen. Was Lod dead? Was Tarkal? Did the roving bands of peasants give allegiance to either? To both? Or to neither? Sarazin talked it over with Jarl who said:

'All wars are fought blindfold. We know well enough that nobody will thank us if we leave Shin to be burnt by whatever beggar passes this way. That, for the moment, should be enough.'

On the eighth day, a day of downpouring rain, a dawn patrol sighted upwards of three hundred ragged creatures on the outskirts of Shin. Peasants loyal to Tarkal? Or to Lod? Or an anarchist rabble of brigands or beggars?

'If they are Lod's men or Tarkal's then we are safe,' said Jarl. 'If otherwise, then we may have a fight on our hands.'

And the battle-wise Rovac warrior had all his people stay inside the Great House. He had the horses brought within

172

also, to the greater detriment of the floors and the atmosphere. Then he had the doors barricaded. Then he walked through the Great House repeating orders given previously.

'These people may be friends or enemies,' said Jarl. 'Whoever they are, let them reveal themselves to us, not vice versa. If they approach, nobody is to speak to them but me. Let them guess at our numbers. Let them think us a thousand. Let nobody enter a quarrel which may betray our true numbers.'

As the ragged mob outnumbered the defenders of the Great House by six to one the concealment of the true state of affairs was, in Jarl's opinion, of the utmost importance.

Sean Sarazin himself had command of the roof of the Great House. He had a dozen men with him, all armed with longbows. And he had his dwarf Glambrax, who had persuaded some handy fellow to make him a crossbow. A small instrument but lethal all the same, at least at close range.

Since there was no point in risking the rain unless the Great House was actually attacked, Sarazin and his men sheltered under a tarpaulin, trying to warm themselves by the heat of a couple of charcoal-burning braziers. For a long time nothing happened. As Thodric Jarl was wont to say, wars are mostly a matter of waiting.

The rain sundered from sodden skies, washing the earthwealth of Chenameg into the Velvet River, where it would be carried downstream for league upon league, eventually to silt up the dams built downstream in the Harvest Plains, or, flooding past such barriers, to flow on past Selzirk and eventually stain the waters of the Central Ocean, far to the west.

Glambrax looked at the skies, grimaced, then said:

'Ah! Democracy!'

'What mean you?' said Sarazin.

'Why, that the heavens piss on prince and peasant alike.'

'You've got a crude mouth,' said Sarazin coldly.

'Yes,' said Glambrax, with a grin, 'but good teeth.'

So saying, he popped a walnut into his mouth and

cracked the shell. Sarazin winced. Glambrax tore bits of shell from the walnut kernel. He held it up.

'This is shaped like a brain,' said Glambrax.

'So?' said Sarazin.

'So we have to make the day pass somehow.'

'It'll pass soon enough,' said Sarazin, 'once they attack.'

'If they attack,' said Glambrax. 'They may be friends, may they not? Gathered for a birthday party or such?'

But the dwarf spoke in jest, and everyone knew it. These could not be Tarkal's men, or Lod's, for, if they were either, they would long since have approached to declare themselves. So things looked grim. But at least the sky promised unbroken rain for the foreseeable future, which meant the enemy would have trouble torching the Great House — an important consideration since that house was of timber construction entire.

Towards noon the rain eased to a drizzle. A little later, a woebegone peasant stumbled through the quagmire to the door of the Great House. He was not admitted. In fact, he could not be admitted, since that door had been so thoroughly barricaded it would have been a major operation to open it. However, he was allowed to speak through a fresh-cut arrowslit.

Sean Sarazin and the others on the roof of the Great House peered down at the fellow, wondering what he was saying. He was certainly taking his time about it. Glambrax cocked his crossbow.

'Don't you dare!' said Sarazin. 'It may be a stinking peasant but it's an ambassador for all that.'

'Yes,' said Glambrax, 'it is an ambassador as you are a prince.'

'Tsh!' said Sarazin in disgust, and tried to cuff Glambrax.

Who darted away then made a face which provoked Sarazin into giving pursuit. Glambrax scuttled away to the far side of the roof. Then stopped. Turned. Shouted:

'Ware! Attack!'

Was it a joke? Half a dozen heartbeats later Sarazin knew it was not. While the peasant ambassador parlayed at the front of the Great House his fellows were assaulting the rear. Hundreds of them! They dragged with them siege ladders hastily made from the limitless materials available in the lumber yards of Shin.

'Ware! Ware!' screamed Sarazin. 'Attack! Attack! Attack!'

As his men stumbled across the roof to join him a throaty roar of wrath arose from the oncoming mob. Which began to charge. Sarazin's bowmen began to shoot — then one slipped, fell, tumbled from the roof.

'Watch your footing!' shouted Sarazin.

'He was shot!' cried another of the bowmen. Then cried again as an arrow took him in the gut.

Moments later, the first siege ladder was hoisted. One of Sarazin's men — a fool or a hero, call him what you will — tried to displace it. He put his boot to the ladder, pushed it away, saw it fall. Then a flight of hate-slung arrows raped home and, gasping, clutching, flailing, he fell.

The rest of Sarazin's men were already running.

'Come back!' shouted Sarazin, flat on his belly on the roof from fear of enemy arrows.

But they slipped away down the hatch which led from roof to attic. Sarazin screamed at them again. With no result. What should he do, what should he do? He must do something!

'Should I kill you for mercy perhaps?' said Glambrax, a bolt at the ready in his cocked crossbow.

'Don't point that thing at me,' shouted Sarazin.

'You've no escape, you know,' said Glambrax, with an evil grin. 'I can shoot you down like a dog. Unless by chance you can make yourself invisible.'

'Pox!' said Sarazin, remembering, and unslung the chain which he had till then been wearing round his neck.

As Glambrax chortled Sarazin struggled to remove his magic silver ring from its silver chain. But his hands in panic found it impossible to prise open the tight-wound

coil of metal. Perhaps it was not silver at all but something harder, stronger, fiercer. Another siege ladder
slapped home.

'Here,' said Glambrax, 'give it.'

And the dwarf tore the chain-bound ring from Sarazin's
grip and, swiftly, deftly, liberated ring from chain. Then
dropped the ring so it fell in front of Sarazin's nose. Sarazin
grabbed it. Put it on.

And felt his entire body shaken by unmusical vibrations
which put his teeth on edge. The ring was cold on his
finger, bitter cold, like a band of ice. But his body was
warm already and heating further by the moment. He drew
the brave blade Onslaught. The ring denied him daylight.
He walked in a world of shadows as he dared his dread
towards the edge of the roof.

Where things of thick darkness were already scrambling
up from below. Nightmarish things, uncouth shapes of
bloody hate, of jealous death, of guttural-grunting
obscenity. The enemy. The Enemy! But a hero was there
to meet him, swinging his sword already and screaming
as he swung:

'Wa — wa — Watashi!'

Sweet sliced his blade, sweet, ripping a ragged wound
through the nearest shambling thing, the wound gleaming
red amidst the darkness as the stinking ouns of the thing
outspilled from its walking corpse.

And Sarazin screamed again, and hacked, and chopped,
and kicked away one ladder then another, and heard
gabbling voices roused to horror by the death invisible
which attacked them, and knew then the battle-joy.

He was amok now, berserk, no man left, only battle.
But the heat was rising, he was hot, too hot, he was
burning, scalding, to breathe was pain, and the heat and
pain together made battle give way to the man.

—*One ladder left!*

Sarazin strode to the last ladder, hacked away a bulbous
shadow, put boot to the ladder, pushed, felt it slide, saw
it fall, heard shadows wail away. Then turned. This way.

176

That. Scanning the roof. One shadow remained, a shadow too tall to be Glambrax.

Sarazin advanced.

The shadow—

Saw him? Heard him?

It put itself and its weapon on guard. But Sean Sarazin, invisible, smote the filthy thing, saw red sliced open, yes, he had wounded it sore, had opened its polluted belly. Should finish the job now. But the heat was almost at killing point.

Smartly, Sean Sarazin stepped backwards. Drove his sword into the roof's timbers to free both hands.

Then tore the ring from his finger.

Ice-cold it felt while he was wearing it, but the moment he got it free it felt red-hot. He dropped it sharply, grabbed his sword with both hands, wrenched it from the timbers, then stood on guard. Blinking and gasping. Blinking at light near blinding, gasping for heat and for sweat.

Where was his enemy?

The thing was there, in front of him. Tottering on the edge of the roof. Not a near-shapeless shadow, not a hell-fiend Enemy, but a man. Hands clutched to his gut, red blood outspilling between his fingers. Face deformed by agony, wrenched by pain, but the face, the face, it was—

'Fox!' screamed Sarazin.

He dropped his sword and raced forward. Fox was teetering on the edge. Sarazin slithered on the greasy wood, slipped, fell. Reached. Grasped. Clawed. Grabbed at his father's ankle. And, trying to save him, toppled him. Clutched, held — then lost the man to a jerk which nearly dislocated his arm.

'Father!'

Thus screamed Sarazin. For his father was gone, falling, doomed, dead. And it was Sean Sarazin who had killed him.

CHAPTER TWENTY-THREE

The prophecy: that a prince will return from exile to
Selzirk, will be scorned and reviled when he proposes a
way to save the city from dangers unleashed by wicked
and witless men, will endure great hardship and greater
danger, will win the name Watashi, will marry the princess
of an ancient kingdom, will win the power he needs to save
Selzirk by killing his own father in war, will save the city
and win great praise and everlasting glory.

Still fell the rain, drowning down from grey eternities of
sky while Sean Sarazin lay abed. By night he lay there and
by day also, rousing out reluctantly to use the chamber
pot and for no other purpose. He supped on broth which
Glambrax brought him and, on occasion, ate a little fish
fresh-caught from the Velvet River.

Otherwise he lay almost as if catatonic, a huddle of half-
dreaming flesh slow-breathing and mostly motionless. And
all the while the rain fell without the Great House, drench-
ing down to the mud, to the streets of Shin, to the dank
forest, to the broad-backed river.

With time, Sarazin roused himself. Not to action, but
at least to thought. At first, his thoughts were near as
incoherent as his dreams. A jumble of grief, guilt, regret.

—*My father dead!*
—*I killed him!*

Thus ran the burden of his thoughts.

At first.

But, with time — and a few days are a long time in the

life of an active intellect — Sarazin began to rationalise what had happened. He had killed Fox, true. Fox must be dead, what with the gut wound and the fall from the roof, though the enemy had dragged away all their dead when they beat a retreat. Sarazin had killed him. Had killed his father.

But had excuses.

Item: Fox was doomed to die in that manner anyway, for prophecy had proclaimed that Sarazin would kill him.

Item: Regardless of prophecy, Fox had long been marked for death, for when Fox rode forth with Benthorn and others to attack an embassy at Smork he had made himself an outlaw.

Item: Sarazin had not known it was Fox he was fighting until the fight was already over.

Item: Sarazin had then tried to save his father's life. His strength had been unequal to the task but then . . . he was only human.

Sarazin toyed with those ideas and with others for some time, and was almost satisfied. But not quite. Then he considered the recent events in more depth and detail, and slowly realised that Fox had chosen his fate.

If Fox had truly valued survival then he would have fled far further than Chenameg after he was declared an outlaw. If he loved life he would have gone far south to Drangsturm or across the seas to the Scattered Islands. Instead, he had lent his strength to a sordid uprising of the disorderly elements in Chenameg . . .

As Lord Regan had often said, we do choose our own fate. We are responsible for what happens to us. The lives we lead are shaped by our own free will. Ultimately, though Fox had died by Sarazin's sword, it was the decisions Fox had made which had led to his death.

Sarazin remembered . . .

The hunt for the girl through the forest of Chenameg. The exhilarating excitement of the chase. The girl caught, fallen, captured, his. Then, before he could truly claim his prize, Fox had appeared to steal away the woman.

Was that not evidence of choice?

The girl must have had a victim mentality otherwise she would not have become a victim in the first place. Lord Regan's teachings made that plain. Victims must bear full responsibility for their own fate for, as Lord Regan had often said, history cannot pardon the defeated. If Sarazin had raped the woman then he would have been doing no more than help her work out the fate she had chosen for herself.

The victims have made their choices. Those who suffer, those who are sick, those who are poor, those who are enslaved, those who are ignorant, have chosen their suffering, their sickness, their poverty, their servitude, their ignorance. To say otherwise is, surely, to deny the reality of free will.

So Fox, by linking his fate with that of the victim class, had doomed himself by an act of his own free will. First by allowing Sarazin's lawful prey to escape, then by joining a mob of ragged anarchists making war on lawful authority in Shin.

Yet . . .

When Fox rode from the forest to rescue the woman there was something lordly in his bearing. Something noble in the gesture. And Sarazin had felt . . . had felt like dirt. Had known shame. Had been humbled.

But . . . was that rational?

In any case, there was nothing noble about the attack on the Great House in Shin. The criminal mob had assaulted the Great House while one of their number was at the front door pretending to negotiate. A shameful thing to do. In that battle it had been the defenders who were noble, if not heroic, fighting off an attack by an enemy vastly superior in numbers.

In any case . . .

Sarazin remembered a fine summer's day in Voice, years ago, and Lord Regan saying:

'When something has happened it has happened. You must then realise exactly what has happened so you can

180

take advantage of the situation. But grief, sorrow, pity, regret — those are useless emotions. Worse, they cripple us, they make us useless for action.'

With that remembered, Sarazin considered his own behaviour. Had he not made himself a cripple? In truth, he had. He had killed his father, he had won himself the name Watashi in battle and now, if he seized his opportunity, he could surely marry his princess and thus take one more step towards fulfilling the fate which was prophesied for him. Yet he lay in bed an invalid, though in battle he had sustained but a couple of cuts and a few bruises scarcely worth mentioning.

After a brief but rigorous session of self-criticism Sarazin rose from his bed and went to work.

As yet, nobody knew what had become of Tarkal or of Lod. But the immediate situation was clear enough. A small army of ragged criminals, anarchist outlaws all, was still within striking distance of Shin. If Sarazin and Thodric Jarl marched away and left the city undefended then doubtless those outlaws would seize it.

'So,' said Sarazin, 'we should make command of Shin and, indeed, the governance of all of Chenameg our price for staying here.'

Then he told Jarl exactly what he wanted.

'You want to marry Amantha?' said Jarl. 'You want to set yourself up as king?'

'Nothing less will do,' said Sarazin.

'I caution you against it,' said Jarl, his voice serious, his mien severe.

'Why?' said Sarazin, who, for the life of him, could not see why the Rovac warrior should be taking this line.

'Because,' said Jarl, 'as things stand, all our actions are lawful. We do but defend property in Shin against criminals. That can but win us praise in Selzirk and elsewhere. But if you set yourself up as king in Chenameg then you usurp the law of the Harvest Plains, for the kingmaker herself must approve the crowning of any new king of Chenameg.'

'Impossible,' said Sarazin, 'for Chenameg lies beyond the jurisdiction of the Harvest Plains. My mother Farfalla is called kingmaker only on account of her powers of appointment within the Harvest Plains itself.'

'You may think so,' said Jarl, 'but I believe the law of Selzirk holds things to be otherwise.'

'How so?' said Sarazin.

'Details I cannot give you, for I am no lawyer,' said Jarl. 'But trust me. Things are as I have said they are.'

Sarazin laughed.

'You disbelieve me?' said Jarl.

'Friend,' said Sarazin, 'why so serious?'

'Because it takes but a single witless error to put your life at risk,' said Jarl. 'Believe me, to reach for the crown of Chenameg is to make such an error. Selzirk will punish you for such a breach of the law.'

'I trust you not, at least not in this,' said Sarazin, 'for what you have said is absurd. All know Chenameg to be a state in its own right, an entity entirely separate in law from the Harvest Plains. No law of Selzirk can claim to rule in Shin.'

'You are wrong,' said Jarl.

'In this I trust to my own judgment,' said Sarazin. 'The question now is whether you are for me or against me.'

'I am neither,' said Jarl. 'Whatever you do I will remain here with my men, but only to protect Shin against outlaws.'

'Will you seek to restrain my actions?' said Sarazin.

'I will advise you again against kingship,' said Jarl, 'making sure that my men witness such advice. That much I must do for my own protection. But I will not restrain you, no.'

Thodric Jarl would not restrain Sean Sarazin because there was a chance — not a strong chance, but a chance regardless — that Sarazin could triumph. Winning the throne itself would, of course, be the easy bit. The hard part would be retaining it in the face of the wrath of the Harvest Plains.

The big question was simply this: would Lord Regan send an army from the Rice Empire to Chenameg to support Sean Sarazin? Thodric Jarl had no way to answer that question. In his secret coded despatches to Lord Regan, Jarl had often enough asked for guidance. He had asked directly:

— *What, Lord Regan, are your plans for Sean Sarazin?*

— *Would you send an army to support any coup staged by Sean Sarazin in Selzirk?*

— *If I cannot know the answers to these questions now, when can I know?*

But, since Lord Regan had not seen fit to grant Thodric Jarl an insight into his intentions, Jarl still faced the future blindfold. But of this he was sure: a lot of blood would be spilt before the rule of Chenameg was finally decided one way or another.

Sean Sarazin found it very easy to bargain with Amantha. She believed that Thodric Jarl was Sarazin's oath-bound servant, and would obey him in all things. She believed Jarl would quit Shin and leave the city defenceless if Sarazin but said the word. Nightmares had troubled her lately, and, in the worst of those nightmares, she found herself the victim of a lust-crazed mob of verminous anarchists.

If Sarazin abandoned her, she was doomed.

On the other hand, if Sarazin stayed and married Amantha, order could be restored, her life guaranteed and Shin itself saved from the anarchists.

'We'll marry then,' said Amantha, after a very brief discussion indeed.

'Tomorrow,' said Sarazin, with determination.

'Not so fast!' said she. 'I need a few days' grace at least.'

'Why?' said Sarazin.

'Well, if you really must know, I'm having my period right now.'

'Oh,' said Sarazin, entirely defeated by Amantha's most eloquent argument.

And he agreed to a postponement of five days.

During those five days, much happened, some good, some bad. The bad was very bad. Anarchists slipped into Shin by night and set a dozen buildings alight, and the Great Hall was one of those which burnt to the ground.

The good, on the other hand, was quite good. The manager of a mine some fifty leagues north, alerted to the trouble in Shin by a lone refugee, had exacted an oath of allegiance from the men under his command then set off to march for the capital. This little army arrived two days before the wedding and put itself under Jarl's command.

With his forces thus bolstered Jarl chanced a reconnaissance in force of the surrounding forest, a reconnaissance which brought good news: the enemy appeared to have withdrawn.

'Doubtless,' said Jarl, 'they have been unable to feed themselves, for all the stocks of food worth mentioning are under our command.'

This was some comfort. Even though, of course, Sarazin's kingdom would have to face threats far worse than that posed by a ragged gang of criminal anarchists. Jarl began making plans for a war to defend Shin against Selzirk. And began assessing his men, wondering which of them — if any — could be trusted to take a message all the way to the Rice Empire to alert Lord Regan to the latest developments in the life of his protégé Sean Sarazin.

CHAPTER TWENTY-FOUR

Amantha: second-oldest child of King Lyra of Chenameg and, therefore, heir to the throne if Tarkal is dead (as he is presumed to be).

*   *   *

At dawn on his wedding day, Sarazin was woken by a big, sloppy wet kiss.

'Gaaa!' shouted Sarazin, flailing wildly.

Chuckling, Glambrax ducked and dodged. Sarazin leapt out of bed and pursued him. But, by the time he had driven Glambrax into a corner, the dwarf had armed himself with Sarazin's chamber pot. Which was far from empty.

'I'll let you off this time,' said Sarazin.

'Just as well,' said Glambrax, 'for dead dwarves are the worst of luck at a wedding feast. As it is, the omens are not the best.'

'What do you mean?' said Sarazin.

In answer, Glambrax waddled to the shutters and threw them open. The sky was bruised black and orange. It was raining blood.

'Call off the marriage,' said Sarazin. 'We'll try again tomorrow.'

The next day brought another sodden dawn. But at least this time the rain was water and not blood.

'Today's the day,' said Sarazin.

Since the Great Hall of the House of Chenameg had been burnt by anarchists, Amantha and Sarazin were married in a barn. The roof leaked, but strategically placed buckets caught the worst of the drips. First the wedding guests gathered in the barn, then Sarazin and Amantha entered.

Sarazin wore his battle-leathers. Thanks to his upbringing in the Rice Empire, he still thought of leather as an ugly, uncouth, obscene material — but nothing better was to be had in Shin. So, though uneasy, he made do with what he had.

Amantha, for her part, arrived at the barn dressed in a bright-hued sontag, which was comely enough, but did not match his imaginings, for he had dreamed of her arrayed in silks and gorgeous with diamonds. She looked

185

somewhat sullen, which made him uncomfortably aware that she was not marrying him for the glamour of his cock, but as a matter of pure survival.

As Sarazin entered the barn with Amantha, the guests cried:

'Ave Amantha! Ave Sarazin!'

He could not help resenting the fact that they called Amantha's name before they called his.

The wedding ceremony then commenced, but they had got no further than sacrificing a chicken to the Household Gods when there was a crash of thunder and the door to the barn split asunder.

Then into the barn walked a heavy figure, bringing to the shocked assembly a reek most foul. It was King Lyra! His scalp dangled from his skull, there was mud in the sockets of his eyes, yet he was on his feet, walking, pointing, trying to speak.

'Og-gorog,' said King Lyra.

Upon which Thodric Jarl hurled a hatchet. It took the dead king in the head. The skull exploded in a spray of dirt, stench, pulp and shattered bone. King Lyra's corpse swayed on its feet then crashed to the ground. Amantha screamed hysterically. She did not stop until Jarl slapped her across the face.

Once. Twice. Three times.

Then:

'Get that thing out of here!' said Jarl.

Two of his men each grabbed a leg of the corpse and dragged it outside into the rain. Jarl turned to face the silent audience.

'A corpse walking,' said Jarl. 'That's no great trick. I've seen it done often enough before. It takes but little power — any tenth-rate necromancer can arrange as much. Such a one must have chosen to play a practical joke on these young lovers here. But that tells us nothing of the king's opinion, for the corpse is not the king himself.'

But one of the stable hands spoke up and said:

'The king is angry because Sean Sarazin has never made the quest.'

And others, muttering, said as much themselves. Whereupon Sarazin, realising what he was talking about, said:

'I take upon myself the duties of the heirs of Chenameg as well as their rights. I will make the quest. Ten days hence I will set forth just as Tarkal in his day set forth. I will quest beyond Drangsturm to the terror-lands of the Deep South. I will dare the dangers of the Swarms until I find the tectonic lever and throw the same.'

He meant what he said. He felt drunk with his own heroism, and Jarl's frown did not dampen his exultation. Certainly Sean Sarazin had said the right thing as far as the audience was concerned, for cheers greeted his proclamation.

The rites proceeded without further interruption, and Sean Sarazin was duly married to Amantha of Chenameg. Since he had wed the only surviving daughter of the ruling house of Chenameg, and since there was no male heir in evidence, he was, of course, now king of Chenameg himself.

It was true!

Yes, Lord Regan was right. You can have whatever you want. You can get whatever you wish for. You can be whatever you want to be. The will is free, so all things are possible. All that you need is ambition.

With ceremony done, feasting began, the slaughter of sick horses having provided plentiful meat for the same. After feasting came dancing to the tune of various instruments musicking. Then, finally, late in the evening, Sarazin and Amantha were bundled through the rain to the Great House, there to take their nuptial rites to their logical conclusion.

CHAPTER TWENTY-FIVE

love lovingly enchants (delicious)
your eloquence of perfumes as i
(more moth than butterfly, more dream than silk)
strip (elegance by elegance) these petals
till quite (my sweet) your weather can embrace
and all infoldings clasp us to their task.
                    —n. n. nooth, 'love loving lovingly'

Amantha and Sarazin, wet from the rain, dripped their
way to their nuptial chamber deep within the Great House.
Servants went before them, bearing candles. When they
reached the Great Bedroom which used to be King Lyra's,
Amantha supervised the disposition of the candles, then
dismissed the servants.

Sean Sarazin was alone at last with his true love.

'This,' said Amantha, unnecessarily, 'was my father's
room. Do you like it?'

'I love it,' said Sarazin, with enthusiasm. For it was a
part of a royal palace, and therefore much to be admired.
Still, it was not exactly what he had expected.

For a start, it stank of dogs. Scarcely surprising, since
there were a great many dogs in attendance. Large dogs.
The way they looked at Sarazin made him uncomfortable.
It suggested they had large appetites, and were not fussy
about how they satisfied those appetites.

The room was huge. Overhead were bare rafters. Somewhere beyond, lost in the shadows above, there must be
a ceiling, but Sarazin, who could not see it, felt as if he

was standing in an enormous cave. He waited for Amantha to embrace him in rapture. But she was busying herself with the job of trimming the candles.

'Amantha, darling,' said Sarazin, stealing up on her.

He slid an encircling arm round her waist. But she shook him off.

'Can't you see I'm busy?' she said.

Somewhat taken aback by her brusque reaction, he backed off and sat down on the bed, which was massive. The yellowed skulls of ancestral enemies were perched on the finials at each of its corners.

On the walls of the room were the glowering heads of wild animals slaughtered by King Lyra, by King Lyra's father, and by his father's father before him. Triumphs of taxidermy they were: the heads of stag, wolf and bear. Sarazin was acutely conscious of the fact that in all his hunting he had never personally killed any animal so noble.

'Why are there so many dogs in here?' said Sarazin.

'These are the king's dogs,' said Amantha.

'Couldn't they sleep outside? At least for tonight, I mean.'

'Who are you to change a royal custom?' said Amantha.

Sarazin, who did not want to begin their night of bliss with an argument, declined to answer. Instead, he stripped off his clothes, threw them on to a chair — which was made entirely from interwoven antlers — then began to dry himself vigorously with a towel which had been laid out on the bed.

Then Amantha, having finished trimming the candles, began to take off her clothes. A huge moth with wings the colour of copper and bronze danced dizzy around the candles. A muscular mastiff watched the two humans. Waiting for what? An order? As Sarazin was wondering, a monstrous hound of uncertain breed jumped on to the bed.

'Hey! You!' said Sarazin. 'Get off the bed!'

He grabbed the dog's collar and hauled on it. The brute did not budge by so much as a fingerlength. Instead, it bared its teeth and growled. Sarazin hastily let go and stepped back.

'Sheeba!' said Amantha, sharply.

And clapped her hands twice, in anger.

The hound hastily decamped from the bed and slunk into a corner, where it lay sulking as Amantha towelled herself.

'Don't watch!' she said, catching Sarazin in the act. 'You embarrass me.'

So Sarazin turned away, humming to himself, trying to pretend he felt gay and jaunty. Rain drummed against the shutters. It was cold. He wanted. Warmth, yes. Amantha was warm, surely. What did Lod say? Slippery when wet . . .

Sarazin turned to Amantha, who had swaddled herself in her towel. He tried, gently, to remove it. She resisted. He suddenly became less gentle, and wrenched the towel away from her. She stood there naked, one hand guarding her vulva, the other clasped across her breasts.

'Why look at me as if I were a rapist?' asked Sarazin, hurt.

'All men are rapists,' she said.

Sarazin had not come prepared for political argument, so did not know how to reply. Instead, after a moment's hesitation, he invaded her defences, his hands eagering over her breasts.

'Don't maul me!' said Amantha, pulling away from him.

'But I'm your husband!' protested Sarazin.

'That's got nothing to do with it. My breasts are sore. They're tender. Understand?'

'Like little birds,' said Sarazin, attempting to lighten the mood with a little romance, a touch of poetry.

'Quite possibly,' said Amantha, sourly. 'Well, come on! Let's get it over with!'

So saying, she slid herself under the bed's vast duvet. Sarazin tried to draw it back.

'Stop that!' she said. 'Are you perverted?'

'To see pleasure is part of the pleasure of pleasuring,' said Sarazin.

'Only peasants want to see the flesh in action,' retorted Amantha. 'You want to watch? You're disgusting! That's

190

a filthy low-bred perversion. You must have learnt it from whores.'

Sarazin, abashed, face burning, made no reply. Instead, he crawled under the duvet and coupled with Amantha, going about his business as he was accustomed to, striving like a conqueror.

Amantha cried out in alarm:

'Gently! Gently! You're hurting me!'

Sarazin felt himself deflating. He grasped, wildly, for erotic visions to help him with his thrust. In the end, to his shame, it was Bizzie he conjured into his mind to help him drive and strive until lust was appeased.

'Are you finished?' said Amantha.

'Darling,' said Sarazin, kissing her, tenderly.

'You're finished,' she said, emphatically. 'Take it out!'

'My cherished sweet,' he said, kissing her again.

In terms of pleasure, their coupling had been a disaster. So he wanted to at least indulge his pride. To lie there in possession of his princess, a woman of the Favoured Blood, the woman who guaranteed to him his glorious future.

'Take it out,' she insisted. 'You're finished.'

So Sarazin withdrew, whereupon she rolled away from him. Soon she was asleep. Snoring with a high whine. But Sarazin lay sleepless, restless. Unable to settle. This was not at all what he had expected. He had expected gasping raptures, silken pleasures, panting excitement, eager hands. Instead, he had met with the most grudging welcome imaginable.

'But I'm Lord of Chenameg now,' said he, trying to console himself about his disappointment.

Then he started to wonder where the Lord of Chenameg should go to take a piss. Was there a chamber pot in the room? There must be. But, when he got out of bed, he could not see it.

So he went to the window and opened a shutter. A gust of cold wind buffeted inside, blowing out most of the candles. The shutter tore free from his hand and banged heavily. Hastily, he grabbed for it. Cold rain splattered against his nakedness. He got control of the shutter and hauled it in, leaving just enough space to piss through.

As he relieved himself, Sarazin heard a heavy thump behind him. Glancing over his shoulder, he saw that the hound Sheeba had taken possession of his side of the bed.

'Sss!' hissed Sarazin.

He closed the shutters firmly against the night then went to deal with the hound. Who growled, baring teeth at him. He backed off, warily, looking for a weapon. At which point a draught blew out the last candle, leaving him in utter darkness.

'Bugger!' said Sarazin.

'Yes!' said Amantha, speaking from her dreams. 'Bugger me, bugger me, take me, force me, rape me, shaft me, hold me, clasp me, oh, Tarkal, Tarkal, do it, dig, do it, dig, oh Tarkal, dig, dig, dig, dig . . .'

Her voice trailed away. From outshouting frenzy to a mothdust whisper. Then she shuddered, as if in pleasure. Then, after a moment's silence, gasped as if stabbed. Then groaned. Long and low. Then whimpered. Then no sound came from her but that of regular breathing.

Sarazin stood in the dark, shocked and trembling. What lustful monster lived within the snowpetal skin of his princess? From where had come that foul, dark, demanding desire? And why had she cried her brother's name? Could she . . .? Did she . . .? Surely not!

'He's dead, anyway,' muttered Sarazin, 'so it makes no difference.'

Then made for the bed. He tripped over a mastiff, which lurched to its feet, barking. Amantha screamed:

'Tarkal!'

'It's me,' said Sarazin, 'me, me, Sean Sarazin, your husband, your lover, your friend.'

'Oh,' said Amantha. Then, puzzled but not unduly upset: 'Who turned you into a dog?'

'Nobody,' said Sarazin. 'That's Sheeba beside you. I'm over here.'

'Oh,' said Amantha. Then, still puzzled: 'Pray tell, why? Why are you standing over there?'

'I'm meditating,' said Sarazin.

'Meditating!' said Amantha, with impatience and fury mixed. 'What did I marry? A clown? Come back to bed. Sheeba! Get off!'

Sarazin navigated towards Amantha's voice, got under the duvet and curled up next to his true love. By now his ardour had recovered, and was fleshing out his pizzle with hot young blood. He put a hand on Amantha's shoulder and tried to turn her privacy towards him.

'Not again!' she said, irritated. 'Not now!'

'But . . . darling . . .'

'I have a headache.'

Rebuffed, Sarazin lay staring into the darkness, while Amantha slipped off to sleep. After a while, he realised there was something moving among the rafters overhead. A spider. Glowing phosphorescent in the dark. A monstrous spider.

—*Can't be. Must be dreaming.*

So thought Sarazin. To check, he put a finger into his mouth and bit it. Yes, he was awake all right. So the spider must really be up there. But it was huge! As big as a dog! Should he scream for help? No: the sound might draw the spider. It might leap down and fang them.

He would have to wake up Amantha. Then they would have to creep to the door, very quietly. Then open it, and make a dash for safety. Trembling with fear, he shook Amantha awake.

'All right, you sex maniac,' she said, in something approaching a shout. 'Rape me, then.'

'Keep your voice down,' he said.

'Are you ashamed then? Are you—'

'Amantha! Amantha! Look! Up there! Look! There's a—'

'A spider,' said Amantha, with a complete lack of interest. 'What of it?'

'But it's — it's huge!'

'They only eat bats, stupid. Go back to sleep.'

Sarazin sank back in bed. But he did not dare shut his eyes, not with that hideous monstrosity on the loose above him. Maybe it did hunt bats. Usually. But what if it slipped? And fell? Slap bang into their faces!

In the end, weary beyond belief but still fearful of the spider, he crawled deep under the duvet, down to the darkness somewhere near Amantha's feet. Which were unwashed, and smelt accordingly.

As the wise have elsewhere remarked, there are two disasters which can befall one: getting what one wants, or not getting what one wants. Sarazin felt that, somehow, he had managed to get the worst of both worlds.

CHAPTER TWENTY-SIX

Celadon: Farfalla's second-born child, the brother of Sarazin, Peguero and Jarnel (who is the youngest). An unsubtle soldier dedicated to his military career and to very little else.

Celadon was a military attaché in Shin when Sarazin arrived in the autumn, but was ordered by King Lyra to return to Selzirk with news that Sarazin was forbidden to depart Shin until Lod's trial was concluded.

Sarazin lay dreaming of Amantha. In his dream, she promenaded naked in a marble-colonnaded xystus. Her body shaved. All hair lower than her eyebrows gone entirely. He—

He woke, as a servant slammed the door open.

'Blood's grief!' said Sarazin, staring at the shocked and panting man. 'What is it?'

'My lord,' said the servant, 'soldiers are coming. From the west.'

194

'From the west?' said Sarazin.

'Yes, my lord,' said the servant. 'From the west.'

'Great,' said Amantha. 'Is breakfast coming from the west, too? It should be here by now. Where is it?'

'It will be here soon, my lady, soon,' said the servant. 'But, my lord — the soldiers. The soldiers!'

'How many soldiers?' said Sarazin, already out of bed and shovelling himself into his clothes. 'How many and how far distant? Who saw them? Do they come by road or by forest?'

'They march down the North Road, my lord. Some charcoal burners sighted them yesterday at dusk. They went not near enough to count them but hastened to Shin by night. Ere the sun rose they persuaded the ferrymen to bring them across the river that they might give us the news. They ask now for reward.'

'Hold them!' said Sarazin. 'Death will reward them if they've told us untruths. Where is Jarl?'

'Yes, and breakfast!' said Amantha.

'Breakfast is coming, my lady, coming soon,' said the servant, obviously more fearful of Amantha than he was of Sarazin — something scarcely calculated to improve Sarazin's temper.

'Jarl!' said Sarazin. 'Where is Jarl?'

'He is nowhere to be found, my lord.'

'Then get Glambrax,' said Sarazin.

'Glambrax?'

'My dwarf, you fool!'

In preparation for the wedding, at which he had thought he might possibly get drunk, Sarazin had given his ring of invisibility, his magic mudstone, his dragon bottle and his green candle into the care of the dwarf. In the event, Sarazin had stayed sober, so this precaution against drunken accidents had been unnecessary.

However, Glambrax still had charge of Sarazin's magic.

And Glambrax, it seemed, had made himself very scarce indeed.

Shortly, however, Thodric Jarl was found, lying dead

drunk in one of the stables. Ear-pulling, rib-kicking and a dousing with cold water failed to rouse him. Furthermore, Jarl's condition was far from unique. Few men were fit for battle as all had celebrated Sarazin's wedding feast in uproarious style.

Sarazin swore in his most soldierly fashion then assembled the few capable men at his command.

'We ride on patrol,' said Sarazin. 'If those from the west are friendly then all is well. If not, then we will return to the Great House and flee forthwith.'

The ferrymen took Sarazin and his patrol across the Velvet River to the start of the North Road, a wide trail of mud with forest uprising on either side. Soon Sarazin was leading his men westward. It might be that they rode to their deaths, yet none of their demeanour admitted dismay.

They had not gone far when they sighted a single avant-courier. The man drew rein when he saw them. Whereupon Sarazin cried, in a loud voice:

'Who is it who marches on the realm of Chenameg?'

'Me!' answered a voice which was not entirely unfamiliar. It was his brother Celadon.

Sarazin rode forward. Then the two brothers sat on their horses eyeing each other with disfavour. They did not know each other very well for their past acquaintance had been but short. However, what they knew they disliked.

To Sarazin, Celadon was an uncouth militarist whose concern for the future was strictly limited to the provenance of his next beer and his next whore. To Celadon, Sarazin was a severe embarrassment, a wildly reckless adventurer whose self-serving ambition threatened the careers (if not the very lives) of everyone who had the misfortune to be related to him.

'What,' said Sarazin, opening the hostilities, 'are you doing here? Moreover, how many men do you have at your back?'

'I have four hundred men,' said Celadon, 'and I ride to ensure the lawful succession of the throne of Chenameg.'

'That has been decided already,' said Sarazin, 'for I

196

have married the fair princess Amantha and am myself king in Chenameg.'

'You!' said Celadon, gaping.

'Yes,' said Sarazin proudly, pleased with the obvious impact his new status was making on his brother.

Then Celadon said:

'You're mad! Mad, yes, and shortly dead, unless you flee. 'Tis well I rode first. With no witness to this warning I can let you escape. I thought you ready for some lunacy — but never something so witless as this!'

'Have a care how you speak,' said Sarazin, a warning in his voice, 'for you are talking to a king.'

'Tarkal is king, fool!' said Celadon. 'He rides in our ranks.'

And Celadon explained.

Celadon had of course been sent to Selzirk with news that King Lyra wished Sarazin to remain in Shin for Lod's trial. Unbeknownst to Sarazin, King Lyra had also given Celadon secret dispatches complaining of the activities of outlaws, brigands and anarchists, and asking Selzirk to send Celadon back to Shin in due course with a force sufficient to restore law to the countryside.

Celadon had left Selzirk on Midwinter's Day, which was, in Shin, the first day of the Phoenix Festival.

When King Lyra died on the second day of the Phoenix Festival there had been fighting between men loyal to Tarkal and those loyal to Lod, as Sarazin knew well. The fighting had been inconclusive, and, while Tarkal had won temporary control of Shin, he had been uncertain of his ability to hold the city.

Therefore Tarkal had evacuated Shin and had set off for the Harvest Plains, ferrying every man, woman, child and servant within his power to cross the Velvet River to the North Road then marching them westward. Lod had pursued all the way, and many of the evacuees had died on the slow and bitter retreat.

Then the sore-pressed Tarkal had met Celadon's men, who had been advancing eastward along the North Road at a leisurely pace. Celadon, with gusto, treated Sarazin to a sanguinary account of the action which had followed.

'Lod may well be dead,' concluded Celadon, 'though we have not seen his corpse. But Tarkal is definitely alive, and my duty is clear. As he is King Lyra's oldest son I must see him seated on Chenameg's throne.'

'You have no authority to do so,' said Sarazin savagely.

'On the contrary, I have every authority,' said Celadon. 'My warrant for this foray into Chenameg commands me to obey King Lyra, or, in the event of his death, his son Tarkal.'

'But I am king!'

'Then Selzirk will kill you on that account if you allow yourself to be captured,' said Celadon, 'for Selzirk sees fit to order the succession in Shin.'

'What cause has Selzirk to meddle in the affairs of Chenameg?' demanded Sarazin.

'That is for our rulers to say,' said Celadon. 'I am but a simple soldier and do what I am told. So far, brother mine, I do not know you have made yourself king. We did not meet here, neither did we speak. But soon enough I will know all, then it will be my duty plain to hunt you down and drag you back to Selzirk in chains, there to meet the justice which will doubtless be your death.'

There was no time left for further argument, for Celadon's troops were not that far behind him. Sarazin therefore fled to Shin with his patrol. Once he was back on the southern bank of the Velvet River his first thought was to destroy all water transport. But the ferrymen refused to do the burning and sinking he ordered and his men refused to execute those ferrymen for disobedience.

Sarazin, realising what authority remained to him was rapidly vanishing, ran to Amantha and broke the news to her.

'Therefore,' concluded Sarazin, 'we must flee. I think right on my side but cannot argue the point with Celadon and four hundred swords.'

'You flee,' said Amantha. 'I stay.'

'Come!' said Sarazin, imperiously.

'Don't be ridiculous,' said Amantha. 'I'm in the middle of breakfast, as you can see for yourself.'

'But,' said Sarazin, 'our lives will be forfeit if we stay.'

'Your life, perhaps,' said Amantha, 'not mine.'

'But — darling! We're married!'

'What's that got to do with the price of fish?' said Amantha. 'Tarkal is my brother and I await him here. Take your hands off that! That's my egg!'

A pretty plight was Sean Sarazin's.

Jarl was still incapable, Glambrax was still missing, Amantha refused to be reasonable — so what was he to do? Run, obviously! But, as news of Tarkal's impending return had already spread through Shin, there was not one man — not one! — ready to ride with Sean Sarazin.

So Sarazin saddled the best horse left in Shin and rode forth alone, making for the east. And, since luck was with him, it was a full ten days before he was caught and marched back to Shin. From where he was sent onward to Selzirk to face justice.

CHAPTER TWENTY-SEVEN

Let Wisdom flee and Justice hide its face
For we have entered into a Court of Law.
(Proverbial)

Several days later, Sarazin found himself in a dark dank cell in a dungeon in Selzirk. The cell was made for one, but must perforce hold two when Sarazin was closeted with his lawyer, Childermass Imbleprig. Once again Farfalla had chosen Imbleprig as Sarazin's lawyer and was paying the bills.

'This is bad,' said Imbelprig, shaking his head. 'Very bad.'

199

'You call it bad?' said Sarazin. 'I call it ludicrous. A charge of high treason? How can that be justified.'

'In several ways,' said Imbleprig.

'How so?' said Sarazin. 'I put down a revolution. I saved Shin from being burnt to the ground by a mob of peasants. I preserved the life of the lady Amantha. Then married her, that the rule of law might be restored to the kingdom.'

'You set yourself up as king,' said Imbleprig. 'That was unlawful, not least because Tarkal still lived.'

'How was I to know he lived?' said Sarazin. 'I didn't think him such a coward as to run so quick.'

'Whether his action was cowardice or caution is not for us to say,' said Imbleprig. 'He was King Lyra's oldest child. Furthermore, he was the man Selzirk wanted to see succeed King Lyra. Clearly, by making yourself king, or trying to, you opposed the wishes of Selzirk. That is high treason.'

'What I have done I have done in Chenameg, which exists outside the jurisdiction of the Harvest Plains,' said Sarazin. 'Thus I cannot be called to account for my actions in any court of Selzirk.'

'You are wrong,' said Imbleprig, 'for the Harvest Plains have long claimed jurisdiction over Chenameg. While Selzirk finds it expedient to rule through Chenameg's royal family, our law holds Chenameg to be as much a part of our own nation as Kelebes or Androlmarphos.'

'This is news to me,' said Sarazin.

'No!' said Imbleprig. 'It is not news to you at all, that is the worst part of it. The Rovac warrior Thodric Jarl was at pains to tell you as much in front of witnesses. Or so he says. Do you say otherwise?'

'I . . . well . . .'

'It matters not what you say, anyway,' said Imbleprig, 'for many will witness against you.'

'Who?' said Sarazin. 'Name them!'

'Thodric Jarl himself, for one. Some men of the Watch

200

whom he commanded in Shin. There is also a dwarf, Glambrax. And there are others.'

There were indeed others, and Sarazin heard them all at length during his trial, which lasted for months. It took place in front of Judge Qolidian and seven professional jurors. It went on for so long that Sarazin could scarcely remember any other way of life. It seemed he had spent a lifetime standing in the dock listening to self-justifying witnesses and prating lawyers.

Sarazin's dark despair was only increased by the behaviour of the jurors who paid not the slightest attention to the proceedings. They appeared to think the outcome of the trial a foregone conclusion, for they spent their days gambling with dice, cards and knucklebones.

Meanwhile, lawyers enriched themselves by arguing the finer points of the Constitution interminably.

Was Chenameg part of the Harvest Plains? If it was, then Sarazin, by seizing power in Shin, had committed an act of High Treason. If it was not, then, since Sarazin's actions had taken place beyond Selzirk's jurisdiction, he should rightly walk free.

Farfalla herself was one of those who gave evidence.

'Yes,' she said, in answer to a question from the prosecution, 'Chenameg has always acknowledged the authority of the See of the Sun.'

And she looked on Sarazin coldly, as if he were a stranger. That night, alone in his cell, Sarazin wept. In his dreams he crawled back to the womb and found it cold, stony, haunted by bats and studded with iron.

As the days went by he had other occasions for weeping, for it became clearer and clearer that he was guilty and doomed to death. He no longer doubted that Chenameg was indeed a part of the Harvest Plains. The Constitution held that Selzirk's law ruled all the territory of the ancient empire once commanded by the evil wizard Ebonair. Historians proved to the court that Chenameg

201

had indeed been a part of that empire.

Sean Sarazin, as a son of the kingmaker, was forbidden by the Constitution to hold power in the Harvest Plains. Yet he had tried to seize power in Chenameg. Therefore, since Chenameg was part of the Harvest Plains, he was guilty of high treason.

Late in the spring, evidence and argument were at last concluded, and the jury withdrew to consider its verdict. Sarazin, thinking the jurors an idle pack of derelict fools, expected a prompt decision. However, he had badly midjudged these upright citizens.

This jury was not a random-picked panel of seven plucked from the streets. No, these jurors were professionals, and highly conscious of their responsibilities, for in Selzirk juries were only used in the judgment of the most heinous of crimes.

Here, with so much complex data to consider, the jury had a real job on its hands. Day after day the jurymen deliberated, often sending out for a little something to keep themselves going. Roast dinners, for instance, and skins of wine. Sometimes, to prop up their ebbing morale, they collaborated in a jolly song. The stress they laboured under was evidenced by the sounds of drunken singing which often wafted from the jury room long after midnight.

At last, after the jury had been out for twenty days, the foreman appeared in court. The shadows beneath his eyes testified to the strain under which he had been working, as did his unsteady gait and the tremor in his hands.

'What have you decided?' said Judge Qolidian.

'Guilty,' said the foreman. 'Guilty. He's a nasty piece of work and as guilty as hell. Throw the book at him.'

Then the foreman burped, swayed on his feet, and collapsed insensible in full view of the court, thus exciting considerable sympathy from all members of the legal profession who were present and who alone were properly qualified to sympathise with the hardships of such professional jurors.

Once the foreman had recovered, Judge Qolidian

thanked the jury for their sterling efforts, and expressed a touching concern for the obviously heavy toll which this trial had taken upon even such hardened professionals. Then Qolidian turned his attention to Sean Sarazin.

'Sean Kelebes Sarazin,' said Judge Qolidian. 'The jury has found you guilty of high treason. Have you anything to say before I pass sentence?'

'My client has nothing to say,' said Imbleprig.

'But—' said Sarazin.

Then said no more, for he was suppressed. Judge Qolidian smiled grimly as the suppression proceeded. Then, seeing things were getting out of hand, he said:

'All right, all right, that's enough! You can take your boot off his throat.'

Sarazin, somewhat the worse for wear, was restored to his proper place in the dock. Then Judge Qolidian smiled again. Then laughed with manic glee. Then coughed, and brought himself under control. Then said:

'Sean Kelebes Sarazin, I sentence you to be taken to a place of imprisonment and there to be held until Midsummer's Day.'

Sarazin looked up, startled. Was that all? Imprisonment till Midsummer's Day? That was nothing! However, the judge was not finished yet . . .

'On Midsummer's Day you are to be taken to the westernmost part of Unkrana. There you are to be hung from the neck until near dead. Then you are to be dragged through the streets to Libernek Square, there to have your intestines torn from your body, after which your body itself is to be cleaved into quarters.'

Sarazin smiled, faintly.

He did not believe it.

He did not believe it until the following night, when he woke from nightmare. Screaming.

Long he lay in the darkness, sweating, shivering, near dead from dread. Then, towards dawn, he remembered. Of course! The kingmaker could exercise the prerogative of mercy. That, like the power to appoint city and regional

203

governors, was one of the kingmaker's inalienable powers.

'My mother will save me,' said Sarazin. 'She will. She must!'

Seeking Farfalla's mercy, Sarazin drafted an appeal himself at dawn and had it sent to her. After thirty days a reply came from Farfalla's personal secretary:

'The kingmaker Farfalla, mother of all the peoples, ruler of the See of the Sun, instructs me to advise you that your petition for clemency has been rejected.'

And Sarazin reacted first with anger, then hate, then grief.

The days dragged by until, in due course, Sarazin learnt that the judge who had sentenced him had been appointed governor of Androlmarphos. Judge Qolidian had condemned Sarazin to suffer a dreadful death. And Farfalla had shown her gratitude by making him a king.

Sarazin screamed in rage, screamed and screamed and battered the door of his cell with his fists. Which did him no good, of course. Shortly his lawyer, Childermas Imbleprig, came to say they would be appealing against his sentence. But Sarazin, no longer believing anything could help him, lapsed into a deep depression.

Even when he was brought into court on the occasion of his appeal — which was heard before the eminent Judge Syrphus — he was still too depressed to take much cognisance of the proceedings. After outlining the course of Sarazin's trial and detailing the sentence, Childermass Imbleprig (having thus earnt sufficient sanarands to temporarily quell his loquacity) finally got to the meat of the matter.

'The defence, my lord,' said he, 'asks the court to lay aside the sentence on the grounds that it was improper.'

'Wherefore is it improper?' said Judge Syrphus. 'To hang, draw and quarter a man is a perfectly respectable procedure.'

'With all respect, my lord,' said Imbleprig, 'the proper form of the sentence requires that the prisoner's intestines be burnt in his sight while he is still living. This was omitted from the sentence. I have notarised transcripts of the trial with me if you wish to see them.'

His lordship scrutinised the relevant documents.

'Dear me,' he said. 'Dear dear! Dear dear dear me! You're quite right! The judge of the case entirely failed to make mention of the burning of intestines.'

Days of legal argument followed.

The prosecution claimed the sentence must stand, since it was 'contrary to reason for a prisoner still to be alive while his intestines are burnt'.

But Imbleprig cited the notorious case of Brute Dargzon, who, 'after his intestines were torn out, had strength enough to rise from the ground, pick up a piece of his own lower bowel then hit the executioner in the face with it.'

Furthermore, continued Imbleprig, it was well known that the Orfus pirates would often nail a section of a man's bowels to a mast then chase that victim with red-hot irons, causing him to unravel his own intestines.

'A disembowelled man, then,' said Imbleprig, 'is not a dead man, so the prescribed form of execution for high treason is not, despite the prosecution's claims, absurd. Besides, even if it were absurd, that would be beside the point. The rule of law requires the letter of the law to be followed in all things, and, as the wise have often re-marked, if the law were cleansed of patent absurdities there would be little of it left at all, and precious little work for lawyers.

'The defence, then, has an unassailable argument. The law allows only one form of punishment for the crime of High Treason and that form prescribes the burning of the prisoner's bowels in the prisoner's presence as a compulsory part of the ritual.

'If the defective sentence handed down by Judge Qolidian were to be carried out then a miscarriage of justice would have taken place. For, if Sean Kelebes Sarazin were executed without seeing his own guts thrown on a bonfire, then he would be the victim of an entirely unlawful and unprecedented sentence.

205

'Therefore, since the sentence was improper, the defence asks the court to lay aside that sentence.'

Judge Syrphus reserved his decision, and three days of tension followed. Then the learned judge presented his judgment, which took half a day to deliver. Sarazin understood none of it for Syrphus spoke in Legal Churl, which is more difficult than Field Churl, City Churl and High Churl all rolled into one.

Finally, his business done, the judge took his leave and all those in the court began to disperse.

'Come on,' said Imbleprig, taking Sarazin by the arm. 'Let's take you home.'

'We . . . we won?' said Sarazin, scarcely daring to believe.

'Of course we won! You heard the judgment yourself.'

Indeed, they had won. The judge had ruled that the sentence imposed on Sean Sarazin by Judge Qolidian was defective, hence was illegal. The law allowed only one way for such situations to be rectified: the prisoner must be allowed to walk free.

However, in practice it did not prove that simple.

While Judge Syrphus had been delivering his verdict a mob had been gathering outside his courtroom. A hundred men of the Watch, commanded by Thodric Jarl, were on hand to help convey Sean Sarazin to his mother's palace. But they had a struggle for the mob shouted, roared and threw things.

It was terrifying!

Sarazin was almost crushed to death in the press. It was as bad as his first day in Selzirk, when he had almost died in a mob-trample in the confines of Kesh.

At last, Jarl and his stalwarts brought Sarazin safe into Farfalla's palace, and the gates were closed against the mob. Which promptly began to storm the palace.

Since Farfalla's palace was a converted wizard-built castle, and since the original moat of flame which had ringed that castle still existed, it had the potential to be a formidable fortress. However, its defences had been compromised (in the interests of convenience) by a number

206

of bridges which arched to the battlements from four-storey towers built without the flame moat.

Farfalla's few guards could not defend so many approaches against enemies in strength.

Sean Sarazin — shocked, dazed, bewildered and appalled by the hatred of the mob — was bustled through the palace and up the many stairs to Farfalla's throne room. High was that throne room, so high that it overlooked the four-storey battlements of the palace and afforded a view of Selzirk and the lands of the Harvest Plains beyond the city.

The throne room was packed already with hysterical serving girls, wounded guards and assorted riff-raff. Out of the press came Sarazin's mother who assaulted Sarazin before he could even think of defending himself.

Farfalla embraced Sarazin, squeezing him, crushing him, holding him tight, tight, saying not a word. Indeed, any word she said could scarcely have been heard above the clamour within the throne room, the mob's uproar, the sounds of battle in the stairwell below, the hoarse voice of Thodric Jarl screaming orders.

Was this the end, then? Were they doomed to die here? Jarl's men, whatever their heroism, could only hold the stairwell for so long. As Sarazin was thus thinking, someone kicked him in the shins. Glambrax! Who had a canvas bag in his hands. Sarazin broke free from Farfalla and grabbed the bag.

Within were the magical gifts he had received from the druid Upical. His ring of invisibility on its silver chain. His magic mudstone. His dragon bottle. His green candle. Which should he use? The candle? No, because he had no fire with which to light it — and not the slightest idea what it would do when lit. The dragon bottle? No — unleashing dragons in the throne room might kill them all. His ring? No, for invisibility could scarcely save him now. The mudstone, then! When he used it, the legions of the Dreaded Ones would come to his aid.

Hastily, Sarazin slung the ring-bearing chain round his

207

neck, then pocketed the dragon bottle and the candle.

'Water!' said Sarazin. 'I need water!'

'We none of us need water,' said Farfalla grimly. 'We need a miracle.'

'That's what I need the water for. This is a magic mudstone, see, if I dissolve it in water . . .'

Sarazin explained.

Farfalla was dubious; the mudstone looked very much like a lump of mud to her. In any case, they had no water. No water, no wine, no vinegar, no nothing.

'Glambrax!' shouted Sarazin. 'Get me water! Now!'

'Your wish is my command, master,' said Glambrax.

The dwarf bowed low, then waddled to the nearest wounded guard and confiscated the man's helmet. Within was a velvet lining which he tore out. Below was a single ilavale, which he pocketed. Then he spat on the bare metal. Then started to pass the helmet round.

When Sarazin added his urging to Glambrax's begging Farfalla's people started sucking their fingers, chewing their cheeks, dreaming of blood-squirting steak, tongue-shuffling worry beads or whatever else they had to do to conjure up saliva.

'Quick! Quick!' shouted Sarazin.

For the brazen battle-brawl uproar from the stairwell suggested Thodric Jarl's men were losing. Belatedly, it occurred to Sarazin that perhaps urine would have served. Or blood. Both could have been got far quicker. But it was too late for that because:

'Almost done,' said Glambrax.

Then passed the helmet to Farfalla who looked with distaste on its much-bubbled frothy burden, swilled spittle round her mouth then spat.

'This had better be good, son of mine,' she said, and passed the helmet to Sarazin.

Who, with shaking hands, crumbled the magic mudstone to the spittle-broth. The mud sank out of sight. And did nothing.

'Come on, come on!' said Sarazin.

208

But nothing happened.

Till a serving maid screamed. Others took up the scream as fast-bleeding guards staggered into the throne room, retreating from the stairwell. They were losing.

The influx of guards, the screams, the panic — it was too much for Farfalla's people to take. They became, on the instant, a desperate jostling mob, brawling for air, for space, for an impossible liberty. The helmet was dashed from Sarazin's hands. He stumbled, almost fell, clutched, grabbed a handful of somebody's hair, then was squeezed.

As if in a vice.

It was the same nightmare all over again. He was going to be squashed! Crushed to death by a mindless mob. Killed by the brute weight of bodies. He could not breathe. Then, suddenly, he sighted space to his right. Space, daylight, fresh air, sun. In a thoughtless panic he brawled towards it, striving, shouldering, hauling, punching and kicking.

And, with shock, realised he had fought his way to an open arched window so huge it took up half of one wall. The crowd in the throne room convulsed. Sean Sarazin was forced right out of the window.

'Gaaa!' he screamed.

Clutching. Grasping!

Screaming, he clung to someone's collar and someone else's ponytail, a death-drop beneath his feet.

'Sarazin!' yelled Glambrax in his wart-ugly voice. 'To me! To your left! Look left, look left!'

Sarazin risked a quick glance to his left. Glambrax was clinging to the stonework on the outside of the throne room. Easy enough to do, for the throne room's exterior walls were lavishly sculptured with dragons and such.

'Come on!' said Glambrax. 'What are you waiting for?'

But he had no need to shout, for Sarazin was already moving. Hand over hand he went, clutching to people who were in turn clutching others to save themselves from the death-drop. He gained the stonework, seized the head of a platypus, found a boot-hold on a sculptured skull, then bawled:

'Out on the roof, you morons!'

Screams answered him. Screams of a terror entirely different from anything he had heard yet. Anguished sounds of lacerated horror — as if knives were at throats already. A moment later, people were fighting to escape to the roof. Some made it. Others slipped, fell. Wailing, they plummeted down, down, down—

To smash, to break, to fracture, to wreck their lives on the awaiting stoneslab doom far below. Broken teeth, splintered jawbones, smashed eggshell skulls . . .

Some of those who made it to the exterior began to climb down immediately, descending hand over hand by way of stone-carved unicorns, gryphons, taniwhas, eels, onions, mermaids, seashells and the occasional basilisk and hippogriff and so forth.

But Sean Sarazin climbed instead to the very summit of the exterior of the kingmaker's throne room, determined to make his last stand there. Glambrax followed.

'Glambrax,' said Sarazin, 'get me a sword.'

But Glambrax grinned, giggled, then shook his head.

'Very well,' said Sarazin, 'when my enemies come I must perforce defend myself with a dwarf. A dead dwarf, if a live one proves too unwieldy.'

'Oh, that's a famous weapon, master, a famous weapon!' said Glambrax.

Then he chortled, making a hideous sound half like laughter and half like somebody swallowing blood.

Sarazin, nested in surprising comfort between the uprearing stone dragons which crowned the throne room, closed his eyes and tried to relax. He would need his strength for the battle to come. However . . . that battle proved a long time coming.

Finally, Sarazin realised that he was almost alone on the roof. Most of those who had joined the exodus from the throne room had climbed down, or else had gone back inside. He could still hear sounds of panic but they were faint, distant. Looking down — a long way down! — he saw concerned figures clustered around the corpses of the stone-smashed fallen.

'We'd best be going inside,' said Glambrax, starting the descent.

Sarazin watched him go then, puzzled, followed. On regaining the throne room he found it almost empty. A small boy child was sitting on Farfalla's throne, sucking his thumb. A couple of wounded soldiers sat slumped against a wall. And there were half a dozen servants and such.

And—

Snakes, some dead, some wounded and writhing. Scorpions, some mashed, others holding their ground in fury. Centipedes. Toads. Huge, filthy cockroaches. And what was that in the centre of the room? Dung? No! A heap of bubbling mud!

As Sarazin watched, out from the mud there plopped first a toad, then an adder, then an asp. They were the last of the legions of the Dreaded Ones which had indeed come to his aid, albeit tardily.

A little later, Sarazin discovered that tens of thousands of verminous creatures, most poisonous, still commanded the stairwell. And, in the end, he too had to descend to ground level by climbing down the exterior walls, with Glambrax giving him unwanted advice for every choice of handhold.

Sean Sarazin had two questions which needed urgent answers.

First: why had Selzirk's mob tried for his blood?

Second: did his mother still live?

'Glambrax!' said Sarazin, 'find me Farfalla!'

But the dwarf, who had been trotting at his heels but a moment before, had vanished himself.

211

CHAPTER TWENTY-EIGHT

Drangsturm: flame trench guarded by Confederation of Wizards. Lies 500 leagues south of Selzirk. Runs length of narrow isthmus between Inner Waters (to the east) and Central Ocean (to the west). Divides Argan North from terror-lands of the Deep South where lurk the monsters of the Swarms.

Sean Sarazin had failed.

He had pursued his ambition relentlessly, had won his princess and his kingdom, and then had lost both. He had only been saved from deadly peril by a legal technicality. How humiliating!

Could he still succeed?

Could he still be a hero triumphant, a conqueror, a leader of men, a ruler, a king? Could he — to come right down to specifics — regain the throne of Chenameg which Tarkal had stolen from him?

Perhaps.

If he quested to the terror-lands, found the tectonic lever and threw it then he would be a hero true. With such heroic status, a few mercenaries and a good public relations expert surely he could seize and retain the throne of Chenameg.

The beauty of the plan was that the Harvest Plains would be unable to interfere with such an ambition, for if he threw the tectonic lever then Selzirk's lands would be drowned by the Central Ocean. But how would he find the lever? He had never formally researched the subject but, nevertheless, was aware that precious little was known of the geography of the terror-lands south of Drangsturm.

Besides, the more he thought about it, the more the notion of throwing the tectonic lever seemed absurd. A criminal madness, even. To sink Argan? To drown the Harvest Plains? To kill people by the million? Impossible to justify! He had been taught by Lord Regan that ambition was good: good for the individual, good for the world. But there were exceptions to every rule.

Yet he had sworn himself already to the quest. At his wedding with Amantha he had taken an oath to go questing for the tectonic lever. He had no choice!

'Stop talking nonsense,' said Thodric Jarl, when Sarazin spoke to him about it. 'You did not swear to find the tectonic lever, or to throw it. Your vow was to go on the traditional quest undertaken by all heirs of Chenameg.'

'But that is—'

'Is to quest until wounded, and no further. Surely you got a couple of scratches or such between arrest in Shin and safety here.'

Sarazin thought Jarl would have made a good lawyer, but dared not venture an insult so unpardonable. Instead, he said:

'You call this safety? The mob has stormed the palace once. Why not twice?'

'Mobs cannot be roused to anger on a daily basis,' said Jarl.

'Yet the mob attacked once,' said Sarazin, 'so surely hates me fiercely.'

'The mob hates Farfalla more than you,' said Jarl.

'Farfalla?' said Sarazin, puzzled. 'But why?'

'Because she perverted justice for her family's benefit,' said Jarl.

'I don't understand,' said Sarazin.

'Did you think your judge botched his sentencing by chance?' said Jarl. 'No. Qolidian wasn't made governor of Androlmarphos by accident. That was a bribe.'

'Did — did Farfalla tell you this?' said Sarazin.

'I've not asked her about it,' said Jarl. 'But share my opinion with all Selzirk. How else did Qolidian become governor?'

Sarazin, seeing the inescapable logic of this, was profoundly shaken by this proof of his own ignorance. Shortly, pursuing the truth to the death, he challenged his mother over the matter.

'Of course I bribed Qolidian,' said Farfalla. 'Everyone knows it. Everyone! The people, the courts, the Regency, Lord Regan of the Rice Empire, yes, and the pirates of the Greater Teeth for all I know. My credibility is zero.'

'Will the Regency . . . will they . . .?'

'What?' said Farfalla. 'Impeach me? Over this? No. They can prove nothing. They'd lose in the courts. But, Sarazin my son — watch yourself! Before, they merely suspected you of ambition. Now they have proof of it. Sean Sarazin, king of Chenameg — what on earth were you thinking of?'

'Myself,' said Sarazin simply. 'My duty to myself. To be what I can be.'

'At what expense to others?' said Farfalla. 'Do you realise what you've cost me? Leaving aside that—'

What followed was another long, exquisitely painful lecture. From which Sean Sarazin learnt at least a temporary caution. Thus when certain members of the Watch approached him directly — having given up hope of getting to him through Thodric Jarl — he rebuffed them.

In his new mood of caution he did not trust anyone from the Watch, even though it was members of that organisation who had defended him when the mob rioted. He did report the approach to Jarl who commended him for his caution.

'Your one task at the moment is to get fit,' said Jarl. 'So you're ready for whatever position Imbleprig wins for you.'

'What are you talking about?' said Sarazin. 'Imbleprig is but a lawyer. How can he win me position?'

'So you've not been told,' said Jarl. 'Well then, listen, and a tale I will unfold . . .'

Thus Sarazin learnt that his entanglement with the law was not yet over. Childermass Imbleprig was seeking damages to compensate Sarazin for having been wrongfully sentenced. Imbleprig sought not just money for his client but status and position as well.

'For,' argued Imbleprig, 'my client has been victim of such a cruel injustice that unless the court intervenes it will be impossible for him to fulfil his talent and follow the career which should by rights have been his.'

Imbleprig laid it on so thick that Sarazin was positively embarrassed. Sarazin, in his innocence, fully expected the court to throw out his case on the grounds of its patent absurdity. But, as it happened, the intricacies of the Constitution, the details of law and regulation made since and the court rulings on the seventy-seven relevant precedents were all on Sarazin's side.

Midsummer's Day arrived, initiating the year Alliance 4326. Sarazin, reminded by his mother, did his duty to the sungod. And his court case continued.

After much palaver, the court ruled that Sarazin had indeed been grievously wronged, and was therefore due for compensation. The court declared that the state must pay Sarazin's legal costs and, furthermore, give him a position of high responsibility. It directed the Regency to see that this was done.

There followed a secret conference of the Regency after which Plovey, spokesman for the Regency and one of the most powerful players in the politics of Selzirk, approached Sarazin to offer him command of an army tasked with destroying marauders presently active near the source of the Shouda Flow.

'These invaders,' said Plovey, 'are pretending to be barbarians from the Marabin Erg, but our spies tell us they are in fact from the Rice Empire.'

'No matter,' said Sarazin. 'I'll harry them hard then drive them south with their heads between their legs.'

215

'With their what?' said Plovey, not quite understanding this foreign idiom.

'Never mind,' said Sarazin. 'What I'm saying is that I'll do the job. How many troops do I have?'

'Five hundred horse,' said Plovey. 'But we're thinking of increasing the number by adding some infantry.'

Indeed, the Regency was thinking very hard. It shortly made a public announcement to the effect that there would be a pardon for anyone in prison who would march with Sean Kelebes Sarazin as a foot soldier. This met with an enthusiastic response from the prisoners, and every convicted pickpocket, rapist, perjurer and cock-cutter in Selzirk flocked to Sarazin's banner.

Sarazin, meanwhile, had discovered to his dismay that the five hundred cavalrymen who formed the core of his army were the remnants of the notorious Kelebes mutiny. Judging by their reputation, they would be more dangerous to him than the enemy.

Then, to multiply the confusion, the Regency proclaimed that any and all citizens who wished to march with Sean Sarazin's army were at liberty to do so.

A mistake!

For, along with the assorted psychopaths, lunatics and apprentice boys who took advantage of this offer, the Master of Combat for the Watch volunteered to follow Sean Sarazin on his campaign. A hundred members of the Watch promptly decided to follow Thodric Jarl to war. Sarazin, acting on Jarl's advice, promptly swore them in as his military police.

Sarazin's need for such was dire indeed, as he saw when he reviewed his troops with Thodric Jarl. Disgruntled veterans, convict scum, human refuse from the streets, mumbling lunatics and dolt-eyed idiots.

Still, he faced them bravely and made a speech.

'Death or victory!' said Sarazin Sky.

And his men cheered, for the sun was shining, the enemy were very far away, and they were happy — at least for a moment — to fancy themselves as heroes.

Then Sarazin went on to say:

'As token of my dedication to battle I take for this campaign the name Watashi.'

A grim name indeed! Sarazin's men greeted it with further cheers, for he had given himself a name truly fit for battle. It meant blood, death, fear, murder, slaughter.

And Sarazin exalted. For he had taken another step to fulfilling his prophecy. He was now known to all the world as Watashi.

In the end, Sarazin's army amounted to 500 cavalrymen, 400 skirmishers and 100 military police. Thodric Jarl, with a lifetime's experience of war behind him, had no trouble organising this paltry force, and, late in the summer, they were ready to march to war.

The night before Sarazin's army quit Selzirk, Sarazin sat up late debating with himself. Should he or should he not take his ring of invisibility, his dragon bottle and his magic candle to war? Once more, he read through the intelligence reports. The enemy, whoever they were, were not in strength sufficient to threaten Selzirk.

This invasion, then, was not a matter of great moment. If Sarazin won, that victory would win him, at best, a transitory popularity. If he lost, the disgrace would be bearable, and he was unlikely to lose his life.

He decided his magic was best reserved for a crisis which severely affected either his own life or the very survival of Selzirk. So he hid his magical artefacts away behind a loose stone in one of the walls of his own quarters, thinking that hiding place as safe as any.

And, the next day, he marched from Selzirk with his army.

217

CHAPTER TWENTY-NINE

Shouda Flow: river rising in foothills of mountains little more than a hundred leagues east of Selzirk. A waterway of little importance since, unlike the Velvet River, it is not navigable, seldom floods, and tends to run dry in summer.

Thus it came to pass that in the summer of the year Alliance 4326 the young warlord Watashi rode forth at the head of his troops. As he rode to war, Thodric Jarl let him bear the blade of firelight steel which had been Lord Regan's gift to him. His dwarf Glambrax, who rode beside him mounted on a donkey, carried the same crossbow with which he had done battle in Shin, in Chenameg.

Sarazin's army moved a march a day — ten leagues between sunrise and sunset — keeping to the north bank of the Shouda Flow. Soon after passing the only dam on that river they received fresh news of the marauders, and quickened their pace. On the ninth day, when they were nearing the river's headwaters, their lead scouts spotted enemy outriders on the opposite bank.

'What now?' said Sarazin. 'Should I cross the river and give chase?'

'Given the quality of the troops under your command,' said Thodric Jarl grimly, 'your best hope is that the enemy will run away. I suggest you halt here to give them the chance to do just that.'

Sarazin, with some reluctance, eventually agreed, and

the army camped for the night. On the morrow, they rose to find the enemy on the opposite bank. Jarl did a quick headcount and estimated that Sarazin's men were outnumbered three to one.

'Should we run now?' said Sarazin, on hearing this.

'If they attack across the river, then yes,' said Jarl, 'definitely yes. But let's try to bluff them first.'

'But if our bluff doesn't work,' said Sarazin, 'they could be on us in a moment.'

'Could they?' said Jarl. 'Examine the river.'

Sarazin did so.

This close to the mountains, the Shouda Flow had shrunk in the summer heat to a weed-green creek. The bank on this, the northern side, was the height of a man. On the southern side it was lower. The enemy could charge into the river easily enough but, to get up the man-high bank on Sarazin's side, would have to leave their horses behind.

'I wasn't thinking,' said Sarazin. 'Now — how are we going to try to bluff them?'

'You work it out,' said Jarl, who thought the question too elementary to deserve his attention. 'But think fast — there's a herald coming across the river now, possibly to parley.'

There was indeed a herald from the enemy camp walking across the river, a green bough in his hands as a sign of peace.

'How does he do that?' said Sarazin, fascinated by the sight of the herald's feet twinkling across the surface of the water.

'Ask him when he gets here,' said Jarl.

Then the pair of them withdrew to Sarazin's tent and waited until the herald was shown in. Whereupon Sarazin asked the man the secret of his water-walking.

'I am descended from the High Elves of Izlarkloza,' said the herald proudly. 'Hence my ability.'

Whether he was telling the truth or not is, of course, another story. Sarazin was inclined to believe him, for

219

he liked the herald on first acquaintance — not least because the man addressed him in the Geltic of the Rice Empire, language of his childhood, language of his youth.

'Now to business,' said Jarl, also glad to be speaking that same Geltic.

'Yes,' said Sarazin, beginning the work of bluff. 'First, you'd better know that this isn't my whole army. This is just the advance guard. In fact—'

The rest of what Sarazin said is predictable enough. The herald listened, took it all in, then said:

'Your message will reach my commander's ears in undiluted form.' (Or, to quote the herald more exactly: with no tea in its coffee.) 'But,' continued the herald, 'whether he chooses to believe it or not is nothing to do with me. My own duty is to deliver a message to you from my commander.'

'What is that?' said Sarazin.

'My commander is prepared to send forth a champion to meet a champion of yours in single combat in the middle of the river. Both will fight with bare blades, no shields and no armour. Combat will be to the death.'

'How much do you stake on this fight?' said Sarazin.

'Much,' said the herald. 'If your champion wins, we will withdraw back to the Marabin Erg from whence we came. If our champion wins, your army will march away and let us cross the river unhindered.'

'What then?' said Sarazin.

'Then you are at liberty to attack us. All we want is to get across the river without a fight. Is it a deal? A duel to decide whether our side retreats or crosses the river unhindered. What say?'

'Yes!' said Sarazin. Then, feeling heroic: 'I myself will champion the Harvest Plains.'

Yes! This was the ideal way for a war to be decided. By single combat between champions. More importantly, Sarazin could thereby win personal renown from this campaign. A military enterprise which had till now seemed the most unpromising of routine operations suddenly offered him a chance of deathless fame and glory.

'Bare blades,' said the herald, reminding him. 'Oh, and did I mention helmets? No helmets.'

'Fine,' said Sarazin. 'We will meet unhelmeted in midstream with bare blades and no armour.'

'Be ready soon,' said the herald.

And departed.

'Did I make the right decisions?' said Sarazin, turning to Jarl.

'That's for you to say, not me,' said Jarl. 'You're the boss.'

Then Jarl got to work. Already there was a buzz of noise outside the tent. For the herald had given Sarazin's soldiers news of the agreement in turn for a few twists of tobacco, and now those same soldiers were laying bets on the outcome of the forthcoming fight.

Sarazin had been wearing his best silks when he met the herald, but Jarl ordered him into his sweaty old leathers. Then, working swiftly, Jarl prepared Sarazin for combat by wrapping so many turns of cloth round his middle that it seemed he had a veritable paunch.

When Sarazin saw Glambrax grinning at him — a wicked, knowing grin was his — he felt forced to protest.

'The agreement was no armour,' said Sarazin.

'Armour is stuff made out of steel and such,' said Jarl.

'But cloth in such quantity can often turn a blade,' said Sarazin. 'Armour is defined—'

'You're here to win a war,' said Jarl. 'You're a soldier, not a lexicographer.'

'As a soldier,' said Sarazin stiffly, 'I have my honour.'

'Yes,' said Jarl, 'and your men have lives of their own which they'd rather not lose for that honour.'

'If I die that's my business,' said Sarazin.

'If you die,' said Jarl, 'many of your men will die trying to stop the enemy crossing the river.'

'What are you talking about?' said Sarazin. 'I agreed to the herald's terms! If I die, my army withdraws then the enemy—'

221

'Shut up! Here, put on this cloak, it'll hide the cloth. Here. Rope for a belt. Tie the cloak in close, you don't want it catching on anything. Got your sword? Good. Take this.'

'What? Mud!?'

'Mud, yes, mud!' said Jarl fiercely. 'Mud in his eyes, that's the first thing. Mud and blood, that's what wars are made of.'

Then he led Sarazin down to the river's edge where hundreds of loud-talking soldiers were already waiting. They cheered hoarsely when he unsheathed his sword. On the opposite bank was a similar boisterous congregation. Sarazin had no time for second thoughts, for Jarl was already hustling him into the water. Glambrax followed.

'Back, mannikin!' said Jarl, swiping at him with the back of his hand.

Jarl missed.

And Glambrax, chuckling, dodged past the Rovac warrior and hastened after Sarazin, who was swiftly sinking as he waded forward. Ankle deep. Then knee deep. He would be up to his waist if this went on! His one consolation was that his foeman was having similar problems.

'Let go of me!' said Sarazin, as Glambrax clutched at him from behind.

'I can't,' answered the dwarf. 'I'm in love with you.'

'Tough,' said Sarazin. 'You're the wrong sex.'

'Ah!' said Glambrax. 'So that's the secret! I was wondering what won your horse your favours when all my efforts—'

Sarazin tried to cuff him, and almost lost his sword while doing so.

'Attend to your front!' yelled Jarl from the riverbank.

Sarazin's enemy, waist-deep in mud and water, was labouring steadily towards him. The man's elegant silks were torn away by an underwater snag, revealing the blood-red lacquered armour which he wore.

'Blood!' said Sarazin. 'He's in armour! Glambrax, will you let go of me!?'

'If I let go I drown.'

'Drown, then!'

'I would if I could, master, but it's against my religion.'

'Gah!' said Sarazin, gripping his sword more tightly.

Onward came his foeman, brawning through the water with lumbering strength invincible. By now, Sarazin's men had seen that the enemy challenger had cheated by wearing armour. They began to jeer, to beat spears against shields. Sarazin scarcely heard the noise, for his concentration was devoted to his foe.

Then—

He put down a foot but felt nothing. Betrayed by a pothole, he struggled for balance. Teetered one-footed on the edge of the pothole. Then felt the edge crumble. He snatched a breath — then the river swallowed him.

Spluttering, Sarazin surfaced. Glambrax was riding on his shoulders, legs locked around his neck. His sword? Gone! And his enemy was close, closing, white teeth grinning.

'Shit!' screamed Sarazin.

He ducked beneath the surface. The sword! The sword! It had to be there! In confusions of water, weed and mud he thrust, probed, raked, grappled — and laid his right hand open as he found his weapon's blade.

With the sword secured, Sarazin struggled to the surface. Stale air exploded from his lungs. He gasped, gasped again, spat, squidged water from his eyes. Gripped his sword's hilt double-handed. Blood streaming between his fingers. Coughed harshly.

'You die,' said his challenger, ponderously, raising his weapon to strike.

Then floundered backwards, clutching his throat. Sarazin seized the opportunity, and stabbed. His dying enemy flung wide his arms: and Sarazin saw a miniature crossbow bolt buried in the man's throat.

'You!' said Sarazin.

223

'Good shooting, eh?' said Glambrax, with a grin in his voice.

The men on the northern bank were hooting with triumph. Were mounting their horses. Sarazin turned and — too late! — saw what they were doing. With a scream of triumph, Sarazin's cavalry squadrons charged. Straight down the bank to the swampmud river.

'No!' he screamed, waving his arms frantically. 'No! No! No!'

But it was useless.

Soon, half a thousand horse were floundering in the river, some already starting to drown. With wild halloos, the Rice Empire's heroes attacked their helpless enemy, despite the best efforts of their officers to restrain those heroes.

Soon both armies were helplessly bogged in the mud.

'Shit!' said Sarazin, punching his head from sheer frustration.

Where the hell was Jarl?

The answer came a bare ten heartbeats later when Thodric Jarl led Sarazin's skirmishers on the attack.

'Ahyak Rovac!' screamed the Rovac warrior.

Clad in nothing but a loin cloth, Jarl leapt down the bank and into the river, sword in one hand and a knife in the other. The skirmishers, most as lightly dressed as he, followed like so many rabid rats. Barefoot they came, screaming in excitement:

'Wa-wa-Watashi! Wa-wa-Watashi!'

Some of the smarter of the boot-burdened enemy cavalrymen were already struggling out of their heavy mud-logged battle-gear. But the skirmishers were on them before all but the quickest could escape their burdens.

In what was more or less a waist-deep swamp, the half-naked skirmishers had the edge and then some. Knives, hatchets and sickles flashed bloody in the glittering sun. Men bubbled blood, clutched hands of mud to gaping intestines. Mud-blind, blood-blind, a swordsman staggered, was struck by a rock, pierced by an arrow, was—

But Sarazin could watch no longer.

Some considerable time later, the Rovac warrior Thodric Jarl found Sean Kelebes Sarazin sitting dazed on a rock some five hundred paces distant from the river. Glambrax sat at his feet, barbecuing a frog over a frugal fire.

Silently, Glambrax tore free a frog's leg and offered it to Jarl, who accepted it with a nod and ate it slowly while he studied Sarazin. The young man's leathers were damp, his legs clagged with mud. He had not cleaned his sword.

'We dine at twilight,' said Jarl. 'Roast horsemeat. And, for those who like that kind of thing, long pig.'

Then he turned and walked away.

But shortly sent one of the army's barbers to cleanse Sarazin's swordhand, anoint the wound with the crushed garlic which Jarl favoured as an antiseptic, then bind it with clean white cloth to protect it from the summer dust and the summer flies.

CHAPTER THIRTY

Tyte: province in north-west of Harvest Plains. Most prominent feature is some 2,500 square leagues of swamplands lying north and south of the River Iggle.

'It was horrible,' said Sarazin. 'Blood, filth, screams. And — and the horses. That was the worst of all, the horses. I saw the skirmishers — well — I saw—'

Lost for words, he threw up his hands in disgust. Here,

in the Voat Library, amidst the dusty smell of ancient books and manuscripts, it was harder than ever to understand such barbarity.

'You must have seen things as bad in Chenameg,' said Epelthin Elkin. 'I understand that peasant revolt in Shin was a moderately sanguinary affair.'

'Yes, but that was against peasants. One might expect a brawl with the mob to be ugly. But this — this was army against army. You know. Honoured foes and all that. I expected—'

'Honour? Glory?'

'Something! Not . . . not deaths so indecent. What's worse — they ate the dead. Thodric Jarl organised it. At least half of the men took part. They were — they were disgusted with themselves, yet at the same time they were grinning. Laughing. It was — it was obscene.'

'So,' said Epelthin Elkin, resting an old hand on a treasured book.

Sarazin waited for revelation, but none came.

'Is that all you can say?' said Sarazin.

'I could say many things,' said Elkin. 'But what would be the point, when you know them all yourself? You know, for instance, that warfare is not your métier. You were not born to be a warlord. However, with effort, you might yet make yourself a tolerable poet.'

'But that's just the thing!' said Sarazin. 'They want me to do it again. War again. In Tyte, this time. They want me to bring the anarchists to heel. To collect back taxes for the last ten thousand years or whatever it is.'

'Jarl's going with you, I suppose,' said Elkin.

'No,' said Sarazin. 'He says I don't need his talents. He says the job's too simple. What he really means is that it's hopeless however brilliant the general.'

'Why so?' said Elkin.

'Because tactical brilliance is useless when your soldiers are neck-deep in mud!' said Sarazin. 'So Jarl won't help. But I thought maybe you could give me some ideas. Either to cope with the situation. Or else to get out of this fix.'

'I thought your brother Celadon was taking care of Tyte,' said Elkin.

'No,' said Sarazin. 'Celadon was in Shin till I got there, and now he's been sent back there again. Jarnel was supposed to conquer the anarchists, but he failed. It's a hopeless job. Right now he's off with Peguero hunting bandits in the Spine Mountains.'

'Well,' said Elkin, 'I'm sure they're having the time of their lives.'

'Oh, doubtless,' said Sarazin. 'They're like kids playing at orcs and elves — only they're getting paid for it.'

'Doesn't that suggest anything to you?' said Elkin.

Sarazin thought about it.

'No,' he said, finally. 'It doesn't.'

Elkin sighed.

'When you go to collect taxes in Tyte,' said Elkin, 'you'll have young lieutenants equally as eager as your brother. So! Unleash them. Let them go sloshing through the mud in pursuit of the anarchists. Meanwhile, you find a nice, dry spot by the seaside and camp there till it's time to come back to Selzirk.'

'You're brilliant,' said Sarazin.

But he spoke only from politeness, for he doubted things could be so easy.

Once Sarazin had left Elkin's presence he gave way to despair. He had fought at the headwaters of the Shouda Flow; now he was doomed to go campaigning in Tyte; when that campaign was over no doubt there would be further military duties awaiting him elsewhere.

All his ambitions had come to nothing. He was a prisoner of the system. He had tested his ambition, will and ability against the social order: and he had failed. He was condemned to exactly the fate the Constitution prescribed for him: an endless life of soldiering.

Would he win fame through his sword? Fame, glory, renown? Would he make a name for himself? Perhaps. But it would make no difference. For some reason, he lacked the ability to change the world to suit himself,

227

even though Lord Regan had always made it very clear that any determined person could alter reality at will.

—*Maybe I'm not trying hard enough.*

Thus thought Sarazin.

But, such was his state of doubt and depression that he lacked the will to try at all.

Sarazin's military lifestyle had brought him at least one advantage: an improved relationship with his mother. Now he was conforming to society's expectations, and no longer trying to reshape the world for his own benefit, Farfalla was prepared to indulge him to a certain extent. Indeed, it was a pleasure for her to do so: she took no joy in disciplining her long-lost son.

One of her little indulgences was the present she gave him before his departure to Tyte.

'This is for you,' she said, handing him a little package. 'With my love.'

'What is it?' said Sarazin.

'Something practical,' she said.

He opened the package and, finding a purse of money, duly tendered his thanks. But what was he to do with this money? He was not in the mood for whores, gambling or drink.

In the end, it was Sarazin's half-brother Benthorn who took the money off his hands. Benthorn sold him an amulet which was, or so he claimed, an heirloom from an ancient elven kingdom now remembered only in legend.

This intriguing trinket was a flawless lozenge of glossy black on a necklace-chain of similar colour. On one side was a gold sun disk, while seven silver stars and a sex-sharp silver moon adorned the obverse. Sarazin, unable to resist this bauble, bought it for fifty skilders.

Then marched for Tyte.

CHAPTER THIRTY-ONE

Epelthin Elkin: elderly scholar who serves in the secret service of the Rice Empire and works as Archivist in Voat Library in Selzirk.

Sean Sarazin knows Elkin to be a wizard of the order of Ebber, but does not know him to be a spy. The Rovac warrior Thodric Jarl, a spy himself, knows of Elkin's intelligence work, but, though he dislikes Elkin, does not know him to be a wizard.

Once Sarazin reached Tyte with his army he tried to put Elkin's advice into practice. The trouble was, his fiery young lieutenants lost all their enthusiasm the moment they saw Tyte's hopeless bog-mud tidal flats.

Still, Sarazin did his best. He camped by the seashore and occupied himself with busy work, such as sending out endless patrols to 'gather intelligence'. He wrote long reports. He had his picture painted by a soldier eager to prove his artistic talent if that would keep him out of the swamps for one day longer. Then, on a whim, Sarazin had that same soldier design a coat of arms for him.

'This coat of arms,' said Sarazin, improvising a story to protect him against any possible accusation of treasonous intent, 'is a toy for the son of a friend of my half-brother Benthorn.'

The 'toy', when it was finished, was a shield emblazoned with a black rustre, with seven stars and the crescent moon on the surrounding red. Sarazin, in his dreams, conjured with images of a fabulous future in which this coat of arms would be recognised as the emblem of his line, and all of Argan would recognise his suzerainty.

So far, Sarazin's campaign had been comfortable enough. However, after ninety days of timewasting, boredom got the better of him, and he started a major drive to seek out anarchists and (with luck) capture some so they could be tortured till they paid their back taxes.

The campaign that followed is best described as follows: mud, swamp, bog, quicksand, rain, wind, swamp fever, blood fever, blue fever, green coughing fever, toad fever, eel fever, yellow frog fever and vomit fever.

Sarazin campaigned right through the autumn and into the depths of the following winter, by which time he had caught two anarchists (both of whom had leprosy) and had lost over 700 men to assorted diseases. As he had started his campaign with an army of only 900, this made it somewhat difficult to continue operations.

At this point he was recalled to Selzirk and chastised severely by his superior officers.

He scarcely cared, for he had come down with hepatitis, and was too sick to worry. The army surgeons were called in and sent him home to recuperate. There he stayed through the rest of the winter and the spring which followed, on a strict regime of bland meals (no spices, no alcohol) and bedrest.

His social circle was very small. Bizzie attended him constantly, and his dwarf Glambrax was always underfoot. His mother saw him daily. Jarl and Elkin dropped by now and then. His half-brother Benthorn paid him the occasional social visit, and offered to sell him sundry treasures which he could not possibly afford to buy.

Apart from that, he saw nobody.

Glambrax twice smuggled in notes from Jaluba. So Sarazin knew his delectable whore was still in Selzirk, still working for Madam Sosostris. But Sarazin had money and appetite for neither fortune telling nor woman-chasing.

Plovey zar Plovey visited him once. The spokesman for the Regency was happy to find Sarazin subdued, depressed and — without a doubt — tamed. Plovey had not succeeded in encompassing Sarazin's death as he had planned but was, nonetheless, happy with the way things had turned out. Sarazin, it seemed, was going to live out his life as an obedient, apolitical soldier, just like his three brothers.

Occasional word reached Sarazin of the doings of those brothers. Celadon was still in Shin, while Peguero and Jarnel were still campaigning against bandits.

As for the other people in his life, Tarkal — now King Tarkal — ruled the Chenameg Kingdom. Amantha still dwelt in Shin. There was no word of Lod, who was generally believed to be dead.

As summer approached, Sarazin was at last allowed to get up and about. His recovery thereafter was rapid, so the army surgeons shortly pronounced him once more fit enough for war. Before very long, he was back at the Voat Library, again seeking advice from his elderly tutor, Epelthin Elkin.

'What is the army doing to you this time?' said Elkin.

'They're sending me to Hok,' said Sarazin. 'There's a marauding ogre on the loose in the province with a gang of bandits.'

'What do you want from me?' said Elkin. 'More tactical advice?'

'No!' said Sarazin. 'I want you to get me out of this mess! It's intolerable! Unless you can help me, I'll spend the rest of my life chasing round the provinces after assorted dograpists and delinquent lawyer's clerks.'

'So what can I do?' said Elkin.

'Get me out of it!' said Sarazin. 'You can change minds.'

'One at a time,' said Elkin, 'and with great effort. But minds do not stay changed.'

'You can't — can't you change people's minds so they stay changed?'

'You can't make bricks out of jellyfish,' said Elkin, shaking his head.

'Then — would it change matters if I killed someone? Just one or two people? Plovey of the Regency, perhaps?'

'I don't understand,' said Elkin.

'What I mean,' said Sarazin, 'is simply this: can I win rule of the Harvest Plains by a couple of murders? Killing off key people, I mean.'

'You're not up against individuals,' said Elkin. 'You're up against a social dynamic. Kill Plovey tonight and the Regency will have another spokesman talking the same by tomorrow. You are not struggling with men but with an organisation. Unless all its members are killed at once, the Regency is immortal.'

'So I'm doomed,' said Sarazin woefully.

'Ease up on the self-pity!' said Elkin. 'You're doomed to go to Hok, but that's no big deal. After all, I'll be going to Hok myself.'

'You?' said Sarazin.

'I am being blackmailed,' said Elkin, quietly.

'Blackmailed?'

'You know very well who I am and what I am,' said Elkin. 'You know all Selzirk would turn against me if it was known that I was a wizard of Ebber.'

'Very well!' said Sarazin. 'Kill your blackmailers! I'm sure you have the power. I well remember what you did to me.'

'Ah,' said Elkin, 'but you are but one person. Those who now contend against me are many. This is an underworld conspiracy I'm up against. The gangsters concerned are four score in number — far more than I could handle at once.'

'You underestimate yourself,' said Sarazin. 'Why, you nearly killed me when I . . . when I tried to force your will for my benefit.'

'But you were close,' said Elkin. 'It is easy to control people who are close. As distance increases, so does the

232

problem of control. I cannot get all four score of my enemies under one roof to control them.'

'Then turn one against the others,' said Sarazin. 'Make one a weapon of murder.'

'I cannot do that,' said Elkin.

'But you made me ride to Smork to attack Tarkal!' said Sarazin.

'Nonsense!' said Elkin. 'You wanted to go. You demanded to go! Against my best advice you insisted on going.'

'True,' conceded Sarazin.

'It was very minor magic I worked that night,' said Elkin. 'You expected to go. So I only had to give you the illusion that you were doing what you had chosen to do.'

'But,' objected Sarazin, 'Fox came along with us. You persuaded Fox to the mission to Smork.'

'No!' said Elkin. 'I did no such thing. You yourself did the persuading when Benthorn wanted to kill his father Fox.'

'So I did,' conceded Sarazin. 'But — you had to create the illusion of my presence in the minds of all the people there.'

'Easy!' said Elkin. 'It was night, so I conjured you in their minds simply as a voice and a shadow. Both shadows and voices are trivial illusions. Fox sought to grapple with you. If he had grabbed you — why, I could not have conjured the flesh. He would have found himself holding smoke.'

'It was, still, a powerful illusion,' said Sarazin. 'For, while I lay insensible in Selzirk, my experience was that I rode with Benthorn and the others to Smork.'

'Ah!' said Elkin. 'But remember what happened before I launched you into the illusion!'

'I had that funny turn,' said Sarazin. 'I feared . . . I feared the epilepsy.'

'Yes,' said Elkin. 'A standard trick of the wizards of Ebber! Before launching someone into a world of illusions, give them cause to think themselves very sick indeed. Then they will read any flaw in the illusion as a symptom of their sickness.'

'Cunning!' said Sarazin.

'Necessary,' said Elkin, 'for this magic is exhausting to exercise and limited in its effects. You see, the night of the raid on Smork I never made you see or do anything contrary to your expectations. Nor did I tamper with your will. You acted that night of your own free will.'

'I see,' said Sarazin.

'So,' said Elkin, 'I cannot oppose an extensive criminal conspiracy with magic. I could not make one criminal murder his fellows. At best, I could kill a few of them — but then the survivors would betray me promptly. So I have a choice: to stay here and be blackmailed or to come with you to Hok.'

'Why not go to Drangsturm?' said Sarazin.

'The southern sun is too hot for my liking,' said Elkin.

'Really!' said Sarazin.

'Well,' said Elkin, 'if you must know, I have political enemies in the Confederation of Wizards. I cannot return to the Confederation's castles at Drangsturm because those enemies would prove my death. I am an outcast. A pariah. An exile.'

'But what will you find in Hok?' said Sarazin.

'The most valuable commodity in all the world,' said Elkin. 'Time! Time to plan my next move. Whatever that might be.'

CHAPTER THIRTY-TWO

Tor: a ferocious blood-drinking ogre whose brutal rule made Stokos a sink of iniquity, its coarse, licentious society characterised by devil worship, lawless debauchery, feuding torture and death.

Then Salvation arrived. A religion arose to free Stokos from the ogre's cruel oppression. Guided by notions of purity, chastity, Universal Benevolence and other High Thoughts equally as beautiful, the priests of the Flame overthrew Tor, and now are leading Stokos towards a radiant future under the guidance of Gouda Muck.

Unfortunately, the ogre Tor refuses to die. He dwells as a bandit in Hok, a mountainous province of the Harvest Plains just a few sea-leagues from Stokos. Moreover, he does not live quietly, but proves his unprincipled depravity by sending kamikaze squads to infiltrate Stokos, subjecting the nascent utopia to the worst kinds of terrorist outrage: arson, kidnapping and assassination.

In early summer in the year Alliance 4326, Sean Sarazin — now known to the army as Watashi — marched forth from Selzirk with six hundred troops under his command. He was bound for the province of Hok, there to do battle against the dreaded Tor, a man-demolishing ogre from Stokos, the swordsmiths' island.

This time, Sarazin had good, reliable troops, so doubted he would need any military police. Nevertheless, a three-way agreement between Regency, army and Watch saw Thodric Jarl join the expedition with twenty volunteers from the Watch, all sworn to maintain discipline.

Each day, Sarazin took the place of honour right at the front of the army, ahead of the dust and stench of his trampling troops. Epelthin Elkin rode there also, and they talked idly of this and that as they made their way southwest towards Hok's distant mountains. Glambrax, mounted on a donkey, and armed as usual with a crossbow, rode to the rear, diligently memorising the army's repertoire of scatological songs.

Day by day it grew hotter and hotter until one day Sarazin finally stripped to the waist and rode on half-naked, luxuriating in the sun's heat. His amulet, catching the glitter of the sun, excited Elkin's curiosity.

'What is that?' said the wizard.

'A great treasure,' said Sarazin, passing it over. 'I bought it from Benthorn. It's an heirloom from an ancient elven kingdom.'

'I doubt it,' said Elkin. 'For no elves have dwelt in Argan for the last ten thousand years or more. If, indeed, there were ever such things as elves at all.'

'You mean . . . you mean I was conned?' said Sarazin. 'I was tricked? This is worthless?'

'Yes,' said Elkin. 'It's just a trinket.'

And he pocketed it. Casually.

'Give me that!' said Sarazin, suddenly furious.

Elderly wizards — and grim, ascetic elderly wizards like Epelthin Elkin in particular — do not take a childish interest in worthless baubles.

'You want this?' said Elkin. 'Very well! Have it!'

And he tossed it to Sarazin, who snatched it from the sky, his hand a hawk-swift talon striking.

'All right,' said Sarazin, breathing heavily. 'Tell me. What does it do? Does it command minds? Rule armies? Conjure dragons? Break mountains? Raise storms? Summon the dead? Or what?'

'Nothing like that,' said Elkin dourly.

'Then what?' said Sarazin.

'If you'll trust an old man with your toy for another moment or two, I'll show you,' said Elkin.

Sarazin hesitated, then handed over his amulet. Elkin studied it with care, then nudged one of the silver stars, and a man's voice began to speak in a sonorous, long-winded language which Sarazin strongly suspected was the High Speech of wizards.

'This,' said Elkin, 'is the bard.'

'A bard?'

'The bard. Scholarship knows of only one. This must be it: the lost bard of Untunchilamon.'

'Untunchilamon?' said Sarazin, startled.

236

Thus the druid Upical had named the leader of the dread of dragons which lurked within Sarazin's magic snuff bottle of leaf-green jade.

'You've heard the name, have you?' said Elkin.

'Yes,' said Sarazin.

He wondered whether the wizard would pry within his brain for the details. The thought of such intrusion made his flesh crawl. But Elkin simply said:

'That's not so surprising, for Untunchilamon has fame in the east, though it is little known in this part of the world.'

'Pray, then,' said Sarazin, 'tell me of Untunchilamon, and of this bard for which I paid all of fifty skilders.'

As he stressed his ownership thus, Sarazin held out his hand for the bard. Reluctantly, Elkin gave it back to him.

'This is no instrument of power,' said Elkin, 'but I lust for it, since it is of limitless value to scholarship. The lost bard of Untunchilamon holds the voice of antiquity's greatest poet, Saba Yavendar.'

'Saying what? Secrets of magic? Of treasure? Of power?'

'Reciting his Warsong and his Winesong in their entirety,' said Elkin.

Sarazin, who knew of these famous epic poems, understood why a scholar like Elkin would long to own the bard.

'It is known as the bard of Untunchilamon,' said Elkin, 'because Untunchilamon is where it was last seen. It was lost within living memory when a time of troubles came upon that island.'

'Where is this island, Untunchilamon?' said Sarazin.

'It lies mid-ocean between Argan and Yestron,' said Elkin. 'There the magic of the east meets the power of the west. The wizards of Argan are the stronger, but the sorcerers of Yestron command effects more subtle and various. The conjugation of these—'

'Do they breed dragons on this island?'

'What? I was talking about sorcery.'

'Yes, but. Dragons. Do they breed them? On Untunchilamon?'

237

'I have no idea what meats they raise on the island,' said Elkin testily. 'Perhaps they eat dragons, perhaps chickens. Or perhaps they breed both. If you wish to know what blood adorns their table, then a long journey awaits you.'

'Dragons are not bred for the table,' said Sarazin. 'I know that already.'

'You speak in ignorance,' said Elkin. 'For the imperial dragon of Yestron is a dish most valued at banquet. The flesh, however, is rank and rancid unless the beast has been fed for the most part upon honey. Hence imperial dragons are usually raised in the vicinity of beehives, which is unfortunate because—'

'Do they have imperial dragons on Untunchilamon? Are they fierce?'

'What's wrong with you?' said Elkin. 'Your mind's all over the place. For the truth of Untunchilamon, I suggest you quest to the island yourself. I'd be interested myself in your report, since much of the rumour which has come to the attention of scholarship is, I suspect, untruthful.'

They were then interrupted by Thodric Jarl, who wanted to discuss arrangements for their camp that night. And Sarazin did not thereafter question Elkin about bards, dragons and Untunchilamon, for, much as he wanted information, he feared the wizard might become too curious.

Sarazin's ring of invisibility and his dragon-bottle were treasures beyond price. His magic candle also perhaps had its value. He feared that the wizard of Ebber, if he learnt of their existence, might be tempted to steal them. Admittedly, the valuables were safe from instant theft, since Sarazin had left them behind in Selzirk — just as he had for the campaign in Tyte.

But he did not trust Elkin.

Perhaps — though he denied it — Elkin did indeed have the power to change minds permanently. He might be able to force Sarazin against his will: to send him back to Selzirk to retrieve the dragon bottle, the ring and the candle, and to bring these treasures to his lair in Hok.

Even the bard, which held nothing but poetry, had tempted the old wizard powerfully. So the greater treasures must stay a secret lest they prove to be Sarazin's death.

CHAPTER THIRTY-THREE

Hok: fair land of sky-soaring peaks adorned with beauty in dawn and twilight alike (a poet's opinion); a barren land of sheep farts and peasants impressed by the eloquence of the same (opinion of a cosmopolite); a bitching hole, a galgize sludgeon, a regular sunth (opinion of a long-suffering footsoldier who actually had to march through the place with a pack on his back).

Thus Sarazin marched south towards Hok. His mission was simple: to meet the ogre Tor in battle and kill him, capture him or drive him out of Hok.

Tor's territory was the Willow Vale, a substantial valley opening on to Hok's southern coast. To get there, Sarazin would have to march his army over the Eagle Pass, which was high, narrow and easily defended. His maps of the pass were poor and long out of date, but he decided against sending out scouts to reconnoitre the place, fearing this might alert the enemy to his approach.

Near the mountains, the land became flat and marshy. Pools of stagnant water rankled with insects. Fat, slow, bumbling flies the size of a fist droned through the long, hot, sweating afternoons. They settled upon necks, arms and faces, unwelcome as the hand of a child molester.

'Graap groop greep greep,' sang a million million freckled frogs, welcoming the conquering hero.

Sarazin shuddered.

This place was all too much like the approaches to Tyte. Then he raised his eyes to the mountains and was reassured. Good rock awaited: not filthy wastelands of slime where cackling anarchists could mock his blundering scouts by day and night alike.

—But how much mud parts us from the mountains?

The foremost soldiers were already walking ankle-deep in mud. At first the rest followed in a column, but this meant the last of the men were walking through mud trampled to knee-deep liquid filth, and the baggage wagons were getting hopelessly mired. So Jarl had the army spread out in a line abreast.

In its wake, the army left bog-sprawling footprints and slovenly wheelruts which slowly filled with the glitter of water.

'Where do we sleep?' said Sarazin in something like despair, for he saw nowhere dry.

Once, on his long campaign in Tyte, he had spent nine days up to his waist in liquid mud. He had scarcely slept at all — though he had hallucinated often. If he had to endure that again, he would — he would—

—I would die!

Mud, mud, mud! Everywhere! No wood for fires, either. Just the evil green of luxuriant grasses growing hot, rank and feverish. A hallucinatory flash of kalaidoscopic colour from the wings of a dragonfly.

'We sleep in liquid mud,' said Jarl.

Then, without warning, dismounted. His hand lunged for something, throwing up a spray of mud and water. He hauled a pink snake to daylight. A snake? No, it was an eel. An eel? A worm! A worm as thick as a wrist and as long as a leg.

Sarazin opened his mouth to say something — and a fist-sized fly tried to wing its way into the slubbering warmth within. Sarazin battered at the thing with such

240

force he nearly broke his jaw. He swigged a little sun-hot water from a leather bottle, swooshed it round his mouth then spat. He shuddered, imagining he still felt the fly's touch upon his lips.

'What happened?' said Jarl, who was bundling the struggling worm into one of his saddlebags.

'A fly kissed me,' said Sarazin, doing his most heroic best to joke about his trauma.

'Fun!' said Jarl, mounting up. 'Sandpaper your lips and they'll be right enough.'

Sarazin wondered what Jarl wanted the worm for — then decided he would rather not know. As his horses plodded on at baggage-wagon speed, the young commander studied his soldiers. He heard the occasional coarse guffaw, the odd snatch of song. His men were happy enough. But . . . after a night in the mud?

'Tonight,' said Sarazin.

'Yes?'

'Tonight we won't stop. We'll march for the mountains — we can hardly get lost. I reckon we'll be there by dawn. Hard rock and, with luck, some firewood with it. What say?'

'It's your decision,' said Jarl. 'It all depends on whether the mud deepens closer to the mountains. If you'd sent scouts forward to reconnoitre then we'd know. I can't for the life of me think why you haven't done so.'

'You never suggested it!' said Sarazin, stung.

'You shouldn't need me to hold your hand,' said Jarl.

'A great help you are,' said Sarazin bitterly, and signalled his heralds to come to him that they might receive his orders.

Then screamed with rage and slapped his cheek, splattering a huge fly which had been pestering at his sweat. He looked at the ghastly mess on his hand then swore, then dismounted and, for want of anything better, wiped both hand and cheek against the flank of his horse.

At least there had not been monstrous flies in the marshlands of Tyte. Flies of regular size, yes. And leeches,

241

swamp snakes and bad-tempered eels which bit. But nothing quite so disgusting.

At dawn they reached the mountains which rose in walls from the mud. The sheer escarpments were interrupted by a narrow, steep-rising valley. This led to the Eagle Pass — and it was obviously impassable by baggage wagons.

'What now?' said Sarazin.

'You work it out,' said Jarl.

Sarazin considered. Then spoke.

'My campaign fails if the enemy can hold the pass against me. So my priority is to seize the heights. I need speed. Surprise. Every day's delay increases the chance that the enemy will discover my advance and reinforce the pass. So we'll leave all our baggage here and march light and fast now, today, immediately.'

'Not immediately,' said Jarl. 'Let's have breakfast first.'

They breakfasted. Then marched. At dayfail, they were near the top of the valley. And early the next day they reached the heights. A hundred of the enemy defended the pass, but these — to Sarazin's disappointment — surrendered without a fight in the face of overwhelming odds.

Still, he was delighted by his success. He had seized a major objective. His bloodless victory had given him a taste for more. Conquest, triumph, glory. It was good in itself. Beautiful, beautiful!

Sarazin had the enemy's commander dragged before him. This was a big blond peasant who, after being cuffed a couple of times, admitted that he spoke Galish. His name, he said, was Heth. Interrogation proceeded.

'We thought attack unlikely from the north,' said Heth. 'Why do you march against us? We're not at war with the Harvest Plains. Our enemy is the usurpers who have overthrown the rightful rule of kings on Stokos.'

'Don't give us that nonsense,' said Sarazin. 'You're

supporters of the evil ogre Tor, as well we know. You fight with an ogre against human beings. You should be ashamed of yourself!'

'Ashamed of what?' said Heth. 'Of honour? Of loyalty? Of patriotism?'

This argument could have gone on for a very long time indeed, but Jarl, with something of a growl, interrupted. Then demanded to know the disposition of Tor's forces.

'Most of our men guard the coast,' said Heth. 'We always feared attack from Stokos, hence women, children, animals and stores are kept in a camp in the northernmost part of the Willow Vale. If you descend from the Eagle Pass then you will come upon that camp directly.'

'Good news,' said Sarazin, happy to believe it. Then it occurred to him that Heth might be lying. So, watching Heth carefully, he said: 'But it could be a trap.'

'Trap or no trap,' said Jarl, 'we have to come down from the Eagle Pass if we're to finish off Tor. Either we descend or we end our campaign right here and now.'

'What do you recommend?' said Sarazin.

'I make no recommendations,' said Jarl, 'for I am but a simple military policeman who knows nothing of war.'

'Don't be like that!' said Sarazin. 'Have I done something to offend you, or what?'

He was upset that Jarl should be so dour and sour when he, Sarazin, was happy, victorious, on top of the world.

'There's no quarrel between us,' said Jarl, 'but here I'm as ignorant as you are. I've never been to Hok, I know nothing of this Tor and I cannot predict the future. Perhaps we'll find the camp Heth speaks of. Perhaps we'll find an ambush. We don't know. Such is war — and you must live with it.'

Whatever decision Sarazin took he must take it quickly, for his men had but a single day's rations left. He longed to order all his men to march south to war and victory. But memories of various disasters in Tyte made him cautious. His seizure of the Eagle Pass might be a single isolated lucky stroke, a one-off fluke. He decided to hedge his bets.

In the end, Sarazin sent a third of his soldiers back to the baggage wagons with the prisoners (though Sarazin kept Heth with him, thinking the peasant potentially useful as a hostage). When that party reached the baggage wagons, some would stay to guard the prisoners while the rest returned with food.

Meanwhile, all Sarazin's soldiers divested themselves of all their rations. These rations were then divided among the one third of Sarazin's men who would stay to hold the Eagle Pass.

The remaining third would march without rations under Sarazin's command to attack the unprotected camp which, so Heth alleged, lay not far to the south. If the camp truly existed they would be able to feed off its supplies, while if the enemy lay waiting in ambush food would be no help to them.

'What do you think of my plan?' said Sarazin.

But Jarl refused to comment until Sarazin had given his orders and the lead contingent was marching south with Jarl and Sarazin at its head. Both Glambrax and Elkin insisted on coming with them.

As Sarazin and Jarl marched at the head of the invasion force — both leading their horses, for the ground was too rough for them to ride — Jarl said:

'What do you hope to achieve by your orders?'

'Why, to make sure that whatever I lose I don't lose everything. This way I at least keep control of the Eagle Pass, even if I lose my life.'

'Fair enough,' said Jarl. 'But what was your mission?'

'To seek out Tor and destroy him.'

'True,' said Jarl. 'Doesn't that mean you must inevitably force a major battle? All your men against all of his?'

Sarazin was already regretting his caution. He should have taken all his men on this march to the south. This was how a hero would have done it. To save face, he said:

'I've decided on a scorched-earth policy. I'm going

244

to starve the ogre out. That's the way I'll destroy him. This raid is the first move in my scorched-earth campaign.'

Jarl absorbed that in silence. After a while, Sarazin said anxiously:

'Am I doing the right thing or the wrong thing?'

'It's not what you do,' said Jarl, 'it's how you justify it when you get back to Selzirk. I've seen a lot of famous victories which were actually no more than draws — a couple of them were in fact defeats!'

'We'll worry about Selzirk when we get back there alive,' said Sarazin.

'No!' said Jarl. 'Start writing your history now. This is what happened. By a skilful forced march you took the enemy by surprise. You seized the Eagle Pass. You established a base on the heights. Then you yourself led a reconnaissance in force while your subordinates were busy bringing up the supplies necessary to support a determined thrust deep into enemy territory.'

'Why,' said Sarazin, in admiration, 'that sounds really good.'

'Of course it does,' said Jarl. 'With the right line in storytelling, you can make the worst defeat into a triumph of courageous, dynamic soldiering.'

Then Jarl — apparently taking this very seriously — drilled Sarazin endlessly on precisely what he should say on his return to Selzirk. This surprised Sarazin greatly. Jarl was a soldier through and through, and, under the circumstances, Sarazin would have expected him to be concentrating all his attention on the here and now.

Finally, unable to restrain his curiosity, Sarazin asked:

'Why do you care how our history is told in Selzirk?'

'I care,' said Jarl, 'because of the political implications of the telling.'

And he refused to be drawn further on the subject.

Sarazin's men came down from the Eagle Pass into the Willow Vale, an expansive valley of rough-grass sheeplands,

245

studded with outcrops of grey granite and clumps of trees and shrubbery. They found the camp Heth had spoken of — a hutment of a hundred or so shacks.

The enemy were evacuating the camp when Sarazin's men attacked. The foemen fled, leaving Sarazin in uncontested possession of the camp. The spoils of war amounted to a dead dog, two crippled crones, a bawling baby with two heads, a considerable amount of rice, flour, mutton and salt fish, and, of course, the huts themselves.

Sarazin was exhilarated. This was completely unlike the baffling, despairing campaigning he had done in the marshlands of Tyte. He was winning. Again he wished he had all six hundred of his men with him instead of just a third of them.

'Let's take what we can carry, burn the rest and go back where we came from,' said Jarl.

'No,' said Sarazin. 'There were women and children here. Valuable hostages. They can't have gone far. We'll give pursuit.'

He had won two victories without losing a single man. He was ready to dare. And his soldiers, when they knew it was women they were chasing, happily dared with him. Dragging Heth with them, they pursued the refugees south.

But found them not.

By dayfail they had overtaken — and captured — five enemy warriors. Then, exhausted, they set up camp under some trees. It rained all night; the trees gave little shelter; and, in the sodden dawn, Sarazin found his high spirits had evaporated. Now he paid heed to Jarl's counsels of caution and marched his men back towards the Eagle Pass, taking along Heth and the handful of prisoners won on the previous day.

But, on retreating, they found the way to the Eagle Pass barred by four hundred assorted enemy footsoldiers and cavalrymen. The enemy had outflanked them by night, cutting off their escape.

'You're doomed!' said Heth.

'Rubbish!' said Jarl. 'The forces are equal, and the odds in battle equal also.'

'Better force a fight quickly then,' said Heth, 'for Tor commands three thousand men, many more of whom will be here shortly, doubtless.'

'Nonsense!' said Jarl.

But Sarazin could tell he was worried.

Since delay would only worsen their position, Sarazin ordered his men to attack immediately. They refused. While Jarl stoutly maintained the odds were even, any fool could see the enemy outnumbered them two to one.

Sarazin and Jarl faced the untrusty two hundred.

'What do you want to do?' said Jarl. 'Stand here and die?'

'No!' cried an unhero, anonymous amongst his comrades. 'Stand here and surrender!'

Sarazin was most unhappy. From conqueror glorious to miserable captive in a single day — the thought was unbearable. He looked at Elkin, who shook his head. Doubtless, if asked for a display of wizardry, Elkin would say that no single wizard of Ebber could subvert the will of hundreds of belligerent, determined enemy soldiers.

'Very well,' said Jarl. 'But let's at least get the best terms we can for our surrender.'

'What kind of terms?' yelled someone.

'Wine rations, bread rations, fish rations, women rations,' said Jarl. 'The basics. Let's march away west lest we're attacked on the spot. Then we can stand our ground amidst the rocks and negotiate.'

Jarl eventually cajoled the men into withdrawing west rather than surrendering. Why west? Sarazin could not guess, but hoped Jarl had something in mind. He watched, anxiously, to see what the enemy would do. The foe followed. A steady rain fell from dismal death-grey skies. It was summer, but that was the merest technicality: it had grown cold enough to pass for winter easily.

The enemy never showed the slightest intention of attacking — which suggested to Sarazin that the enemy commander was content to wait for reinforcements and expected to receive such shortly. Sarazin's men grumbled incessantly, and a couple wept. The prisoners — except for Heth — were quiet and apprehensive, doubtless fearful of being murdered.

Heth, cheerfully telling Sarazin about the beating he could expect if he delayed surrendering, was silent himself after Jarl clouted him a couple of times.

By late afternoon, it was clear the retreat was taking them into a steadily-narrowing western arm of the Willow Vale. The sheer escarpments to the north offered no prospect of escape. Finally, at dayfail, Jarl revealed his plan.

Jarl made some prefatory remarks about duty, courage, heroism and such — he was speaking, perhaps, with the history books in mind. Then he mentioned sacrifice.

'You want a sacrifice?' yelled someone from the rear ranks. 'I'd give you my mother-in-law to sacrifice, only the bitch is dead already.'

There followed laughter — which had nothing nice about it.

'Who said that?' demanded Sarazin. 'What's that man's name?'

'His name is legion,' said a shout.

'Legion, legion,' roared half a hundred throats.

Upon which all two hundred took up the nonsensical one-word slogan. This was the battle-cry of outright mutiny.

'Never mind who said it,' declared Jarl, as the noise died down. 'Let's talk survival. Westward, this arm of the Willow Vale narrows further. Eventually we run into a cliff. But there is a gate in that cliff. The gate opens into a tunnel. The tunnel leads to safety.'

An anonymous unhero declared that nobody was in any mood for fairytales.

'This is no fairytale,' said Jarl. 'The secrets of gate and tunnel were researched by old Epelthin Elkin in Narba. He—'

248

But Jarl was shouted down by the men, who thought he was bluffing, and meant to march them on hoping to chance upon a path over the mountains. None of the cat-bath-bedraggled foot sloggers were prepared to go another step on such an offchance.

Finally, Sarazin appealed for silence.

'There are two ways we can handle this,' said he. 'You can mutiny here and now, which means you'll be tried for high treason if you ever get back to Selzirk.'

That provoked some rock-throwing. Some of the rocks were quite large — but Sarazin ducked efficiently. When permitted to speak again he said:

'Alternatively, I can order you to surrender. Not now, but tomorrow morning. Then you'd be safe on your return to Selzirk. What's more, as prisoners you'll get one day's pay for every ten you spend in captivity. Not a fortune — but money in your pockets all the same. So what do you want? Mutiny now, and exile from Selzirk forever? Or surrender tomorrow and take prisoners' pay if you ever get back home?'

'What's the catch?' cried a man.

'No catch,' said Sarazin. 'Just hold this ground till dawn while I race for the west. With me will go Thodric Jarl — and any other man who lusts for freedom.'

'You've got a deal,' declared one of the soldiers, and this sentiment was duly seconded, voted on and confirmed.

Thus Sarazin and Jarl escaped to the west by night, taking with them Heth — their most valuable prisoner. Their only other companions were Epelthin Elkin and the dwarf Glambrax.

Sarazin was shocked by the speed of events. He had gone from being a victorious commander to a hunted fugitive in scarcely no time at all. Anxiously, he asked Jarl:

'This gate, this tunnel — do they really exist?'

'Ask Elkin,' said Jarl. 'He's the scholar.'

Was Elkin's scholarship accurate? It must be! Otherwise,

Sean Sarazin might shortly die. He said as much to Elkin when they halted about midnight to rest their horses.

'Your life?' said Elkin. 'My life is at stake here too.'

Then drew Sarazin away from the others and said to him, in an urgent whisper:

'Remember, Jarl thinks me a scholar. Only you know me as a wizard. If Jarl learns as much it will prove my death for certain. Whatever we find to the west, remember — never speak to me as a wizard. To do so would be to slay me.'

'You can trust me,' said Sarazin.

Thoroughly bewildered by this. What would they find to the west? Something other than a gate and a tunnel? And why would their discovery spark talk of wizardry? And why would Jarl kill Elkin if he knew him for a wizard?

Towards dawn — a miserable dawn of driving rain and rising wind — Sarazin finally remembered Jarl's first audience with Farfalla. The Rovac warrior, offered the position of Master of Combat for the Watch, had taken umbrage because the salary was denominated in wizard coinage. He had spoken of a feud of long standing between wizards and the Rovac.

Great! Not only was Sarazin running for his life, but he was also embroiled in a mysterious feud between the ruthless wizards of the Confederation and the homicidal mercenaries of Rovac!

Through dawn's grey rainlight they roughed on over rain-slide rocks until their mounts broke down entirely and had to be turned loose. On they went by foot.

'Cut me loose,' said Heth, whose hands were tied behind his back. 'I need my hands to steady myself.'

'All right,' said Jarl, cutting Heth free.

Immediately, the peasant sprinted for freedom.

'Stop!' shouted Sarazin.

But Heth ran on.

Thwap!!

A bolt from Glambrax's crossbow slammed into a sapling just to the left of Heth's ear. Waterdrops thick-splattered down from the sapling's leaves. Heth glanced back, saw Glambrax already recocking his crossbow — and halted.

'I give up,' said Heth.

Jarl advanced on him looking grim.

'Don't kill him!' said Sarazin.

'I will, unless he swears himself to our escape,' said Jarl.

'By all means!' said Heth hastily.

And duly swore to do all in his power to help the fugitives escape alive and uninjured (and, for Jarl was thorough when it came to formulating oaths, unhexed, unfrightened and in the best possible state of health and wealth), and not to try to escape himself no matter what the temptation or provocation.

'Unth!' said Glambrax, cursing in an uncouth tongue unknown to any of the others. 'A hunting party comes! For us, I warrant!'

Indeed, looking back they saw a full three dozen soldiers in the distance. Friends or enemies? Probably Glambrax was right and they were enemies.

'So our men betrayed us,' said Sarazin bitterly. 'They surrendered as soon as we were gone.'

'Don't be so quick to judge,' said Jarl. 'Mayhap one crept away from the rest to betray us. Or the enemy attacked once we had left. Or perhaps among our enemies there are wizards or witches who read our thoughts and acted accordingly.'

'Friend Jarl has a mind with analytical powers formidable,' said Elkin. 'But—'

'Save it,' said Sarazin. 'We know the rest.'

And he set off for the west, thinking to set a cracking pace. But geography conspired against speed. They shouldered through thickets, fought brambles and dared uprearing rocks. Were they still being pursued? Was

251

the enemy gaining on them? It was impossible to say.

They marched till old man Elkin was utterly exhausted, and the others not much better. Even though life and liberty were at stake, they could go no further. Jarl led them into the thickest undergrowth available, and there they huddled like so many pigs.

The daylight faltered as the rain worsened. The ground ran wet with water. The wind came sluicing and slicing from all directions, swirling away all chance of dreams with gusts and buffets of water-slap. The dullsky day darkened at length to night — a night of sleepless misery which beggars description.

By dawn, Sarazin felt a good half century older. But roused himself to his feet, helped eat the last of their food, then bravely led the march onward. It was march or perish: for unless they reached sanctuary soon they would die on their feet. He was sure of it.

He was right.

CHAPTER THIRTY-FOUR

The fugitives: Sean Sarazin (the man who would be king); Thodric Jarl (Rovac warrior and military policeman); Epelthin Elkin (scholar and wizard of Ebber); Glambrax (Sarazin's dwarf servant and son of the witch Zelafona); Heth (blond peasant from Stokos, a commander loyal to the ogre Tor and now Sarazin's hostage). These five are heading west up a steadily narrowing arm of the Willow Vale, hoping to find escape through a gate known to Elkin through scholarly research.

Through pelting rain they stumbled, harried by the rough-fingered wind. The skies above, near black with the burden of cloud, birthed thunder. The thunder at first was distant. Then near at hand it spoke:

THUMBLUMABLOM.

Sarazin flinched, though he knew lightning comes first and thunder after. He heard the thunder so he was safe. For the moment. Then, close at hand — too close! — a tree shattered. Forked apart by lightning. He slipped, fell, thinking himself struck. A rock swung heavyweight into his head as thunder fisted the air apart.

—*Who? What?*

—*Night? Or am I blind?*

That much he (gasping) asked, or thought he did. Heard incoherence reply, perhaps because the light was dazed, the sky still herding elephants, the river rain . . .

'. . . all right?'

—*Of course I am.*

Yet there was a drunken discourse of stones beneath his feet, then and for some time after. The rains sluicing from grey to black. The strength of friends lugging, shoving, pushing and hauling, helping him onward, panting.

Sick, bruised, stunned and stumbling, Sarazin mouthed surrender. But if anyone heard, they paid him no heed. Desperation ruled their will. He was driven onward like a slave being flogged to a place of execution.

Several nightmares later, they halted.

—*To rest?*

No. To stare. Gawp. Gape.

At a sheer-rising cliff topped by a bone-white pinnacle half a league high. Around that pinnacle coiled a dragon, its sheens and shines of jade and jacinth glittering as lightning writhed around it. Against such a monster, what sword could prevail? For the moment, it was looking north. But if it turned their way . . .

Then Sarazin, with some sense left to him despite the blow to the head which had almost demolished his consciousness, realised the dragon was at least a hundred times too large to be alive. The brute was the work of hands.

Statue?

Sculpture?

No word fitted.

'I heard a man speak of this once,' said Heth. 'But he was drunk at the time. I thought the drink to be talking.'

'Blood!' said Jarl. 'You never told me about this. What is it?'

'Dragon, pillar, and many workings delved deep in the cliff are all part of Castle X-n'dix,' said Epelthin Elkin. 'It was built by the Dissidents, of whom you may have heard.'

None denied knowledge of the Dissidents, for none wished to provoke a lecture.

'Let's be finding this gate,' said Jarl. 'The sooner we get out of the rain the better.'

Shortly they were at the foot of the heights, which rose above them in terrors of precipice and overhang, bare cliff and frowning tor. The rock was near awash with rain, for the sturm und drang of the day's advent had given way to a sullen, unrelenting downpour.

And there was the gate, a squarebuilt door five times man height. Raindrops shunned its surface, which was a dark, dark blue stained with streaks of opaline iridescence. Sarazin ventured his fingertips forward. Found the surface smooth, warm, dry, and alive with tentative vibrations.

'Is this the door to the dragon castle?' said he.

'This is but the Eastern Passage Gate, giving access to a way beneath the castle,' said Elkin.

'Explanations later,' said Jarl. 'Open it!'

'Stand Heth some distance hence,' said Elkin. 'It would not do for him to learn the Word.'

Glambrax menaced Heth with his crossbow, and the bandit withdrew while Elkin muttered. But whatever the Word was of which he spoke, Sarazin heard it not.

Nevertheless, the door . . . vanished. One moment it was there: the next it was gone.

Sarazin stared down the passageway within, which was lit by a flickering blood-red light. To his horror, he saw the heads of dragons in legion staring at him.

'Onward!' said Jarl.

As the Rovac warrior strode past the nearest dragon head, Sarazin saw it was but a lamp of bizarre make jutting from the wall at manheadheight.

Soon all five — Jarl, Sarazin, Elkin, Glambrax and Heth — were in the passage. Then Elkin muttered another Word, and the door manifested itself, sealing out the windclap rain and leaving them in a sudden silence.

Silence?

Dripping clothes . . .

Epelthin Elkin still breathing harshly . . .

'Well,' said Sarazin, lamely. 'So we're safe.' Then, with a degree of apprehension: 'But where does the tunnel lead?'

'Onward,' said Jarl. 'The sooner we get going, the sooner we'll find out.'

'I don't know about you,' said Heth, 'but I'm poked.'

So saying, the bandit from Stokos sat himself down beneath one of the dragon lamps. Glambrax, war-roaring, bounded up and down before another such lamp, making faces at it.

'Glambrax!' said Sarazin. 'Enough of that! Sit down!'

'No time for sitting,' insisted Jarl. 'Onward!'

But the vote was against him, so, with the others, he sat. Glambrax then began to scratch himself. In a frenzy, his hands clawed through his hair, as if legions of lice had infested his locks. Then his hands delved beneath his clothing, groped in his armpits, fumbled his crotch. All the while his heels drummed on the floor. Sarazin could not be bothered to shout at him.

'You were speaking earlier,' said Jarl, 'of the people who built this place.'

'Ah yes, the Dissidents,' said Elkin. 'The Dissidents, you

255

see, were those wizards who refused to join the Alliance
of wizards and heroes formed back in the days of the Long
War when the Skull of the Deep South threatened all of
Argan with the menace of the Swarms.'

That had been many years ago indeed.

'Well,' said Heth, 'go on. What happened to them?
They're not here now, that's for sure. Did the Alliance go
to war with them, perhaps?'

'It is written in the Chalobshadala Chronicles,' said
Epelthin Elkin, 'that the Dissidents kept themselves to
themselves all through the Long War, which lasted over
two hundred years. When the war was over, the Dissidents
were nowhere to be seen.'

'So where did they go?' said Heth.

'Your guess is as good as mine,' said Elkin. 'Some claim
the Dissidents fled to another plane of reality, while others
hold that they removed themselves to Veda, and live
hidden among the Sages even to this day.'

'Tell me,' said Heth, 'these Chala-whatsit Chronicles. Are
they wizard writings?'

'The Chalobshadala Chronicles are indeed wizard
writings,' said Elkin. 'I came to know them well in
the years of my youth, when I worked as a scribe in
Narba.'

'So you're a scribe!' said Heth.

'What did you take me for?' said Elkin. 'A bootblack?
I trained in Narba as an all-round scholar. Both scribe and
translator, and accountant as well.'

Sarazin, knowing Elkin to be a wizard, thought the lie
so obvious as to be unbelievable. Surely Jarl must realise
by now that Elkin was a wizard., But Jarl showed no signs
of doubt. Neither did Heth, who said:

'So you were trained in Narba. What brought you to
Hok with an army?'

'Scholarship is difficult for my aging eyes,' said Elkin,
'so I thought war might give me an easier living.'

It was not much of a joke, but Heth, who had a ready
sense of humour, fell about laughing.

'It's not that funny,' said Jarl, who in fact found it not funny at all.

'I know, I know,' said Heth. 'But, still . . .'

In truth, he was exhausted beyond endurance, and if he had not succumbed to laughter then in all likelihood he would have given way to tears.

'Those fit enough to laugh are fit enough to march,' said Jarl.

And eventually persuaded the refugees to dare on down the passage.

After every hundred dragon lamps, they passed yellow doors to left and to right.

'These doors lead to the Underkeep,' said Elkin. 'Great are its wonders, but they are known by hearsay only, for but a single man ever managed to open those doors. He explored the Underkeep for days — but died shortly after exiting its labyrinth.'

After five hundred dragon lamps — a long and weary march indeed — they found a pair of white doors standing opposite a matching pair of black doors.

'These are also mentioned in the ancient writings,' said Elkin. 'If the writings can be trusted, the black doors give access to a room which flies from here to the heights of the Greater Tower of X-n'dix. The white doors give access to the Lesser Tower likewise. But the secret of opening both black doors and white has been lost.'

'So you say,' said Jarl, 'but it seems you know little of wizards. On Rovac we know full well that the archives of the Confederation of Wizards run unbroken back to the days of the Long War. Indeed — to certain events which preceded that war.'

'There are such things as moths,' said Elkin mildly. 'Moths, fires, floods and so forth. In any case, remember it was the Dissidents who built this complex, not the wizards of the Confederation.'

'Do the surviving records tell us,' said Heth, 'how much further we must march to reach this tunnel's end?'

'Why, we are half way along this passage,' said Elkin,

'for the white and black doors mark its midpoint. At the end we'll find a door which exits to daylight.'

'You mean,' said Sarazin, in dismay, 'we can't get into the castle at all?'

'We are within Castle X-n'dix already,' said Elkin, 'for this passage, like the Underkeep, the Lesser Tower and the Greater Tower, are all parts of that stronghold. But certainly for the moment we're limited to this passage only.'

'And later?' said Jarl.

'If we can climb to the Lesser Tower, I believe I can open a door to the interior of that tower,' said Elkin.

'What will we find then?' said Jarl. 'What will we gain?'

'That,' said Elkin, 'I do not know.'

At last they reached the gate at the end of the Passage. Elkin opened it, and they stumbled outside. Blinking at brilliant sunshine. While they had been toiling underground, winds from the sea had cleaved the clouds, and the sun slashed down from a breach of blue sky.

After the close, oppressive blood-lit gloom of the dragon-lamp passage, the world of day was an amazement of wide-flung vistas, of blood-hot greens and simmering blues, of a million million glints and reflections.

They had quit the Passage through a gate set in the base of a west-facing cliff. At their feet, leagues of rock-tumbled goat-footed pastureland tumbled away to a mirage-bright sea which lay at least a day's march distant.

It was hot. Hot and steamy. The rain-washed world was being baked dry by the sun. Sarazin incautiously glanced at that luminary. His eyes flinched from the blazing white disk. Luxuriant mauve and purple blossoms flared across his landscapes as his watering eyes tried to adjust to the world.

Elkin was closing the gate. Heth, without being asked,

had already distanced himself from this ceremony: the bandit had wandered off towards a nearby stream. Thodric Jarl was following him. And Sarazin, realising he was quite thirsty, joined them.

The wrist-thick yet energetic rivulet bubbled up from the rocks at the cliffbase, then went bounding away through its own miniature fern-fringed gorge. Sarazin's knees creaked as he squatted to the water.

He dipped his hands into the (cold!) water, slushed it round his mouth, gargled, spat, coughed up phlegm, spat again, then handcupped more water and drank. Slowly. Letting the water warm in his mouth before he swallowed it, remembered times in the past when he had greeded down cold water to comfort hunger, only to suffer the iron-uncomfortable weight of it griping in his gut.

'See-see-swaasoo!' sang a nearby bird.

Inviting itself to dinner, perhaps? Snails as the hors d'oeuvres, bird as the main course, worms as dessert.

'Swasoo swilasoooo . . .'

Sarazin searched for the bird. Saw it perched some seven paces distant on the ruinous bare-bough remnants of what had once been a tree. It was no bigger than his fist, yet as gaudy as a thousand-league emperor. Its white-striped walnut-brown head was crowned with a flame-red ruff; its throat was adorned with emerald; the plumage of its back was gold seeded with sunglints of silver; its breast was a pale blue and its feet were gold again.

It was immaculate.

How did birds manage to look so perfectly turned out so soon after the worst of weather? Sarazin himself looked a mess, and, even without a mirror, he knew it. His thorn-torn dirt-grimed travel-worn hands were evidence enough.

'Swasoo-too-loo!' sang the bird.

The edible bird?

Only one way to find out.

'Glambrax,' said Sarazin, in a low and earnest voice. 'Shoot me that bird.'

259

'What bird?' said Glambrax, bounding towards him, crossbow in hand.

By the time the dwarf had assaulted across the terrain to Sarazin's position the bird had, of course, long since flown.

'Never mind,' said Sarazin, in disgust. 'Go and see if you can find something we can eat.'

Glambrax obeyed, and was soon back with a handful of sheep droppings.

'Are you out of your mind?' said Sarazin.

'These are fresh!' said Glambrax. 'The turd implies the sheep, does it not?'

'And the sheep the shepherd,' said Jarl.

'Truly,' said Heth, 'and the sky smokes.'

'What mean you by that?' said Sarazin, thinking Heth was using some obscure, eliptical idiom of his native Stokos.

'Don't you see it?' said Heth. 'Look where I'm pointing.'

Yes. Indeed. A thin thread of smoke was rising from a coomb some thousand paces distant.

'Let's not worry about shepherds and their fires,' said Epelthin Elkin. 'Let's be getting to the Lesser Tower.'

Now, for the first time, Sarazin turned and looked up. Up at least a league-length height of cliff and crag, of thornbush outcrops and lean-grass scrambles to the bone-white sungleam of the dragon-encumbered pinnacle half a league high which was the Greater Tower of Castle X-n'dix. He thought he could see also a smaller structure which might be the Lesser Tower, but:

—*Whatever's up there can wait.*

'I'm in no hurry to go mountaineering,' said Sarazin. 'Let's check out this smoke.'

'There's no mountaineering required,' said Elkin, eager to see more of this Dissident stronghold. 'Look close! You'll see a way to the heights which a very child could climb.'

'Well,' said Jarl, 'you being closer to your second childhood than we are, feel free to go on without us. Meanwhile, we're going with Sarazin.'

Outvoted, Elkin fell in with the rest, and, after a long and uncomfortable walk in damp, chafing clothes, they came upon five huts tucked in amongst the trees of the coomb. Approaching this hamlet, they savoured the smell of woodsmoke, which Sarazin for one found most suggestive of cookery, mulled wine, warm beds, dry clothes and other pleasant things.

After disputing their right to life with half a dozen mangy curs, Sarazin and his comrades became an object of fascination for thirty-seven peasants, most of whom were blond like Heth.

'Anyone got any food?' said Sarazin in his best Churl.

Laughter and the eager gabble of quick-talking children greeted his cry.

'What did they say?' said Sarazin in bewilderment.

'Hush,' said Jarl. 'Here's the headman coming out to talk to us.'

Indeed, the oldster now approaching was the resident patriarch, who went by the name of Ugmug, and had taken it upon himself to deal with the strangers. He spoke a language incomprehensible to all but Heth, who knew it to be the Ligin of Stokos. With Heth as translator, the travellers learnt that the locals called their country X-zox.

Elkin, his philological curiosity aroused, was ready to swear that the name X-zox, given to this coastal enclave, must be a corruption of X-n'dix, the ancient name for the castle. That suggested a continuous human presence in the enclave for thousands of years.

(So at least thought Elkin, in his fatigue. Though there are of course other possibilities — such as, for example, that a passing wizard might lately have named X-n'dix to the locals, thus making the corruption recent rather than ancient.)

'What name do the locals give to the Greater Tower of X-n'dix, and to the Lesser?' said Elkin.

Heth asked, but, when the answer proved to be grossly obscene, answered that the locals left them unnamed. At

261

which point fatigue overcame philology, and Elkin pursued the matter of names no further.

Jarl, on the other hand, had questions yet to be answered, so, with Heth still serving as translator, he asked them. What was the coastline like? It was a reach of unbroken cliffs, offering certain death to any ship which tried to hazard a landing. Who ruled the valley? The heads of the families between them. How many people dwelt there? Some five fists of families — perhaps two or three hundred individuals at most.

'Good,' said Jarl.

'What about food?' said Sarazin.

Heth asked if they might please be given a little food, since they had gone days unfed through all the weathers.

But here they struck difficulty, for the traditions of capitalism were strong in X-zox, so nothing was forthcoming by way of hospitality. Sarazin and his people were invited to trade, but none of their gear was surplus to requirements. They lacked, of course, the strength to demand by force.

'Do they know,' said Sarazin, 'that X-zox is but a part of the province of Hok, which is in turn but a fraction of the Harvest Plains, and that I am a warlord of the empire of which they are but the smallest part?'

Hunger, frustration and fatigue had left Sarazin with a bloody temper. He was ready to punch someone. Thodric Jarl wisely led Sarazin away, leaving Heth to do the negotiating.

'Please,' said Heth to Ugmug, 'I can see you're of Stokos stock just like myself. We've ancestors in common, that's doubtless, let alone race and language. As a son of your people, I'm begging you. Couldn't you spare us just a little bread? Some old crusts, perhaps? Some meat meant for the dogs. Your most worthless rubbish would be a feast to us.'

Ugmug wavered.

'Well . . .' said he.

But then his niece stepped forward. Miss Inch. She was

young, fierce, beautiful, and ferociously intelligent. Ugmug fell back a pace, for he was more than a little frightened of her.

'Don't listen to these people,' said Miss Inch. 'They've got goods to trade. Swords. Jerkins. Boots.'

'Well then,' said Heth, 'I suppose I can go barefoot if I must. Would my boots buy a meal for the five of us?'

'Yes,' said Ugmug.

'No!' said Miss Inch. 'We can do better than that. Charge what the market can bear! He'll sell his boots for half a meal just for himself. He has to. He's got no choice. So why should we sell our foodstuffs cheaper?'

'Woman,' said Heth, appalled at her attitude, 'have you no charity?'

'Altruism,' said Miss Inch, 'destroys the basis of economic prosperity, which is that I should be free to exchange my best for your best at terms agreeable to us both. So give us your boots! You'll get a fist of bread in return.'

'Those terms,' said Heth, slowly, 'are not agreeable to me.'

'Ha!' said Inch. 'Wait till tomorrow! Hunger will bring you to agreement by then if not sooner.'

'Do you think to enslave me through hunger?' said Heth.

'What's this nonsense about slavery?' said Inch. 'You're perfectly free to come and go as you please, buy or sell, borrow and lend, go into business, open a bank or float a company. You call that slavery?! Rubbish!'

Heth thought her a cold, cruel, vicious woman. But he was wrong. She was an economist of the laissez-faire variety, dedicated to the highest principles of individual freedom and personal responsibility. She refused him charity since she knew such welfarism would undermine his initiative, take away his incentive to work, and make him into a lazy good-for-nothing dole bludger.

As Heth had never met an economist before, he entirely

failed to recognise what he was up against. He still thought he could beg at least a little bread before sunset.

'Woman,' he said, 'think what you would want for yourself if you were in my position.'

'I'd never be in your position,' said Inch smugly. 'I'd never emigrate until I had sufficient means to support myself in a new country.'

'I'm not an immigrant!' said Heth. 'I'm a soldier, a fighting man, a patriot. A supporter of King Tor.'

'Tor!' said Inch, in a voice which made Heth realise immediately that he'd made a big mistake. 'The ogre?! You support him? Don't you realise his government built roads and sewers, ran lighthouses, opened a university and built a hospice in Cam?'

'Is that so terrible?' said Heth.

'Of course it is!' said Inch. 'Government should take care of the law and the defence of the realm, and that's that. Let the market look after the rest! These Flame-worshippers have got the right idea. They're not spending so much as a clipped spring on the roads.'

'Then the roads,' said Heth, heavily, 'will fall into ruin.'

'If they do,' said Inch, 'that will prove there was no justification for them in the first place, in terms of the market.'

This debate could have gone on all day, as Heth, despite his wretched condition, had found fresh and fiery energies for debate now that his beloved King Tor had come under attack. However, at that stage Jarl returned, and, with help from Elkin and Glambrax, dragged Heth away.

So, still hungry, and disgusted by their reception, Sarazin and his party began to trudge back the way they had come, heading for the Towers of X-n'dix.

'What happened?' said Sarazin.

Heth explained.

While the doctrines espoused by Miss Inch were alien to Heth, they were well known to much of the rest of the world, for their originator was of course the great

264

Yan Nard, one of the Nine Immortals of history. These ideas were not entirely unfamiliar to Sarazin, for Lord Regan's own beliefs owed much to Yan Nard's teachings.

'What this ignorant peasant woman doesn't understand,' said Sarazin, 'is that such arguments only apply within a stable social context. They don't hold good in emergencies.'

An interesting assertion! What would Miss Inch have said in reply? It would have made, perhaps, a historic debate — but Jarl refused Sarazin permission to return to the hamlet to start it.

'We'll not get anything out of these people whatever we say or do,' said Jarl. 'So let's make do with what we've got.'

'Which is nothing!' said Sarazin.

'No,' said Jarl. 'We must have got some information, at least. Well, Heth — what did you learn?'

'A little,' said Heth. 'Boats must run from here to Stokos, for all that they claim a landing's impossible on the shores of X-zox.'

'How did you find that out?'

'Because the talk turned to Stokos, and it's clear these people know what happens there. Worse, they see no wrong in Gouda Muck and his gang of lunatics.'

'Tell me more,' said Jarl.

Sarazin, now sulking, paid little heed to the conversation which followed. He was busy conjuring with fantasies in which he wrecked bloody vengeance upon the people of X-zox. He only abandoned these playdreams when his party began the sweat-gasping climb up the near-sheer league-length heights of the Towers of Castle X-n'dix.

Evening shadows were falling by the time the five made it to the nearer of those Towers: the Lesser, which stood to the west of the Greater, and was therefore invisible to the east. Seen from a distance, the Lesser Tower looked tiny. But up close it was impressive enough in terms of size — though the style left more than a little to be desired. Sarazin thought:

—It looks like a weapon. A giant's club.

The Lesser Tower was circular in section, its diameter widening from roughly thirty paces at ground level to thrice that at the top, which was ten times manheight from the ground. Those proportions made the tower seem heavy, unwieldy, overbearing. For a moment, Sarazin thought it was falling — then realised that the impression of movement came from the slow-streaming evening clouds.

Glambrax scampered ahead of the others, grabbed a dark-purple thigh-bone which projected from the tower, hauled himself up and kissed a skull the colour of polished mahogany. In the dying light of the evening, Sarazin saw the entire tower was built of skulls, bones, gargoyled heads, fangs, claws, veined wings, and other pieces of both human and alien anatomy.

Painted?

His fingers caressed the nearest skull. It was dark, dark red, dark as blood drying towards black. Anatomically correct, right down to the close-stitched joints between the skullbones. His fingernail bent as he tried to scratch away the colour. He tried it with the tip of a knife.

'Metal,' he said.

'Or pottery,' said Epelthin Elkin.

'Pottery!' said Sarazin. 'I'm not daft enough to believe that.'

'The Dissidents,' said Elkin, 'were masters of ceramics.'

'Did they work ever in Selzirk?' said Sarazin. 'This reminds me of the roof of my mother's High Court. Also of a certain monument in Libernek Square.'

'The Dissidents were patrons of the arts,' said Elkin. 'They may well have fostered talent which later expressed itself elsewhere.'

Sarazin — wondering if perhaps Elkin had been a Dissident himself — studied the gloomy colours of the wallwork. Waterweed green, squid purple, murder red, mahogany, lead, anthracite, pumpkin and plum.

'Whatever this is made of, one could have wished that

the colour scheme had been somewhat more sophisticated. If this was the art they patronised it leaves much to be desired.'

'Ah,' said Elkin, 'doubtless they would have welcomed a maven like yourself to advise them in matters of taste.'

'Are you mocking me?' said Sarazin, the touch of anger in his voice suggesting the final triumph of hunger over wit, of fatigue over tolerance.

'Doubtless he means,' said Jarl, 'that only a fool would stand here talking colours when we've our lives to lose and a world, perhaps, to win.'

With that, he began circling the Tower, looking for a gate. He found nothing, and returned to the others disgruntled.

'Where's the door?' said Jarl.

'Right in front of us,' said Elkin.

So Jarl tried the wall with a word:

'Open!'

But no door opened.

'Lead friend Heth out of earshot,' said Elkin, 'and I'll attend to this.'

That he did, a single Word of his causing part of the sculptured wall to melt away. Within, red light breathed from dragon mouths in legion, showing them the interior of the Lesser Tower of Castle X-n'dix.

They entered with swords drawn, for they had no idea what they might find within.

CHAPTER THIRTY-FIVE

X-zox: enclave on western coast of Hok.
X-n'dix: complex built by the Dissidents which dominates the heights separating X-zox from the Willow Vale.

Willow Vale: valley opening on to the southern coast of Hok.

Inside the Lesser Tower the heroes found . . . silence. Dust. More dragon-mouth lamps. Stairs climbing in tight spirals to the heights. Arrow slits and spyholes invisible from the outside, so cunningly were they hidden among the tower's decorations.

Guided by Elkin, the explorers soon found food: siege dust held in ancient bronze-coloured urns adorned by obscure alphabets and inscrutable hieroglyphics.

'We can live on this forever,' said Elkin, exhibiting this wealth to his comrades.

'Is this a joke?' said Sarazin, dabbing a finger in the fine-ground grey dust then touching that finger to his tongue.

'No joke,' growled Jarl. 'I've heard of this stuff in Rovac. Iron rations for bare-bone survival.'

'We could trade it to the local peasants,' said Heth brightly.

'Oh yes!' said Glambrax, chortling. 'For roast phoenix, baked basilisk, fresh virgins' blood and all.'

'If we offer this in trade,' said Sarazin, 'we'll lose all goodwill in X-zox forever.'

But Heth persisted, so on the morrow the others let him attempt a trade. Miss Inch opposed purchase, claiming the dust had no utility. But she was overruled for once, and the locals, thinking the siege dust to be the ashes of the Time Lords whom they believed had built the local landmarks, willingly bought it for the magical properties they thought it to contain. They paid in food in plenty, and Sarazin started to think rather better of Heth.

That, however, was before Sarazin had tasted the local food, some of which threatened to quell all appetite forever. But at least it kept the adventurers going while they explored the Lesser Tower from top to bottom, always hoping to find treasure, or implements of power which would allow them to master the world.

They found many doors, cupboards and chambers which they could not open. In his dreams, Sarazin broke into them to discover oranges which metamorphosed into dragons, flowers which spoke then romanced him, a sceptre which exulted him into clouds of gold and incense . . .'

A sea-smooth cowrie shell, wet with wave, which warmed to perfume, which licked his nipples erect, which buttered his orchids then twisted itself into a woman . . .

'Sarazin,' she said, breathing his name . . .

She was none other than Amantha. And Sarazin thereupon dreamt of amation, of his own flesh deliciously conjoined with Amantha's slick humidity, her grasp persuading him, his blood engorged. On the verge of satisfaction, he woke.

'Shtig,' he said.

Swearing softly, in order not to wake his companions, for it was after midnight and he would not be thanked if he roused them.

Once awake, Sarazin could not get back to sleep. He was hungry. He was bedded down on a grossly uncomfortable pile of branches. Glambrax was snoring hideously. But what really kept him awake was an uncomfortable awareness of his own predicament.

He was alive, true.

But, other than that, his situation was disastrous.

He had been defeated by the ogre Tor. Two hundred of his men had mutinied and had doubtless been taken prisoner. By now the rest of his army was probably on its way back to Selzirk — unless it had been destroyed by the ogre. Worse, to get home Sarazin would have to return through the Passage, steal through the Willow Vale and try to sneak across the Eagle Pass without being caught.

A grim state of affairs indeed!

Sarazin was sleepless till dawn. Breakfast did not improve his temper, for a very few days in X-zox had left him thoroughly sick of the local provender. In X-zox the staples were fish, potatoes, and unleavened bread made from flour ground from millet. The luxuries were mutton, sparrows and fricasseed vipers.

Mutton made Sarazin nauseous, sparrows frustrated him with their high bone-to-bite ratio, while snake meat left him with agita, which was once so severe that he misinterpreted acid indigestion as a heart attack. So much for the luxuries. As for the staples . . .

'As an army commander,' said Sarazin, that morning, 'I have a duty to return to Selzirk to report. Sluggardry ill befits a hero-prince.'

'Save lectures on hero-princes until we meet one,' said Glambrax, thus earning himself a kick. Rubbing his backside ruefully, he then said: 'Why be in such a hurry to get us all killed? We've a thousand enemies or more between here and safety.'

'He has a point,' said Jarl.

'I think we could get back to the Eagle Pass if we took Heth with us as hostage,' said Sarazin.

'Good thinking!' said Jarl. 'They'll think much better of us in Selzirk if we bring back at least one prisoner.'

'Steady on!' said Heth, in alarm.

The young peasant had no wish whatsoever to be dragged back to that distant alien city, of which he had heard the most ominous rumours imaginable (many of them, let it be added, quite true).

'Sorry,' said Sarazin, 'but we don't have much option. We have to get out of here somehow.'

'Then leave the way the locals do,' said Heth. 'They don't know the secret of the Passage, so they must have some way in and out of here, either by land or sea.'

'But will they tell it to us?' said Jarl. 'They constantly disclaim knowledge of any such route, obviously hoping to raise its market value.'

'We can't wait around,' said Sarazin. 'We should leave today. I'm sorry, Heth. I quite like you — but you'll have to come with us.'

'If you let me stay,' said Heth, 'I'll — I'll swear lifelong loyalty to you. I can't disown my oath to King Tor, but once Tor is dead I'll follow you forever, to death and beyond.'

'What good is that to me?' said Sarazin. 'This ogre is in the prime of life, or so I've heard. By the time he's dead, I might be dead myself — and you too. Anyway, if we don't have you as a hostage we'll never get out of here alive.'

'I can grant you safe conduct,' said Heth. 'As regional commander for the north of the Willow Vale I have the authority. I'd come with you as far as the Eagle Pass. I'd see you safely out of Tor's territory.'

'Tor's territory!' said Sarazin. 'You've got a cheek! No, you're coming back to Selzirk with us.'

Heth drew a deep breath. Then:

'If you take me back to Selzirk I'll tell everything I saw. How your troops mutinied. How you lost all authority. How you—'

'You dare!' said Sarazin, on the edge of losing his temper.

'I will!' said Heth, defiantly.

While the two glared at each other, Jarl exchanged glances with Elkin, sucked on his lower lip, then said:

'I think Heth's offer is reasonable. We get out of here alive — if he is to be trusted, which I think he is. You, Sean Sarazin, then have a man bound to your service by an oath, albeit an oath not immediately effective.'

'But now he knows the secrets of X-n'dix!' said Sarazin.

'He knows only that the place exists, which is no great secret since he had heard of its existence before he met us,' said Elkin. 'He knows not the Words to open the Passage Gates or the Lesser Tower, though you yourself have been trusted with them. I will be staying here. You can be sure nobody will wrest this tower from my control. But, if you doubt — then let Heth swear to leave me here in peace.'

The matter did not end there, but, after lengthy

deliberations which would have done credit to a coven of lawyers, Sarazin agreed that they had devised oaths to bind Heth so firmly that he could not be a danger to them.

Heth consented to swear these oaths.

Then, that very same day, Jarl, Sarazin, Glambrax and Heth descended from the Lesser Tower, returned through the underground passage to the Willow Vale, and set off towards the Eagle Pass.

CHAPTER THIRTY-SIX

Sarazin's career: as the public sees Sean Sarazin's life, since his return from Voice he has been (1) an invalid, (2) a prisoner of terrorists, (3) a usurper of the throne of Chenameg, (4) a successful army commander who won a victory at the headwaters of the Shouda Flow and (5) commander responsible for a minor military disaster in Tyte.

None of this is sufficient to make him a figure of note. But the outcome of his campaigning in Hok is about to change that entirely . . .

While Sarazin had been in X-zox, bloody fighting had taken place in Willow Vale. Tor's troops, who had cut off escape to the Eagle Pass for two hundred of Sarazin's men, had been drawn away by an urgent message from the south telling them that they were needed to fight off an invasion from Stokos. Thus Sarazin's two hundred never surrendered to Tor's men.

The 'invasion' from Stokos proved to be but a probe, easily beaten off by Tor's forces on the coast. Couriers brought news of this to Tor's four hundred men who were in the north of the Willow Vale, and they promptly turned back.

By this time, Sarazin's two hundred had retreated to the top of the Eagle Pass to link up with their fellows. They then defended that pass in a truly sanguinary battle. Losses on both sides were so heavy that each, taking fright, thought itself defeated, and retreated.

When Sarazin and his companions reached the Eagle Pass, corpses alone commanded the heights. Thodric Jarl made appropriate comments — most of them obscene — then Heth said goodbye and departed.

Once the peasant was out of sight, Jarl hacked savagely at a grey-haired corpse. Sarazin, nauseated by the stench, the blood, and Jarl's battle-grunting frenzy, turned away. Finally Jarl decapitated the corpse and put the head into a nose bag taken from a dead horse.

'Right,' said Jarl, shouldering the nose bag. 'Let's be going.'

Sarazin didn't ask what he wanted with the head. He didn't really want to know. So, with Glambrax trotting behind them, they began the descent to the marshland plains north of Hok.

By the time they got there, most of Sarazin's surviving soldiers had already started for home. A few of the sick, the lame and the lazy remained behind, feeding off the contents of abandoned supply wagons. Jarl interrogated them, made a number of uncomplimentary observations, then organised them for the march back to Selzirk.

'Let's leave the sick and chase after the main body of the army,' said Sarazin. 'If we catch them, we can turn them around. We could still secure the Eagle Pass.'

'No need,' said Jarl. 'Enough men have been killed already.'

'Are you afraid of bloodshed?' said Sarazin, amused to hear such apparently pacifical sentiments from the fierce-tempered Rovac warrior.

'You've lost enough men to make people believe you did

some serious fighting,' said Jarl. 'As things stand, you can claim victory, but if you lose more then people might suspect defeat.'

'But we are defeated!' said Sarazin.

'Not so,' said Jarl. 'You invaded Hok and, despite the machinations of the evil wizard Elkin, you dealt Tor's army a dreadful blow. All that is necessary is a mopping-up operation. That's the story you'll tell in Selzirk, anyway.'

Sarazin was bewildered. So Jarl knew Elkin was a wizard!

'How — how did you know Elkin was a wizard?' said Sarazin.

'He's not!' said Jarl. 'I'd have killed him out of hand if he was. But our story will make your name in Selzirk. It was mostly Elkin's invention, I must admit, but some of the finishing touches are my own.'

'Story?' said Sarazin, quite lost. 'What story? What are you on about?'

Jarl, obviously very pleased with himself, explained. Here is that story:

Sean Sarazin personally led the invasion of Hok, and did very well indeed until the evil wizard Elkin, a master of the Black Arts of the order of Ebber, subverted the will of his soldiers by sorcery most foul. When the troops had thus been brought to the brink of mutiny, Elkin lured Sarazin away by a further exercise of the same magic.

Soon, Sarazin, Jarl and Glambrax were prisoners in a dark and evil castle in the west of Hok. There they endured unspeakable tortures as Elkin tried to subjugate them entirely to his will. At last, however, the heroic Sean Sarazin broke loose, killed the wizard and hacked off his head.

'A second-rate fairy tale!' said Sarazin. 'Who's going to believe that?'

'Everyone,' said Jarl. 'After all, the killing was witnessed by myself and Glambrax both. Plus we have proof. The very head of the wizard himself. Admittedly, the features will be somewhat the worse for wear by the time we reach Selzirk, but there's no helping that.'

Sarazin remained doubtful, but agreed to tell things Jarl's way. As he did once they caught up with the main body of his fast-retreating troops.

To Sarazin's surprise, the men who had almost mutinied against him readily agreed that they had been under a wizard's spell. Some claimed to have seen auras of thunder and blood-rot entwined about the wizard's head. Some had heard his voice speak in the thunder. Many claimed they had suffered uncanny nightmares since.

Sarazin, shocked and bewildered by this, asked Jarl for explanations.

'Where is the puzzle?' said Jarl. 'Before you told them your story they were furtive mutineers fearful of prosecution and the weight of military discipline. Now they're righteous victims of a magic of great evil — aye, and maybe heroes too.'

'But — but people can't just misremember like that!' said Sarazin.

'Can't they?' said Jarl. 'You'd be surprised what people can do when it suits them.'

'Are all my men liars then?' said Sarazin.

'They none of them lie at all,' said Jarl. 'The only liars here are you, me and Glambrax. The rest merely believe what we tell them to believe. The brain is soft, Sean. Memory is soft. Both can be shaped by the will.'

'Perhaps,' said Sarazin. 'But I doubt that we'll shape belief in Selzirk so easily.'

So said Sarazin. But a surprise was in store for him.

CHAPTER THIRTY-SEVEN

The Watch: organisation responsible for maintaining law and order in the cities of the Harvest Plains. Has long been involved in a bitter (and bloody) rivalry with the army, which has more power and prestige, and gets better pay and pensions. Many of the Watch are so discontented with their lot that they are willing to support a coup if this promises to improve their careers.

While Sean Sarazin was campaigning in Hok, members of the Watch raided the Voat Library following an anonymous tipoff. They found private papers belonging to Epelthin Elkin which revealed an astonishing story to the city.

Elkin was a wizard!

Not any wizard, but a wizard of Ebber.

A truly evil wizard, for his papers detailed monstrous plans to enslave Sean Sarazin in Hok, subvert the will of Sarazin's army, throw in his lot with the ogre Tor, then lead an invasion of the Harvest Plains.

When this was revealed, rumour ran rife in Selzirk, and the city was soon close to panic. There were reports that Tor had invaded with half a hundred legions of orcs, ogres, trolls and mutants under his command, that Elkin marched with him and was rousing the dead from their graves to join the war, that the slaves had revolted, that the anarchists of Tyte were marching from their swamplands to join the carnage.

Many worthy citizens fled the city.

Then, to the great relief of those who remained, Sean Sarazin returned at the head of his army with news of a great victory. He had defeated the evil wizard Elkin, had chopped off the wizard's head, and brought that head with him now as a trophy. His men had dealt Tor's army a devastating blow. The ogre himself was said to have been wounded in battle — perhaps fatally.

The streets rang with cheers for Sean Sarazin.

'Watashi!' screamed the mob, shouting his battle-name. 'Wa-wa-Watashi!'

He was famous. A popular hero who had won a victory worthy of the greatest warriors of legend. Jarl and Glambrax recounted time and time again the bloody details of the death of the evil wizard Epelthin Elkin. His men told of their successes in battle in every tavern in Selzirk.

Even Farfalla was impressed by her son's triumph. And Plovey zar Plovey, spokesman for the Regency, was — though he maintained his composure — severely shaken. He had not known Sean Sarazin had it in him. The young man was more dangerous than he had thought!

At first, Sarazin was content to glory in his triumph, to attend banquets as the guest of honour, to make speeches, to ride in parades, to review troops, to lecture his fellow officers on the problems of doing battle with a master of the Dark Arts, to lay his hands on the sick, and to bed certain female fans who longed for the lips of a hero.

Perhaps the most satisfying sign of his new status was that his mother and Thodric Jarl allowed him to keep his blade of firelight steel with him always. They no longer feared he would sell it to cover his expenses. Indeed, he had no temptation to make such a sale, for some grateful merchants had clubbed together to present their city's saviour with a gift of a considerable sum of money.

However . . .

What nagged at Sarazin constantly was his knowledge

277

that this gigantic fraud had been organised long in advance without any reference to him whatsoever.

Elkin, who had documented his 'plans' in elaborate detail, must have been in on it from the start. And Jarl likewise. And Glambrax? Not necessarily, but quite possibly! And, since someone had tipped off the Watch, thus prompting the raid on the Voat Library, the conspiracy must own at least one other person.

Sarazin positively boggled when he saw how neatly he had been manipulated. Military misadventure had made the diversion to X-zox perfectly natural, but Jarl and Elkin must have planned to go there anyway. And what was next on their agenda?

Finally, thinking he had better find out, Sarazin summoned Jarl to his quarters. They sat themselves down on opposite sides of a large wooden table covered with maps and documents, then Sarazin began. First he stated the obvious: that the outcome of their mission to Hok had been finalised before he ever left Selzirk.

'That,' said Sarazin, 'was why you never took much interest in whether we defeated Tor or not. It scarcely mattered either way. I'd be a hero as long as I got back to Selzirk alive.'

'Right,' said Jarl.

'But what I want to know is this,' said Sarazin. 'What does Elkin get out of it?'

'The deal is,' said Jarl, 'that once you've made yourself master of the Harvest Plains, Elkin will get to rule Hok.'

'You mean to make me ruler of the Harvest Plains?' said Sarazin in amazement.

'Isn't that what you want?' said Jarl.

'Yes, but — but for a start, what gives you and Elkin the right to decide who gets Hok?'

'It's but a small payment for a big sacrifice,' said Jarl. 'The old scholar had to leave all the comforts of home to arrange this for you. Do you grudge him the rule of some rocks and wilderness? He's an old man. He can't have long to live.'

278

Wrong! Sarazin knew that Elkin, as a wizard, might live for thousands of years yet. Furthermore, Elkin's story about having to leave Selzirk on account of blackmail might well be true. Whatever his precise motives, the wizard had undoubtedly acted entirely in his own interests.

'Leaving aside the fate of Hok,' said Sarazin, 'what gives you the right to arrange all this without consulting me?'

'It's what you want, isn't it?' said Jarl. 'First we make you a hero. We make you popular. Then we make you ruler. Men are ready to obey you if you are ready to be obeyed.'

'What men?' said Sarazin.

'Before I tell you that,' said Jarl, 'you must agree to go along with our plans.'

'You can't use me like this!' said Sarazin, his voice rising almost to a shout. 'I'm not — not a puppet, a doll. I'm not a child. What gives you the right to run my life?'

'It's not me who is running your life,' said Jarl. 'It's Lord Regan.'

Sarazin was so startled by this claim he thought he must have misheard.

'Lord Regan?' he said.

'What are you?' said Jarl. 'Some kind of echo?'

'But what's Lord Regan got to do with it?' said Sarazin.

'Everything,' said Jarl. 'He planned to make you ruler of the Harvest Plains right from the very start. Right from when you first came to Voice when aged — what was it? Four? Five?'

'Four, I think,' said Sarazin, automatically. Then, recovering himself: 'I can't believe this.'

'Lord Regan raised you, didn't he?' said Jarl, with manifest impatience. 'Who made you think yourself a prince? Was it me? Was it Elkin? No — it was Regan himself.'

'Because he thought of me as his son,' said Sarazin.

'No. Not his son. A weapon. A weapon with which to conquer Selzirk.'

279

'What are you trying to say?' said Sarazin. 'Lord Regan never meant to send me to Selzirk. He thought of me as his son. It was only political pressure which made him expel me from Voice.'

'What political pressure?' demanded Jarl. 'There never was any such pressure! Lord Regan is an absolute ruler. Nobody opposes his wish. You came to Selzirk because this is where he wanted you.'

'But — but if — but why did he never tell me what he wanted?'

'He did.'

'Not so!' cried Sarazin.

'Lord Regan told you exactly what he wanted,' said Jarl, his voice a hammer. 'What's more, you did as you were told.'

'You're mad!' said Sarazin, alarmed. Was Jarl insane? Quite possibly! 'I was never told anything. Least of all by Lord Regan.'

'You were told you must make yourself great through war then set yourself up as ruler in Selzirk. It was all written down in the book of prophecy the Sosostris woman showed you. That was Lord Regan's message to you.'

Sarazin was so surprised he almost stopped breathing. He protested. Faintly.

'But . . . but . . .'

He was dizzy. Disorientated. How could this be true? He gripped the edges of the table, hard, as if trying to keep in touch with reality. He felt like a man who has just been turned into a woman. Like a dog which suddenly realises it is really a cat. His entire worldview had been turned upside down.

It was too much to take.

It couldn't be true!

Sarazin took a deep breath then said:

'Are you trying to tell me that the book of prophecy was forged at Lord Regan's behest?'

'No, no,' said Jarl. 'The book was centuries old. There's heaps of such rubbish available if you know where to look.

280

That particular text suited Lord Regan's purposes so he made sure you got your hands on it.'

'Impossible,' said Sarazin. 'For a start, it implies Sosostris was in league with Lord Regan — and maybe Madam Ix too. But that can't be true. Sosostris set me up. She sold me to that Turbothot woman, that old slag who hauled me into her bed then had me arrested for debauching her. That almost cost me my life!'

'So perhaps Sosostris plays a double game,' said Jarl, 'working for Lord Regan and Regency both. Trust nobody!'

'What about Jaluba?' said Sarazin. 'Did Lord Regan send her here to . . . to lure me to the Sosostris place?'

'I wouldn't put it past him,' said Jarl. 'It explains much which would be hard to explain by coincidence.'

'Indeed,' said Sarazin, feeling dazed.

Could it be true? Had his whole life really been planned and manipulated by Lord Regan? If it was true, why . . . then he had been but a pawn in a game of players more powerful when he had thought himself a free agent acting in perfect liberty.

Gods!

'You,' said Sarazin. 'You — you're — are you Lord Regan's agent?'

Jarl grinned a wolfish grin. Then said:

'The Rovac are mercenaries. Does a battle-hardened mercenary follow a penniless boy into exile for the sake of a whim?'

The answer was hard to deny.

This was a severe blow to Sarazin's ego indeed! He remembered his own innocent delight when Jarl and Elkin had first told him they were coming with him to Selzirk. He had thought himself the most marvellous young man because he was capable of commanding their loyalty.

Now . . .

Now he saw they had followed him only because Lord Regan had ordered them to. When they quit Voice, Jarl had been in a truly filthy temper, which had scarcely improved by the time they reached Selzirk. Suggesting he had not wanted to come at all.

'Why did you never tell me any of this?' said Sarazin in anger. 'Why? I have a right to know! It's my life! You knew everything, everything! But told me nothing!'

'I knew nothing,' said Jarl, spreading his hands. 'I was told to watch, to wait, to spy. That was my brief. Nothing more. I never knew what plans Lord Regan had for you. I asked, mind! But was told nothing.'

'A strange way to do business!' said Sarazin bitterly.

'On the contrary, a way most sensible,' said Jarl. 'It minimised risks. I could betray myself as a spy, but could never betray you because I knew nothing worth the telling. Lord Regan is a patient man. He let you establish yourself, test yourself, find the limits to your ability. All the while, he was doubtless watching me too. Watchers to watch the watchers!'

'Then?' said Sarazin.

'Then, when you came back from Tyte as an invalid, Lord Regan acted. He saw you'd gone as far as you could without help. So he let me into his confidence and conspiracy began in earnest. Oh, we were busy while you lay sick! Lord Regan sent men and money both. We've been building the organisation you need to launch a coup to put you on the throne of the Harvest Plains.'

'But . . . I don't quite see this,' said Sarazin. 'How does my ambition benefit Lord Regan?'

'Sarazin,' said Jarl, 'the Watch is ready to rise at your command. We've purged it of men like Qid — an enemy of yours, for he was one of the Regency's men, whether you knew it or not. We've tempted, bribed, blackmailed, threatened and murdered. The Watch is ours. But that is not enough.'

'We need the army,' said Sarazin.

'Of course,' said Jarl. 'But you'll never get it. Oh, some men will come to your banner, doubtless. But not all. There'll be civil war in the Harvest Plains. You can only win with Lord Regan's help. There'll be a price for that help.'

'Selzirk will be to Galtras Laven what Shin is to Selzirk,' said Sarazin.

'Something like that,' said Jarl. 'Certainly the Harvest Plains will be obedient to the wishes of the Rice Empire. But you yourself will rule from the See of the Sun. You will rule in your own right, as king. As emperor! Well — do you like the idea?'

There was a challenge in Jarl's voice. And Sarazin, looking Jarl in the face, realised something about the man had changed. The Rovac warrior was alive, alert, fierce-faced, more of a wolf than ever. His nostrils flared as he breathed.

Jarl was ready to kill.

Sarazin had a choice.

He could say yes, yes, make me emperor. He could betray his people to the ruler of the Rice Empire. He could make himself Lord Regan's pawn for real. Or he could say no — and die on the spot. Doubtless Jarl had instructions from Lord Regan: kill Sean Sarazin if he refuses. Kill him, quit Selzirk, and return to the Rice Empire for your reward.

'Well?' said Jarl. 'Must I repeat myself? Do you like the idea?'

'Yes!' said Sarazin.

Blurting out the word in an access of terror.

No sooner had he spoken than he realised what he had done. In horror, his mind a churning turmoil of mingled fear and disgust, he realised he had agreed to betray the land of his birth to a foreign power. He had agreed to become Lord Regan's creature, Lord Regan's pawn.

Or had he?

'So you like the idea,' said Jarl, slowly.

Sarazin forced himself to smile.

'It — it's a great idea,' he said.

Trying to buy himself time. There was something else he should be remembering. But what? The dragons, that was it! The dread of dragons in his green snuff bottle. And his ring of invisibility, his magic candle. He could

283

win battles with those, could win a civil war with them.

Suddenly, he saw what he had to do, and said:

'This is such a great idea that I accept it with all my heart. I will swear to it. I will put my heart and soul into this conspiracy. But — with one reservation.'

'What?' said Jarl.

'We will not seek military help from the Rice Empire until we really need it,' said Sarazin. 'I would like you yourself to agree as much, as well.'

'Done!' said Jarl.

Without hesitation. For he was sure Lord Regan would not wish to commit troops to this struggle until events were very far advanced indeed. Jarl knew nothing of magic dragons or a magic ring and a magic candle. In his ignorance, he was easily tricked.

Both then solemnly swore themselves to the oaths that would bind them to their decisions. Then Jarl said:

'I don't believe I've ever got drunk with you, have I?'

'Getting drunk,' said Sarazin, 'is not one of my hobbies.'

'That's as may be,' said Jarl, 'but today you'll get drunk with me.'

As ever, Sarazin could not resist the will of the Rovac warrior, and they went forth and got drunk in a really major way.

CHAPTER THIRTY-EIGHT

Salt Road: trading route running from Drangsturm to Narba, through the Rice Empire, past Veda, north to Selzirk and Runcorn, then through the kingdoms of Chorst and Dybra to Estar and the far north of Argan.

* * *

Midsummer's Day arrived, bringing the start of the year Alliance 4327. By then, Sarazin was so busy he scarcely had time to say his annual prayers to the sungod.

His military duties were demanding. By now, disturbing rumours from the far north of Argan had been confirmed. The evil Khmar, the Red Emperor of Tameran, had invaded Argan. His armies had already conquered the northern nation of Estar, and were expected to march south down the Salt Road to invade the Harvest Plains.

While the reports were confused, it seemed dragons and wizards were mixed up in this warfare. Some reliable eyewitnesses had indeed seen Khmar's armies commanding dragons against the defenders of Estar, doubtless through magic provided to them by wizards.

Since Sean Sarazin had personal experience of fighting against wizards, he was made a member of an army council charged with planning the defences of the Harvest Plains against Khmar's monstrous regiments.

Meanwhile, he was actively engaged in Jarl's conspiracy. He was meeting members of the Watch and other people, and taking personal oaths of fealty from them. The coup was timed for the following year.

The Watch was diligently investigating the past lives of all the most important political figures in the Harvest Plains, eager to see if any were vulnerable to blackmail. They were turning up a lot of interesting information about Qolidian, king of Androlmarphos.

Farfalla was not the first person to bribe Qolidian, and not all of those who had bought justice from that corrupt judge had been so discreet in their dealings. With luck, Qolidian could be blackmailed into handing over control of the city of Androlmarphos when the coup finally took place.

In the little time remaining after the demands of army and conspiracy, Sarazin devoted himself to the disposal of the wealth which had come his way. Some of it went on things Benthorn brought him. Always things connected with royalty, nobility. Illuminated texts on heraldry and

285

courtly manners. Ancient scrolls dedicated to poetry such as Saba Yavendar's Victory of the Prince of the Favoured Blood. And other items of a similar nature.

Late in the summer, Sarazin's brothers Jarnel and Peguero marched away at the head of an army which was to have a second crack at destroying the ogre Tor. Sarazin wished them luck, then forgot about them, for he had seen his brothers so seldom that they were still very much strangers to him. Celadon he had scarcely seen at all: the man was still in Shin.

To his surprise, Sarazin found he envied his brothers' simple lives. They lived free from the doubts which had lately begun to plague both his waking moments and his dreams. All they had to do was put in a day's work then get drunk in the evening.

Some of those doubts were entirely natural. He feared for his life, and not without reason — for many things could go wrong with the complex conspiracy he was involved in.

Well, he could steel himself against fear.

But it was harder to deal with his growing doubts about the ethics of the conspiracy he was involved in. He could not say where doubt had come from. Was it a symptom of senility, perhaps? Despite his best efforts to ignore it, he could not. What right did he, Sean Sarazin, have to overthrow the present government and impose his will on the Harvest Plains?

—*I could govern the country better. That's the main thing.*

So he told himself.

Indeed, he was sure he could improve things. By now he knew full well that many important problems were ignored because Selzirk's power brokers were absorbed by the long, slow, agonising political struggle between Farfalla and the Regency.

Once Sean Sarazin had swept away both the Regency and the institution of kingmaker, once he had made himself absolute and unopposed ruler of the Harvest

Plains, why then surely he could end inflation, abolish unemployment, bring the criminal classes to heel, get dung-dropping animals banned from the streets (or at least put an end to the taxes on dung carts) and take the thousand and one other initiatives necessary for the health of the nation.

So why this doubt?

Things had been much, much simpler back in the old days, when he had believed absolutely in the prophecy. Of course, once Jarl had revealed the prophecy to be but Lord Regan's instrument of communication, his belief had been destroyed.

Still . . .

He longed to see the ancient book in which the prophecy had been written down.

At last, unable to resist the temptation any longer, Sarazin took himself off to the premises of Madam Sosostris. He was wary, knowing the woman might (possibly) be an agent of the Regency. Yet how could it be a crime to want to look at an old book?

He asked after it.

'Oh, that old thing,' said Sosostris. 'I sold that by auction months ago. But there's something on the premises which might interest you. Jaluba is her name.'

Sarazin was bitterly disappointed at the loss of the book. But gained some reward for his enterprise nevertheless, for Madam Sosostris allowed him to hire out Jaluba for half a day at a time. Thus he once again enjoyed Jaluba's delights, often smuggling her right into his quarters in Farfalla's palace — easy enough to do, for Bizzie collaborated with him in this enterprise.

Of Sarazin's relationship with Jaluba there is little to tell. It was a repetitive and predictable affair, a matter of haunch and nipple, cock and quim, lips and tongues, pants and grunts, tensions and spasms, teasing and giggling, laughter and lies. Enjoyable, to be sure — but of no consequence whatsoever.

Physical lust is an itch most easily scratched. But

Sarazin's lust for the old book could not be so easily satisfied. He saw it in dreams and daydreams alike. He somehow felt that, if only he could read those ancient words again, all would become clear.

Eventually, he took Benthorn into his confidence. He described the book, then said:

'From its contents, I judge it to be at least in part a cookery book. However, if I recall rightly there was stuff in it about wizards, which might aid my present military research.'

Benthorn undertook to seek it out and find it.

Then, in the autumn, Benthorn delivered the book to Sarazin. Who bargained hard — for he did not wish to betray the volume's true worth to his half-brother — and bought it for a reasonable price. (A reasonable price being, nevertheless, a very high price, for the workmanship which had gone into the book was alone enough to make it a treasure of great value.) And took it back to his quarters.

And opened it with trembling hands.

It was just as he remembered. Marvellous, marvellous. A glory of glowing colours, of fantastical animals and imaginary landscapes illuminated in miniature. Sunset orange, aubergine purple, dragon-flame red. Pictures of eagle-winged cats, of grouchy basilisks with smouldering eyes, of—

But never mind!

It was the prophecy which counted.

Swiftly, Sarazin found again the relevant passage. After all this time in the Harvest Plains, he had no trouble reading (or talking, or thinking in) Churl. Even the antiquated Spiral Style orthography gave him no problems. Here again was the prophecy, with its several parts:

—*That a prince of the Favoured Blood would be exiled from Selzirk in his youth, then would return to the city.*

Well, that fitted the facts of the life of Sean Sarazin, no doubt about it.

—That wicked and witless men would unleash great dangers threatening Selzirk's survival, and that the prince would be scorned when he revealed the solution.

Maybe, with a little prodding and poking, the past events of Sarazin's life could be made to fit that part of the prophecy. Or perhaps that part had yet to come.

—That he would earn the name Watashi, would marry the princess of an ancient kingdom, would war against (and kill) his own father.

All true. All that had happened. His public knew him now as Watashi. He had married Amantha. And he had killed Fox in a rooftop battle in Shin — something he regretted but which was not his fault, for the ring of invisibility had made it impossible for him to recognise his father as they did battle.

—That his father's death would give him the power he needed to save Selzirk.

Did that fit? Not exactly. But maybe he had gained some power from his father's death which was not yet revealed to him.

—That he would rescue the city from danger, and would be praised with great praises, his name enduring forever in glory.

What did that mean? Doubtless it referred to the future, because so far he had saved the city from no real danger, only from the sham danger posed by Epelthin Elkin. Presumably, his moment of greatest glory lay in the future. And, while the prophecy did not specifically promise him rule of the Harvest Plains — he could see that now, though in the past he had somehow deluded himself into believing it did — surely such rule was implicit in its promises.

After all, surely he could parlay great glory into a leadership position. He was Sean Sarazin, was he not? Sarazin the bold, the brave, the valorous!

So thought Sarazin.

Then abruptly pushed the book away from him.

'What was I thinking of?' said he. 'The whole thing's a

con. It was Lord Regan who sent me the book.'

Then the most marvellous thing happened. Sarazin remembered that, while Lord Regan had sent him the book, Lord Regan had not had it forged. The text was genuine — and very old.

Then . . .

Sarazin felt as if his consciousness was expanding. His mind was getting larger and larger. He understood everything, in scarcely the time it takes to swallow a mouthful of bread.

The text was genuine. The prophecy was no forgery. Furthermore, it fitted the facts of Sarazin's life. While Lord Regan had sent it to him, surely the facts implied that Lord Regan was but a tool of destiny. Sean Sarazin was fated to have the prophecy revealed to him, and the fates had worked themselves out by means of Lord Regan.

'Fools!' said Sarazin, hammering the table with his fist.

He laughed.

Exulting.

All these people thought they could control him, use him, manipulate him. Lord Regan thought as much when he sent Sarazin the prophecy by a tortuous route. But Lord Regan was not using the prophecy — no, the prophecy was using him! Jarl thought Sarazin condemned to (eventually) pledge his allegiance to Lord Regan in return for military assistance. But Jarl was wrong, for Sarazin had the ring, the candle, the dragons.

'I am no pawn of theirs,' said Sarazin. 'They are now players in my game!'

His doubts were gone, now. He had to act as he did because it was fated. It was no use fighting against fate.

That night, before Sarazin slipped off to sleep, he remembered walking with Lord Regan long ago in the Sunrise Gardens in the elegant city of Voice.

'In the final analysis,' Lord Regan had said, 'you can have whatever you want. You can be whatever you want to be. You can win whatever you want to win.'

That was what free will meant.

Lord Regan had spoken thus because he was manipulating Sarazin, working on Sarazin's sentiments, shaping Sarazin to be a weapon to use against the existing order in the Harvest Plains.

—But what he said is true.

—I can be what I want to be. I can have what I want. The will is free so all things truly are possible.

So thought Sarazin.

Later, when he was almost asleep, it finally occurred to him that such a faith in free will was in conflict with his faith in fate. He trusted Lord Regan's doctrines because he believed free will shaped the future. Yet allowed himself to be comforted by prophecy because it suggested the future was fixed already.

That woke him up properly.

'Have I got it wrong?' he said.

He sat in bed thinking about it for a long, long time, his thoughts getting more and more tangled all the time. Happily, he was able to bring things to a nice conclusion:

—These are philosophical questions and I no philosopher. Who am I to say that fate and free will cannot exist in the same world? Surely it is a dichotomy, like light and dark, right and wrong, good and evil, up and down. Who can deny that such opposites exist? The one is necessary for the existence of the other.

—The contradiction, then, is not there at all. It only seems to be there. If I were a better philosopher, I would see how the one world supports the two opposites. One room supports both light and dark, does it not, when a candle burns at midnight?

—When I am older, when I am wiser, when the prophecy has worked itself out, then I will understand. I must live for that day. I must work for it.

With that settled, Sean Sarazin fell asleep, and slept more soundly (and with sweeter dreams) than he had ever done before in his life.

CHAPTER THIRTY-NINE

Jaluba: Sarazin's doxy, who pleasured him first during his exile in the city of Voice, and who later came to Selzirk to take employment with the fortune-teller Madam Sosostris. Circumstance suggests that it is highly probable that she is an agent in the pay of Lord Regan of the Rice Empire, though Sarazin has never seen fit to ask her about this.

Autumn brought wind and rain. The open arches of Farfalla's throne room were boarded up, as they always were in bad weather. With the views shut out, it became a dim, dull, draughty place. Sarazin went there twice that autumn — once when his mother had an audience with the king of Kelebes (who was, of course, her appointee) and once when she received Plovey of the Regency and discussed the budget for her palace for the following year.

Dull stuff.

And what Sarazin was doing from day to day was equally dull. His work on the military committee preparing for an invasion by the Red Emperor Khmar had almost ground to a halt, for it was clear by now that the invasion was not going to take place.

Reports from the north were contradictory.

One said the Lord Emperor Khmar had been eaten alive by the dragon Zenphos. Another said that mountains of fire had arisen in the north, blocking the salt road and drowning Khmar and his armies in molten rock. A third said the Red Emperor had been killed by wolves in the forests of Penvash.

But all agreed that there would be no invasion.

The military committee was preparing its final report. The public, for its part, had almost forgotten about Khmar altogether. As for Sean Sarazin — his battles in Hok had become part of ancient history. His triumph against the evil wizard Epelthin Elkin had been but a five-day wonder.

He was bored. Even the routine work of conspiracy was just that — routine. But Jaluba — ah, she was never routine. She was not just delicious but exciting as well. Sarazin romanced her, boasting of his achievements and his potential. To his delight, she believed his every word.

Unlike some people one could mention, Jaluba knew her demon lover was a strong, brave hero who was destined for great things. She said as much. Sarazin then became at least half-convinced he was in love with her, for her protestations of praise told him his own opinion of himself.

In daydreams of the future, Sarazin imagined marrying Jaluba and making her queen of Selzirk. He would name a month of the year in her honour, would raise statues to her praise on every street corner, would turn Libernek Square into a walled garden where she could walk naked in summer amidst butterfly sunlight, delighting in the possession of her own beauty.

Thus Sarazin dreamed: while others worked, schemed, plotted, and prepared his downfall.

One autumn morning, Bizzie admitted Jaluba to Sarazin's quarters as she was accustomed to. The morning then passed in love and games. Sarazin for the first time showed Jaluba his bard; he also almost went so far as to read to her from his prophetic book.

Then, shortly before noon, the lovers were disturbed

when Bizzie arrived with a message: Sarazin was wanted by Farfalla.

'How long will this take?' said Sarazin.

'I don't know,' said Bizzie. 'I've no idea what your mother wants with you this time.'

Sarazin exchanged kisses with Jaluba and told her to wait.

'Will you leave me this toy, then?' said Jaluba, dangling the bard from one of her dainty fingers.

'By all means,' said Sarazin.

Then was off, hoping he would not be away from Jaluba for long. He hurried to Farfalla's High Court where his mother was in conference with several men. To his astonishment, he found they were discussing the possibility of building a new capital to the east, near the border with Chenameg.

'How can I help?' said Sarazin.

'You are our military expert,' said Farfalla. 'You will advise us on this project's strategic implications. You also know Voice, of which you have spoken highly. We are particularly interested in these aqueducts which you have praised so freely.'

'Well, yes,' said Sarazin.

He was no longer in a hurry to get away. Jaluba, after all, would still be available on the morrow. But to have people of importance attend seriously to his opinions, his knowledge, his expertise — well, that was a pleasure which rarely came his way.

It was late afternoon before Sarazin finally returned to his room. As he had only rented Jaluba from Sosostris for the morning, he was not surprised to find her gone. Unfortunately, one or two of his possessions appeared to have departed with her. His bard, for example. And his prophetic book. Worse, a whole armload of documents was missing.

'The minx must have hidden them,' muttered Sarazin.

He looked under the bed, under the blankets, in his travel chest . . . but found nothing. His valuables were gone for real!

'I've been robbed!' exclaimed Sarazin.

Shocked, hurt and alarmed. How could Jaluba do this to him? More importantly — why had she done it? Where had his valuables gone? If she had decided to flee the city and had stolen his bard and his book to sell for cash — why, then there was no harm done.

'I'd not grudge her those trinkets,' said Sarazin bravely, though in fact he already knew he would mourn the loss of his book and bard for years. 'But the documents! What could she want with those?'

Of course, he knew the answer already. He was simply trying to deny his own awareness. But, in the end, that proved impossible. Jaluba must be planning to blackmail him with those documents.

Some were innocuous — maps, official briefing papers and so forth. But on some there had been his own notes. Lists of names. Records of dates, appointments, passwords, safe houses and so forth. To most people, such cryptic notations would mean nothing. But if they fell into the hands of someone who already suspected conspiracy — Plovey, for example — they might prove his death.

'Gods!' said Sarazin.

'There are no gods to help you here,' said Plovey zar Plovey, striding into his room.

A dozen thug-faced brutes with truncheons followed close behind. They seized Sarazin and threw him against the nearest wall.

'Hey!' said Sarazin.

One of Plovey's brutes hit him — hard! — in the solar plexus. He expostulated no more, but stood there gasping, fighting the pain.

Meanwhile, Plovey gave calm, crisp orders. Obedient to these, his men shovelled all of Sarazin's remaining books and documents into capacious sacks. Then searched his room. They tore apart his mattress, smashed his furniture, explored the stones of the wall and—

'No!' cried Sarazin in anguish.

For one man had found the loose stone which guarded his magic treasures: his dragon-bottle, his ring of invisibility and his eldritch green candle.

'Aha!' said Plovey. 'So there's something in there, is it? What is it, darling boy? What have we found?'

'Nothing, my lord,' said the searcher, who had explored the hole and had found it empty.

'Let me see!' said Plovey.

But there was truly nothing to be found behind the loose stone. Another thief had been there before them.

'This will suffice, then,' said Plovey, kicking one of the sacks. 'I'm sure there's enough within to hang our pretty young friend. Ah yes, hang him — and draw him and quarter him as well. Come! Let's be gone!'

Plovey's men grabbed Sean Sarazin and dragged him from the room. He screamed for help, and help came — but Plovey had a warrant for Sarazin's arrest on a charge of high treason and that warrant was sufficient to repel the would-be rescuers.

Plovey escorted Sarazin to the Regency's headquarters and there a ferocious interrogation began. Plovey's very first question told Sarazin that all was lost:

'Name your fellow conspirators.'

'I don't know what you're talking about,' said Sarazin bravely.

And remained obdurate while the afternoon wore away, while evening darkened to night, while dawn stained the sky with blood. By that time, he was too exhausted to be frightened any longer. Just as well: for Plovey had assumed a truly frightening mien.

'You set me up, didn't you, darling boy?' said Plovey, in a voice of snakes and scorpions.

'Set you up?' said Sarazin, bewildered. 'I don't know what you're talking about.'

'You take me for a fool?' said Plovey.

And, giving way to his own anger, Plovey zar Plovey slapped Sarazin. Once. Very hard. But did not hit him again, for at that moment Thodric Jarl burst into the Regency's headquarters. Jarl had twenty men of the Watch at his back — and, more importantly, he had Childermass Imbleprig with him.

Imbleprig had a warrant signed by Judge Syrphus himself, ordering that Sean Sarazin be released by the Regency immediately. Shortly, Sarazin was stumbling through the streets, dazed by the morning sunlight, supported by Jarl.

'We've got him now,' said Jarl savagely. 'We've got him for real now.'

'Who?' said Sarazin. 'Who have we got?'

'Plovey!' said Jarl.

'I don't understand,' said Sarazin. 'I thought he had us.'

'No, no, no,' said Jarl. 'He thought you were part of a conspiracy to launch a coup. So he raided your quarters.'

'But I am part of a conspiracy!' protested Sarazin.

'Yes, yes, yes,' said Jarl. 'But he can't prove that. So we've got him for false arrest.'

'But he had a warrant!' said Sarazin.

'It was a forgery,' said Jarl. 'He had to move fast, for his informant told him you were about to burn the Conspiracy Papers and flee the city. So he didn't have time to get a warrant sworn out, so he forged one, so we've got him for that too. Forging a warrant is a capital offence.'

'Say all that again,' said Sarazin, by now completely disorientated.

'Later,' said Jarl. 'Once we're safe in Farfalla's palace.'

Once they were indeed safe in that palace, Jarl went through the whole story again.

For a long time, Jarl had been developing contacts within the Regency. These contacts had warned him of Plovey's impending raid on Sarazin's quarters.

'But I don't understand,' said Sarazin. 'What were these Conspiracy Papers supposed to be? And who told Plovey I was supposed to have them in my possession?'

'We don't know who Plovey's informant was,' said Jarl. 'The Conspiracy Papers are of course that informant's invention. They were alleged to hold all the details of our conspiracy. That's why Plovey took every document he could find from your room. Of course he found nothing suspicious.'

'How do you know that?' said Sarazin.

'If he'd found proof sufficient to have you arrested,' said Jarl, 'you'd be in a dungeon right now, and Plovey would be persuading a judge to validate his forged warrant retrospectively. That's been done before now.'

'So . . . so Plovey knows nothing.'

Jarl laughed.

'On the contrary,' said Jarl. 'Plovey knows everything. But he can prove nothing! That's the important thing.'

'Jarl,' said Sarazin, slowly, 'there's something you ought to know.'

'What?' said Jarl.

'There were some things . . . some things that went missing. Before Plovey raided my quarters. There was a book, a bard, and . . . some documents. I think . . . I think Jaluba's taken them.'

For a moment, Jarl was silent, thinking. Then, his voice grim, he said:

'Tell.'

CHAPTER FORTY

Sarazin's stolen possessions: the prophetic book telling of his return from exile and his rise to glory; the Lost Bard of Untunchilamon, holding a complete recital of the 'Warsong' and the 'Winesong' by Saba Yavendar himself; a ring of invisibility; a magical green candle; an enchanted bottle holding a dread of dragons; sundry documents, some of which hold potentially incriminating notations by Sean Sarazin.

Sarazin told Jarl most of the truth — but not all of it. He did not mention his magic candle, his dragon bottle or his ring of invisibility. Those things were secret. Only Glambrax knew about them. Sarazin had kept them hidden from Bizzie, from his mother — even from Jaluba.

And he could not tell Thodric Jarl of those implements of power, for they were the surprise he was keeping in reserve. The power he meant to use to win the civil war which would surely be the end result of the conspiracy he was engaged in.

Only those enchanted objects could save him from finally having to resign himself to becoming Lord Regan's pawn. They were the key to his independence, his ambition, his dreams. If Jarl found them he would have to reclaim them — without letting Jarl know what they were.

Meanwhile . . .

'It's the documents which worry me most,' said Jarl.

The documents, yes.

Sarazin had been careful. He had never committed to paper anything which could be incriminating in its own right. Nevertheless, the notes which were among his stolen documents might be enough to destroy his conspiracy.

'All Plovey needs is a list of names in your handwriting,' said Jarl. 'Then he'll move heaven and earth to get warrants to interrogate everyone on that list under torture.'

That was not just Jarl's opinion — it was also the truth. Plovey obviously did not have the documents as yet — but somebody did! The conspirators were doomed if Plovey got to the papers before they did.

So the conspirators went hunting.

First, Thodric Jarl raided the premises of Madam Sosostris. He took twenty men, armed, masked and hooded. They smashed their way in, ransacked the place, interrogated the staff — but found no trace of the documents.

What they did find was that Jaluba was missing. She had disappeared, and Madam Sosostris had no idea where she had gone. Sarazin bethought himself of Madam Ix — but a raid on that fortune-teller's lair proved equally fruitless.

Sarazin briefed Glambrax, then sent his dwarf into the taverns of Jone to listen for rumours. But someone stomped the hapless mannikin in a tavern, and he was put to bed with a set of broken ribs.

Then Sarazin thought of Benthorn. His half-brother, yes! Little trusted, and little deserving of trust. He had not seen him around for the last few days. Why?

Sarazin conferred with Jarl, then the two led a raid on Benthorn's residence. But Benthorn was not there. Diligent enquiries — conducted at swordpoint — established that Benthorn was in Androlmarphos. Sarazin's half-brother had departed for the trading port days before Sarazin's goods had been stolen.

'So it wasn't Benthorn,' said Sarazin.

'It might well have been Benthorn,' said Jarl. 'He'd know we'd suspect him. He might well have briefed a thief to do the dirty work while he absented himself from the city. Likely we'll hear from him sooner or later demanding blackmail money.'

'I think it would be better if we heard sooner,' said Sarazin.

'Right!' said Jarl. 'For then at least we'd know where the danger lay.'

At Glambrax's suggestion, to force Benthorn to show his hand, they sent a courier to Androlmarphos to deliver to him a brief, anonymous note. It said:

'To love me is to love life. And vice versa.'

Then, when Sarazin's fear and panic had reached its peak, Jarl came to him by night.

300

'What is it?' said Sarazin, startled from dreams of blood-stump torture and public execution.

'The Watch has caught the thief,' said Jarl.

That had Sarazin sitting up in a hurry.

'Good!' he said, spitting out the word with explosive force, punching his open hand with his fist. 'Have we got it all back? The book? The papers? The bard? The—'

'Was there something else missing?' said Jarl.

'A few trinkets,' admitted Sarazin. 'Souvenirs of travel. A little jade snuff bottle and a couple of other things.'

'Well, nothing like that's turned up,' said Jarl dourly. 'We haven't even got the papers back. Or your pro-phetic book. But we've recovered the bard. The thief was wearing it.'

'Where is he?' said Sarazin.

'The Watch are holding him prisoner,' said Jarl.

'Let's go and see him. Now!'

'No,' said Jarl. 'We wait. Give him time to stew in his own juices. Then we have him brought to us. Then we work him over in a really major way. Torture, that's the thing. We'll have the truth soon enough. He's not going anywhere in the meantime.'

'How long?' said Sarazin, desperately. 'How long before we can start torturing him?'

'Oh, three days . . . maybe four,' said Jarl, watching Sarazin sharply. 'There's no hurry.'

There was in fact every reason for the most urgent hurry imaginable. But, by insisting on this delay, Jarl was putting pressure on Sarazin. Jarl suspected — rightly! — that Sarazin was withholding important information. With enough pressure, Sarazin would crack.

'So,' said Sarazin, taking a deep breath, 'we wait, then.'

And the two glared at each other.

Sarazin suspected — and he was of course correct in his suspicion — that Jarl suspected Sarazin of holding out on him. Moreover, Sarazin suspected that Jarl suspected Sarazin of suspecting Jarl of such suspicion.

301

'While we wait,' said Sarazin, 'how about telling me the thief's name? Is it anyone we know?'

'No,' said Jarl. 'He's Drake Douay. Nobody I know.'

'Nobody I know either,' said Sarazin.

When he finally fell asleep, he dreamt of this Drake Douay who was now his enemy. The thief who had made off with his bard, unique treasure of Untunchilamon. And with his prophetic book, his documents . . . and his enchanted valuables.

'Douay,' said Sarazin, in his dreams, 'when we meet, you die.'

CHAPTER FORTY-ONE

Drake Douay: a man arrested by the Watch after a brawl in Libernek Square, and subsequently found to be wearing a piece of jewellery which his captors recognised as Sarazin's bard.

After Drake Douay had been in captivity for three days, Jarl concluded that Sarazin was not going to crack and confess whatever secrets he was hiding. By this time, Jarl was near cracking himself, for every day's delay increased their danger.

So Jarl had the thief Douay brought to Farfalla's palace. Jarl and Sarazin dressed up in their most impressive costumes — princely silks for Sarazin and ornate armour for Jarl — and, after letting Douay stew for a while, proceeded with the interrogation.

Sarazin had imagined that Douay would be a dark and dirty inarticulate thief with a scowling mien. Instead, Douay proved to be blond and dirty. And young, smooth-tongued and as cocky as they come. Both Jarl and Sarazin were infuriated by his attitude.

Douay seemed completely unaware of the enormity of his crime. Worse, at first he refused to confess his guilt, and told the most absurd lies. The young punk claimed, for example, that he had once won dozens of bards by fighting in some place called Ling. Of course Sarazin was not fooled by such a tale for even a moment, for he had learnt from Epelthin Elkin himself that the bard was a unique object, there being only one in all the world.

Two things in particular annoyed Sarazin.

First, that Douay had managed to damage the bard in the short time it had been in his possession. There was a gouge ripped through the skin of the precious thing, suggesting the punk Douay had tried to cut it open to see what was within.

Second, that Douay had not the slightest idea who Sarazin was. Sarazin's dearest wish was to have his battle-name, 'Watashi', on the lips of every citizen of the Harvest Plains. But to Douay the name appeared to mean nothing. The fact that the Watch had reported that Douay was also ignorant of Farfalla's existence was scant consolation.

Eventually, after a most unsatisfactory interview, Douay was gagged and taken to an abandoned store room. Over the last three days, this had been converted into a horror house. Many ugly instruments of iron had been gathered together; a torture bench had been installed; and Jarl had slaughtered a chicken in the room to make sure it was suitably blood-bespattered.

Sarazin did not follow Douay to the torture chamber. To tell the truth, despite his anger Sarazin was somewhat fearful of what might happen in that ugly room. Torture was an acknowledged road to the truth, of course, and was much used by Selzirk's judicial system. Even so . . . somehow Sarazin did not like the idea.

However, nothing dreadful happened inside the torture

303

chamber. Once Douay was ungagged he started talking very, very quickly. Then, as soon as a saw was applied to his ankles, he screamed — and confessed. According to Douay, Sarazin's quarters had been burgled by criminals from Jone. Douay named and described the ringleaders — and said where they could be found.

Whereupon Jarl had Douay thrown into solitary confinement, conferred briefly with Sarazin, then organised a raiding party to capture those ringleaders and bring them in for interrogation.

Jarl's raiding party left for Jone at nightfall. Sarazin waited anxiously for the raiders to return.

He waited for a long time.

What could be keeping them?

Sarazin doubted that anything serious could have happened to Jarl, and suspected the Rovac warrior had faked a delay simply to put more pressure on Sean Sarazin.

—*He'll play head games till I crack and tell all. Well, let him! For I won't crack!*

Jarl knew Sarazin had a secret, but had no idea what it was. And could not possibly guess.

—*But what if Douay gets tortured more? What if he tells of the bottle, the ring, the candle? Well, let him. Mention of such means nothing to anyone ignorant of the magic of such things.*

Surely everything stolen from Sarazin would eventually be recovered? His prophetic book, his documents and his enchanted objects. It would then be a delicate job to regain possession of his magic without anyone else realising it was magic . . .

—*I'll say those things have sentimental value. That'll do it. If only . . . if only I could get the truth from Douay myself.*

Unfortunately that was impossible. Sarazin could not steal Douay away and torture him for the full truth in private, because Sarazin commanded no men in his own

304

right. He had to work through Jarl. Which, since he was playing a double game, was perilous indeed.

At last, some time after midnight, Sarazin gave up waiting, and went to sleep.

'What do you want?' said Sarazin, groggy with sleep.

'Your mother wants to see you,' said Bizzie.

'Now? Is she crazy?'

'Thodric Jarl has been arrested.'

'What?!' said Sarazin, now very much awake.

Very shortly, he was in his mother's High Court, hearing the dreadful truth.

Thodric Jarl had taken a dozen men on a raiding mission into Jone. They had captured two of Douay's criminal confederates, had put them into sacks, had thrown the sacks onto a dung cart, and had started the return journey from Jone to Santrim. But in Kesh they had been ambushed by some of their captives' gangster friends.

Unfortunately, the gate-tower at Kesh was not controlled by the Watch but by the army. Soldiers had broken up the fight, and had taken Jarl and his men prisoner.

'Shortly,' said Farfalla, with grim satisfaction, 'they will doubtless be tortured by judicial order. Then the truth will come out. All of it.'

'What truth?' said Sarazin.

'Don't play innocent with me!' thundered Farfalla. 'I know you've been playing games of treason and conspiracy. Plovey knows too. I've called him to a conference. He'll be here soon.'

'Plovey!' said Sarazin.

He looked around wildly. There was no escape. Farfalla's guards would cut him down if he tried to flee.

'Calm down!' said Farfalla. 'I'm not betraying you. I'm trying to save your neck — and Jarl's. So tell me what you know. Everything!'

Sarazin prevaricated, but Farfalla soon had the truth out of him — or at least a part of the truth. He denied taking

305

part in a conspiracy, but admitted that he had had some potentially incriminating documents in his possession. That these documents had been stolen. That one of the thieves, Douay, was a prisoner in Farfalla's palace at this very moment. And that Jarl had gone hunting for Douay's confederates.

In due course, Plovey arrived, and Farfalla went to work. Sarazin learnt a lot that night about negotiations — negotiations of the toughest kind imaginable. Talk was still going on after sunup.

In the end, a deal was struck.

As things stood, Plovey was due to go on trial on a charge of forging a warrant, a charge of false arrest and three dozen associated charges relating to assorted technical infringements of the law. If these matters came to court, Plovey would likely be found guilty and be executed.

So: charges against Plovey would be dropped, and, in return, there would be no charges laid against Jarl or any of his men. Farfalla and Plovey, working in concert, could easily arrange this.

'You agree?' said Farfalla to Sarazin.

'There's still the matter of these thieves,' said Sarazin. 'I want them put to the torture.'

'That could be embarrassing,' warned Farfalla, unable to understand why he insisted on taking such a risk.

'We have to do it,' muttered Sarazin.

Unwilling to tell her about his missing magic. But equally unwilling to lose the chance of recovering that magic — whatever the risks!

Farfalla was undecided.

'Dearest colleague,' said Plovey, showing no fatigue despite the arduous negotiations they had been through, 'we could easily reach agreement on this matter.'

'What kind of agreement?' said Farfalla.

'To torture all our criminal prisoners without reference to courts of law. This unlawful act would bind us together in criminal conspiracy. Let us agree that the fruits of our

306

crime will remain our private property, not to be disclosed to outsiders.'

Farfalla did not like the idea. It was too dangerous! Who knew what truths might be exposed? And she could not trust Plovey — whatever he said.

But . . .

Sarazin proved adamant, Plovey was persuasive, and, at length, Farfalla finally gave way. Fatigue, for once, had undermined her good judgment.

Plovey promptly arranged for torture to begin. They started with the criminals Jarl had captured, and learnt things so startling that by noon all else had been almost forgotten.

CHAPTER FORTY-TWO

The first men put to the torture were Andranovory and Erhed, a pair of criminals captured by Jarl on his raid into Jone. Not much was needed to get them talking: a couple of jabs from a bodkin and they were talking as fast as they could. And a truly remarkable tale they told.

In spring, they had been living in Estar, in the north of Argan. When Estar had been invaded by the evil emperor Khmar, they had fought valiantly in the defence of the realm. Thanks to help from certain wizards — Phyphor, Garash and Miphon — the forces of evil had been defeated.

Then the wizards had persuaded the men to travel with them to hunt down the evil wizard of Heenmor, who was in possession of a death-stone, a wizard weapon which could turn men to rock and bring rocks to life.

Led by two Rovac warriors — the heroes Elkor Alish and Morgan Hearst — the men had endured wild adventures in the interior of Argan. Many of their comrades had been killed by dragons, basilisks or giant scorpions, by battles with two-headed barbarians, or by the dreadful punishments meted out by the Rovac for the most trifling offences.

Finally, Andranovory and his comrades had mutinied. After a savage battle against the wizards and the Rovac, the mutineers had managed to kill the wizard Phyphor, and had made their escape. That had been in early summer.

For some time, Andranovory and his comrades had lingered by the shores of the Araconch Waters, the great lake deep in the heart of Argan. There they had enjoyed the delights of the Temple of Eternal Love where the trees were of gold and the gardens of diamond.

'Many men,' said Andranovory, 'died there of pure delight.'

'Aye,' said Erhed. 'So we who were left fled.'

'How many of you were left alive at that stage?' said Farfalla.

'About four hundred,' said Andranovory. 'But many died on the journey from Araconch to here.'

Then he described the terrors of that journey down the Velvet River through the wilderness, through the Manaray Gorge, through the Chenameg Kingdom, and then at last to Selzirk. If Andranovory was to be believed, they had met with dragons, ghosts, monsters, plague, man-eating plants and worse before they finally reached sanctuary.

'Then what?' said Farfalla.

Many of the surviving mutineers had already left Selzirk. But Andranovory and Erhed provided the names and locations of several who remained. Farfalla and Plovey gave Sean Sarazin the job of hunting down these people and arresting them.

'Meanwhile,' said Farfalla, 'Plovey and I will talk with this Drake Douay, and see if he confirms his comrades' tale.'

* * *

308

Thus the interrogation of Drake Douay resumed, and almost immediately proceeded to torture. Sarazin heard all about it from one source or another. He took the keenest possible interest in this interrogation, for he lusted to recover the enchanted objects which he knew Douay had stolen from him.

However, Sarazin was to be disappointed, for Douay did not confess his sins. Unlike Andranovory and Erhed, he lacked the sense to cooperate, and told nothing remotely resembling the truth.

The much-scarred Douay claimed, as if expecting to be believed, to have seen combat against so-called Guardian Machines of improbable construction, against heroes of Hexagon, the Ling of Ling (whatever that was), Collosnon warriors, lizard monsters, crocodiles, the dragon Zenphos and a legion of monsters of the Swarms.

Depending on what story he was telling, Douay claimed his birthplace variously as Estar, Stokos, the Greater Teeth and the Lesser. His very name was uncertain, since he admitted a string of aliases, such as Narda Narkin, Shen Shen Drax, Arabin lol Arabin and Demon-son Dreldragon.

It was almost impossible to get anything resembling the truth out of Douay. However, Sean Sarazin — commanding Farfalla's guards, some Regency guardsmen and some men of the Watch — eventually managed to catch another ten of the mutineers who had gone questing in the wilderness with the wizards and the Rovac.

When isolated from each other and interrogated separately, these prisoners gave testimony proving that the broad outline of the tale told by Andranovory and Erhed was true. Khmar had been defeated by an alliance of wizards and Rovac; those wizards and Rovac had gone questing for a death-stone possessed by the evil wizard Heenmor; soldiers under their command had finally mutinied near the Araconch Waters.

At the time of the mutiny, the pursuers had been chasing Heenmor towards the north-east of Argan. If the wizards and the Rovac eventually defeated Heenmor and won command of the death-stone, then they would take it to the Confederation of Wizards.

'Probably,' said one quick-witted mutineer, 'their route would take them through Selzirk. So you could arrest them, seize their death-stone, and make yourselves lords of the universe.'

Farfalla laughed when she heard this.

'Absurd,' she said.

Then thought some more, and went to see Plovey, and put a certain proposition to him. They came to an agreement, and started using their influence to get what they wanted.

They were successful.

And, shortly, Sean Sarazin was dismayed to find himself placed in permanent command of the gates of Selzirk. His mission: to wait until the wizards and the Rovac came through the gates. Then to arrest them, and take from them the death-stone.

'Why are you doing this to me?' said Sean Sarazin, knowing this task to be both futile and absurd. 'Is this punishment? If so, then punishment for what?'

'Plovey and I have decided,' said his mother, 'that we must keep you out of mischief. We neither of us want civil war in the Harvest Plains.'

'Civil war?' said Sarazin. 'What are you talking about?'

'Civil war,' explained Farfalla, 'would be the inevitable result of your conspiracy.'

Sarazin knew by now that he had managed to keep virtually nothing secret from his mother. Nevertheless he said, as a matter of form:

'I don't know what you're talking about.' Then: 'Anyway, leaving aside this conspiracy nonsense — what about these things which were stolen from me?'

'None of our prisoners knows anything about that,' said Farfalla. 'The burglary must have been the work of Douay alone.'

'Then let me have Douay!' demanded Sarazin. 'I must

have him! I must get the truth out of him! By torture to the point of death, if nothing else will avail.'

'Oh, that's been taken care of already,' said Farfalla.

'What do you mean?' said Sarazin.

'I mean that Douay has been tortured to death. He confessed himself to be a pirate, so, when we'd got all we could out of him, we turned him over to the law. The legal penalty for piracy is to be tortured to death — and his execution was yesterday.'

Sean Sarazin was desolate.

Douay was dead, and the secret of the whereabouts of the magical treasures had died with him. Sarazin's hopes of retrieving his ring of invisibility, dragon-bottle and enchanted candle were finished. Thus his hopes of ruling the Harvest Plains in his own right were shattered.

What's more, he could no longer hope to rule even with Lord Regan's help, for, since both Plovey and Farfalla were alert to his ambitions, conspiracy had become too dangerous.

The great game was over.

And Sean Sarazin was condemned to stand at the gates of Selzirk day in, day out, always with one mutineer or another at his side, waiting for the wizards and the Rovac to come past bearing the death-stone they had won from the wizard Heenmor.

Life passed, slowly.

Then Sarazin's view of the world began to change.

First, he learnt that Drake Douay was still alive in one of Selzirk's dungeons. On cautious enquiry he found Plovey of the Regency had arranged for Douay to survive.

Why?

Sarazin could not figure it out, so asked Jarl.

'Douay doubtless blames you for his torture,' said Jarl. 'If not you, then certainly me, for I helped teach him the meaning of pain. Plovey doubtless thinks to use him some day as an assassin.'

311

'Assassination,' said Sarazin, 'plays no part in the politics of Selzirk.'

'It is not traditional,' agreed Jarl, 'but things may change. Particularly if Plovey learns that our conspiracy has been renewed.'

'But it hasn't!' said Sarazin. Then: 'Has it?'

Jarl laughed.

'This time,' said Jarl, 'we're going very, very carefully. The less you know, the better.'

So the conspiracy was still afoot. Douay still lived. The enchanted objects could still be retrieved. There was still hope!

But Sean Sarazin was still condemned to the never-ending monotony of gate-guard duty.

In spring, the absurdity of that duty became manifest when terrifying news came from the north. A new power had arisen in Argan. The Rovac warrior Elkor Alish had killed the evil wizard Heenmor, had seized control of the death-stone himself, and had used the power of that weapon to conquer the city of Runcorn.

Now Alish was demanding the surrender of the Harvest Plains. If such surrender was not forthcoming, then Alish would invade — and any army which stood against him would be turned to rock by the death-stone.

Refugees from Runcorn arrived in Selzirk — survivors of a battle which had been fought against Alish. Some had hands of stone, arms of stone, legs of stone. Some had faces partly transmuted to rock. Some died not long after reaching Selzirk. Dead or alive, they were proof of the disaster which threatened the Harvest Plains.

Panic gripped the capital. Many people fled Selzirk. Some committed suicide. There was a great conference attended by Farfalla, the Regency, the guilds and the army — and nobody could see how to stand against Alish.

The Regency now made its nature clear. There were brave men in its ranks — Plovey zar Plovey, for example, who feared little and confessed his fear of nothing. But most members of the Regency were cravens, and this majority passed an Emergency Executive Decree appointing the kingmaker Farfalla as Supreme Warlord for the duration of the war, this appointment to terminate ninety days after an Official Declaration of Peace.

The implications were clear. Since Farfalla now had total command of the Harvest Plains, the shame of surrender must fall upon her. Furthermore, if the invader Elkor Alish decided to execute Selzirk's ruler, then it was Farfalla's head which would roll.

Farfalla acted quickly.

'Elkor Alish,' she said, 'is armed with a weapon of wizard make. The heroes who sought to wrest that weapon from Heenmor were charged with the duty of returning it to the Confederation of Wizards. We know the Confederation wants this death-stone, and would not permit Alish to wield it in his own right. Therefore let us send messengers to the Confederation asking for help from that quarter.'

It was truly extraordinary for the Harvest Plains to seek help from wizards, for that realm had suffered much in the past from the rule of such. However, the times were desperate, so this expedient met with no resistance.

'Send me!' said Sean Sarazin.

But Farfalla refused him.

'You,' she said, 'I no longer trust. You will stand guard at the gate. Your people will watch still in case wizards come south. Or spies — spies in the pay of Elkor Alish. That is your duty.'

Then Farfalla recalled Sarazin's brother Celadon from Shin, and it was Celadon she sent south to take word to the Confederation of Wizards. Peguero and Jarnel could not be sent, for they had not returned from Hok. Their fate was unknown, for the army they had led to Hok to fight against the ogre Tor seemed to have disappeared entirely.

CHAPTER FORTY-THREE

On an afternoon when the spring weather was hinting at the heat of summer to come, Sarazin was sleeping off a hangover in a room built above Selzirk's northern gate when he was awoken by Erhed.

'What is it?' said Sarazin.

'They're coming!' said Erhed, frantic with fear and excitement. 'They're coming, they're coming!'

'Who?' said Sarazin.

'Hearst is coming. Miphon is with him.'

'You're kidding,' said Sarazin.

But Erhed was all sincerity. Sarazin scarcely had time to arm himself and get down to ground level before the Rovac warrior Morgan Hearst came through Selzirk's gates in company with the wizard Miphon. They and their two companions were all mounted.

'He's lost his hand,' hissed Erhed, astonished.

'Who has?' said Sarazin.

'Hearst! That's him! The one with the hook for a hand! The green-eyed one is Miphon. Those other two — one's a woodsman from Estar, the other I don't recognise.'

'We'll know soon enough,' said Sarazin.

And stepped forward to challenge the strangers.

'Halt!' cried Sarazin.

Before the strangers could flee or fight, Sarazin's men grabbed the reins of their horses. What now? Were the strangers spies, refugees, enemies, allies? Were they in flight from Elkor Alish or were they in his pay? Sarazin's men were looking at him, waiting for orders.

—*Plovey must not know of this.*

That was vital. Plovey would know shortly, of course. But Farfalla must know first. If these uitlanders became allies against Elkor Alish they must be Farfalla's allies, not Plovey's.

'You,' said Sarazin to Hearst, 'come with me.'

'Who are you to command me?' said Hearst, his hand already on the hilt of his sword.

Sarazin, who knew the temper of the Rovac from long acquaintance with Jarl, feared a fight then and there. Adopting his most lordly voice, he said:

'My name is Watashi. I'm eldest son of the kingmaker, Farfalla, highest power in the Harvest Plains. Mark me well: I'm the best swordsman in Selzirk, and my blade is faster than yours.'

The bluff held Hearst — for the moment.

'I've been here before,' said Miphon. 'Then, Farfalla's eldest son was Sarazin Sky.'

Sarazin was furious. How had the wizard learnt of that pet name? He hated it! Through gritted teeth, he said:

'So men have called me. But names may change with the times. Watashi is my name now, as I have told you. Come.'

And, to Sarazin's surprise, the strangers obeyed, and gave him no trouble as he escorted them to Farfalla's High Court. He had their names by the time they arrived.

On admitting the strangers to Farfalla's presence, Sarazin felt a pang of shame at the manifest poverty of his mother's throne room. It should have been rich with gold, silver, tapestries and ivory; it should have been filled with music and incense, with slaves in silks and supplicants crowding round the throne.

Instead, it was the same old place as ever, with just a few guards in cheap grey, a couple of scribes and a handful of serving women keeping his mother company. To Sarazin's mortification, Farfalla's skin was dyed red. How gauche! He was furiously embarrassed, since the fashion for red skin had already been fast-fading since

315

the year before. Worse — Farfalla was wearing clunky copper earrings and peasant bracelets which belonged to a phase of fashion older yet.

—*What did I do to deserve such a mother?*

Sarazin knew the strangers must be sniggering behind their mask-stolid faces, but suppressed his embarrassment, and, in his grandest style, said:

'To the kingmaker, mother of all the peoples, ruler of the See of the Sun, greetings. Here before you stands the Rovac warrior Morgan Hearst, and here, the wizard from the south, Miphon. This one here we believe to be a peasant from Estar, Blackwood. And this one, perhaps with truth and perhaps not, tells me he is a Galish merchant by the name of Ohio.'

Farfalla took her time assessing Hearst and his companions. Then she began to interrogate him. She let him know that some of his erstwhile quest companions had been interrogated, and had betrayed their knowledge of his pursuit of the wizard Heenmor, his quest for the death-stone.

'We have received an ugly little embassy demanding our surrender in the name of Elkor Alish and the death-stone,' said Farfalla. 'Knowing this Alish to be sworn to the service of wizards, and lacking any evidence of a death-stone slaughter said to have taken place near Runcorn, I have chosen to disregard this threat. Yet I see this Alish is not of your party. So is he dead? And if not, does he indeed command the death-stone?'

Sarazin thought he could understand his mother's strategy. There was panic in Selzirk — a panic made all the worse by very tangible evidence of the death-stone's work. Farfalla was concealing this from the strangers to strengthen her own negotiating position.

But what did she hope for?

They most certainly did not have the death-stone itself, for that was in Runcorn with Elkor Alish.

While so thinking, Sarazin had not been paying attention

316

to Morgan Hearst, who had been talking all the while.
Sarazin caught just Hearst's last word:

'. . . intelligence.'

Then Hearst's companions disappeared. They vanished!
One moment they were there, the next they were gone.
Two bottles rang as they hit the stone floor: a red bottle
and a green bottle. And Hearst was uncovering something,
was holding it aloft.

'The death-stone!' cried Hearst. 'Move and you die.'

'Die yourself!' snarled Sarazin.

And drew his sword, attacked, glimpsed something
flying towards him—

Then staggered into stars, blundered into darkness, and
collapsed.

Unconscious.

CHAPTER FORTY-FOUR

Sean Sarazin, knocked out by the death-stone which
Hearst had thrown at him, played no part in the negotiations which followed between Hearst and Farfalla. By
the time Sarazin recovered, it was all settled. Hearst
would organise the defence of the Harvest Plains against
Elkor Alish, and would then be allowed to go south with
his companions and with the death-stone.

Those companions spent some time in the magical red
and green bottles into which they had retreated. The
mutineers who had been tortured for information in the
autumn and winter had spoken of a magical green bottle
which could hold an entire army within its depths, but the
interrogators had discounted that tale.

Now they knew better.

'But it's too late,' raged Sarazin, cloistered with his

mother for a very private conference. 'You've thrown away our best opportunity. We could have killed Hearst, we could have taken the death-stone, we could have made ourselves rulers of the Harvest Plains.'

'So you think,' said Farfalla impassively.

'You're not really going to let him go south, are you?' said Sarazin. 'You're not really going to let Hearst walk out of here with the death-stone? How could you? This solves all! With the death-stone, we could master all of Argan. You won't let him go. You mustn't! You won't, will you?'

'Wait and see,' said Farfalla.

A little later, certain ugly rumours came to Sarazin's ears, and he confronted his mother again, invading her private quarters for the purpose.

'Is it true,' said he, 'that you've taken Hearst to bed?'

'That,' said his mother, her face momentarily looking as if the death-stone had been at work on it, 'is a most improper question.'

'But someone has to ask it!' said Sarazin defiantly. 'You can't take up with this — this wandering mercenary. He's the worst kind of lowlife imaginable.'

'You'd be surprised what I've taken up with in my time,' said Farfalla.

Then ordered Sarazin to depart. When he did not, she threw him out.

Back in his own quarters, Sean Sarazin lay on his bed, heartbroken. Was this how it was going to be? After all his planning, his scheming, his conspiring? Was it all going to come to nothing? Was this wretched Rovac warrior going to make himself lord of the Harvest Plains?

If Sarazin judged aright, his mother planned to romance this Rovac warrior, to make him and his death-stone hers, to proclaim herself empress, sweep away the Regency, abolish the Constitution and make herself absolute ruler of the Harvest Plains.

And for Sean Sarazin?

318

For him there would be, at best, a livelihood. For his mother did not trust him.

Sarazin was still brooding about it when Thodric Jarl came to see him. The Rovac warrior arrived unannounced, looking extremely weary. He was dirty, unwashed, and stank of horses. There was blood on his clothing.

'Jarl!' said Sarazin. 'I haven't seen you for days! Where on earth have you been hiding?'

'I've been down in Androlmarphos,' said Jarl, 'pursuing the recruitment of Qolidian.'

'Qolidian, yes,' said Sarazin.

That was the judge who had sentenced Sarazin to death, botching the sentence as a favour to Farfalla, who had rewarded him by making him king of Androlmarphos. Since then, Jarl had been following various leads, seeking sufficient material to blackmail Qolidian into supporting Sarazin's cause.

'Has any word reached you yet?' said Jarl.

'Word of what?' said Sarazin. Then, without waiting for a reply: 'What do you think of Farfalla's new guests? Morgan Hearst — have you met him?'

'I haven't and I won't,' said Jarl, with mingled contempt and disgust. 'A Rovac warrior in league with a wizard! That's an abomination! Elkor Alish, that's the man I admire.'

'Alish betrayed his comrades,' protested Sarazin. 'He quested for the death-stone in their company, then tried to take it for himself.'

'He was true to his duty,' said Jarl. 'He did what a Rovac warrior is sworn to do. He moved against the wizards when the time was right. This Morgan Hearst is the traitor. Hearst should have thrown in his lot with Alish. Instead, Hearst stole the death-stone from Runcorn and brought it south.'

'If you think so highly of Alish,' said Sarazin, 'why don't you go to Runcorn to join him?'

'I've no need to go to Runcorn,' said Jarl. 'Alish is already in the Harvest Plains. He's seized Androlmarphos.'

319

'What?!' said Sarazin.

'It's true,' said Jarl, wearily.

And explained.

Jarl's men had finally got the material they needed to blackmail Qolidian. Then they had explained to Qolidian that he had but two choices: to commit suicide or to throw in his lot with them.

Unfortunately, Qolidian had a third option.

He had taken it.

He had accepted bribes from Elkor Alish, had arranged for the garrison to be poisoned, and had helped the foreign marauder invade the city from the sea.

'I was the first person out of 'Marphos,' said Jarl. 'I took a string of horses and I rode. Three drowned in river crossings, two dropped dead beneath me — but I got here. I'm the first to bring the news to Selzirk. And you're the first to hear.'

'I don't understand,' said Sarazin. 'How could Alish come by the ships to move an army? Spies suggest—'

'The pirates are in on it too,' said Jarl, bluntly. 'Alish is in league with the Orfus pirates of the Greater Teeth. That's where the ships come from, there's no secret about that.'

'He's doomed himself!' said Sarazin. 'We'll take the death-stone and trash his army in an instant.'

'And trash 'Marphos as well?' said Jarl. 'Would your mother permit that? Alish has the whole city as hostage. This business will not be swiftly settled. But we must make a decision — and swiftly.'

'What decision?' said Sarazin.

'Do you not see it?' said Jarl, so weary he was almost weeping. 'All hopes of conspiracy are gone. Power is no longer split between kingmaker and Regency. Your mother has won that battle in her own right. If we could have won 'Marphos we could have had a chance. But as it is . . .'

'We could throw in our lot with Alish,' said Sarazin drily.

320

'Yes!' said Jarl, with sudden fervour. 'I didn't think you'd be game to do it, but that's it, yes, that's the way.'

'I was joking!' protested Sarazin. 'Fight with Alish? When Selzirk holds the death-stone? That's craziness.'

'Then I really have failed,' said Jarl, his voice flat. 'I thought I'd taught you some fighting spirit, but I was wrong. You haven't got what it takes. You never will have. You're a disappointment to me — and, I warrant, to Lord Regan.'

Jarl turned to go.

'Wait!' cried Sarazin, in anguish. 'How can you say something like that? I tried, didn't I? I won Chenameg, didn't I? If only for a day! Don't go! Don't leave me! I — I—'

Wordlessly, he clutched at Jarl.

But Jarl shook him off, and left.

And was never again seen in Selzirk.

CHAPTER FORTY-FIVE

Soon preparations for war began in earnest. And this was like nothing in Sarazin's experience. For it was not a matter of sending away one or two thousand men to fight somewhere beyond the horizon. This was the mobilisation of an entire nation for a war to the death.

Morgan Hearst was unlike Thodric Jarl in many ways. For a start, Hearst was very tense — as if he were on the edge of a nervous breakdown. He was labouring under an immense mental burden, and he was very, very bitter. That Sarazin saw easily, though he could not decipher the source of the bitterness.

But, in some ways, Hearst was exactly like Jarl. He had the same habit of command, the same ruthless style, and gave the same impression of being extremely dangerous. What's more, when Hearst commanded, men obeyed.

Sarazin, knowing he could never hope to command the same obedience himself, was intensely jealous. This was the day of Selzirk's greatest danger. And Sean Sarazin was doing nothing for the city: instead, this foreign adventurer was winning all the glory.

After a lot of hard thought, Sarazin came up with a little scheme which he personally thought brilliant. He proposed that Drake Douay be brought from his dungeon and sent to 'Marphos to offer Alish safe conduct and a massive bribe if he surrendered. This might just work. And, even if it didn't — Sarazin would feel safer with a potential assassin out of the city.

To Sarazin's surprise, Plovey supported this scheme, and it was eventually put into practice. But Alish made no reply to this overture, and Douay did not return to Selzirk.

Meanwhile, Hearst carried on organising for war.

His performance was impressive indeed.

Until the day when he made a reconnaissance of the plain to the north of Androlmarphos, where he planned to fight Elkor Alish. Despite Jarl's predictions, Farfalla had proved ready to have the death-stone used against Androlmarphos. But Hearst, for inscrutable reasons of his own, had refused to employ that devastating magic. So the two armies would meet without the benefit of magic.

This was ideal cavalry country, and Alish was known to have plenty of horses. But, to Sarazin's dismay, Hearst had no grasp of cavalry tactics whatsoever. Sarazin tried to help the Rovac warrior, but Hearst declined the enlightenment so readily offered, refusing to admit his own ignorance.

Thus, as the day for battle approached, things looked to be shaping up for a regular disaster.

All too soon, the battle-day arrived. Elkor Alish marched forth with his troops. Army engaged army. And, to Sarazin's bewilderment, Hearst smashed the enemy, winning a victory on a field of blood and gore.

A little later, Hearst used just enough of the death-stone's magic to breach the walls of 'Marphos, and drove Alish from the city.

The Rovac warrior had won a great victory for the Harvest Plains, and had made himself a hero. Selzirk rejoiced. And Sarazin, with shock and horror, shortly learnt that his mother planned to make Morgan Hearst ruler of the Harvest Plains in his own right.

CHAPTER FORTY-SIX

Rumours of what was to happen soon brought crowds of supplicants to the door of Morgan Hearst — even though he, for the time being, thought it politic to deny the rumours and play the part of the simple soldier.

Sarazin hears these rumours not, since he was busy brooding over maps of Stokos, and of the Greater and Lesser Teeth. He was hoping to find a way to win power and glory for himself. And, since the pirates had been broken in battle, surely the next logical step was to seize those territories from the sea reavers. Sarazin had no experience of war at sea, but was prepared to learn.

'A power base, that's what I need,' he said. 'Some men loyal to me, a reputation, and . . . and . . .'

He knew he was dreaming.

Hearst had won what Sarazin had always wanted. Hearst would soon be ruler of the Harvest Plains, and Sarazin would be nothing. Nevertheless, he could still dream. And did.

His daydreams were interrupted by an unexpected and

peremptory summons from Morgan Hearst, which he obeyed. To his shock and horror he found Drake Douay closeted with Hearst.

'You!' said Sarazin.

'Nay,' said Drake, 'I died at sea some many days ago. What you see here is none but my ghost.'

He would have said more, but Hearst cut him off.

'Business,' said Hearst. 'Elkor Alish is playing a trick with this fellow. A trick he learnt from Selzirk. He holds two of the man's friends as hostage, requiring, for their release, proof of delivery of two letters.'

'How does that concern me?' said Sarazin.

'One of those proofs must come from me,' said Hearst. 'But the other needs come from you.'

'I give no proofs to this thieving whoreson bastard,' said Sarazin.

'You will give proofs,' said Hearst, waving a letter, 'or I will give this document to the Regency.'

'What says it?'

'This letter from Alish to you invites you to join with him in making war on the Regency and installing yourself as emperor of the Harvest Plains.'

Sarazin was horrified. This was like one of his worst dreams coming true! What would his mother think if she saw such a letter? Let alone Plovey! He did his best to shrug it off:

'That speaks of no crime on my part. It's no crime to be made an offer, no matter how criminal. Crime lies only in the acceptance, which I'd never make — and which none could prove against me.'

But Hearst persisted, and, in the end, Sarazin consented to give Douay a signed and dated piece of parchment saying simply that the petition of Drake Douay had been refused. Then Sarazin was dismissed by Hearst, and retreated to his own quarters to think things through.

Once more — this was the story of his life! — he was embroiled in conspiracy. And, once again, he was the last person to know what was going on. Why had Douay returned to Selzirk? Why had Alish sent letters to Selzirk with Douay? If one letter had been an invitation to conspiracy directed to Sean Sarazin, what had the other letter said?

Was Douay in league with Hearst? If so, how? Why? Since when? And what would the outcome be? Perhaps Sarazin should denounce Hearst. But for what? And what proof did he have?

The more Sarazin thought about it, the more he was sure of only one thing: his life was in danger. He thrice considered fleeing the city immediately and thrice rejected the notion.

'This is impossible,' muttered Sarazin.

He wished he could talk it over with someone. But Elkin and Jarl, the tutors of his youth, were no longer with him. Jaluba was long gone — and where she was nobody knew. His father was dead, his mother was scarcely on speaking terms with him, so who was left? Benthorn, whom he did not trust. And Glambrax.

'It's hopeless!' groaned Sarazin.

He was utterly alone and helpless at the most critical juncture of his life. Soon there would be a formal banquet in the Hall of Wine, which had been refurbished especially for the ceremony. At that banquet, Morgan Hearst would be consecrated as one of the Favoured Blood in sacred ceremony.

Then he would be proclaimed ruler of the Harvest Plains.

And what if he then set about ridding himself of obvious rivals — such as Sean Sarazin?

Sarazin was still thinking about it when word reached him that Qolidian had surrendered to the Harvest Plains. The renegade governor of Androlmarphos had escaped to Runcorn after Hearst defeated Alish in battle. But now he had given himself up. He was currently in Kelebes, far to the north, but would soon be brought to Selzirk for interrogation and the administration of justice.

Was he coming back to die?

Not likely — that was not Qolidian's style!

So he must have some plan to preserve his life.

But what could save him in the face of such crimes?

Surely, only the exposure of a greater treason, a greater crime. The crime of Sean Sarazin, conspirator, plotter, traitor, the man who had long sought to make himself master of Selzirk in defiance of the Constitution.

How had Qolidian come by details of the conspiracy? There were many possibilities. After all, Qolidian would have had freedom of action while Elkor Alish ruled 'Marphos. Jarl had escaped from the city alive, but many men of the Watch who knew details of the conspiracy would have been trapped in the city. Qolidian could have won details of Sarazin's treason by torture.

—*One way or another, he knows. And I must flee.*

—*But what if I'm wrong? What if he doesn't know? What if I'm mistaken?*

An easy solution presented itself. When Sarazin wanted to go to Chenameg, he had let the world think he had been kidnapped by terrorists. All he needed to do was fake another kidnapping. Glambrax could help him. Yes, that was it!

Sarazin was resolved.

On the night of the banquet in the Hall of Wine, Sean Sarazin would be kidnapped. Glambrax would bear witness to the kidnapping, and would then follow Sean Sarazin to his chosen destination.

Which was the city of Voice, far to the south in the Rice Empire.

CHAPTER FORTY-SEVEN

Sean Sarazin arrived in Voice with his sword, his dwarf,
a stolen horse — and a lot of information. Lord Regan was
resident in the city when Sarazin arrived, and soon the
ruler of the Rice Empire was methodically pumping the
young refugee.

Sarazin told all.

Well, almost all.

He breathed not a word of the instruments of enchant-
ment which had been stolen from him, but he told the rest
of his tale to the full. Lord Regan knew most of it already,
having received regular reports from Thodric Jarl, Epelthin
Elkin and other spies.

But the latest events were new to him.

'So,' said Lord Regan, when Sarazin was finished.
'Morgan Hearst is to be ruler of the Harvest Plains.'

'By now he will be,' said Sean Sarazin. 'The very night
I fled he was to be consecrated as one of the Favoured
Blood. Doubtless today he lords it over Selzirk, and plans
conquest. After all, he has the death-stone.'

'Which you say he had sworn to take south to the
Confederation of Wizards.'

'Elkor Alish had sworn an identical oath,' said Sarazin,
'yet yielded to temptation. I do not think Hearst a greater
man. After all, he has already delayed long in the Harvest
Plains. Besides, I think my mother has ensnared him in
a love-web.'

'So,' said Lord Regan, 'lust and ambition will make
Hearst the master of the Harvest Plains. Doubtless his
thoughts will soon turn to conquest. When that happens,

I cannot stand against him. Not if he is armed with the death-stone.'

Then Lord Regan explained that he already had a refuge prepared against a day of trouble.

'It is a place in the Ashun Mountains. There I can flee if my world comes to an end. You could go there now, if you chose. Or you could go to Chenameg.'

'Chenameg?' said Sarazin, startled.

'Yes,' said Lord Regan, briskly. 'I have long sponsored a little . . . a little trouble in Chenameg. Men fight there against the tyranny of Tarkal of Shin. One of those who stands in opposition to Tarkal is Lod.'

'Lod!' said Sarazin, in amazement. 'So Lod lives!'

'Why does that surprise you?' said Lord Regan. 'Have you ever heard that he was dead? No? Then what did you hear of Lod?'

'That he escaped from Shin when Tarkal sought to execute him,' said Sarazin. 'Tarkal, rightly thinking himself unsafe, then left Shin himself and set off for the Harvest Plains. Lod harried Tarkal's retreat. Then Tarkal joined up with an army led by my brother Celadon. Together, those two defeated Lod's forces. I know nothing of Lod's fate after that.'

'He came to me,' said Lord Regan. 'He came to me with the remnants of his forces. I gave him what he needed — armour, weapons, military advisers. I saw him established in the hills in the south of Chenameg. Since then, he has ever been a thorn in Tarkal's side.'

'And you would have me join him?' said Sarazin.

'You do as you will,' said Lord Regan. 'You can go into refuge in the Ashun Mountains or join Lod in Chenameg. But you cannot stay here. Not when Morgan Hearst rules in Selzirk. For, if Hearst learnt that I was sheltering you, he would think my ambition was to set you on the throne of the Harvest Plains.'

Lord Regan paused, then, laying his hand on Sarazin's shoulder, he said:

'It is, of course. It always was. For, as I have told you

328

before, I have long thought of you as my son. But I judge that this is not the moment to try the move.'

There were times in the past when Sean Sarazin had hated Lord Regan. Who had lied to him. Used him. Tricked him. Manipulated him. Fooled him. But, now that he was face to face with the man, Sarazin could not doubt his sincerity.

Lord Regan did care for him!

Lord Regan did think of him as a son!

And, one day, Lord Regan would put him on the throne of the Harvest Plains. Not just to serve his own ends — but because he truly valued Sean Sarazin. How could Sarazin return such love? He knew how. He knew what would please Lord Regan. So he said:

'My lord, you have given me a choice of flight, refuge or war. I choose war! I will go to Chenameg and there join Lod's fight against Tarkal. Then, in the fulness of time, if another fate presents itself — I will be ready!'

CHAPTER FORTY-EIGHT

Sean Sarazin set off the very next day with Glambrax and half a dozen soldiers as guards and guides. Lord Regan came to farewell him, and brought him a goodbye present.

'Open it later,' said Lord Regan. 'It's a trifle. A small token of my appreciation.'

Sarazin resisted the temptation to open the present until evening. Then he tore away the wrapping, eager to see what Lord Regan had given him. When he caught sight of a small green bottle, his spirits soared.

Then fell again.

It was the wrong bottle!

329

This gift bottle was made of glass, and held a high-class cologne. Also in the present-package was a brand new razor, a block of perfumed shaving soap and a camel-hair shaving brush.

'I suppose it's the thought that counts,' said Sean Sarazin, trying to persuade himself that that was the case.

Then he spotted one last item: a small note in Lord Regan's handwriting. It said:

'Another surprise awaits you in Chenameg.'

What?

Sarazin could hardly wait. He was up at dawn the next day, and had his party on the move the moment breakfast was over. He was more eager than ever to get to the secret guerilla camp in the southern highlands of Chenameg, to meet Lod — and to discover the nature of the surprise.

The guerrillas had their headquarters in an old hunting lodge in the foothills of the mountains which formed the southern border of the Chenameg Kingdom. It was a huge building of black logs. Lod's great-grandfather, who had caused it to be erected, had hunted on a most immodest scale.

Sarazin smelt the lodge before he saw it, because the state of the outdoor latrines left a lot to be desired. Apart from the latrines, he could also smell food — fresh baked bread! — and firesmoke.

When the lodge came in sight, he saw it was washing day. A dozen outdoor fires were burning, heating huge iron cauldrons in which water was warming. Clothes were being washed, and bodies also. Sarazin saw Lod, and hailed him:

'Lod!'

'Friend!' said Lod, in a joyous voice, running towards him.

'So you got here,' said a loud-voiced man.

Sarazin knew that voice.

'Jarl!' cried Sarazin. 'What are you doing here?'

'Fighting a war,' said Thodric Jarl. 'What else would a Rovac warrior be doing?'

Thodric Jarl was indeed at war. But he was running very little danger, for he was acting as a military adviser, not as a combatant. And he was getting very well paid — his pay being banked in Voice with the Monastic Treasury of Inner Adeer. It would be ready for his return — and, with luck, it would be enough to finance his retirement.

Jarl had little to say to Sarazin — after all, they had not been parted for very long. But Lod and Sarazin had a great deal to say to each other. Finally, when they had just about talked themselves out, Sarazin said:

'Well, Lord Regan said there was a surprise waiting for me in Chenameg, but I thought it would be something more worth the journey than Thodric Jarl. You don't by chance know the whereabouts of a pretty young wench named Jaluba, do you?'

'No,' said Lod, with a sly grin. 'But I know the surprise Lord Regan was talking of. Thodric Jarl wasn't it. Come this way.'

And Sarazin allowed himself to be led to the back of the hunting lodge. There a man was practising kata with a heavy-bladed sword. He was naked to the waist, and had his back to them.

'Fox!' said Lod.

And the swordsman turned. Sarazin saw his scar — a thick welt slashed across his belly. Saw his face, his astonishment, then — his delight. It was Fox, yes, it really was, his father, not dead at all but here, here, alive and fighting fit, and—

Glad to see him!

The next moment, Fox had cast aside his sword and was running towards Sarazin. A moment later, they were embracing. Laughing, weeping, slapping each other on the back. Alive, alive — and exultant.

CHAPTER FORTY-NINE

When Fox told his story, there were no startling revelations. Sarazin had last seen his father falling from a roof in Shin, wounded by Sarazin's blade.

As Sarazin now knew, Fox had of course been alive when he hit the ground. He had been the leader of the raggle-taggle mob which had tried to take control of Shin, and his people had taken their wounded commander with them when they finally retreated into the wilderness.

Eventually, Fox had linked up with Lod after Lod returned to Chenameg. Fox was now commander of the National Liberation Front currently engaged in the People's Struggle to overthrow the monarchy and establish the Democratic People's Republic of Chenameg. When they finally conquered Chenameg, Fox and Lod would rule jointly.

'Two kings for one nation?' said Sarazin.

'No,' said Fox. 'Two presidents.'

Then he tried to explain the difference between a president and a king. But, as far as Sarazin could see (and in this case he saw very well indeed), there was no difference worth mentioning.

'Well,' said Sarazin, 'and how is the war going?'

'Slowly,' said his father. 'But we're winning. We lose very few men because our people are very highly trained. You'll be an expert yourself once we've finished with you.'

'I'm a trained soldier already,' said Sarazin, proudly.

'Not quite,' said his father.

And, in the days that followed, Sarazin learnt what his father meant by that. Sean Sarazin thought of himself as a battle-hardened veteran, for he had fought near the headwaters of the Shouda Flow, in the marshlands of Tyte, in the mountains of Hok and on the plains before Androlmarphos. But he was but a beginner at the kind of warfare his father was involved in.

For a start, he was largely ignorant of archery. But, since the bow was the basis of forest warfare, he had to do his best to master it. He learnt, also, silent killing with knives, garottes and hands alone; the making of booby traps such as spiked pits and deadfalls; tracking and travelling without leaving tracks; signal codes based on birdcalls; and the art of living off the land.

'Remember,' said one of his instructors, 'you need meat to fight. The best source of meat is a dead enemy. Don't forget!'

Sarazin remembered a certain feast Thodric Jarl had organised after a battle by the banks of the Shouda Flow. And he shuddered.

'Never mind,' said his father, when Sarazin spoke to him about it. 'Cannibalism isn't compulsory in our ranks. But it's always an option. Never forget that.'

Sarazin was shocked. But this scarcely diminished his pleasure at regaining his father. He had been alone for so long! Only now did he realise how intensely lonely he had been in Selzirk with nobody he could truly trust, nobody he could truly talk to.

But his father — his father welcomed him, trusted him, valued him, was open and frank with him. And Sarazin was delighted. He strove to be worthy of his father, and threw himself heart and soul into his military studies.

In Chenameg, Sarazin changed some of the habits of a lifetime. For example, he had always worn his sword by his side. But Fox's men spent much of their time down on their guts, sneaking or spying or waiting in ambush. So much so that they called themselves 'snake fighters'. Sarazin learnt that, in the war of the snake, a sword is

333

better slung over the back in company with bow and quiver.

Without complaint, Sarazin endured all the rigours of his training. Salt-meat monotony. Lice. Forced marches. Downpour skies. Pain. Monotony. Fatigue.

—*For it all has a purpose.*

—*It prepares me.*

—*The blade is being tempered.*

Sarazin was sure that his father would lead them to victory, that they would conquer Chenameg, would kill Tarkal, would capture Shin and set themselves up as rulers. It might take ten years — but victory would be theirs. And, though Sarazin would not rule in Shin, he would at least have a real role in the world. He would no longer be idling his life away for no purpose as he had in Selzirk.

—*The future is radiant.*

Thus thought Sean Sarazin.

And was happy. Training with friends, eating with friends, swapping war stories of hair-raising ferocity, and speculating on what might be happening out in the big wide world. Their sources of information were zero, for they were entirely isolated from all the world's routine commerce. Fresh news would reach them next at the start of winter, when they would receive fresh supplies from the Rice Empire.

'News can wait,' said Sarazin. 'But can the war?'

His father laughed at his puppy-eager enthusiasm.

'We have a big campaign planned for the spring,' said Fox. 'Till then, we train, we plan, and we wait.'

That autumn, Sean Sarazin went on his first big tactical exercise in the training area. This was in the mountains a few leagues south of the hunting lodge.

Those engaged in this exercise tramped into the area with heavy packs and practised setting up a camouflaged encampment with as little noise as possible — ideally none.

334

Then they left their heavy packs at this encampment and went on manoeuvres.

They split into parties which practised ambushing each other, tracking each other, attacking and raiding each other. And so forth. They got very tired, very muddy — and, naturally, had the time of their lives. This was the fun part of war. Good comrades, plenty of excitement and total safety.

Then came the night manoeuvres. They were to split into seven separate parties, tramp all night through the forested highlands, and regroup in the morning at the base of a notable mountain to the south.

And it was on these manoeuvres that Sarazin received his first intimation that the world as he knew it was coming to an end.

CHAPTER FIFTY

Night, and rain as dark as the night. Men travelling softfoot, true to the discipline of silence. Keeping close, very close, near enough to touch, near enough to smell. In the dark, it would be the easiest thing in the world to get lost.

Actually they were lost, for it was impossible to tell one's location on a night so dark. But while they kept going uphill they were getting closer and closer to their goal. At dawn they would send someone up a tree to establish the precise direction to the mountain where they would rendezvous with their fellows.

So, while it was dark, and cold, and wet, and raining, they were far from disheartened. They were dressed for the weather. And, as their packs were back at their encampment, they were travelling light, carrying only their weapons (swords, knives, bows and quivers of arrows), a single waterbottle each, and a day's rations.

Easy work!

And, since they had been on the march for half the night already, they had long since worked themselves into the rhythm of travel. One and all, they felt they could walk forever. A novice had the lead, Sarazin was in the middle, and Fox (who had joined these exercises so he could judge his son and gauge his suitability for a command responsibility) was taking up the rear.

There were ten of them. Ten fit, healthy men who were — though a civilian might not think it possible — content with their lot. Though, if any of the ten had suddenly been granted three magical wishes, he would doubtless have used one as a matter of urgency to kill off his lice.

Then the nightmare started.

One moment they were moving along nice and easy through the night rain. The next moment, there was a scream. Then a shatter-crack as a tree was torn apart.

Then—

Bubbling cries of agony from the leading man. Screams of panic from the others. A shout from Fox:

'Scatter!'

A superfluous shout, since they were running already. All of them — save the leading man, who was dying.

Sarazin fled as fast as the others.

Then was snatched by a monster.

'Yeh-garn!' he screamed, kicking and struggling.

The brute smashed him around the ears. He grabbed its — arm? Limb? Tentacle? No: its branch. He had run into a tree. He stooped beneath the branches, went to ground, then lay very still, listening, staring fearfully into the dark.

He tried to hush his own harsh breathing. His chest was tight. He could hear pattering rain. Sounds of violent retreat, already diminishing. Some of his comrades were still running.

What had happened?

Something had attacked the leading man. But what? A boar? Wolves? An enemy marauder? A vampire? A werewolf? A gigantic wildcat?

—*Whatever attacked him smashed a tree.*

—*I heard it! The tree was torn apart!*

—*Not a wolf, then. Not a werewolf, even. Or a vampire. Or a cat. Or a man. A bear? Could a bear smash a tree? Don't think so. Not a bear-type thing to do, anyway.*

—*So what was out there?*

—*Giant? Possibly. The boot!*

Yes. Sarazin remembered the gigantic boot in which he had once sheltered for a night during earlier travels through Chenameg. The owner of such a thing would be able to smash trees with ease. What else had such strength?

—*Dragons. Perhaps. But there was no roar, no flame.*

—*So it was a giant. Must have been! Nothing else makes sense.*

So thinking, Sarazin began to shudder.

He waited for a long time, listening. He could no longer hear any sounds of flight, struggle or agony. Only the wind, the rain, the night-talk of the forest. He was very cold by now.

—*What to do?*

In the end, he could no longer bear simply to lie there, waiting helplessly. He got to his feet. Then, shadow-silent, he eased away through the forest. Then halted. Which way should he go? Cautiously, he gave an owl-voiced code-call. Then thought:

—*Do owls hunt in the rain?*

No matter: the rain was dying down. Sarazin waited until he thought it had stopped — the constant rain-drip from the trees above made the precise moment difficult to judge — then gave the owl-voiced call again.

Listened.

—*Answer me, answer me!*

337

No reply.

Sarazin called again. An owl-voiced reply came. Distant. The others must have moved off quickly. Sarazin called again. Listened.

—*Speak to me!*

He was answered.

Stealthily, he headed towards the signal. After going for some considerable distance, he stopped. He was about to call again when one of his comrades called to him. From somewhere very close at hand.

—*Where are you? Where?*

He listened intently. Finally, the call came again. From a tree directly above. Sarazin looked up. Up through the dark scaffolding of branches lit here and there by stars. And saw a small, dark shape. Which called to him, giving an owl-voiced cry. Then spread its wings and flapped to the next tree.

—*Pox! Pox and bitches! Dog-dung soup!*

What now?

He was lost by night in unfamiliar territory to which he had no map. He had food — though not much — but no tent, no tinder box. For once, he did not even have an ill-mannered dwarf bumbling around at knee-height, for Glambrax had been left behind at the hunting lodge. He was utterly alone. His comrades were out there, somewhere, in the darkness. But then so too was a large, bad-tempered giant with a homicidal disposition.

—*How long till dawn?*

—*Half a night? Less, by my judgment.*

Sarazin analysed his situation by applying the Rule of Objectivity: if someone else was in your predicament, what advice would you give them? He drew a blank. Then he remembered Thodric Jarl lecturing on the Laws of Panic:

'When all else fails, try doing nothing.'

It had sounded stupid at the time, but now, recalled in a time of dire need, it sounded uncommonly sensible. Sarazin settled himself down at the foot of the nearest tree.

He hoped to sleep — but unfortunately, it was far too cold for that. He was shivering again, and would shiver till dawn unless he died of it.

Dawn. The sun rose into a blue sky from which all traces of cloud and rain had vanished. Sean Kelebes Sarazin set out for higher ground, taking care to leave clear tracks of scuffed footmarks, bent twigs and torn leaves which could be followed by his comrades — and by himself, if he had cause to retrace his steps. He hoped giants could not stoop low enough to read a trail.

After a while, he came upon a tree which looked good for climbing, and shinned up it. Long before he reached the top, the branches grew too thin to support his weight. Still, he thought he glimpsed a mountain.

He climbed down again.

—*Keep on uphill, that's the thing.*

Indeed. He'd sight the rendezvous mountain sooner or later. Or come across a trail-sign to point him to his comrades. To tell his own people where he was going, he broke up some rotten branches and laid out an arrow on the ground, pointing in his direction of travel. With luck, a hostile giant would never notice such an insignificant mark.

—*Now let's be moving.*

So thinking, Sarazin set off again.

He had gone scarcely a hundred paces when, as he was about to step into an open glade, he halted.

He thought he had seen something move.

—*Yes. Just ahead. In the grass.*

The grass lay green and innocent in the autumn sunlight. But something was moving in the grass. What? Sarazin stared at the grass fearfully.

—*A snake, that's all.*

Sarazin smiled, relaxed, advanced. The slim green snake reared up in front of him, swayed this way and that, then sank back to the ground. He took another step forward.

339

The snake went into reverse, weaving itself through the grass almost soundlessly. Its every movement perfectly fluid. Effortless.

For as long as he could remember, Sarazin had always admired snakes for their beauty, their poise, their sophistication, their perfect mastery of style. Now that he had met the snake the forest no longer seemed so alien, so lonely.

—*A good omen.*

The glade opened on to another one where the grass was higher, more plentiful. Sarazin stretched, yawned, grinned at the sunlight, waded into the tall grass, put a foot into something soft, into—

—*mud?*

But was already committed, his weight following his foot, something crunching under his weight, grass parting beneath his hands as he saw, to see was to know, to know was—

—*to die?*

Then someone screamed.

—*Me?*

No, it was not Sarazin screaming, even though he stood with one foot firmly planted in the carcass of a ruptured man-corpse, even though that corpse was a comrade's, eyes death-staring at the sky.

—*Blood?*

—*Tracks?*

Neither. No blood. No tracks. Nothing to show how the man had got here. And his legs were missing. So he hadn't walked here. And the arms were gone. Something had been hungry! Or angry. Very angry. And had dropped the corpse from the sky. Or had thrown it.

—*Which?*

—*Dropped? Thrown?*

—*By giant? By dragon?*

—*And who screamed just then?*

Sarazin looked up. Overhead were a few slim branches which could have supported nothing heavier than a nest-raiding hedgehog.

Another scream ruptured the forest.

Sarazin was shocked to realise he was totally exposed to view. He dropped to his gut. Dropped straight down to the wet green grass. Then, emulating the snake, he writhed through the grass to the trees. He crawled into the nearest bit of rough and tangled undergrowth. Then peered around, seeing very little since the same shrubbery which sheltered him cut down his vision in all directions.

Then he saw a man running.

A man fleeing, all weapons gone, an empty quiver bouncing on his back. Running, running, running, then—

Down went the man.

He had tripped, had caught his foot on a root and had gone down hard. But he was up again on the instant, up and off. Ten paces, twenty. The forest ahead of him was thick and dark. He plunged in without hesitation. And the forest—

Thrashed. Tore itself in tumult. Screamed. Raged in demolition.

—*The trees! It's the trees! Eating people!*

Sarazin shrank to the earth in terror.

Amidst the shatter-thrashing forest there was the graunch of rending wood. Then a tree was falling, falling, crashing towards him, no chance to run—

Branches in all directions—

Sarazin flung his arms around his face to save his eyes, wrapped his fingers into fists, ground arms and fists to the ground, and gasped—

And was lashed by whip-quick branches flailing against his scalp, his leathers, back, arse and ankles. He lay still. Listening to his body. He felt nothing. He was paralysed! His back was broken! No, not so — he could still feel his toes in his boots. His left foot was sore where the nail of his great toe, ingrowing, had started to become inflamed and infected.

His knees hurt, too.

A good sign. An excellent sign. Pain! Ah, most beautiful sensation! But where was the rest of the pain? The lacerating

341

agony of smashed flesh and cracked bones? Absent. For a good reason, too. Only the thinnest, uppermost branches of the tree had fallen as far as his body.

Sarazin, remembering the tree was a man-eater, flinched from those branches. Then came to his senses. Possibly there were such things as man-eating trees. He lived, after all, on the continent of Argan, where it is always dangerous to claim that a given improbability is impossible. However — a suicidal man-eating tree? That would be compounding the improbabilities beyond reason.

—*Something knocked this tree over.*

—*Something big. Very big. Very very big.*

—*Our giant. Our dragon. Or whatever our enemy is.*

It could hardly be a bear, for a tree the size of the one which had fallen could have made the keel of a sizeable ship, a keel capable of standing the storm-stress of a major sea. No bear could demolish such.

—*A giant. I'd lay odds to it.*

—*No. Two giants. Minimum.*

For a man had come running from danger and had run straight into death waiting in undergrowth ahead of him. So there were at least two monsters on the loose in the forest. Maybe three.

Sarazin shuddered, remembering the walking rocks which had run amok in the streets of Androlmarphos after the death-stone had destroyed part of the walls of that city. He had toured the ruined city afterwards, had seen the devastation wrought by their strength. Was it rocks, then? Rocks and not giants? If so, then a death-stone must have been used in the neighbourhood to bring the rocks to life.

—*Is it wizards, then?*

Through long acquaintance with Thodric Jarl, Sarazin had learnt at least a little of the Rovac warrior's fear of wizards, those Powers in the World of Events who were not bound by ordinary human limitations.

—*So I still have a choice of enemies. A couple of giants. Or some walking rocks. Or a duo of dragons.*

342

So thinking, Sarazin lay still. Waiting. Listening. He slid a hand to his crotch to harass the lice which were tormenting him. He could have sworn he had successfully deloused himself before setting off from the hunting lodge. But lice spread rapidly.

—*Never mind. Once I'm back safe I'll boil them to death. My own body in boiling water if that's what it takes!*

He waited. Watching. Listening. Thinking.

—*We of the Common People, in symbol of our Revolutionary Ideals, share each with each these our Holy Lice, in token of the pledge of our blood to overthrow tyranny and rhubarb our bullshit, to wank our turnips and cream off our peas.*

—*Gah!*

—*I hope this Common People nonsense ends quick when Fox is king of Chenameg. Or president, or whatever it is. Same difference. Anyway, we'll see.*

Then a dreadful thought occurred to him. What if Fox was dead? Killed by the giant, the dragon, the rock or whatever it was? That would be unendurable. To have regained his father — then to have the man snatched away again.

—*Blood!*

—*What was that!?*

Something big, heavy, tree-crunching clumsy, was smashing its way through the vegetation towards him. He snake-crawled through the undergrowth. Slowly, for twigs snatched at him, roots juddered against his knees, swatches of leaves must be pushed aside. Then he put one fist straight into a patch of nettles, swore, heard the world rupture behind him, got to his feet and fled.

Like a stone hurled from a slingshot Sarazin bolted from the undergrowth to the sunlit clearways of the forest. He ran. Tiring rapidly, for he was running uphill and the slope was steep.

—*Must turn.*

He did turn. Saw what was behind him. A lurching grey

343

creature blotched with orange. A lichen-patched rock? No, some kind of animal. A sausage-shaped body terminating in a gaping mouth, a mouth of sun-white teeth a shark would have envied. Sarazin had plenty of time to observe all this, for the creature had slowed, perhaps because he had halted.

While it had slowed, it was still advancing. How? On legs? It had no legs! It flowed over the ground. But not like a snake, oh no, for such was its weight that the ground quaked beneath it. Length? About that of a sea dragon. Girth? About that of a man's outstretched arms. Weight?

Whatever it weighed, it had muscle to match its bulk, for, having leisured uphill for a bit (getting its breath back?), it began to put on speed again. Sarazin fled in panic. Still uphill, uphill, for to turn might be to die. But his strength was gone. Guts cramping. Breath sobbing. Feet stumbling.

—*Trees clear ahead.*

—*The top of the rise.*

Sarazin, with the top of the slope just a few paces uphill, dug in for a final sprint. He darted between close-packed trees. Sunlight opened up in front of him. He leapt for the sunlight.

'Shit!'

He had jumped over a cliff. He was falling. Arms flailing, he tumbled. Then crunched himself into a ball. Not a moment too soon! For he smashed through the wide-flung branches of a cliff-clinging tree. Still falling!

'Waaaa!'

Skloush!

Water demolished his world.

Half-stunned, Sarazin flailed feebly, and surfaced. Blinked, gasped, thrashed, put his feet down, touched no bottom. Looked left, right, up, down, his eyes everywhere, like a brute beast which fears the immediate theft of its meal.

He was afloat in a deep pool in a miniature valley

with cliffs to left and to right. Atop one of those cliffs was the brute which had so recently chased him through the trees.

— *Jump, then, you bastard. Jump!*

The thing paused, then vanished.

— *Does it know a way down?*

— *Doubtless! Otherwise this would be my lucky day, which it surely isn't.*

Sarazin floundered to the edge of the pool. Sloshed through the shallows. Stumbled to the dry. Big tracks were in the dry. Some blunt. Some clawed. Some inscrutable.

— *Monsters came this way. Men, too.*

Men and beasts. Monstrous beasts which had torn turf, had left fresh scratches on granite. Some hundred paces up the valley, something caught the sun. Metal. An arch of metal. Sarazin stumped towards it, hands meantime slapping at his gear, checking what was there and what was missing.

Sword at hand. Quiver still there. Bow gone. Water bottle torn free. Knife present and correct. Win some, lose some. Now what's with this metal thing?

Sarazin halted a good thirty paces short of the metal arch, not keen to go any closer since it was the focus of all the jumbled tracks which were in evidence in the valley. The tracks all went to or came from that arch. Why? It was as wide as a man's outstretched arms, true, but nothing could go through it, surely, for the way was blocked by a sheet of shimmering metal.

There was a humming in the air.

— *Bees?*

— *Monsters?*

Sarazin dared a glance behind him. Nothing there. He turned back to the arch. He was coming to the opinion that the arch itself — or the marble plinth on which it stood — was making the humming sound. He dared himself forward. Then halted abruptly as someone stepped out of the doorway, stepped right out of the grey shimmering metal.

It was Fox.

His father.

'Fox . . . ?'

Disorientated, Fox looked left, looked right. Stared at Sarazin. Seemed to have trouble focusing. Then saw him, and staggered towards him. Then another man stepped from the arch. A soldier of the National Liberation Front. Wounded, his scalp half torn away.

Then out through the arch crawled a centipede, a green brute nearly too big to get through that Door. Fox and his companion did not hear the monster as it hauled itself into their sunlight.

'Fox!' screamed Sarazin. 'Behind you!'

His father turned. Saw the centipede. Which was gaining on his companion. Who tried to run. But slipped, tripped, fell. With an inarticulate cry, Fox turned. Lurched towards the fallen man. Then collapsed and went face down in the muck.

The centipede loomed over Fox's doomed comrade, who mewled with fear then screamed in unutterable agony as the monster forked into his flesh. The demolition job would surely distract the centipede for a few moments at best. Then it would turn its attention to Fox. Sarazin, sobbing with terror, scuttled towards his father's comatose body.

A dozen paces and he was there.

'Fox! Fox!' said Sarazin urgently.

Slapped his father's face. Shook him. Glanced from shock-pale Fox to the sun-glittering centipede. Which reared upward, blood dripping from its fighting mandibles. It screamed with a sky-rending ululation. Then, dread by dread, hauled itself over the ground towards them.

'You can't have him!' screamed Sarazin.

The scream made the centipede pause. As it wavered, Sarazin made his decision. He would save both their lives. Or they would die together. Sarazin scooped up Fox, slung the man over his shoulder and staggered away towards the pool. Could water save them? It must! It must! How far? Seventy paces?

—*Oh shit, shit, no, no no!*

There was something between them and the water already. A lesser brute than the centipede, but death all the same. A creature the same as the legless hulk which had chased him through the forest before his cliff-jump. Perhaps the self-same brute.

Sarazin dropped his father.

The centipede was nearest, so Sarazin turned to face that threat first. Drew his sword, but could muster no battlecry to match the steel. The weapon-weight was shaky in his hands. He was panting, sobbing, was but a straw's-blow away from collapse.

Smooth, the monster was moving smoothly now, perfectly articulated, graceful even. It closed the distance. And Sarazin struck. Delivering a blow which missed, overbalancing him. The point of his sword dug deep into the turf. He hauled it out, glanced up at the brute, which was striking—

'Gah!'

Sarazin swung.

One of the monster's fighting mandibles clipped the sword. Threw it into the air. Where it spun, tumbled in the sun, and flashed into intolerable fire. And the centipede screamed, writhed, thrashed upward, blasted by that fire. Sarazin flung himself to the ground, covering his father with his body as heat washed over them.

Though the bulk of the centipede protected them from the full fury of the flame-wrath, the heat was nearly unbearable. The ground shook as the centipede, mad with pain, beat its body against the ground. Whence came such flame?

—*From dragons?*

Sarazin lifted his head a fraction. The centipede had ceased its head-banging, and was writhing in helpless agony. Dying. Lurid flames danced over its body, purple and red, gold and amber. The other monster? The hulk of its body lay but twenty paces away. From its corpse, a heavy smoke ascended to heaven.

'Fox?' said Sarazin, softly.

His father was unconscious.

So who was that talking?

Someone was, for he could hear voices: not ghost-soft like the hallucinations which sometimes muttered the odd word to him during a sleepless night of sentry duty. No — these were the harsh, curt voices of the workaday world. Of men in a very big hurry. Foreign voices speaking an angry language which clattered brusquely through the sunlight.

Sarazin got to his knees, then to his feet. Sidestepped clear of the centipede and saw a bustle of people gathered around the archway, with more joining them every moment. People were simply stepping out from the shimmering grey screen of metal, as had Fox and his comrade.

One pointed at Sarazin and shouted.

Sarazin, temporarily unable to speak, flung his hands wide apart to show he was unarmed. At that moment, there was an ominous roar from one of the clifftops. Turning, Sarazin half-saw a monster there, a long-legged thing obscenely fashioned. Then one of the strangers gathered by the steel arch lifted his hand and spoke a Word.

Fire flashed from hand to cliff.

Clifftop, clifftop trees and monster exploded into flame. The monster thrashed through the air, burning, falling, tumbling. Hit the ground. Stood up, staggered, lurched towards them, fire seething from its flesh. Another Word. Another blast of fire. And the monster dropped, most definitely dead.

Carbonised.

—*Wizard work.*

—*So these are wizards.*

Some of them were, at any rate. But as they came striding down the valley — in Sarazin's direction! — he saw most of them were spearsmen dressed in sky-blue uniforms, which had evidently been designed for ceremonial display, but were now severely battle-stained. These soldiers were heavily burdened with packs, and some led donkeys which laboured under weights still greater.

As they drew level with Sarazin, one of the wizards halted by Sarazin.

'Galish?' said the wizard.

'I speak it,' said Sarazin.

'Death.'

'This is a threat?' said Sarazin. 'Or a promise?'

'Death comes. Leave to live.'

With that, the wizard strode away in the company of the sky-blue soldiers. When the last of them had gone by, Sarazin turned back to Fox, who had recovered consciousness and was sitting up looking at them.

'Got any water?' said Fox.

His voice a husk. Voice of a man uncertain of his own existence. Hurt. Frightened. Shocked.

'Sorry, no,' said Sarazin.

Feeling his own need. Sweat hot on his forehead. Stinging in his eyes. Throat parched. Limbs shaking.

'There's water close, though,' said Sarazin. 'Muddy, but that's no worry. I'll get some for you.'

'Good,' said Fox, making an effort to play the manful leader. 'We'll drink then be gone. That Door opens to disaster. More of the Swarms may dare their way into Chenameg if we linger.'

Thus spoke Fox. But, by the time Sarazin had returned with water, Fox had fainted again. And it was some time before he was fit to travel.

349

CHAPTER FIFTY-ONE

All of the groups which had been involved in the night navigation exercise had been attacked in the forests by monsters of the Swarms. There were few survivors. However, Sarazin, Fox, and a dozen other exhausted men eventually straggled back to headquarters with tales of death and horror. Fox, the only survivor who had dared the Door, was infuriatingly vague about it.

Drake Douay, the thief who had stolen Sarazin's bard, had told stories of Doors in Penvash and elsewhere. Sarazin now deeply regretted disbelieving those stories. If he had believed, he might have paid attention to what he was being told. What had the pirate said of the management of such Doors? The details escaped his memory.

'This Door,' said Sarazin, when all at the hunting lodge were discussing the disaster in common conference, 'I heard someone talk of such. You know who I'm talking about, Jarl. The man Douay. What did he say about Doors?'

'That he went through such,' said Jarl. 'That's all I remember. Do we know where this one goes? Fox?'

'It goes from one place to another,' said Fox.

'Like a dog pissing,' said Glambrax.

'Shut up, you!' said Sarazin. Then, to his father: 'What places were these? Where might they be?'

'I've no idea,' said Fox.

'Then what did you see?' said Sarazin.

'Through this Door,' said Fox, 'I saw tree and stone, rock and sky, earth and water.'

'This was all . . . real?' said Lod, who had not seen the Door.

'If illusion, then illusion is life,' said Fox. 'Do you think our monsters mere nightmare? They killed!'

Lod shook his head.

'It was the Door I doubted,' said he, 'for I've never heard of such. But your monsters, which must surely be creatures of the Swarms, are famous in Chenameg since the eldest sons of our kings are bound by tradition to quest as heroes to the lands south of Drangsturm.'

'So this Door, then,' said a dark-bearded soldier, 'must open to the terror-lands of the Deep South.'

'For all we know,' said another warrior, 'it could open to another world entirely.'

'Swarms are creatures of our world,' argued a third. 'Besides, young Sarazin here spoke to a wizard in Galish. The Door opens to a place of wizards beyond Drangsturm.'

'Not necessarily,' argued a fourth. 'It could be a gateway through time, to a past or a future where the Swarms rule all of Argan.'

'No—'

'But—'

'I say—'

'Silence!' said Fox, thumping his fist on a table. As his men hushed, he looked from one to another. Red-eyed. Exhausted. He marshalled words with care, then spoke. 'Whatever the nature of this Door, wherever it goes, without doubt creatures of the Swarms come through it.'

Slowly, compensating for fatigue with an exaggerated precision, he detailed their task. They must shut the Door. How? He had dared the Door himself yet knew of no way to close it. So help must be sought, either to seal the Door or to guard it with gates and walls, lest monsters invade all Chenameg and the lands beyond.

'We lack the numbers to defeat such brutes,' said Fox. 'They have killed some of our best already. We should withdraw from our headquarters, now, today, lest we wake tomorrow to find ourselves besieged by nightmare.'

He proposed sending embassies to Shin, Selzirk and the Rice Empire to sound the warning. Sarazin was about to volunteer to journey to Voice when Fox said:

'I myself will warn the Rice Empire. I have the confidence of Lord Regan, who will believe me where he might not believe others. Jarl will go with me.'

'Then I will risk the wrath of Tarkal in Shin,' said Lod. 'As I have said, we know much of the Swarms here in Chenameg. Tarkal will doubt, but he will check before he disputes.'

Silence.

Sarazin realised Fox and Lod were both looking at him.

'Oh well,' said Sarazin, 'I suppose that leaves me with Selzirk. I mean, I'm the logical choice. Okay, I'll go.'

He was glad now that he had carefully arranged things so that the people of Selzirk would think he had been kidnapped. That limited the amount of explaining he would have to do on his return. He could simply say his kidnappers had dragged him to Chenameg, that he had been held prisoner, had broken loose, had staggered through the forest — and discovered the Door!

A thin tale.

But no more incredible than the truth.

—*Aye. There's the rub. Will anyone believe me? They must! Otherwise Chenameg is finished. The Harvest Plains will fall to the Swarms next. Then all of Argan!*

—*But has Selzirk strength sufficient to close or secure such a Door?*

Could the death-stone destroy the Door? Perhaps. But could Morgan Hearst be persuaded to make the attempt? If Hearst refused to believe the tale Sarazin told, what then?

—*Then we are doomed.*

But . . . yes, of course! There were transcripts of Drake Douay's interrogation in Selzirk. Douay had known the secret of commanding Doors. Given that knowledge,

Sarazin might be able to close the Door in Chenameg on his own, even if nobody in Selzirk believed his grim tidings.

Later that day, Sarazin was in a barn packing for his journey to Selzirk when Glambrax came to him.

'Out of my way, mannikin!' said Sarazin. 'I'm busy.'

'Aha!' said Glambrax. 'But not too busy to satisfy your heart's desire!'

'You mean, to cut out your liver and hack off your head?' said Sarazin. 'Why, I can do that any day. Scram!'

Instead of fleeing, Glambrax grinned and produced a rope of woven bark which was knotted round a glittering silver ring (still attached to its silver chain) and an ornamental bottle of leaf-green jade.

'Give me that!' said Sarazin, shocked, startled, snatching for the enchanted treasure.

But Glambrax ducked away, pocketed the valuables, dodged a blow from Sarazin and sprinted outside. There, Jarl, Fox and Lod were conferring over a map of Argan which Lod had drawn with a stick in a patch of dirt.

'Stop him!' cried Sarazin.

His father collared Glambrax.

'What do you want with the dwarf?' said Fox.

Sarazin hesitated. He could reveal all. He could have the ring of invisibility and the dragon-bottle taken from Glambrax. But then the secret would be out. And Jarl and Fox would doubtless want to use his magic dragons to destroy the Door.

But they were his, his, his alone! Special treasures given to him by the druid all those many years ago. They were his weapon of last resort in his campaign to win himself an empire. He would not squander such simply to close a Door. Since pirate scum like Douay had mastered Doors, Sarazin knew he could do as much himself without help from magic dragons. Once he knew the secret.

'I wanted,' said Sarazin, 'merely to get some work out of this mannikin.'

'Then take him,' said Fox, in good humour, giving Glambrax a shove which sent him staggering towards Sarazin.

As Sarazin grabbed for the dwarf, Glambrax jinked, evaded him, and sprinted back to the barn. Sarazin stalked him with murder clearly written on his face. By the time Sarazin gained the barn, Glambrax had nimbled into the rafters and was sitting there out of reach, kicking his heels.

'Come down,' said Sarazin, picking up a pitchfork. 'Down, mischief! Or it will go ill with you.'

Glambrax grinned, then ran along a rafter to a little bat-high window. He could jump and be gone in a moment. Sarazin sighed, and threw down the pitchfork.

'What do you want?' said Sarazin.

'Your oath,' said Glambrax.

'To do what?' said Sarazin. 'To buy you the favours of six dogs a day? Or what?'

'To ask no questions,' said Glambrax, grinning.

'Don't be ridiculous!' said Sarazin, speaking with explosive force. 'I have to know what happened! It's my right. You — you buggered my chances, you filthy piece of cheese-shit! I could have won, could have ruled, could have conquered. But you — you—'

Sarazin was so angry that words failed him.

'But it wasn't me!' protested Glambrax.

'What do you mean, it wasn't you?' said Sarazin. 'You were the thief! You were the one who ruined my conspiracy!'

'No, no,' said Glambrax, with a rare display of urgency. 'The thieves came before me. They took your bard, your book, your precious papers, ah, all of it, all of it.'

Sarazin, in reply, picked up a hardened piece of dung and hurled it at the dwarf. It hit the rafter below Glambrax's feet and exploded into pieces.

'You were the thief!' said Sarazin. 'You and Douay,

354

in league together! You stole the magic, he stole the bard!'

'Not so, not so,' protested Glambrax. 'There were other thieves. They took your stuff then gave me a chance to take more.'

'You admit it!' said Sarazin. 'You thieved my magic!'

'They warned me Plovey was coming,' said Glambrax. 'If I hadn't taken it, then Plovey would have.'

'You could have told me!' said Sarazin. 'I was in conference with my mother. You could have warned me.'

'But I was made to swear not to,' said Glambrax. 'I was made to swear many things, oh yes, not to warn you, never to give you the names—'

'The names?'

'The names of those who took your bard, your book, your papers. I swore I would not. Thus you must swear to ask me no questions.'

Sarazin stared at Glambrax. Could he tempt the dwarf within pitchfork range? If so, then he would kill him!

Then Fox came into the barn.

'Are you ready to go?' said Fox. 'Your escort is nearly ready.'

'Almost,' said Sarazin.

Then embraced his father, who slapped him on the back and called him a man. Then left to supervise other activities. Whereupon Sarazin turned to Glambrax and said, with venom:

'All right then. I swear. I'll not ask you questions. I'll not harm you, either. Not for this. But if you step out of line again, I'll — I'll — I'll stuff your guts with biting vermin then broil you alive.'

Glambrax feigned fear, then laughed, and dropped both ring and bottle to Sarazin. Who, swearing softly to himself, tore those items free from the rope of bark. He put the ring's chain round his neck and pocketed the bottle. Then Glambrax produced the magic green candle and tossed it to Sarazin.

Who finished packing then went outside, meaning to

seek out the escort which was to accompany him to the border of Chenameg. Glambrax jumped down from the rafter and came jog-jog-jogging up behind him.

'M-m-mathter, m-mathter,' said Glambrax, faking a lisp and a stutter simultaneously, 'd-d-don't leaf us, don't leaf us.'

'Nara zabara jok!' said Sarazin, using the crudest Galish he knew.

Whereupon Glambrax, giggling, skipped in front of him, dared his boot, laughed when it missed, then started skipping backwards, keeping just out of range of Sarazin's wrath.

'I was very good, you know,' said Glambrax. 'I didn't meddle with ring or bottle, though I was tempted, tempted, oh, you can't imagine the temptation.'

'It's well that you resisted it,' said Sarazin, 'for this magic would have been your death if you'd tampered with it. It kills dwarves and mutants, and you're both!'

'Will it kill monsters, too, if we meet such on our journey?' said Glambrax.

'Our journey?' said Sarazin. 'No, my journey. You're staying here. The last thing I need right now is a delinquent ankle-biter scuffling around at my heels.'

'You'll die without me,' said Glambrax.

'That's all right,' said Sarazin, with unfeigned non-chalance.

And Glambrax protested no more, for their colloquy had brought them in sight of the escort.

Shortly, Sarazin set out — without Glambrax! He had an escort of a dozen men to accompany him through the forest, and he had a string of four horses. Once they reached the border of Chenameg then Sarazin, with the forest's dangers behind him, would ride for Selzirk alone, with all possible speed.

Many dangers lay ahead. But surely nothing could defeat Sean Sarazin. Not now that he had recovered his magic.

His anger was already fading, and he was beginning to experience something close to joy. The power, the power! It was his! Again! And, this time, he would not lose it. His implements of power would never again leave him. He would keep them with him always.

Sarazin took his leave of Fox, Lod, Jarl and several soldiers he had come to know well during his sojourn in Chenameg, then swung up into the saddle, and, singing a snatch of a hunting song, rode forth into the future.

CHAPTER FIFTY-TWO

One bloodshot dawn some long days later, Sean Sarazin sighted Selzirk's towers in the distance. Surely he would reach the city by noon. Then he would have news of all the world's affairs. He had spoken to nobody on his frantic journey, fearing recognition and arrest by some petty bureaucrat.

—*In the city I'll find men who will believe me.*

Or would he?

His tale was fantastic, like something out of legend. A tale of wizards and Doors, of fire-magic, of desperate danger in forested uplands, of combat with gigantic monsters. Sarazin had uncomfortable memories of his utter disbelief of similar stories told under torture by the pirate Drake Douay.

—*But they must believe me. Selzirk itself is in danger!*

It was then that he remembered the prophecy. Long ago he had dismissed it. Yet — perhaps he had been a fool to do so. For, after all, the prophecy fitted his life in ways which could scarcely be explained by coincidence.

—*It might be true. It might be!*

Was this then the time for the prophecy to be fulfilled?

With a sense of elation, he realised it quite possibly was. The fools in Selzirk who were likely to disbelieve him: those were doubtless the wicked and witless men he must overcome to save the city.

—But what of Fox?

Sarazin was dismayed when he remembered the fate of Fox, which was to die.

—To be killed. By me!

Sarazin knew, truly, he had no wish to murder his father.

—But it is written! It is fated through prophecy! So how can I help it? Yet Fox is far from Selzirk. So perhaps that's how I murdered him. By letting him dare the leagues to Voice. Perhaps he's dead already.

But Sarazin could not bear the thought of Fox dying. Fox: the one person in the world who had accepted him absolutely. Who had never tried to trick him, use him, manipulate him, exploit him. His father, his one and only.

—Perhaps Fox did die. When I hacked him open at Shin. It is said men sometimes die, leave their bodies, then return a little later to take up life once more. It is said.

—It could be true.

Sarazin, weary unto death, struggled as best he could with the logic of prophecy, finally persuading himself that prophecy had indeed already been fulfilled as far as Fox was concerned, since he had for so long counted Fox as one of the dead.

—Alternatively . . . since Bizzie is such a wanton wench, perhaps Fox is not the father of my flesh at all. Perhaps some other fathered me. Maybe I've killed such a flesh-father already, in Tyte perhaps, or elsewhere. Or am to kill him, slaying him without ever knowing his identity.

That was possible.

But, the more Sarazin thought about it, the less he liked the idea. He wanted a true father, a real father, not a half-father.

358

—Fox is my father. My one and only. And he will not die! He must not!

So thought Sarazin, and spurred the last of his four horses. When the nag collapsed under him and died a league short of the city, he started walking. But before he reached the city gates he was overtaken by a rider from the east. It was Glambrax, perched atop a pony stolen from the National Liberation Front.

'You,' said Sarazin wearily, without evidencing any surprise.

He knew he had been a fool to think he could rid himself of Glambrax so easily.

'Me,' said the dwarf cheerfully. 'With news! I've talked with villagers en route. I bet you never dared.'

'I'm not free to swap rumours at the beggar gates,' said Sarazin. 'Such is the penalty of fame. Well? Out with it! You're looking uncommonly happy today. So tell! What ails the world?'

'Oh, you'll love this,' said Glambrax, rubbing his hands together. 'Drangsturm has fallen! The Confederation of Wizards has broken apart in war. The Swarms march north. All civilization in Argan is doomed. What a beautiful day!'

'This is no day for jokes,' said Sarazin, too weary to countenance such levity.

'But it's true!' protested Glambrax.

Sarazin punched Glambrax's pony, hoping it would rear and throw the hand-rubbing dwarf. But the poor beast was far too weary. Such was its condition that Sarazin, lest he kill it with his weight, must perforce walk beside it while Glambrax rained the worst of rumour on his head.

Sarazin believed not a word of it. For thousands of years the Confederation of Wizards had guarded Drangsturm, the great flame trench which stretched the length of the isthmus between the Central Ocean and the Inner Waters, preventing the monsters of the Swarms from invading Argan North. Why should things so suddenly change?

But, to Sarazin's shock and horror, they were scarcely within the gates of Selzirk when they met people who confirmed the dwarf's claims.

There were still many people in Selzirk. Some sober, some drunk. Those who were sober were mostly too busy to talk, so Sarazin had to glean information from the drunks. What he learnt set his head spinning.

Drangsturm had indeed been destroyed.

The Confederation of Wizards had indeed broken apart in war.

The monsters of the Swarms were indeed on the march, invading Argan North.

'My mother?' said Sarazin. 'Farfalla, the kingmaker? What of her?'

'Gone,' said a drunk.

'Dead?'

'Not dead. Fled. She ran for the Rice Empire when the Regency charged her with high treason. Flight proves the charge, does it not? Traitorous bitch!'

'A charge of high treason?' said Sarazin. 'On what excuse?'

'Do you not know?' said the drunk. 'She let Morgan Hearst flee the city with the death-stone. It should have been ours, ours, but she let him go!'

Sarazin did not break the man's jaw because he felt more shock than anger. So Morgan Hearst had not made himself ruler of the Harvest Plains. Hearst must have gone to the Confederation of Wizards, then. With the death-stone.

Then Sarazin recalled the terrible anger which Jarl had shown at mention of wizards. On Jarl's arrival in Selzirk he had spoken of a feud of long standing between wizards and Rovac. Later, Jarl had praised the Rovac warrior Elkor Alish for breaking an oath with wizards and seizing the death-stone.

And Morgan Hearst was a man very much like Jarl . . .

Sarazin could see it now. Hearst must have taken the death-stone south to the Confederation of Wizards.

But not to hand it over to that Confederation. Oh no! Hearst must have gone to war with the wizards, pursuing the ancient feud and dooming all Argan in the process . . .

What now?

What should he do?

'Come,' said Glambrax, tugging at Sarazin's sleeve. 'Let's go to your mother's palace.'

'Agreed,' said Sarazin.

At least they could find shelter there. Probably.

So they set off through the streets of Selzirk, and at last reached Farfalla's palace. It had changed. The bridges which had once straddled the encircling flame-moat had been broken down. And a drawbridge sealed the gatehouse keep.

'Open up!' bawled Sarazin. 'Open in the name of the law!'

But, though he shouted until he was hoarse, the lofty walls of the ancient wizard fortress remained silent. Inscrutable. Finally, someone shot at him. They missed, but, fearing more arrows, Sarazin withdrew.

'Somebody in authority, that's what I need,' he said.

'What's wrong with yourself?' said Glambrax. 'You're the king of Selzirk, for all that I know.'

'Listen,' said Sarazin, grabbing the dwarf by the ear and twisting. 'I need memories of the interrogation of Drake Douay. Where should I look.'

'Why do we need such memories?' said Glambrax. 'To close the Door in Chenameg is the least of our problems. The Swarms will come be that Door shut or open.'

'With the world in ruin and the Swarms on the advance, that Door might one day prove our sole route of escape,' said Sarazin.

'But it goes to a place where there are Swarms already!' protested Glambrax.

'No,' said Sarazin. 'It goes to several places. If we can go to a safe place then close the Door behind us . . . that will preserve our lives when all else fails. So . . . use your brain, mannikin! Tell! Who will have memories of Douay's interrogation?'

'Plovey, of course,' said Glambrax, kicking him in the shins and twisting free.

'Right! Of course! Well, let's get moving then! Where does he live?'

'That's your problem,' said Glambrax. 'I'm a dwarf, not a street directory. What do you need his home for, anyway? Go to his offices.'

They went — but found all offices of the Regency empty, their interiors gutted by fire. So they would have to seek Plovey at home, wherever that might be.

'Well,' said Sarazin, wearily , 'I suppose we've got all day.'

CHAPTER FIFTY-THREE

That evening, Sarazin dined with Plovey of the Regency on carp culled from a pool in the courtyard of Plovey's house. They ate by candlelight, consumed a quantity of excellent wine, then got down to business.

'My soul delights in our renewed acquaintance,' said Plovey, dabbing his lips with a napkin. 'But, fair friend, pray tell — what seek you here?'

'Transcripts of the interrogation of Drake Douay,' said Sarazin, urgency harshening his voice as he shook off the languor which had taken possession of him during the meal. 'They're in the palace. I can't get at them. Who has seized the palace?'

'Calm yourself, calm yourself,' said Plovey, manifesting alarm. 'The angers harm the digestion. Some more wine? Come, the night is yet young, and you young with it. Strong in your youth, and handsome with it. There.

Drink. No! Not so hasty. This wine has a bouquet worth savouring for its own sake, even before the liquid itself laps the lips.'

Sarazin sipped the glass which Plovey had freshened, then, with scarcely controlled impatience, said:

'The palace. Who holds it?'

'I've not been that way for several days,' said Plovey. 'I've been supervising the defence of my home against the wicked and the witless. You may have seen gangs of such in the streets — not that they'd touch an inpoverished swordsman like yourself when there's richer game more safely touched.'

Plovey was smiling. Smug with secrets. That phrase he had used: the wicked and the witless. It had come from the prophetic book. Did Plovey come by the words by chance? Or what? An interesting question — and one that Sarazin was determined to ask before the night was through. But other things took priority.

'I need the details of Douay's interrogation,' said Sarazin. 'So I need the relevant transcripts. Or, at least, to know what's in them.'

'Ah!' said Plovey. 'So you've turned archivist. My friend, it will be pure pleasure to assist you in scholarship. Yes — could you indulge your greatest admirer with your reasons for this sudden lust for knowledge? What can you get from Douay now that you didn't get before? You got back your bard, didn't you?'

'Yes,' said Sarazin, who was, as always, wearing the Lost Bard of Untunchilamon around his neck. Though the thing had been damaged by Douay, it still worked: whenever he pleased he could still listen to the great poet Saba Yavendar reciting his Warsong and Winesong in the High Speech of wizards.

'Well then,' said Plovey, 'why bother further with Douay or his history?'

So Sarazin told his long and laborious story.

Concluding thus:

'. . . so I know Drake knew about Doors, and now I

363

have a Door of my own to deal with in the forest of Chenameg. Hence my interest in the interrogation.'

'Why worry about a Door bringing monsters to Chenameg?' said Plovey. 'Sweet silk, the Swarms will conquer all the world soon enough, with or without such a Door.'

So, once more, Sarazin had to explain:

'I see the Door now as a means of escape. If the Swarms truly do conquer, we might be glad of a quick way out of here.'

'That's a thought,' said Plovey.

And, since he had an excellent memory, he told Sarazin what he had learnt from Drake Douay about the mastery of Doors.

'Each Door has a niche in the marble supporting the arch,' said Plovey. 'Place a globe of stars in such a niche. All the Doors of that Circle will then open. Remove the globe and they close. Simple? Simple!'

'My companions who dared the Door saw no such globe,' said Sarazin.

'One sees what one looks for,' said Plovey. 'That, at least, is my experience. I tell you, Sean Sarazin — dare the Door and check the plinth at each station on the Circle. In one niche or another there must be at least one globe of stars, otherwise the Door would not have opened.'

'Describe to me this star-globe,' said Sarazin.

'Green,' said Plovey, toying with a little blue-veined cheese. 'Slippery. Like a frog. Fist-sized yet heavy. Stars glow within. Other than that, dear friend, I know nothing of it. Only that Drake and his comrades had such a globe in Penvash. Some cheese? No? Come! You only live once.'

'All right,' said Sarazin, rat-gnawing on cheese, 'what came of it? The globe, I mean. The one the pirates had.'

'Since pirates are what they are,' answered Plovey, 'naturally they came to blows over it. One of their number then ran off with the treasure, and—'

'Was never seen or heard of again?'

'Precisely. How did you guess?'

'It seems to be the story of our times,' said Sarazin.

'Well then,' said Plovey, 'I've made my decisions already. I believe Selzirk doomed for certain. I leave tomorrow for your Door in Chenameg. If you could help me tonight with detailed directions you can be sure of my welcome on a future meeting.'

'My pleasure,' said Sarazin.

'Then, as a token of my appreciation,' said Plovey, 'I give you my house and everything left in it after I quit the place at dawn tomorrow.'

And Plovey smiled. He was utterly calm. Completely unruffled. Why? Because, all his life, he'd known something dreadful was fated for him and his world. He had endured a sense of impending doom ever since childhood. Now, at last, the worst had happened. Utter and unmitigated disaster. Which had ended the agony of waiting.

Plovey could almost have been called happy.

'So now you know,' said Glambrax, from under the table. 'What now? Do we go with Plovey?'

'No,' said Sarazin. 'We stay here to defend Selzirk.'

'You're crazy,' said Glambrax, banging his head against the underside of the table.

'Not crazy,' said Plovey gently. 'Our dear friend has a prophecy to fulfil. Now is Selzirk's greatest hour, therefore he must defend the city against its enemies.'

There was silence in the room but for the thunk . . . pause . . . thunk of Glambrax's head. And the scrabbling of a rat in the panelling. Sarazin's hands strayed from knife to spoon to meatpick.

'You . . . you knew,' he said. 'Everything. All along. You knew it all.'

'Oh no, dear friend,' said Plovey. 'You underestimate yourself. Despite my best efforts, I found out very little, oh, very little indeed. But I knew you read a certain prophecy in a certain book. Oh yes. Come . . . shall we

365

start work on the map? I should be hard put to find this Door without it.'

'Not till you've told me how much you knew,' said Sarazin. 'And how you came to know it.'

'Ah,' said Plovey, 'Lod told me a little.'

'Lod! Lod worked for you?'

'Lod worked for everyone,' said Plovey. 'Farfalla paid him to be an additional bodyguard to young Sean Sarazin. Oh yes, your mother took good care of you, believe me. Lod was sworn to your defence, thanks to your mother's gold.'

'I never knew,' said Sarazin, appalled by his own ignorance.

'Of course,' said Plovey, smiling, 'Lod also worked for Lord Regan. I didn't know it at the time, but I found out later. Oh, many secrets have come out of the woodwork since the Swarms stormed Drangsturm. People now freely tell secrets they would once have carried to their grave even in the teeth of torture.'

'Lod . . . Lod was Lord Regan's spy?'

'Lord Regan's agent. Lord Regan had many such in Selzirk. Of course, Lod also worked for me.'

'He worked for you?'

'He took my gold,' said Plovey, with another smile, 'and, now and again, gave me just a little information. Not enough to kill Sean Sarazin. Oh no, he didn't want you dead. You were very precious to him. Your life guaranteed him a triple income. But he told me a little, now and then.'

'How about Benthorn?' said Sarazin.

'What do you think?'

'I think he was your creature through and through,' said Sarazin.

'Yet you did business with him.'

'A little, and with great caution,' said Sarazin. 'It did me no harm, did it?'

'You survived,' conceded Plovey.

'And Madam Ix? Madam Sosostris? Mistress Turbothot? How did they fit into the scheme of things?'

'The two fortune-tellers played a double game. They worked for Lord Regan and for me as well. Again — neither of them wanted you dead. They told me enough to earn their pay, but not enough to condemn you. But Mistress Turbothot . . . ah, she was mine. We almost got you, didn't we, darling boy?'

'You were very cunning,' admitted Sarazin. 'But . . . if you wanted me dead, why didn't you just send in assassins? I know it's not traditional, but surely, under the circumstances . . .'

'You were watched, you were guarded, you were a warrior in your own right. You weren't the easiest of targets, darling boy. Besides . . . I am an artist. What's more, two can play at that game. Farfalla had told me as much to my face. Now . . . shall we attend to this map?'

Sarazin stared at Plovey. He needed time to absorb what he had been told. A lot of time. So much had happened, so suddenly. He had learnt that Hearst had not made himself ruler of Selzirk, that it was Hearst who had destroyed Drangsturm, that Farfalla had fled, that Lod had been a spy . . .

'Just one more question,' said Sarazin. 'You raided my quarters. Why?'

'Because I was set up, of course,' said Plovey equably. 'I was told I'd find certain proof of conspiracy which would damn you and your mother both. Instead . . . well, you know the rest.'

'There was in fact proof of conspiracy in my quarters,' said Sarazin. 'Not certain proof, but evidence enough to prove dangerous. Somebody took it before you came. Was it Douay? Or who?'

'That I know not,' said Plovey.

'Jaluba was in my quarters when I left to join my mother in conference,' said Sarazin. 'When I came back, she was gone. Where did she go to? Was she the thief? Was she your spy?'

'Jaluba,' said Plovey, tasting the name. He dabbed his

mouth with a napkin, then said: 'Ah, I remember. Your whore in Voice. Later, a servant of the Sosostris woman. Am I thinking of the right person?'

'You are,' said Sarazin.

'Well,' said Plovey, 'I know nothing of her fate. She was certainly never one of my people, I assure you of that. Now, dear Sarazin, your one question has become three. Have you yet another? Or may we settle to the map?'

'Yes,' said Sarazin. 'We'll work on the map.'

Late at night, the map was finally finished. The next day, Plovey left Selzirk, taking with him servants, slaves, women (some in chains, others not), men at arms and half a dozen relatives. He left his house to Sean Sarazin, as he had promised.

And there Sean Sarazin stayed during the days that followed, with only Glambrax for company. The Swarms drew steadily nearer, and Selzirk steadily emptied as more and more of its people fled. Some hardy souls remained, thinking the Swarms would be delayed by the river.

Then came news that the Swarms were crossing over one of the dams to the east, and were building a bridge to span the river to the south. Then nearly all of the people who had stayed in the city ran for their lives.

But a few diehards stayed on, Sarazin and Glambrax among them.

CHAPTER FIFTY-FOUR

Sarazin polished his ring of invisibility till its silver shone in the sun. He anointed his jade-green dragon-bearing bottle with oil and buffed it up. He sharpened his sword. He did some stretching exercises to free up his muscles.

He was ready for the greatest challenge of his life: to save Selzirk from the Swarms, which were at the gates of the city and were expected to break through those gates before sundown.

'I, Sean Kelebes Sarazin, known to the world of war as Watashi, dedicate this day to the salvation of Selzirk.'

So said Sarazin, who was safe from Glambrax's mockery since the hyperactive dwarf had been locked away in the highest room of Plovey's house.

Stern in resolution, he stepped to the street. And was not overly surprised when Glambrax fell in beside him. He was, neverthelss, curious.

'How did you get out?'

'Out?' said Glambrax. 'Out of what? I got from my mother's womb, I remember, by means of being dragged. Or is it something else you're interested in?'

'Never mind,' said Sarazin. 'Never mind.'

High noon in Selzirk. Sarazin released his ring of invisibility from its chain and put it in a pocket where it would be ready for instant use. If his dragons failed to defeat the Swarms, he might need that ring to survive.

The Swarms were without the gates, and those gates were groaning under the onslaught of the monsters. Some of the diehards who had remained in the city had sworn to stand and fight — but now they were turning and running.

'Hold fast!' cried Sarazin. 'I have magic here! Magic with which to save the city, the world.'

But all the people ran, and he was left alone. He was piqued to think there would be no witnesses to his heroism. Would that spoil the prophecy? And, even in the confusion of the moment, he still found time to wonder how his father's death came into it.

—But I decided that already, didn't I? He died in Shin. Didn't he? He was dead enough as far as I was concerned, *even though he lived. So that satisfies the prophecy. Doesn't it? Please?*

—But what if the prophecy's a lie anyway. Could it be? Do I die here, today?

—Impossible.

For the magical snuff bottle in his left hand was the one the druid had given to him, the one which held a dread of dragons totally obedient to his command.

—But they will live only briefly. That's what the druid said. Will briefly be long enough?

—It must be!

Wood graunched and ruptured. The gates shattered. Through the wreckage came a tunneller, a creature of the Swarms built like a sharp-pointed obelisk. Hundreds of multi-purpose limbs jutted from its body in every direction. Those which happened to be in contact with the ground were presently being used as its feet.

The tunneller quested. Blindly. This way. That.

Sarazin found himself trembling.

—The bottle, man. The bottle!

His fingers stumbled over the polished jade. Grasped. Tugged. The top would not come out!

'Stuck!' he wailed.

A quick-limbed blue ant the size of a calf slipped past the tunneller and advanced on Sarazin, fighting mandibles clicking — 'snick snick snick!' — like castrating scissors from an Oedipal nightmare.

Then the top came — sclop! — out of the bottle. And up roared the dragons, billowing into the air with a rush of fumes and fury, filling the air with the smells of cinnamon and low-grade sulphur. Their wing-clap fury filled the sky. The creatures of the Swarms shrank back, retreating from the dragons.

Yes, there were nine of them.

And nine dragons made an army. It could not be doubted. They were the most dragonish dragons ever seen, fire-winged creatures each a hundred paces from head to tail, and they were his, they were his alone, so strong, so proud, so beautiful that Sarazin wanted to weep and laugh at the same time.

'Well,' said Glambrax, resolutely unimpressed. 'Don't just stand there gaping. Command them.'

The dragons, having flaunted their fury in the skies above, settled to the rooftops. The largest alighted on the battlewall above the shattered gate. Sarazin glanced at the Swarms, which were hesitating in the gateway, then said in a battlefield voice:

'I am Sean Kelebes Sarazin, named in war as Watashi. I stand before you as lord of Selzirk, as prince of the Harvest Plains, as saviour of my people, fulfiller of prophecy, warlord and dragonmaster. Acknowledge my rule!'

The dragon on the battlewall, the largest and most lordly of them all, answered:

'I am the dragon Untunchilamon. Verily, thou art lord of my will. What is thy command, my master?'

Sarazin, face flushed with the heat of the dragon's breath, said:

'Destroy the Swarms and save Selzirk.'

'To hear is to obey,' said Untunchilamon.

Forthwith, all nine dragons launched themselves into an all-out attack on the Swarms. Roaring, dragons grappled with monsters.

But—

To Sarazin's horror, before his very eyes the dragons were torn apart. Their forms shuddered, smoked, decayed to clouds of sulphurous fire, then disintegrated altogether and were blown away on the breeze.

'Your dragons, you see,' said Glambrax, talking sober sense for once, 'were no more than illusion. Beautiful illusion, extravagant illusion — but illusion for all that.'

'I see,' said Sarazin.

Speaking as one dazed.

He realised now that his dragons had been but a form of fireworks. Most beautiful and intelligent of fireworks, capable of speech, and, perhaps — however briefly — of thought. But fireworks for all that. Beautiful, transitory — and ultimately useless.

'Now, my master, lord of my will,' said Glambrax. 'What is your command?' Then, as Sarazin made no reply, the dwarf tugged sharply at his sleeve, and said again, urgently: 'Shall we run?'

'Yes,' said Sarazin, as if waking from a dream. 'Yes, I suppose we must.'

And, as a bevy of blue ants advanced on them, they did indeed run. They sprinted, in fact. Sarazin was fast enough — but Glambrax was not. One of the ants gained on him, seized him.

'Sarazin!' he squealed.

Sarazin turned, saw, swore. Jammed the ring of invisibility on to his finger. Drew his vorpal blade. Strode back and hewed the head from the nearest blue ant. Then grabbed Glambrax and hauled him away. As Sarazin grabbed him, Glambrax too became invisible to the monsters of the Swarms.

The ring was hot on Sarazin's finger. Getting hotter. It hurt, it hurt! It burnt! As they rounded a corner, Sarazin dropped Glambrax then wrenched the ring from his finger. Threw it to the ground. Where it burst into white fire. With sun-bright flames it consumed itself, then was gone, leaving only an ugly rust-red scar on the stonework of the street to show where it had been.

Sarazin watched the immolation of his hopes and dreams from the nearest doorway. Then one of the monsters of the Swarms edged round the corner. A small black and tan dog stood in the middle of the street barking furiously at it. A moment later the dog was trashed to a raggage of blood and bone.

Sarazin slammed the door, bolted it, and joined Glambrax on a quick retreat to the cellar.

CHAPTER FIFTY-FIVE

They dwelt in cellars and sewers, in stormdrains and rat-squeeze underpassages, in crypts and boltholes, in shadow and darkness. The cold rains washed the sewers clean. The Velvet River itself ran cleaner than ever before in living memory.

—What were we then? A pollution on the face of the earth?

—I know not. But know our destiny now. To be rats to our lords, the Swarms.

That was what Sarazin told himself. But he believed it not. Surely some hero would come, some force, some power, to liberate Selzirk from the Swarms. Sometimes, he toyed with his magic green candle, the last piece of magic left to him. Did that perchance have the power to save Selzirk?

The trouble was, he had not the slightest idea what the candle could do. The druid who had given it to him had not known. It might prove dangerous rather than helpful.

—I'd best not use this until I know what it does. Or until my life's so deep in danger that there's no other way out.

Thus thought Sarazin.

In those dismal days, it was some consolation to him that at least his mother's palace still stood fast against the monsters. He approached, sometimes, at night. Flame wrathed up from the moat, no longer quiescent but ferociously alive. Sometimes he saw figures on the battlements. Long after midnight, strange lights sometimes writhed around one of the eight towers which had long been sealed against humankind.

—The wizards have reclaimed their own.

Thus thought Sarazin, and knew it for truth.

He could see, now, what had happened. When the Swarms had invaded Argan North, the wizards by Drangsturm had fled by any means available. Some had come to Selzirk and reclaimed the ancient wizard fortress which had been the foundation of Farfalla's palace.

—Perhaps those who guard the walls are the same wizards who came through that Door in Chenameg.

That would explain much: Drangsturm fell; the wizards fled through a Door north of Drangsturm; the Swarms pursued them through that Door.

—Should I myself try that Door? Is there any hope of safety through such?

Sarazin played with the question, but made no serious attempt to answer it, for he still hoped for Selzirk to be saved, liberated, rescued.

Since the Swarms were more active by day than by night, Sarazin and Glambrax slept through most of the day, waking each evening to begin their activities. On one such evening, they were up in a belfry spying on the Swarms as those monsters settled to take their rest, and planning a raid on a warehouse where they hoped to find something decent to eat.

That was the evening that they saw a mountain moving in the distance, crossing the Harvest Plains like something out of nightmare. Then Sarazin truly knew his hopes for rescue were futile. The world had gone mad. When mountains take to walking, what next? Will the sky take to falling?

'Tonight,' he said to Glambrax, 'we leave the city.'

'To go where?' said Glambrax.

'To Chenameg,' said Sarazin. 'To the Door.'

CHAPTER FIFTY-SIX

After enduring many hazards — the worst of which were in human form — Sean Sarazin and Glambrax finally reached the hunting lodge which had been the headquarters of the guerrillas who had fought under the command of Fox in the highlands of Chenameg South. They found it burnt to the ground, together with all its outbuildings. Nearby, they found a man tied to a tree, but, as he had died of starvation or exposure some days previously, he proved less than informative.

'At least nothing's gnawed the corpse,' said Sarazin. 'That proves there's no monsters hereabouts.'

'Or else,' said Glambrax, grinning, 'that their taste is for fresh meat only.'

'We'll see,' said Sarazin, somewhat uneasily.

And, without further ado, set off for the Door where he had once almost met his death in a confrontation with the Swarms. He had trouble finding the place. In company with Glambrax, he spent three days trekking back and forth through the hills, searching for the deep-cut valley where he had dared his sword against a gigantic green centipede.

They spent the nights in the trees for fear of monsters, and, in consequence, were ragged with lack of sleep by the time they finally found the valley. Fortunately, there were no live monsters in evidence, though the tattered remains of a giant centipede and of one lesser beast showed Sarazin he had not imagined the brutes.

The Door was there, too.

The steel archway, wide as a man's outstretched arms,

still stood on the marble plinth. However, it no longer hummed, and was no longer filled with shimmering grey. Instead, Sarazin could look through the arch to grass and sky.

Glambrax scrambled on to the plinth, hopped towards the arch, then jumped right through. But he did not disappear into another world or another time. Instead, he landed on the marble of the plinth, scarcely half a pace from where he had started. The Door was not working. It was nothing more than a hoop of cold metal stuck in some cold stone.

'Piss on it!' said Sarazin in frustration.

As Glambrax suited actions to his words, Sarazin searched for the niche said to be set in the plinth. He found such a niche, but it was innocent of any star-globe. Sarazin sat on a rock, idly tossing a stone from one hand to the other, pretending he was thinking.

'What now?' said Glambrax.

'What do you suggest?' said Sarazin.

'A night at the theatre, a couple of good ales, then we can catch a dog and rape it.'

As Glambrax grabbed hold of a virginal stone and began to demonstrate his dog-raping technique, Sarazin sighed, and started to think in earnest. There was no sign of any recent intrusion into the valley. Green growth had repaired the blast damage where wizards had used flame against the Swarms. There were no fresh tracks. The Door, he suspected, had been shut for quite some time.

'Do you want to use my rock?' said Glambrax. 'I've broken it in for you.'

'I want,' said Sarazin, 'to start building a house.'

'Whatever for? We're not going to stay here, are we?'

'Got any better ideas?'

'Hok,' said Glambrax. 'Castle X-n'dix.'

'Dunderhead!' said Sarazin. 'It's half a thousand leagues from here to Hok. The full width of the Harvest Plains lies between us and it.'

'Not so,' said Glambrax. 'Hok is but two hundred leagues distant.'

'What a happy little optimist!' said Sarazin. 'I'll split the difference. We'll say it's 350 leagues away. That's 35 marches. Besides, we've no more food, and my boots are finished as it is. This Door may open tomorrow, then we can go through to — to—'

'To meet our ancestors,' said Glambrax, smirking.

'You'll never meet yours,' retorted Sarazin. 'They'd flee from the disgrace on the instant.'

In the end, Sarazin's will prevailed: they would stay. And wait. Hoping that the Door would finally open.

Sarazin's plan was to build a house and live off the land. Erecting a shack proved easy enough, but land-living was a tougher proposition. Then Glambrax confessed to knowing the location of a couple of supply dumps back near the hunting lodge. A raid on those dumps uncovered great quantities of mouldering rice.

Bit by bit, they carried the rice back to the Door.

And ate, and slept, and ate again — and waited.

After many days of eking out a miserable existence by the Door, Sarazin and Glambrax were flushed out of the valley by a keflo, one of the monsters of the Swarms. They eluded it — just! — then narrowly escaped death in the form of another gigantic green centipede.

Clearly, the Swarms had pushed into Chenameg from the Harvest Plains, and were now in the Kingdom in quantity. Sarazin and Glambrax escaped south into rough-torn mountain heights where the Swarms could not venture.

They now had a choice.

First, to stay put and starve in the barrens above the treeline, where a hunter could not be guaranteed success even if the quarry was earthworms.

Alternatively, to march east of south, descending into the desolation of the Marabin Erg then daring a march to the shores of the Sponge Sea. But the Marabin Erg was a man-destroying desert with a fearsome reputation, and the Sponge Sea itself was but a name from legend.

Or . . .

Sarazin recalled the interrogation of Atsimo Andranovory, Erhed, and others. On deserting the quest hero Morgan Hastsword Hearst in the dragonlands near the Araconch Waters, Andranovory and his companions had eventually found their way down the Velvet River which, after flowing through the Manaray Gorge, entered the Kingdom at the Gates of Chenameg — thereafter running westward down to the Harvest Plains and the waters of the Central Ocean.

'This is what we do,' said Sarazin to Glambrax. 'We march widdershins through the mountains till we come to the Manaray Gorge. We follow the Velvet River east into the interior, then dare a passage across the dragonlands till we come to Brine.'

'Then?' said Glambrax.

'We hope for a ship to Ashmolea,' said Sarazin. 'There's no hope left for Argan.'

'Gah!' said Glambrax.

The dwarf was in a bad temper, which did not improve when the violence of the mountain upthrusts forced them to descend once more to the lowlands of Chenameg to dare the danger of the Swarms and seek passage through the wilderness to the Gates of Chenameg. Such were the difficulties of their journey that it was early summer before they finally drew near those Gates.

CHAPTER FIFTY-SEVEN

Gates of Chenameg: western end of Manaray Gorge where Velvet River issues into Chenameg.

*   *   *

Sarazin expected no hindrance to his projected journey up the Velvet River to the Araconch Waters. But, on drawing near the Manaray Gorge, he found hordes of refugees camped at the Gates of Chenameg. Many were newcomers like himself, driven east by encroaching monsters.

The Velvet River, pouring from the Manaray Gorge in a turbulent torrent, could not be ascended — except by salmon. Precipitous cliffs forbade escape to the east but by one narrow path clinging to the southern side of the gorge. The Gates were heavily fortified, and the Lord of the Gates taxed all who used that path.

Sarazin's first impressions were:

Mud, stench and noise.

Mud from unpaved ground trampled by thousands. Stench from sewage unburied. Noise from pranking children, wailing babies, howling dogs, ranting roosters. Everywhere Sarazin looked there was something to offend his sensibilities.

'Why waste our efforts feeding dogs when the world slips to disaster?' said he.

'Because we in turn on dogs may feed,' said Glambrax. 'Look!'

Indeed, at a nearby stall dead dogs were hung up for sale, while others, their hind legs broken so they could not escape, waited for purchase and slaughter.

Other uncouth meats were on sale. Rats, mice, carrion crows, toads, frogs, snails, worms. And stranger things, such as lumps of flesh of phosphorescent blue. Hard jelly tinged with green. Thin sheets of pliable, transluscent red flecked with gold. To his relief, Sarazin saw one could also buy fish.

On enquiry, he found the alien meats he had failed to identify were the flesh of monsters of the Swarms. Men hunted such in highly organised bands of two or three hundred, armed not just with spears and crossbows

379

but also with powerful arbalests originally designed for siege warfare.

'So the Swarms can be fought,' said Sarazin with relief.

'That is scarcely news,' said a stranger. 'For the last three thousand years and more the Landguard have defended the Far South against any monsters from the Deep which fluked a passage past Drangsturm.'

'But now we know the secret of this combat too,' said Sarazin.

'There is no secret, unless you call weight of numbers a secret. A crossbow well-handled can bring down an elephant, so it is no surprise that stray monsters fall to our companies. But when the odds are reversed, when the Swarms come east in their thousands, then we must leave or die.'

'Why linger then?' said Sarazin.

'Why not?' said the stranger. 'The days are no longer in Brine, the sky no more blue in Ashmolea. I work as a hunter in Karendor's company. It won't last forever, but it's a good life while it lasts.'

'Then — you're one of these who hunt against the Swarms?'

'Indeed. Would you care to join us? We're always looking for good men.'

'I'll think about it,' said Sarazin.

'You do that. You'll find us in the stockade downriver from this — this mud. You can't miss it. The stockade's the size of a castle, a huge wall of earth, logs and stones, with the head of a green as a trophy over the gate.'

'A green?' said Sarazin.

'A green centipede,' said the stranger. 'Come, man — you have the look of a soldier. Why hesitate? Join us today. We'd find work for your dwarf as well. Smoking meat and such.'

'I am but newly arrived,' said Sarazin, 'and there are some people I would like to look for first. But if I find them not, you may see me at your door tomorrow.'

Then he parted company with the stranger and explored

the refugee camp further. But saw not a single face he knew. He asked after friends, acquaintances — even enemies. Fox? Farfalla? Lod? Lord Regan? Jaluba? Thodric Jarl? Amantha? Benthorn? Plovey? Tarkal of Chenameg? The quest hero Morgan Hastsword Hearst? The wizard Miphon? Blackwood of Estar? Madam Sosostris?

He heard rumours of some of these, but the rumours were contradictory, so he despaired of learning the truth. Tired and hungry, he considered his options. He must find employment soon, or starve. In this camp, food could only be bought for gold or silver, and he had neither.

At last, late that afternoon, Sarazin decided to present himself to the lord of the Gates. What could he offer such a lord? Why, his sword and his service, of course. He was a trained soldier, an experienced army commander, a veteran of battle. Perhaps, too, he could give the man his bard. It would be a pity to part with such a treasure, but the gift might sweeten the audience should the lord of the Gates prove hostile.

So thinking, Sarazin dared the challenge of the guards of the Gates.

'Who are you?' said the guards.

'Know that I am Sean Kelebes Sarazin, named in battle as Watashi. I demand an audience with the guardian of these Gates.'

'What about the halfling at your heels? Your servant, is it? Or your clown?'

'I,' said Glambrax, proudly, 'am Aldarch the Third, Mutilator of Yestron.'

'A clown, then,' said the guard. 'Enter, the pair of you! Our lord may be amused by clown and clown-master.'

'Who is your lord?' said Sarazin.

'He goes by several names,' answered one of the guards, 'but hereabouts we call him sir.'

Once inside, Sarazin was not asked for his weapon, but was flanked by two armed and armoured guards, leading him to suspect that the warlord he had come to see was not in the habit of trust. Glambrax, however, trotting along behind them, was not flattered with a guard of his own.

Since much of Argan's skill was being funnelled through the Gates of Chenameg, the master of those Gates had no trouble recruiting talent. Many carpenters, stonemasons, architects and labourers had entered his service, and had raised all manner of buildings for his delight. One was a high-gabled throne room with a floor of cold grey flagstones.

On admission to the throne room, Sarazin found it doubled as an armoury: a wealth of weaponwork was hung on its walls. But Sarazin had no eyes for steel. All his attention was given to the blond runt who sat on silken cushions on a throne fashioned from black iron.

—*Oh no!*

The lord of the Gates was grinning.

'Welcome,' said he.

'My lord,' said Sarazin, 'I am at your service.'

And gave his most courtly bow to the master of the Gates, who was none other than the pirate Drake Douay.

CHAPTER FIFTY-EIGHT

Name: Drake Douay.
Occupation: undisputed master of the Gates of Chenameg.
Status: a hero of the Age of Darkness which has come upon Argan with the fall of Drangsturm.
Description: compact body marked by scars from heroic battles with bloodthirsty Yarglat barbarians from Tameran, evil pirates devoid of pity, man-devouring sea serpents and fell monsters too numerous to detail.

382

It is to be regretted that some of the scars which mar the beauty of the noble Douay are the consequence of prolonged torture endured in Selzirk after his capture by minions of a certain ungentleman named Sean Kelebes Sarazin, also known as Watashi . . .

While Sarazin's head was still bowed, Douay snapped his fingers. In response to this command, his guards grabbed Sarazin and relieved him of sword, sheath and swordbelt.

'Search,' said Douay.

This single word provoked a strip search. Sarazin protested at this humiliation. A guard hit him. Hard. In the solar plexus. Sarazin went down on his knees. The pain was paralysing. He could not breathe.

'Not so rough, man,' said Douay, jumping down from his throne. 'I've my own pleasures to take with this bitch.'

Sarazin, kneeling naked on cold stone, found his breath, raised his head and said:

'You call me a bitch?'

'Aye, and a thief,' said Douay, striding forward. Sarazin's few possessions had been piled in a heap. Douay scattered them with a kick, then fished out the bard from the wreckage. 'What's this?' he said.

'The bard,' said Sarazin. 'The Lost Bard of Untunchilamon.'

'My bard!' said Douay. 'Won by me in Ling, aye, from Guardian Machines who screamed for my death as they fought me. Right proper it served me, aye, saved a whole ship from mutiny once, for such is the power of the thing. Then this bitch Watashi stole it from me. A thief, aye, that's what he is. His dwarf's a thief into the bargain!'

With that, Douay scooped up one of Sarazin's boots and hurled it at Glambrax, who, thinking himself unobserved, had been detaching a dagger from a weapon rack on the northern wall. The boot missed, and Glambrax fled.

Taking the dagger with him. Douay did not bother ordering a pursuit.

'I — I apologise for the bad behaviour of my dwarf,' said Sarazin.

'The bitch thinks to apologise,' said Douay. He grabbed a hank of Sarazin's hair and yanked. Hard. 'Apologise! That's what he thinks to do. But for what? For a worthless dagger, that's all. Not for the larger things. Blood, bashings, beatings, threats, kidnap, arrest without trial, torture, unlawful detention, aye, I could go on, but life's too short for the catalogue.'

Such was Douay's anger that Sarazin knew his only hope of survival was to kill his foe.

'May I stand?' said he.

'Our four-legged bitch wishes to perform for us,' said Douay. 'To show us the lesser breeds can dare themselves upright on two feet only. Very well then. Stand!'

So saying, Douay released Sarazin's hair.

And Sarazin rose, knowing he would only get one chance. It would have to be a killing blow. A straight blow to the throat.

Douay struck.

Down went Sarazin, struck while still thinking, still rising. Down he went, hands flailing at the ground to break his fall. And a boot smashed into his ribs. And:

—And I'm going to die!

But he did not die. He was still alive when he was bundled into a bloodstained torture chamber and strapped down to a torture bench.

The torture chamber was warm. The shutters were closed against the day, keeping out the winds. Heavy iron cooked slowly in braziers. Hot. Red hot.

'Comfortable?' said Douay.

'What do you want?' answered Sarazin, speaking with difficulty, half-convinced his swollen jaw was broken.

384

'The truth,' said Douay.

Sarazin, bound to cold wood, looked up at Drake Douay and saw a face as loveless as that of a rapist. Douay was no longer grinning. The beating he had given Sarazin in the throne room had been but a game. Now the real business of revenge was going to begin.

'Torture,' continued Douay, as Sarazin held his silence, 'is an acknowledged road to the truth. They say as much in Selzirk, in any case. Do you dispute it?'

'Selzirk has fallen,' said Sarazin.

'Then regard this as enquiry historical,' said Douay. 'I will prove out Selzirk's methods by iron upon flesh.'

'What do you want to know?' said Sarazin, with a sense of rising desperation.

'Why, the truth!' said Douay. 'Nothing more, nothing less. You will number for me the fish in the sea. Then prove that number or perish.'

'Prove?' said Sarazin. 'How can I prove anything when I'm naked on a breadboard?'

'This is no breadboard!' said Douay. 'This is a butcher's block. As for the how — why, that's your problem. Do well, Watashi. Do well — and you might live till morning.'

With that, Douay turned and departed, leaving Sarazin in the hands of the torturers, who were two in number: black-masked men who looked as if they enjoyed their business. These rubbed their hands, grinned at each other, then picked up instruments variously rough and sharp.

'Come now!' said one. 'You're not going to cut off his toes, are you?'

'Why? What do you think we should do?'

'The teeth! That's the thing to start with.'

'Oh no no no! I can't abide the sound of crunching teeth.'

'Well, you know how I feel about toes.'

'All right then, let's start with the nose.'

'Agreed! The nose!'

385

One of the men opened the jaws of a pair of nose-cutters, loomed over Sarazin, and—

And Sarazin fainted.

When Sarazin recovered, it was night. He was still strapped down, utterly helpless. In terror, he looked for his torturers. They were nowhere to be seen. But dull fire glowed red in a brazier where iron was heating still, ready for their return.

Sarazin's nose was still in place. But they would come back. They would hurt him, would cut him, would beat him. And he had no hope of escape, no hope whatsoever.

Helplessly, he began to cry.

He sobbed, alone, lonely, utterly bereft. Hot tears blubbered from his eyes and coursed down his cheeks. It was not fair! How could they do this to him, to him, Sean Sarazin?

'I did nothing wrong,' he said.

But nobody answered, of course.

The fire glowed red. The darkness creaked. Wind was at work on the shutters of the torture chamber. And Sarazin's tears eased away at last, and he was left cold and shivering. Waiting for his torturers to return. Waiting for his death. More afraid than he had ever been in his life.

At last, the grey dawn came like a cutthroat. The ashes in the brazier were cold. A whisk of wind found its way beneath the shutters, feathered the ashes, shifted a few to the floor. Sarazin shivered. Then heard footsteps. Soft footsteps. Creeping, creeping. He sucked on his tongue, summoned up saliva, moistened his dry throat, then said:

'I hear you, Douay.'

'It's not him, moron,' said Glambrax. 'It's me.'

The next moment, Glambrax was beside Sarazin, cutting him free with a dagger. When Sarazin's bonds had been severed, he got off the torture bench — and promptly collapsed to the floor.

'What ails you?' said Glambrax.

'My back,' said Sarazin, in agony. 'It's given way. I can't get up.'

Glambrax promptly started pounding and pummelling and pounding Sarazin's back like a professional masseur. Under his ministrations, Sarazin gained freedom of movement, and soon had the satisfaction of standing and pissing into the brazier.

'Take a shit while you're about it,' said Glambrax generously. 'We're in no hurry.'

'No thanks,' said Sarazin. Then, by way of explanation: 'Constipation.' Then, seeing Glambrax was making for the door: 'Where are you going?'

'Won't be a moment,' said Glambrax.

He was in fact several moments, but returned in due course with an armful of clothes. Sarazin's clothes. Sarazin dressed, somewhat dismayed to find that his boots were missing.

'What about my boots?' said Sarazin.

'Don't worry,' said Glambrax. 'We'll get you some boots before we get out of here.'

'That raises another question,' said Sarazin. 'Just how are we going to get out of here?'

'Follow me,' said Glambrax.

And led the way through the dawn-quiet building, out through a side door, up one stairway, down another, and out through another door. Glambrax scuttled across an open courtyard, then paused, listening at yet another door. Sarazin joined him. He could hear a demented animal wailing within the building, and was frightened.

'What's that?' he hissed.

'Nothing to worry about,' said Glambrax.

Then Glambrax opened the door. Sarazin slipped through. Glambrax nipped in after him, slammed the door and sidled away. Laughing horribly. And Sarazin, to his horror, found himself back in the throne room where he had confronted Drake Douay the day before.

Douay was now striding up and down the room playing on a skavamareen, which was the source of the abominable noise which Sarazin had incorrectly identified as a demented animal.

The next moment Sarazin was seized by two black-masked torturers. And realised that all the events so far were but moves in a game of destruction being played by the fiendish Drake Douay.

CHAPTER FIFTY-NINE

Skavamareen (aka the Ruptured Cat): an instrument frequently mentioned in discussions of fates worse than death. It is said to have been invented in Chi'ash-lan by the notorious anarchist Han Dran Ilk, who is alleged to have been sentenced to five years' penal servitude after he repented and confessed to the offence.

The veracity of this story is often disputed, on the grounds that the sentence detailed is manifestly grossly inadequate for the crime in question. Be that as it may, Chi'ash-lan was certainly the first place to ban this instrument, though it was later outlawed everywhere from Jatzu to Quartermain.

In all the Ravlish lands, the skavamareen (and the delinquents who played it) could find no refuge. Except in Sung. There it won welcome, for it fitted in well with the discord of the back-thumping sklunk, the honk of the kloo, the crash and scatter of the krymbol and the blare of the bray.

While Sung is many leagues from the Gates of Chenameg, the chances of these troubled times have brought a skavamareen to the ruler of those Gates, and, having plenty of time on his hands, he has set himself to master it. A formidable task indeed, for the skava-mareen is a complicated instrument having the following parts:

* The gut (some say: the demon hole) which is a capacious bag of greased leather. According to the scholarly account given in the 'Protocols of the Pipers of Prion', the gut contains the tormented soul of a murderer (or, in the low-budget version, that of a cat) which has been imprisoned there by sorcery.
* The funnel (alternatively: the strangled python) which is a valved tube used by the player to inflate the gut.
* And, finally, the Three Demons and the Demonmaster, which are, respectively, three reed drones and a special-ised pipe equipped with finger-holes which help the player degrade the environment with a peculiarly horrible form of gratuitous violence which only Sung could welcome as music.

'Do you like it?' said Douay, obviously referring to the music he had been making.

'Since I am human,' said Sarazin, with the bitter courage of a man who is certain of his death, 'I welcome the confirmation of my prejudices.'

'What mean you by that?' said Douay.

'I mean,' said Sarazin, 'I knew you at first sight for a barbarian. To find you embracing a skavamareen does but confirm my opinion.'

Douay grinned again, and patted his trusty skavamareen. Then said:

'Did you sleep well?'

'You know very well how I slept,' said Sarazin, on the verge of losing his temper. 'You had me strapped down for torture throughout the night.'

'Man, why so fierce with the voice?' said Douay. 'I was

389

but searching for truth. Is that not right, that I should seek to improve myself?'

Douay's merry face and effortless bonhomie were the very last straw. Sarazin, who had fear worse than nightmare, thought Douay's merriment the worst kind of mockery.

'You tortured me for fun!' said Sarazin. 'As a joke! What kind of monster are you?'

'I am no monster,' said Douay, sounding hurt. 'I am but a diligent student of the arts and philosophies. 'Twas in Selzirk that I studied in torture. Was I wrong to remember my lessons?'

'Whatever was done to you in Selzirk,' said Sarazin, 'there were grave matters of state involved.'

'Oho!' said Douay. 'Matters of state, is it? The world's excuse for everything. Well, man, get this straight — here I rule. I am the state.'

He started to blow into the funnel of the skavamareen, inflating the instrument for another onslaught on the sensibilities. If Sarazin had restrained himself, speech would shortly have become impossible. But Sarazin lost his temper entirely and spoke:

'You're like every bully,' said he. 'Brave when the numbers are with you.'

Almost immediately, Sarazin regretted having spoken. Such words might well lead to instant death. But the blond-haired Douay did not order his execution. Instead, he stopped inflating the skavamareen, and said:

'Speech is easy, man. But I'd doubt you brave even with the numbers on your side.'

'You doubt my courage?' said Sarazin. 'I tell you this — if I had a sword I'd prove you coward soon enough.'

'You say?' said Douay. 'Truly, you are rash, for I have yet to meet the man to match my blade. In truth, I lately killed a man named Plovey, who counted himself the best swordsman in Selzirk.'

Sarazin knew he must be bluffing, for Plovey had been known in Selzirk as a master swordsman. Surely a bar-

barous uitlander like Douay could never have defeated a sophisticate like Plovey. The young man was over-confident. This might be the way out! If Douay could be provoked into combat, Sarazin could surely kill him.

'Talk, talk!' said Sarazin, urging scorn into his voice. 'I know well the talk of dwarves, for I have one of my own.'

'You called me what?' said Douay, an edge of ice in his voice.

'What do you expect me to call you?' said Sarazin. 'Dare I name you giant when the dog which raped your mother was taller than the brat he spawned?'

Douay laid aside the skavamareen and drew his sword. The thugs holding Sarazin gripped him tighter.

'Is this the way you prove your courage?' said Sarazin. 'Through butchery?'

'Nay, man,' said Douay, with contempt. He selected another blade from the wall, held one in each hand and said to Sarazin: 'Choose. My left or my right.'

'The left,' said Sarazin.

'It makes no difference either way,' said Douay, laying the weapon in his left hand down on the stone floor. 'For the blades are of equal quality.' Then he said to his strong-men: 'Leave. Close the door. Stand without. Let none enter until we are finished.'

Douay stepped back from the weapon on the floor. Sarazin, edgy, heart quick-pulsing, dared himself forward, snatched up the blade and screamed his defiance:

'Scaaa!'

Douay, standing some five sword-lengths' distance, said with indifference:

'No need to hurry. We've got all day. Take your time. Test your weapon to start with. I don't want this to be too easy.'

Sarazin did not know what to think. Was this a trap? He backed off. Then, with a decent distance between himself and Douay, checked the linkage of blade to hilt, and tried the sword for balance.

391

'I cannot fault the weapon,' said Sarazin, trying to keep a tremor of fear from his voice.

He was beginning to think that this was not exactly fair. He had been on short rations for many days. He had not slept through the night. He was still stiff, bruised and sore from the pounding Douay had given him the day before. He was cold, hungry, tired, thirsty. But there was no time to protest for Douay was advancing. Obviously for the kill.

'Scaaa!' screamed Sarazin desperately, throwing himself on the defence.

Douay, still well out of weapon-reach, eased himself to a halt, then, amused beyond measure by Sarazin's evident desperation, threw back his head and laughed.

'This is — is a joke?' said Sarazin, starting to hope that Douay would call off the fight.

'You are the joke,' said Douay softly.

Then graced closer, sword at the ready. His face had become hard, cruel, predatory. He was finished with laughter. Sarazin realised that only one of them would leave this room alive.

—*One chance then. One blow to kill him.*

Thus thinking, Sarazin seized the initiative, putting all his strength into a blow designed to decapitate his opponent.

'Ha!' screamed Sarazin, striking.

Douay ducked. Sarazin's sword hissed through the air, missing Douay's scalp by no more than the black of a fingernail. And Sarazin was for a moment off-balance, wide open and helpless to save himself.

Douay struck.

Douay slammed into Sarazin with his shoulder, hitting so hard that Sarazin was sent staggering backwards. As he flailed for balance, Douay kicked him in the chest. Down went Sarazin, his sword discarding to the air.

Sklang!

Thus sang steel against steel as Sarazin's blade tumbled into cold metal racked on the walls of the armoury. It was

392

well out of reach. And Drake Douay was already standing over him. Sword in hand.

'What sayest thou, Watashi?' said Douay.

And Sarazin found courage to answer:

'I was taught to match my blade against swordsmen, not streetfighters.'

Whereupon Douay said, in a perfect imitation of the voice of Plovey of the Regency:

'Ah, darling boy! But I am a swordsman! Swordsman and streetfighter both.'

Sarazin closed his eyes. Waited for his death. And heard Douay say:

'Take him to the guest room.'

Almost immediately, Sarazin was seized and dragged away to the unknown horrors of the guest room, whatever that might be.

CHAPTER SIXTY

The Favoured Blood: the aristocracy which by tradition rules in Argan. The legends of Argan claim that only those of the Favoured Blood can rightfully rule, and that disaster will befall any state otherwise governed.

While in practice much power in Argan fell to other hands generations ago, concessions have always been made to popular belief. The kingmaker of the Harvest Plains, for instance, has always been consecrated in sacred ceremony as a member of the Favoured Blood.

Even the elections which take place in Runcorn and Provincial Endergeneer are not (in theory) mere popularity contests, but are (again, in theory) an appeal to the populace to decide which of the candidates (if any) shows any trace of descent from the Blood.

*   *   *

The guest room proved to be a quiet bedroom painted pink. It held an enormous double bed. The linen was clean, the sheets smelling of lavender, and Sarazin was shortly sound asleep between these sheets.

He slept right through that day and through the night which followed, only waking when he was roused for breakfast the following morning. Breakfast was good, very good. Fish fresh from the Velvet River. Roast pigeon. Fried potatoes. And a draught of dandelion wine to wash it all down.

Once breakfast was over, Sarazin was led into the presence of the formidable Drake Douay.

'Do you acknowledge me as your equal?' said Douay.

'You are the greater swordsman,' conceded Sarazin.

'Greater by nature and greater by birth,' said Douay. Then he took something from his pocket, held it up and said: 'What's this?'

Douay was holding a jet-black necklace chain from which hung a cool, glossy lozenge of an identical black. The lozenge turned slowly, so Sarazin saw first a golden sun disk, then seven stars and a crescent moon on the obverse.

'What's this?' insisted Douay.

'That,' said Sarazin, wearily, 'is the Lost Bard of Untunchilamon. My bard. Bought with my own money.'

'How do you know it as yours? Maybe it's somebody else's bard.'

'There was but one in all the world,' said Sarazin.

'Are you sure?' said Douay.

'Positive,' said Sarazin.

'Look at it!' said Douay.

Sarazin took the bard and examined it.

'There,' said Sarazin. 'See? There's the damage done when you got my precious cut up in a street fight.'

'So,' said Douay, 'that is the Lost Bard of Untunchilamon. Then what is this?'

394

And Douay dangled before Sarazin's eyes another bard. He let Sarazin take it into his hands. Sarazin tried to make this new bard speak. It did so — in the voice of Saba Yavendar.

'Where — where did these come from?' said Sarazin, bewildered.

'I told you,' said Douay. 'I won many of such from Guardian Machines in desperate battle. All but one were stolen from me in Narba. As lord of the Gates I've been on the lookout for my stolen property. Man, don't look so shocked!'

'But — but Epelthin Elkin — he told me — he said — just one, that's all, that's what he said, only one of these was ever made.'

As Sarazin was blathering, Douay took back both bards, pocketed them, then said:

'You believe everything you're told?'

'Elkin's a wizard!' said Sarazin.

'A pox doctor, then,' sneered Douay. 'Aye, I've had dealings with wizards myself. Man, this magic stuff is fraud, if you ask me.'

'But the Confederation built Drangsturm and—'

'Oh, Drangsturm was pretty enough — I saw it myself before the South all turned to shit and custard. Aye, that and other things, Doors and flying islands and such, not that you believed me when I told. But I doubt that wizards ever made such, for the ones I've met can't do something as simple as a love philtre.'

'So Elkin was wrong,' said Sarazin. 'Or else he lied to me.'

'Whichever way, Watashi, I tell you straight. The bard you owned in Selzirk was but one of many. That I told you true. Yet you believed me not. Aye, tortured me on account of disbelief. I told you of Doors, too. You wouldn't believe those, either. Yet I've people here who've been through such.'

'I believe now,' said Sarazin. 'I've seen monsters come through a Door in Chenameg.'

'Oho!' said Douay. 'What you see you believe, and the rest of the world is a lie. If you weren't ready to believe speech, why torture me for speech?'

'I . . . I'm sorry. But . . . you . . . there were . . . I mean, you told not one story but five. You were . . . I mean, think of the names for a start. First you were Drake Douay, then the son of a Demon, then something else, then . . .'

'Aye,' said Douay, softly.

'Anyway,' said Sarazin, 'it was Jarl who did the torture. Jarl and Plovey and others.'

'But you who condemned me! I was innocent, yet you let me be taken for torture!'

'But . . . but it was so difficult,' said Sarazin. 'So difficult to believe your innocence when you told us so many different names and all.'

'Many names I went by, yes,' said Douay, 'for not all could be revealed. But now the worst has happened, so all may be revealed. It will do no harm.'

'I . . . I should like to know the truth,' said Sarazin.

Then Drake Douay revealed himself to Sarazin as Lord Dreldragon, heir to the Scattered Empire, a seapower realm of the Central Ocean.

'I am of the Favoured Blood,' said Douay, 'for it is the Favoured Blood which rules in the Scattered Empire. Mighty are our weaponmasters and beautiful our women. But, more than either, our kingdom values its honour.'

Then Douay explained that, years before, he had learnt of the doom which threatened Argan.

'I learnt of it through prophecy,' said Douay, 'for we have true prophets in the Scattered Empire. My kith and kin thought Argan doomed, but then I was vouchsafed a prophetic dream. If I came to Argan on my lonesome, I might have a chance to save the place.

'But there was something I had to do, aye, this dream of mine showed me what was needed. There's a price for everything, man, and this is the price I had to pay. I had to come humble like, concealing my true identity.

'This was the burden that was placed upon me. To leave all that was dear to me. To go humble, aye, like a sick cat slinking past a thousand hounds in kennel. Then, when doom came upon Argan, I was to rally the strongest and fight against the Swarms.

'That I have done. Hence you find me here as lord of the Gates of Chenameg. But I've been weakened, aye, weakened by vile tortures, by filthy dungeons, by punishments unnatural and undeserved, and most of all by torture. It was you who did it, Watashi. You punished me in my innocence. You broke my strength. Hence, when Argan's peril came, I lacked the power to save the continent.'

Now Sarazin saw the depths of his own guilt, and he knelt at the feet of the noble Douay and he wept, helplessly. Until Douay raised him to his feet.

'You know me now for what I am,' said Douay gently. 'I am of the Favoured Blood. You thought me a pirate, but I am no pirate, though hardship may have forced me to keep company with such. I am the scion of a noble house. Truly. I am of the Favoured Blood.

'When I came to these Gates, the evil Groth held them against the people, ruling with rape and torture. I overthrew his tyranny which oppressed the people, and now I hold the Gates in justice for all the people. My fee upon the traffic is moderate, for I take but ten per cent of all that moves.

'I rule, as I have said, in justice. Are you ready to receive my justice?'

Sarazin dried his eyes and said in a voice without life: 'I am.'

'This, then, is my justice,' said Douay. 'I will not kill you, though death you richly deserve. Instead, I will let you depart from here with your life. Aye, with your life, and with food for the journey, and new boots for the trail.'

Then Douay led Sarazin to the eastern exit of his fortress palace, where Glambrax was waiting with two leather

397

packs, one sized for a dwarf, one for a man. They were old, weather-scarred packs, smelling of the sweat of many soldiers.

'They're not pretty,' said Douay, seeing Sarazin looking at the packs dubiously. 'But they'll do the job. Strong, see?'

He picked up the larger pack by one of its shoulder straps and threw it to Sarazin. Who was almost bowled over by the weight.

'Grief!' said Sarazin. 'What's in it?'

'Oh, food and such,' said Douay. 'You couldn't travel with less.'

Sarazin thanked the magnanimous Douay for his mercy. And Glambrax, grinning, danced around the noble Douay, capering, bowing incessantly.

'Stop that!' said Sarazin sharply, horrified. This was no way to behave in the presence of one of the Favoured Blood!

Glambrax stopped capering, knelt, licked Douay's boots, then embraced him. At last, Douay slapped at the dwarf. Glambrax slipped away, grinning still.

'Must I leave?' said Sarazin to Douay. 'I would fain put my sword at your service.'

'Aye, mayhap,' said Douay softly. 'But black humours come upon me when I rage at dark and light alike then kill, aye, my blade terrible to behold for it glows with a light like blood. Then no steel can prevail against mine. Aye, stone itself gives way before my blade.'

'How so?' said Sarazin, amazed.

'It is a dark matter of witchcraft,' said Douay. 'This curse has lain upon the ruling house of the Scattered Empire for generations, that their sons will be beset at times with evil. Best you leave, Watashi, before the fit comes on me yet again.'

'You . . . you kill many?' said Sarazin.

'When the fit is upon me my servants feed my blade with victims,' said Douay. 'Aye, throw me cats and such. But, Watashi, despite my mercy there is a part of me which hates you still. I'll not deny it. When next the madness comes, I fear that cats will not suffice. My blade will hunt you, aye. And cut closer than shaving, I promise you that.'

'Perhaps a wizard . . .?'

'Man,' said Douay, 'you think I've not sought help from every quarter? Wizards are frauds, I've told you before. This is witchcraft, the real source of evil. This I must endure. Such is my burden.'

So spoke the noble Douay, his voice unwavering, a tragic courage written in his face. And Sarazin, humbled by such courage, such suffering, such grandeur in defeat, went down on his knees before this scion of the House of Hexagon, who permitted Sarazin to kiss his hand.

Then Sarazin was given back his own sword, sheath and swordbelt, and was given new boots as well. With his equipment complete, he shouldered his pack and set off, with Glambrax as ever just a footstep behind him.

Thus, in early summer in the year Alliance 4328, Sean Sarazin and his untrusty dwarf Glambrax departed from the Gates of Chenameg and trekked east. They hoped to travel beside the Velvet River to the Araconch Waters, the enormous freshwater lake in the desolate heartland of Argan North. From there, they hoped to trek north through the dragonlands to a tributary of the Amodeo River, then follow that river downstream to the far, far distant seaport of Brine.

That seaport was in the north-east of Argan, and from there they could get passage across the seas to foreign shores free from the threat of the Swarms. And to a new life as . . . as what?

That question would, doubtless, resolve itself in due course. For the moment, what mattered was to make the journey. Burdened by their packs, Sarazin and Glambrax laboured up the ever-climbing path clinging to the southern side of the Manaray Gorge. Finally they reached the rough-cut uplands.

On they trekked, forever keeping the Gorge on their left. This was a land of bones, of shadows, of rock and wind, with shambling mountains dominating the horizon. A lonely land, despite the many marks which showed that other refugees had been this way.

Finally, late in the afternoon, when they came upon a rill of water threading its way between jumbling boulders, Sarazin decided it was time to make camp. They had not eaten all day, nor had they drunk. So first they slaked their thirst, then they broke open their packs and rummaged within. Most of the weight proved to be pemmican — rich stuff made not just with meat but with nuts and dried cherries also.

As well as food, they had a change of clothes apiece and several changes of socks and four empty leather water-bottles. They also each had a single oblong strip of canvas with lightweight ropes sewn to each corner. These would provide a little marginal shelter against the worst of the weather.

'No gold,' said Sarazin gloomily.

When they finally got to Brine, they would be stony broke. He would probably have to sell his sword to buy them a passage out of the place.

'Ah,' said Glambrax, with an evil little laugh, 'but we're not entirely without treasure.'

'What do you mean?' said Sarazin.

Then Glambrax showed his master the trophies he had carried away with him from the Gates of Chenameg. During the formalities of the farewell, Glambrax had succeeded in picking the pockets of the noble Douay — and had stolen not just one bard but both of them.

CHAPTER SIXTY-ONE

'How could you?' said Sarazin furiously.

As the dwarf scrabbled to escape from his master's anger, Sarazin grabbed him by the hair.

'You're not going anywhere!' said Sarazin.

'So kill me then,' said Glambrax truculently. 'Where's your gratitude?'

'Gratitude?' said Sarazin. 'For what should I be grateful?'

'The bards! I thought you wanted them.'

Sarazin was ready to weep. Or to pound Glambrax to a pulp. How could he live with the shame? The noble Douay had forgiven him, after all the terrible things that had been done to him after his arrest by Sarazin's minions — and had been repaid by this outrageous act of theft.

Sean Sarazin could not even keep his dwarf in order. Yet he had once had such pretensions of grandeur that he had imagined himself as ruler of the Harvest Plains!

Sarazin shook his dwarf.

Then pushed him away, sending him sprawling to the stones.

'I should kill you,' said Sarazin. 'But it wouldn't do any good.'

Glambrax made no answer, and in fact stayed stolidly silent for the rest of the afternoon.

Evening came, then night. Sarazin, depressed and exhausted, laid himself down to sleep. Though he was sleeping on stones, he was so fatigued that he slept solidly until he was woken at dawn by jubilant birdsong.

He rose and stripped himself. Took a piss. Looking at his cock as he did so. A peasant's cock. Ugly piece of animal anatomy. He had once flattered himself by thinking it intrinsically imperial. Had so deluded himself that he had thought himself worthy of a princess.

Well . . .

He had no delusions left now. He was what he was: a homeless beggar bereft of all prospects.

Carefully, he washed himself with water from the rill. It was cold, and, shivering, he was glad to warm himself by the fire Glambrax had started. The two said nothing to each other as the sun rose, stretching early morning shadows across the landscape.

Sarazin was stiff and sore from yesterday's long hard march — and from the damage done to him by Drake Douay. But, after he had treated some of his aches and pains with a little liniment which some thoughtful person had included in his pack, he felt somewhat better, though his eyes were sore and he had a dull headache.

As he breakfasted on pemmican, he considered his options. They could always turn back, march all the way to the Gates and return the stolen bards to Douay. But what if Douay yielded to one of the black angers he had spoken of, and killed both Sarazin and Glambrax on the spot?

'We'd better go on,' said Sarazin.

Glambrax made no answer. Sulking? Or meditating? No, he was just otherwise engaged: busy grubbing dank clumps of noxious matter from the depths of his nose.

'Up!' said Sarazin. 'Up on your feet and get moving.'

By noon, both man and dwarf were footsore and thirsty. They had filled their waterbottles at their campsite before setting out but durst not drink unless they really had to — for there was no telling when they would next find water. Flies were pestering about Sarazin's face. Irritated, he slapped at them. Hard. Then, after hurting one of his ears, slapped with more care.

He started looking for somewhere cool, somewhere they could shelter to rest. After resting they could push on when it was cooler.

So thought Sarazin. But it was not until late in the afternoon that he spied a suitable place — a deep and dark-shadowed cave. Invigorated by such a welcome sight, he strode towards it gratefully.

'Have a care,' said Glambrax, who by now had decided that he once more knew how to speak. 'There might be dragon or basilisk within. Or ogre — or worse!'

'Worse?' said Sarazin. 'What's worse?'

'A lawyer, perchance,' said Glambrax, and cackled.

But Sarazin went on regardless, imagining cool depths of batstone darkness and chilled water falling drip by drop. He found the cave noisy with flies — and from it breathed a stench which made him retch. But before he could flee, he saw all. The wounds, the heads, the limbs, the corpses deliquescing. He stumbled away from the cavemouth and collapsed insensible in the sun.

He was roused by a boot in the ribs.

Opened his eyes. Saw shadows, boots. Heard voices. Muttering. A harsh laugh.

'. . . meat for the Slavemaster . . .'

He stumbled from the ground, reaching for his weapon. And was hit from behind, bashed, knocked senseless.

He measured his length on the ground and lay still.

CHAPTER SIXTY-TWO

Sean Sarazin had been ambushed by one of the many gangs of brigands which worked the territory between the Gates of Chenameg and the Araconch Waters. If Sarazin and

Glambrax had not been taken there and then, they would inevitably have fallen victim to one gang or another before they completed their journey, for only large and well-armed parties could hope to travel unmolested.

And nobody could hope to travel unobserved.

Once captured, Sarazin's fate was to be sold to the Slavemaster. The Slavemaster was the greatest gangster of them all, a warlord who traded with the lesser gangs and, from time to time, put together convoys which went to the Araconch Waters to trade with the greater warlords who had set themselves up in business there.

Sarazin, sick and sore, asked no questions about the Slavemaster as he was driven east along a track which never strayed far from the Manaray Gorge. At last, he was brought to a walled stockade built without a formidable cave complex.

There he was given leave to rest while they awaited the arrival of the Slavemaster. Rest he did, sprawled full length on raw rock, too weary by then for curiosity, regrets or despair. Glambrax stretched out beside him, for once too wearied for mischief.

For some time Sarazin lay there, almost comatose. Then he heard someone call his name.

'Ho, Sarazin!' said Lod.

Was it Lod? It certainly sounded like Lod. So Sarazin opened his eyes, and looked up, and saw . . . Tarkal.

'Do you recognise me?' said Tarkal, his face inscrutable.

'You are Tarkal of Chenameg,' said Sarazin wearily. 'You are of the Favoured Blood.'

'And you are Sean Sarazin, our honoured guest,' said a familiar voice, and, yes, it was indeed Lod, as large as life and as merry. And before Sarazin knew it he was being stripped of his clothes and bundled into a hot tub. After a bath came a massage, then sleep, blessed sleep in clean linen, as unexpected as his experience in Drake Douay's guest room, and every bit as welcome.

*   *   *

Tarkal of Chenameg, the Slavemaster himself, gave Sarazin two days to rest and recover before he invited him to dine with him. Glambrax attended the meal, as did Lod. Amantha was nowhere to be seen, and Sarazin did not like to ask where she was.

Throughout the meal, Lod and Glambrax made most of the running, chaffing each other, joking and jesting, punning and storytelling, while Sarazin and Tarkal sat in silence, preoccupied by their own thoughts. At that dinner, Tarkal wore one of the bards which had been taken from Sarazin, while Lod wore the other.

Sarazin wondered if he would ever get them back.

During the meal, Glambrax told outrageous stories about the terrible Drake Douay, who, by his account, had tried to torture Sean Sarazin to death. He gave a spirited and improbable account of their escape from Douay.

'. . . and just as well we escaped,' said Glambrax. 'For he'd sworn to cut up young Sean as ratbait.'

'What about yourself?' said Lod.

'Why, no, not me,' said Glambrax, 'for I never tortured him as Sarazin did.'

At that, Tarkal finally spoke:

'You tortured Douay?'

'In Selzirk,' said Sarazin.

For he could not deny responsibility, even though the actual inflicting of pain had been done by other hands.

'You were lucky indeed to escape,' said Tarkal.

'Oh, lucky enough,' said Sarazin, in no mood to tell the truth, since it would have been a laborious process to unstitch all of Glambrax's lies — and, besides, the truth was shameful, involving as it did the theft of Douay's bards. 'Still,' continued Sarazin, 'you've been lucky yourself.'

'What?' said Tarkal. 'To be ruling here? As Slavemaster? There was no luck in that, friend Sarazin. I was in the right place at the right time.'

'Of course,' said Sarazin. 'Ruling in Shin and all.' It

would have been easy for Tarkal to remove himself and his people from Shin to the wastelands long before refugees were on the move in great numbers. 'But why then didn't you set yourself up at the Gates?'

'Oh, I did,' said Tarkal. 'When word reached Shin that the Swarms were invading, I saw my opportunity. I saw what must inevitably happen. There are few routes of escape, and the Gates are one of the best. So I set myself up as lord of the Gates.'

'Then — what? Douay came?'

'No. A brute called Groth pushed me out of the Gates. Douay — or Lord Dreldragon, or whatever you want to call him — came later. I've never met him. Yet.'

'You're thinking of meeting him?' said Sarazin.

'I'm curious,' said Tarkal. 'Curious to see what he might do with Sean Sarazin.'

He said it quietly. Watching Sean Sarazin. Who saw Glambrax wink at him. The dwarf had anticipated this!

'You joke, of course,' said Sarazin, casually. 'For you have honour, surely. Douay is a monster, a brute addicted to slaughter and torture. He hates me as he'd hate a sister-killer. Tarkal, I know there's true nobility in your nature, thus . . . your jest frightens me not, for I know it for what it is.'

Tarkal chewed on some fish, spat out a stray scale, then said:

'Indeed I jest. Tomorrow, Sean, I'll let you go east. I'm running a convoy east to the lords of the Araconch Waters. You'll be my guest of honour on the trek.'

'Tell me then,' said Sarazin urbanely, 'what manner of lords be these? In the history I learnt, the shores of the Waters were empty of human life.'

'Indeed,' said Tarkal. 'Well, Lod can tell you the ins and outs of recent history.'

And Lod obliged, telling of the sanguinary events which had accompanied the mass influx of refugees, of the lordlings who had made themselves suzerain over one wretched piece of rock or another, of war, murder, killing, torture, organised rape, slavery, cannibalism, oppression, treachery and assorted bloodbaths — history in miniature, in fact.

Late that night, Lod came in secret to Sarazin and told him another tale. According to Lod, Tarkal hated Sarazin intensely because, in Lod's words:

'Your marriage to his dear sister Amantha was but a form of rape.'

By Lod's account, in the morning Sarazin would be seized, gagged, tied, taken down through ever-descending caves to one which opened by the shores of the Velvet River, deep in the sunless depths of the Manaray Gorge.

'There,' said Lod, 'you will be loaded on to a raft and taken downriver to Douay. Do you understand?'

'I understand,' said Sarazin, gently, 'that you were ever a joker, Lod, my friend. But tonight I think the joke in the worst of taste. Surely it is an evil thing for you to thus impugn your brother's honour. Why, I remember when once you swore he sought to murder you!'

'So he did,' said Lod darkly, 'but I've purchased my life through the worst kind of abasement.'

'You've roused my interest,' said Sarazin. 'Pray tell!'

'Now you joke!' said Lod. 'Your life is at stake! You must run, run, run tonight or you're doomed, dead, done for!'

Lod became so insistent that, at last, Sarazin realised that Lod was not here on his own account but on Tarkal's. So he allowed Lod to chivvy him into his clothes, and then to lead him to freedom — and, when Tarkal triumphantly ambushed them, Sarazin consented to scream in feigned terror and despair.

Though he found the whole performance hard work, for he was not one of the world's natural thespians.

407

CHAPTER SIXTY-THREE

The next morning, Sarazin was hogtied and loaded on to the raft that was to take him downstream to the Gates of Chenameg. Tarkal and Lod were both coming along for the journey, as were half a dozen fighting men.

'Why does my dwarf run free?' said Sarazin, for Glambrax was capering on the raft.

'He has sworn himself to my service,' said Tarkal. 'At least until we reach the Gates.'

'Glambrax!' said Sarazin. 'How could you? You vile, treacherous, gamos-sucking turd!'

In response, Glambrax simply hauled out his shlong and pissed all over the unfortunate Sean Sarazin. Who screamed in wrath which — this time — was not feigned at all.

Then, mercifully, Sarazin was gagged, which meant he need do no more acting. Tarkal's fighting men untied the raft and pushed it out into the flow of the Velvet River and away they went, bucketing down the swift-flowing river which sprinted between the sullen walls of the Manaray Gorge.

In truth, Sarazin was worried about his reception at the Gates of Chenameg. Drake Douay would doubtless have a lot to say about the theft of his precious bards. However, Sarazin hoped the truth would serve. Glambrax could take the blame — and a whipping, too, if Douay decided that was what he deserved.

Unless the anger of madness was upon the noble Douay, nothing worse should befall Sarazin and Glambrax at the gates.

But then man and dwarf would be back where they had started from, unless Sarazin could turn this situation to his advantage. Unless he judged Douay wrongly, the man, however noble, had a bloody sense of humour. Perhaps Sarazin could tempt him into arranging some gladiatorial games.

—*Me versus Tarkal. That's the thing!*

Sean Sarazin knew he had sinned by his crimes against the Favoured Blood as represented by the noble Douay. But it would surely be no crime for him to fight and kill Tarkal, even though he was of low birth — for Tarkal was a murderer.

Sarazin knew it.

Nothing else could explain King Lyra's mysterious death in a bog in Chenameg on the occasion of that long-ago hunt in winter, shortly after Sarazin had seen the famous phoenix renew itself in a temple in Shin.

—*He murdered his father to win the throne. Therefore his death is due. I would be but an instrument of justice.*

And, with a little help from Douay, after Sarazin had despatched Tarkal he could surely seize the Slavemaster's cave complex, and set himself up as a warlord in his own right. It was all so logical, so natural, so inevitable that it was irresistible.

—*Killing Tarkal. That will be the hard bit.*

Sarazin's confidence in his bladework had been shaken since his clash with Douay in which Douay had defeated and disarmed him. But then, Douay was a greater warlord than the notorious Groth, and Groth himself had earlier displaced Tarkal as master of the Gates, which suggested Tarkal was no great warmaster.

—*Besides, I've fought him before.*

—*And I won.*

Yes. And Sarazin remembered his own post mortem on his first duel with Tarkal. He could have killed the prince of Chenameg if his heart had really been in the fight — rather than in staying alive.

—This time, I will kill him!

So thought Sarazin.

Then thought no more, for the raft hit rapids which made thought impossible, such was the terror of their progress. Terror at least for Sean Sarazin — for, tied and gagged as he was, he had not the slightest hope of survival if he was washed overboard.

Lod and Tarkal, for their part, whooped in exultation as the raft plunged through treacherous turbulence and hissing chutes where water exploded into spray. The raft rocked, kicked, bucked, whirled round and lurched in a sickening fashion.

Wave after wave of cold water swept over the passengers. Sarazin — cold, cold! — shivered and shivered. Wondering if he would die of exposure before they ever reached the Gates. Then the raft nosed into the water and Sean Sarazin was lifted up and carried away entirely. He tried to scream. Gagged, he could not. Then an agonising pain tore at his scalp.

'Got you!' cried Tarkal, hauling Sarazin back on to the raft. Then, leaning close to Sarazin, the Slavemaster said: 'You don't get away that easily. Oh no. For you're very special to me, oh yes, as special to me as Douay.'

Then Tarkal kissed Sarazin on the forehead, gently, gently. Drawing blood was a pleasure reserved for the future.

'Gates ahead!' cried Lod.

Sarazin thought:

—Already?

But of course. For the horseracing river trifled with distances which meant dawn-to-dusk labour for a man slogging along with a heavily laden pack.

He closed his eyes as the raft ploughed down one last water-slope. The raft rocked and bucked as they churned through the final rapids. Then Tarkal screamed in triumph, and Sarazin knew they were out of the Gates.

Or almost.

He opened his eyes. Saw rock-snap spray, a water-

410

splintered sun, and something out of nightmare swooping towards them. Something human screamed as wing-claws snatched it. Tarkal, screaming and swearing, drew his sword. The weapon went spinning as something whipped him away into the water.

Lod drew his own blade — then thought better of it, and dived into the water.

'Kill the prisoner,' said one of Tarkal's surviving men.

A subordinate drew steel, loomed above Sarazin. Who gazed upwards, eyes bulging in terror. And saw the sky shudder to shadow, saw his assailant's body ripped to the sky.

—*Neversh.*

The thought was a scream.

And screams audible split the sky as another man was torn away. A scythe-sweeping tail slashed across the raft, mowing down the survivors. Sarazin closed his eyes.

Then opened them. For:

—*This is the last of life.*

He did not choose to die in self-made darkness.

So he gazed open-eyed at the scene. The Neversh in the sky, two of them. No, three. Four! Five! A full five of the monsters, nightmarish creatures of the Swarms, enormous brutes flailing through the air in front of the Gates of Chenameg, attacking the slow and the foolish with feeding spikes, grapple-hooks and clawed feet, sweeping and slashing with whiplash tails which could kill a horse or break a man in half.

From the battlements of Douay's fortress at the Gates of Chenameg, crossbowers unleashed their bolts, shooting at the low-flying monsters. One floundered, sank low, then struggled for height and flew out of Sarazin's field of vision.

He bit ferociously at the gag in his mouth. He needed his voice, his voice! To scream for help. All it needed was one person to dare the river and tow his raft to safety. But it was not to be, for the gag held. And if the defenders of the Gates looked at the raft, doubtless they saw but a scattering of corpses aboard — nothing worth swimming for when the Neversh were in the skies.

—Tarkal lived.

So thought Sarazin, bitterly. He was almost certain the Slavemaster had been knocked overboard by the same blow from the tail of a Neversh which had sent his sword spinning away.

—Lod too. So who's dead?

Glambrax was dead. That was for certain. Sarazin could see the dwarf lying beneath a man's corpse, blood guttering from a bloody headwound. Three dead soldiers were aboard the raft. The head of one had been smashed to pulp by a whiplash from a monster's tail.

—Gods.

The Gates of Chenameg were already receding into the distance. Sarazin looked left, looked right, scanned the banks for signs of human life. He saw baskets of abandoned laundry, unattended fishing rods, and cooking fires burning without human supervision. Most people had fled — and those who had not were lying as if dead, hoping to escape the attentions of the Neversh.

A little further downriver, the raft drifted past a huge stockade of earth, logs and stones, a fortress raised by a company of men who hunted creatures of the Swarms for a living. As the raft went by, the shadow of a Neversh flickered overhead. And nobody within the stockade even thought of risking life and limb to retrieve that piece of river-refuse.

CHAPTER SIXTY-FOUR

A corpse-laden raft drifted down the Velvet River. Strong and steady ran the river. Not at the horsepanic pace of the Manaray Gorge, to be sure — but the river never paused, never rested. A man could outrun it or, indeed, outmarch it — but only briefly. Nobody could have matched the river's pace for a daylength journey.

Noon came, then night. Then dawn. Then noon again. From the Gates of Chenameg to the city of Shin was, by river, a matter of about a hundred leagues, and, shortly after noon, the raft drifted past the ruins of that city.

Briefly, it grounded on the shore. Then the current eased it away, and it floated downstream, towards the west. Sarazin by then was in agony, for, quite apart from the tortures of thirst, his hogtied body was wracked by cramps.

There was no escape, for he had been tied up by experts. What was more frustrating than anything was the thought of his magic candle, still safe in one of his pockets. His enemies had not recognised it as the magical treasure it was, once a much-valued possession of a wizard. But it was useless to him, for he could not get to it.

—And I had it all figured out.

Tarkal was a fool, and he had been tricked so easily, conned into taking them back to Drake Douay. By rights, Tarkal should now be dead, and Sarazin should be on his way to becoming Slavemaster. But, as it was, Tarkal was probably drinking up large and listening to Douay entertaining his guests on the skavamareen — while Sean Sarazin was doomed on this downriver journey.

Which, in all probability, would terminate in his death.

On floated the raft, into night.

Into nightmare.

It was fifty leagues from Shin to the border between Chenameg and the Harvest Plains. And, while dawn was pinking the sky, the raft slipped across that border. There was no more forest to left or to right, only the flatlands of the plains. The river grew wider, slower, more leisurely.

And Glambrax stirred.

413

Raised his bloodstained head, vomited violently — then collapsed again.

—*Come on, you gutless dwarf!*

So screamed Sarazin. But this experiment in telepathy proved fruitless, for Glambrax had not stirred again by noon. Then the raft drifted through a breach in one of the dams which had once tamed the Velvet River for irrigation.

At some time in the past, heroes had breached that dam, thinking to save their land from the advance of the Swarms. But a smooth grey bridge — manufactured by those monsters — now spanned the gap. On that bridge stood a keflo, a low-slung monster. Silent. Unmoving. Statuesque.

Sarazin lay very still, staring at it.

And Glambrax groaned.

—*Quiet! Quiet!*

Perhaps telepathy worked on this occasion, for the dwarf relapsed into silence again. It was not until noon that Glambrax finally crawled towards Sarazin and, after a struggle, released his gag. Then began to feed him water.

Releasing the ropes was a slow business, which took the weakened dwarf till midnight. But it was done. So, when dawn came, both were free — but neither was good for anything. It was not until the next day that they managed to push the corpses overboard.

On floated the raft. Much of the time Sarazin lay sleeping, dreaming of winter snow on the heights of the Ashun mountains, of voices far distant in time and space. He would wake now and then to a bloodstained raft stinking of offal and vomit, to the steelbright sun glittering on the riverflow.

Overhead, the shadows of vultures.

The riverbanks were empty. No monsters. The monsters of the Swarms were, doubtless, on the fringes of the occupied territories, hunting out humans, killing, slaughtering, ravaging. Here, in the heartland of the new dominions of

414

the Swarms, Sarazin was safe, for the moment.

He had endless time to think. And to sorrow. For what did he lament? For himself? No. For the loss of his world. He experienced . . . not exactly *weltschmerz*, no, not an abstract sorrow for the fate of the world as a whole, but grief for the loss of particular people.

Not dear friends, no, he had been singularly short of bosom companions throughout his life, but perfectly ordinary people — servants, soldiers, tavern keepers, scribes, librarians, members of the Watch, even minor functionaries of the Regency. People he had known in passing, whose faces he remembered, and whose voices.

—*All gone, all fallen, all dead.*

What was amazing was how intensely they had all been involved in their own lives, passionately concerned with the power politics of the various milieus in which they moved, all with their own loves, hates, lusts, fears, joys, ambitions.

—*All now as dust.*

And what was most amazing of all was to realise that the outcome would ultimately have been the same even if Drangsturm had never fallen, even if the Swarms had never come. In time, all would have died, and all their works would have become as nothing. For such is the nature of a world of mortality.

Mortality.

—*Most improbable of all improbabilities.*

So improbable that, even now, Sean Sarazin had difficulty in grasping the inevitability of his own death. He knew it was technically certain, sooner or later. But, while some things had changed, others had not: he was still the centre of his own universe, and found it near to impossible to imagine the universe carrying on without him.

—*Yet it will happen.*

—*Or so theory says.*

Sarazin was much occupied with such thoughts, for Glambrax offered him nothing in the way of conversation. The dwarf had taken an almighty blow on the head, and was fit for very little except sleeping and sunbathing. Fortunately, the skins of both travellers were already suntempered — otherwise they would have been badly burnt on that downriver journey.

For there was no shade, no shelter.

But, of course, limitless water.

Sarazin drank freely. Drinking of the Velvet River had almost killed him when he first arrived in Selzirk, but he had no choice. Besides, the river was much, much cleaner than it had been when people in their tens of thousands lived on the Harvest Plains.

At length, the raft drifted past the walls and towers of Selzirk the Fair. Sarazin was tempted to land — then saw a single uncouth monster standing where there was a hundred-pace gap in the outer battle-wall of Selzirk.

The river gate — that was what Lod had called that gap. Then Sarazin had called it a military obscenity. Or had Lod said that too? Sarazin could not remember. That conversation had taken place on the day of his return from exile, and he could not sort out the details in memory.

But what he could remember was his high excitement, his enthusiasm, his confidence. He had been so certain that life was truly beginning, that power and glory awaited him.

—*Fool!*

That was the judgment Sean Sarazin passed on his youthful self as the raft floated on downstream, leaving Selzirk behind in the distance.

He had been such a fool! So young, so feckless! He had not been destroyed by gambling, boozing, fighting or whores. But a callow pride had nearly seen to his destruction regardless. If it had not been for the advent of the Swarms, he would still have been in the forests of Chenameg, fighting a futile guerrilla war against Tarkal of Lod.

—*But what could I have had if I had been wise?*

He could have had a career in the army. Going out

416

every night to get pissed as a newt (to use Jarnel's death-less phrase). But what kind of life would that have been?

—*No life for me, that's for sure.*

—*So I was doomed whatever I did.*

So thought Sean Sarazin, then forced himself to admit that it was not true. Nobody had compelled him to stay in Selzirk. He could have taken to the Salt Road and could have fled north or south. To Drangsturm. To Chi'ash-lan. Anywhere. He could read and write, he could speak Galish — he could have made some sort of life for himself wherever he went.

—*But that's in the past. Let's think of the future.*

So Sarazin did think of the future. But could see nothing for himself or his dwarf but bare survival. Downstream lay the delta of the Velvet River, a marshy place of tidal beaches, of islands and estuaries. The Neversh might overfly the delta, but it would be difficult for heavyweight monsters to operate in such terrain. There, no doubt, he could grub a living, surviving by eating raw fish, raw shrimp, raw marshbird.

—*Grow old and die, doubtless webfooted before I die.*

So thought Sean Sarazin, then fell asleep to dream of rain, grey and endless, rain spindling down through fog, of his hands old and withered, his spine curving. Old man Sean Sarazin, a living ghost in the marshlands, a dying dwarf croaking at his feet . . .

He woke with the certainty that the dream was pro-phetic, that his future was known and could not be escaped. And he became so depressed that thereafter he roused himself only to drink and to void wastes. His depression persisted until the day he woke to find the raft adrift in Lake Ouija, a tidal bulge in the river just south of Androlmarphos — and realised there were people on the shore.

CHAPTER SIXTY-FIVE

When Sarazin and Glambrax were taken from the raft, they were so weak that they were consigned to an infirmary in Androlmarphos, and there they were fed for days upon broiled fish and the flesh of seabirds. As Sarazin's strength recovered, what he craved was not food but information. However, his keepers gently declined all requests for a briefing, saying it would tire him too greatly.

After three days, however, Sarazin was judged strong enough to see visitors, and was asked if he wished to receive any.

'An academic question,' Sarazin said. 'Surely nobody knows I'm here. And who in 'Marphos would know me?'

'On the contrary,' he was told. 'Everyone in the city knows of your arrival. As for those who wish to see you . . .'

He was given a list.

A long list.

There were people who had known him in Voice, Selzirk and Chenameg. Soldiers who had served under him in Tyte and Hok. Friends of friends and friends of the friends of friends. Servants and tavern keepers, poetasters and minor functionaries of the Regency. The very people whose demise he had so sincerely lamented as he drifted down the Velvet River on his raft.

Now that he knew so many to be alive and kicking, his desire to see them was zero. Though he did want a long talk with someone — anyone! — so he could bring his knowledge of current affairs up to date, he had no wish to be a tourist attraction, which was what he obviously was.

However, two names on the list of would-be visitors demanded his attention: Lord Regan and Jaluba.

'Those two,' he said. 'I'll see those two.'

'When?'

'Now!'

As it happened, Lord Regan and Jaluba did not attend Sarazin until the next day. They came together, hand in hand — and, to Sarazin's startlement, Lord Regan introduced Jaluba as his wife.

'My dearest and nearest,' said Lord Regan, and kissed her.

Lord Regan was wearing a skyblue military uniform, whereas Jaluba was — despite the heat of summer — wearing a coat made of fitch fur.

Sarazin had to admit that Lord Regan had made an excellent choice. Jaluba was but twenty years of age — and she was delicious. Any man would have wanted her. Sarazin did not begrudge Lord Regan possession of the woman, who sat quietly, the very picture of a damsel demure.

Nevertheless, Sarazin begrudged the marriage inasmuch as it made it impossible for him to demand the answers to some of the questions he had had in mind. Such as: where the hell had Jaluba gone to after she disappeared from Selzirk? Why had she disappeared on the day Plovey of the Regency had raided Sarazin's quarters? Had she perchance had anything to do with the theft of a bard, a prophetic book and certain documents from Sarazin's quarters?

However, plenty of other questions remained. And heartfelt greetings were scarcely over before he was asking them:

'How did you come to 'Marphos? And — where is my mother? I heard she'd fled to the Rice Empire. What about Fox? My father was going to seek your help. That was back in the autumn. There was a Door in Chenameg and — oh, it's a long story, but he was coming to see you. Jarl, too. What happened to them?'

'They reached me, one and all,' said Lord Regan. 'Your mother and your father both. And Jarl. When the Swarms came, I went south to Narba to seek a passage to the Scattered Islands. But Fox and Farfalla went with Jarl to Hok. Jarl persuaded them they could find refuge there.'

'It's true!' said Sarazin. 'Didn't Jarl tell you about Elkin, about X-n'dix?'

'Oh, I've heard all about that,' said Lord Regan. 'Jarl told me — and, besides, I've heard all about your war stories thrice over from Jaluba's lips.'

And Lord Regan and Jaluba squeezed hands, then kissed.

'Well,' said Sarazin, 'can I get to Hok?'

'You could walk,' said Lord Regan.

'What about ships?' said Sarazin.

'No ships run from here to Hok,' said Lord Regan. 'We trade with Stokos, to be sure. But not with Hok, for Stokos and Hok are at war, and the wizards favour Stokos.'

'Wizards?' said Sarazin. 'Pray tell, what's this about wizards?'

'Ah. So you don't know the story of today's 'Marphos. Is that how it is? Very well then. Listen, and I will tell . . .'

According to Lord Regan's account, as the Swarms approached, many refugees had been evacuated from 'Marphos. They had fled into the Central Ocean in ships, bound for the Scattered Islands or the Ravlish Lands. When the last ships had departed, there had been lawless rioting in the city, until an uncouth gangster had set himself up as warlord.

Then the city had suffered under the most foul and obscene oppression imaginable. Pack rape and cannibalism had been the least of it.

Finally, two ships had arrived, bearing wizards and

soldiers of the Landguard who were loyal to those wizards. Lord Regan was on one of these ships, having joined it at Narba. War had ensued. After a bitter struggle, the wizards and their soldiers had taken over the city — but their victory had been marred by an outbreak of typhus.

After the depredations of tyranny, war and plague, scarcely three thousand people remained in Androlmarphos. With nets and lines, the people wrested fish from the Velvet River and the sea itself. They hunted seabirds and riverfowl. Or they worked under the supervision of the wizards, who had, among other things, set up a manufactory for siege dust.

Androlmarphos traded with Stokos, exchanging siege dust for firelight steel and other products.

'What for the future?' said Sarazin. 'Will the wizards stay here in 'Marphos? Or take over Stokos, perhaps?'

'I cannot speak for that,' said Lord Regan, 'for these days I am but a soldier of the Landguard. They have given me a commander's rank, but, for all that, my position is lowly. I play no part in the high counsels where matters of state are decided.'

'Then come with me to Hok!' cried Sarazin, fired with enthusiasm. 'There I must go, I can do nothing else. My mother and father are there, the tutors of my youth as well — and others, doubtless. That is my future, if anywhere.'

The depression he had suffered on his downriver journey had vanished. He had a goal, a mission, a purpose. To strive to Hok and join his family, or what was left of it.

Lord Regan laughed.

'I am sworn to the service of the wizards,' said Lord Regan. 'My future is with them. But perhaps . . . perhaps I can arrange your passage to Stokos.'

'To Hok,' said Sarazin, correcting him.

'Yes, yes,' said Lord Regan, rising to go. 'To Hok. I come again tomorrow. Is there anything you'd like?'

'Grapes,' said Sarazin. 'Is that possible?'

'I regret not. But . . . wine? Yes? Sean Sarazin, I'm sure I can scavenge the most excellent wine. Now I must be off, for I've business to attend to — but Jaluba will stay a little longer and keep you company.'

Stay Jaluba did, but, though her presence was enchanting, her conduct was nothing if not chaste. Still, she did vouchsafe Sean Sarazin a single kiss before they parted.

CHAPTER SIXTY-SIX

At first, a passage to Hok seemed impossible to arrange. And Sarazin certainly did not wish to dare the long trek along the coast — not with monsters of the Swarms on the loose. However, in due course Lord Regan brought him the good news. A ship would be made available and Sean Sarazin would be landed on the southern coast of Hok.

'Where precisely?' said Sarazin.

'On the shores of the Willow Vale,' said Lord Regan. 'That, I understand, is the only sensible place for a visitor to Hok to land.'

And Sarazin could but agree.

Nine days after their arrival in Androlmarphos, Sean Sarazin and his dwarf Glambrax set to sea on a barque known as the Green Swan (a name which Sarazin frankly thought better suited to a tavern than to a ship).

Lord Regan was nominally the commander of the ship. Though it was the sea captain who was his subordinate who actually supervised the running of the barque, Lord Regan got the only decent cabin aboard. There he slept at night with his darling Jaluba. And there, during the day, he entertained Sean Sarazin.

Sarazin had been told that the journey from 'Marphos to Hok would probably take them four or five days, or a little longer if they had unfavourable winds. Certainly there was plenty of time for him to talk with Lord Regan and Jaluba.

And talk he did, positively bubbling. He was alert and alive, enthusiastic about life, delighted with the thought of reunion with his father, his mother and the tutors of his youth. So Hok was at war with Stokos. So what? As he looked back over his life, it seemed he had never been much more than a swordstroke away from danger. War in Hok would be no worse than what he had endured already.

And the present was sweet, for he had an admiring audience more than ready to hear all his tales. Once he had exhausted his accounts of hair-raising encounters with tyrants and monsters, he told and retold stories of his past.

Lord Regan, of course, knew that Sarazin had well and truly enjoyed Jaluba in the past. But Lord Regan showed not the slightest sign of jealousy as Jaluba praised Sean Sarazin's skill, bravery and daring.

In time, Sarazin found himself once more telling in detail of his campaign in Hok. In truth, the whole thing had been a shambling disaster. But, as Sarazin told it, the events in Hok had been a true test of heroes.

He told yet again of the storming of the Eagle Pass, the pursuit of the enemy into the Willow Vale, the near-mutiny of his troops when the enemy cut off their retreat, his escape up an arm of the Willow Vale, the long journey underground from the Eastern Passage Gate to the Western Passage Gate.

Then the encounter in X-zox with the madwoman Miss Inch, and the retreat to the Lesser Tower of X-n'dix, where eventually Epelthin Elkin had stayed.

'Tell me again about X-zox,' said Lord Regan. 'Is this underground tunnel the only way into the place?'

'The enclave is surrounded by mountains,' said Sarazin,

'and the locals allege that the cliffs of the coast permit no landing. I suspect an unknown path leads into the valley, but the only way to X-zox which I know is through the Passage Gates.'

'Then what will you do,' said Lord Regan, 'if you find those Passage Gates closed against you?'

'I'll open them, of course,' said Sarazin. 'It takes but a Word to open such a Gate, and but a Word to close it.'

'What Word is that?' said Lord Regan.

But Sarazin, to his horror, found he had forgotten how to control the Passage Gates. Fortunately, Glambrax remembered the Words to command both the Passage Gates and the door into the Lesser Tower of X-n'dix. Lord Regan and Jaluba paid special attention to the memorising of both.

Suggesting to Sarazin that perhaps they meant to accompany him to Hok after all.

CHAPTER SIXTY-SEVEN

The next day, at dawn, the Green Swan slipped past the rugged cliffs of the western end of Hok. Sarazin, promenading on the deck, surveyed the shore, which was barely half a league away. Those cliffs must be those of the enclave of X-zox, and he himself could most certainly see no place which promised a landing.

He looked inland, up a valley rugged but green, to the heights at the head of the valley, some ten leagues or so from the shore. Something gleamed on those heights. Was it the Greater Tower of Castle X-n'dix? What else could it be? The dragon-encumbered tower was bone white and stood half a league tall.

—So that must be it.

But no details could be told from this distance. Still, Sarazin would be there soon enough. A few leagues to the south, the coastline bent away to the east. The ship would turn to follow the coast, and, shortly, would land him on the shores of the Willow Vale. From there he could march overland to X-n'dix.

—*Ogres and such permitting, of course.*

So thought Sean Sarazin.

But, as the morning wore on, the ship did not turn east. Instead, it continued south. What lay due south? Why, only Stokos. That was all.

Then . . .

Sarazin went and confronted Lord Regan.

'As I told you before,' said Lord Regan, sadly, 'in the war between Hok and Stokos, the wizards who are my masters favour Stokos. And I have sworn an oath of fealty to my masters. Now — must I put you in irons below decks? Or will you swear to behave yourself?'

'Tell me first,' said Sarazin, 'are we truly bound for Stokos? And what fate awaits me there?'

'We are indeed bound for Stokos,' said Lord Regan, 'and are more than half way there. Your parents are in Hok, so Stokos can make good use of you as a hostage. Also — Stokos needs the secret of the Passage Gates if it is to conquer Hok entire.'

'This is bitter news,' said Sarazin, 'and much I could say which I will not. Well then . . . I will swear to make no move against you. We will behave as people of breeding should. Till the end.'

'Sean,' said Lord Regan, 'that's spoken as a man. And I will most certainly take you at your word.'

There, then, the matter should have ended. The making of oaths is the most sacred undertaking of manhood, for if men were not true to their word then trust would become impossible. And, if trust became impossible, then only the most barbaric expedients of murder and genocide could secure peace between men and between nations.

Thus Sean Sarazin, having given his word, should have

425

gone into captivity. However, unfortunately Sarazin had long lived in Selzirk, a vicious city given to degenerate ways. And there he had frequented with lawyers, whose crime against humanity is the systematic perversion of language.

Moreover . . . it was not just lawyers who had taught Sarazin bad habits. For even the Rovac warrior Thodric Jarl had once shown him how to worm his way out of an oath. Thus, though Sarazin had once sworn to go questing for the tectonic lever, he had never made the slightest attempt to do so.

So . . .

Sean Sarazin had sworn to make no move against Lord Regan, therefore he would not. However, reasoning like a lawyer, he argued that his dwarf was an entity separate from himself, therefore instructing his dwarf to attack Lord Regan would not constitute oath-breaking.

And even if it did — frankly, after all he had been through, Sean Sarazin was not prepared to be thwarted at the last moment. In Hok there was life, liberty and friendship. In Stokos, only stifling imprisonment, and torture perhaps, and quite possibly death. So Sean Sarazin instructed Glambrax — and gave him the green candle.

The green candle. Oh most precious of enchanted objects! The last of his remaining gifts from the druid he had encountered so long ago in the forests of Chenameg. The ring of invisibility had failed him, the dragon-bottle had proved a bitter disappointment, and the magic mudstone had long since been used, but the candle remained.

What would it do? Summon a dragon, a genie, a ghost, a wraith? Call up ghouls and demons? Satisfy wishes? Or do something miraculous but utterly useless? Sarazin could only hope.

Glambrax acted that evening.

When Lord Regan was dining in his cabin with wife,

dwarf and Farfalla's son, Glambrax took it upon himself to open the lanterns one by one and trim the candles within. When he came to the last lantern, he took out the green candle.

And lit it.

CHAPTER SIXTY-EIGHT

When Glambrax lit the green candle, the result was almost instantaneous. Smoke exploded from the candle in nauseous gouts, a stench worse than skunk and corpse mingled. And Lord Regan cried aloud in wrath and grabbed for the dwarf, but was met with a knife.

Glambrax stabbed once, twice—

Jaluba screamed—

And again and again—

And screamed—

And Lord Regan was falling, toppling, going down, the dwarf hacking, blood spurting and spraying—

Jaluba no longer screaming but retching, and Sarazin writhing on the floor, choked by nausea, the smoke having just about done for him, the stench unendurable—

And the door flew open stormed into—

Smoke boiling, a breath was enough, the men were flailing, gagging, chucking up, wrecked or retreating—

And Glambrax drove steel home once more, once more, but that was thrice more than was necessary, for Lord Regan was dead for real.

The candle still alight, smoke leaping from the wick in a series of coughing explosions. Glambrax had it still in his left hand.

Glambrax stuck the bloody knife in his belt, grabbed Sarazin by the scruff of the neck and hauled him from the cabin. Shortly they were out on deck, the candle still coughing, smoke still exploding, Glambrax himself very green at the gills.

But still upright, for the dwarf was possessed of a toughness not given to men. After all, he was his mother's son — and his mother had been the truly formidable witch Zelafona.

'Put it out!' gasped Sarazin, clawing for the candle. 'Out, or I die!'

Glambrax thumped him, hard. And, as he fell to the deck, put in the boot. Some of the ship's soldiers and sailors were fleeing for the rigging, some trying to hide themselves below, and others launching the ship's boats. All this by the last glimmering light of sunset.

A few tried to attack the source of the smoke — but fell back reeling.

'Gods!' groaned Sarazin.

Then vomited helplessly, stomach knotting up in helpless agony. He upchucked again as Glambrax grabbed him by the collar and hauled him to the side of the ship.

'When I say jump,' said Glambrax, 'then jump.'

Sarazin was incapable of making a reply. Peering down at the night-darkening sea, he made out a boat below, its crew about to cast off. Further spasms seized him.

By the time he had recovered, Glambrax had scrambled down into the boat with the candle still coughing in his hand. The crew had fled, diving to the sea, careless of shark-risk or drowning. The boat was his. Could he but make it.

'Jump!' shouted Glambrax.

Sarazin mustered his strength and jumped. He hit the sea by the side of the boat with a tremendous splash. And, by the time he surfaced, Glambrax had extinguished the candle and was ready to haul him aboard.

There was little left of the candle — just a small stub scarcely the length of a thumbnail. It had got them out of one predicament, but they could not count on it for much in the future.

Sarazin was nearly incapacitated by the after-effects of the candle. If escape had relied upon his strength, then escape would have been impossible. But Glambrax rowed them free of the Green Swan, rowed out into the deepening night, then raised their boat's minuscule sail.

They could have been captured, had the crew been fit to work the ship. But most of the Green Swan's crew were in a state almost as bad as Sarazin's. A few could have manned a small boat and pursued the escaping prisoner and his dwarf — but they lacked anything to inspire them to such a feat.

Thus Sarazin and Glambrax made good their escape, and, in due course, landed on the shores of the Willow Vale.

CHAPTER SIXTY-NINE

By the time Sean Sarazin and his dwarf reached the shores of the Willow Vale, the Green Swan had already sailed to Stokos. While Sean Sarazin was telling his news in Hok, other news was being told in Stokos — with predictable consequences.

But, for the moment, all that mattered to Sean Sarazin was his homecoming. Homecoming? Yes, after the bitterness of exile, a landing on Hok counted as that. Hok was, after all, a part of the Harvest Plains — and, more to the point, was inhabited by friends as well as strangers.

It was strangers that Sarazin met first. He and Glambrax were arrested by a mounted patrol and taken two leagues inland to a small fort. The commander of that fort was Thodric Jarl. The Rovac warrior was dressed as ever in iron-studded battle-leathers, and looked strong, fit and hearty.

'Sean!' cried the bulky-bearded Thodric Jarl, and embraced him.

'Is my mother here?' said Sarazin. 'My father?'

'Both Farfalla and Fox are in X-zox,' said Jarl. 'Most of our people dwell safe in X-zox, for we're often raided by marauders from Stokos, though they've yet to summon up the courage to invade in force. We use the Willow Vale for farming only, and as pastureland for sheep and cattle.'

'Are Fox and Farfalla well?' said Sean Sarazin.

'Both fit, both healthy, both well,' Jarl assured him.

'Do they rule, then?' said Sarazin. 'Are they the lords of Hok?'

'Nay,' said Jarl. 'Hok is ruled by Heth, who holds the land in trust for a greater ruler.'

'Heth?' said Sarazin. 'Did you say Heth, or Hearst?'

'I know nothing of the fate of Morgan Hearst,' said Jarl. 'After Hearst left the Harvest Plains he disappeared to sight. No, it's Heth I'm talking of. Heth. You remember. Don't you?'

But Sarazin didn't.

'Never mind,' said Jarl, with a laugh. 'No doubt once you reach X-zox Heth will explain everything to you himself.'

'I live for that day,' said Sean Sarazin, in a tone suggesting quite the opposite. 'Meanwhile, what about Peguero? Have you news of him? And Jarnel? And Celadon? Has anything been heard of him?'

While Sarazin had never been close to his brothers — indeed, they were still very much strangers to him — he was eager to learn of their fate.

'All three of your full brothers were here once,' said Jarl, 'as indeed was your half-brother Benthorn. But, like others, they have chosen to flee to the west, to the Scattered Islands and lands beyond.'

430

'Why should they flee?' said Sarazin.

'Because our war with Stokos threatens our destruction. But as I say, it's but a matter of raiding for the moment. The mountains protect our people in X-zox. Besides, Epelthin Elkin is still masquerading as a wizard, a bluff which helps us keep Stokos at bay. Intimidation, that's the thing.'

Then Sean Sarazin had to tell his sorry news. Lord Regan was dead — and Sean Sarazin the much-betrayed had wasted not a single tear lamenting his death! — but Jaluba still lived.

'The wench knows the Words,' said Sarazin. 'If she tells all in Stokos, then the enemy can open the Passage Gates and the Lesser Tower itself.'

Jarl saw the danger, and was soon riding for X-zox in company with Sean Sarazin and dwarf, meaning to personally oversee the defences of the mountain-protected enclave and the underground passage which led to it.

Inland went the riders until they had almost reached the Eagle Pass. Then they turned west and marched up an arm of the Willow Vale. Since Sarazin was here last, a road had been laboured through the wilderness, allowing them to travel swiftly to the cliffs in which the Eastern Passage Gate was set.

Sarazin remembered it as being black, but it proved to be a dark blue stained with streaks of opaline iridescence. Squarebuilt it was, and five times manheight. Warm and dry it was, vibrating faintly beneath his fingertips.

'Open it,' said Jarl.

Then Sarazin said the Word, hoping he had got it wrong. But he remembered correctly, for the Word had been something he had diligently committed to memory during his earlier travails in Hok.

And the Passage Gate opened.

By vanishing.

Within was the flickering blood-red passageway lit by dragon-head lamps. Sarazin remembered that all right. He

431

remembered what he would see at the far end of the passage, too, when he exited into X-zox. He would see a rock-tumbled goat-footed pastureland reaching away for ten leagues or so to the sea.

In fact . . .

When Sean Sarazin opened the Western Passage Gate and stepped into X-zox, what he saw was a valley terraced for intensive cultivation, a valley where he could see at a glance at least a half dozen villages.

A proper path had now been cut in the steep-scrambling slope leading upwards for a league or so to the cliff heights where stood the Towers of X-n'dix. The Greater Tower was, as ever, sealed against entry, its bone-white heights soaring skywards for half a league with a jade and jacinth dragon draped around it.

But the Lesser Tower, that pile of sculptured skulls, bones, heads, fangs, claws and other pieces of anatomy both human and alien, was accessible as always. Within dwelt Epelthin Elkin, who greeted Sean Sarazin warmly when he arrived with Jarl and Glambrax in tow.

The old scholar was wearing a faded, much-patched robe of green and purple. Once it had been a truly gorgeous garment, but the rigours of life in Hok had aged it rapidly. Elkin, however, was unchanged. For as long as Sarazin could remember, the old man had looked much the same. Wisp-frail grey beard, grey hair pigtail-plaited, mahogany skin walnut wrinkled, sky-zenith eyes bloodshot but sharp, stance upright as ever.

'I'm afraid I bring bad news,' said Sarazin.

Then bravely told how he had foolishly revealed the secrets of the Gates to Lord Regan and Jaluba. And how Jaluba still lived.

'Then we must expect invasion from Stokos,' said Elkin gravely.

'Magic may perhaps defeat such invasion,' said Sarazin.

'Have you brought magic with you to X-zox, then?' said Jarl, with a laugh. 'Don't look to old Elkin for any! He is but a fraud, as I've told you already.'

Which reminded Sarazin once again that the Rovac warrior did not know that Elkin was truly a wizard. Well? Could Elkin's magic save them from invasion? The old wizard of Ebber had often pleaded weakness in the past — had in fact insisted more on the weaknesses of magic than its strengths.

Of course, a little bit of Sarazin's magic green candle remained, safe in Glambrax's keeping. A potent weapon indeed! But such a fragment would not burn for long. To think that such might repel an invasion was at best a poor joke.

But . . .

Why should Stokos be at war with Hok? There was no reason that Sarazin could see. Perhaps the conflict could be resolved by treaty.

'Elkin,' said Sarazin, 'Pray tell, what quarrel has Stokos with us?'

'Come,' said Jarl, 'this is no time to talk politics. You'll be wanting to meet your mother. And your father, of course.'

When Epelthin Elkin had first explored the Lesser Tower — years ago, in the course of Sarazin's campaign in Hok against the ogre Tor — he had found many doors, cupboards and chambers which he could not open.

Since then, the elderly wizard had sought to open these, hoping to find treasure left by the Dissidents who had built Castle X-n'dix. Elkin had been largely successful in his efforts, and, while the amount of treasure he had uncovered was zero, this did mean that there was plenty of living space within the Lesser Tower.

It meant, for example, that Fox and Farfalla had a room to themselves. A small room, admittedly, but dragon-lamps within gave light, and an arrowslit allowed a view of a fraction of the sky.

Though Jarl had told Sarazin his parents were fit and well, Sarazin found his father ill, his skin an unhealthy yellow. He had hepatitis. Sean Sarazin, who had been long

433

laid up in bed with the same disease after his disastrous campaign in the marshlands of Tyte, knew just how miserable his father must be feeling.

Still, the occasion was joyful regardless. A time for kisses and embraces.

'Do you know,' said Farfalla, 'we're getting married.'

'When?' said Sarazin.

'On Midsummer's Day,' said Fox. 'Not long to go now.'

'Congratulations!' said Sarazin.

Then, after a great deal of talking — he had adventures to tell of, and his parents had tales of adventures of their own — he finally got round to telling the bad news. About the Words.

'The enemy can likely breach the Passage Gates,' concluded Sarazin soberly.

'Then,' said Fox, 'your next step must be to see Heth. Have you been told yet?'

'Told what?' said Sarazin.

Fox and Farfalla looked at each other. Then both broke into laughter.

'What's the joke?' said Sarazin angrily.

There was no joke as far as he could see. He had betrayed a secret vital to the defence of X-zox. Now he was due to confront the ruler of that land, the mysterious Heth, who would surely be most unhappy with him. Sean Sarazin had survived the wrath of other princes, true — he had lived through his encounters with Drake Douay and Tarkal of Chenameg. But could he be sure of surviving a third such encounter?

He was not optimist enough to count on it.

'Go,' said Fox, waving away Sarazin's questions. 'Go. See Heth. The sooner you know, the better.'

Sarazin, brain positively boiling with unanswered questions, was taken by Thodric Jarl to Heth's quarters.

'How does Heth like to be addressed?' said Sarazin anxiously. 'As Lord Heth? King Heth? Lord Emperor Heth?'

'Don't worry about that,' said Jarl firmly. 'Remember

what I told you. Heth is not ruler in his own right. He does but hold Hok in trust for a greater ruler.'

Sarazin was scarcely reassured, but put a brave front on it regardless as Jarl led him into Heth's quarters. There they found the man himself seated on a goatskin-padded chair, sharpening a sword. He looked up as they entered. He was a big man. Blond. And, to Sarazin's eye, undistinguished.

'Hello, Sean,' he said.

'Hello . . . Heth,' said Sarazin uncertainly.

'Don't you remember me?' said Heth.

'Should I?' said Sarazin.

'I was your prisoner once.'

Sarazin began to sweat. Not another person with a grudge against him!

'I've had many people technically my prisoner,' said Sarazin. 'Anarchists in Tyte, though if I remember correctly there were but two of them, and both lepers. But, after a battle by the banks of the Shouda Flow—'

'I was your prisoner in Hok,' said Heth.

Sarazin stared at him.

Then:

'Not . . . not the commander?' said Sarazin. 'The commander of the Eagle Pass? Tor's minion.'

'The same,' said Heth.

And now, of course, it all came flooding back. The capture of Heth when Sarazin's men stormed the Eagle Pass when they first invaded Hok. Heth forced to march with Sarazin and his companions to the Eastern Passage Gate. Heth compelled to travel with them to X-zox. Heth forced to swear . . .

To swear . . .

'You swore an oath,' said Sarazin slowly. 'An oath of fealty, was it not? The words . . . the exact words . . .'

The exact words escaped him.

'I swore lifelong loyalty to you,' said Heth. 'I swore that if King Tor died then I'd follow you forever, to death and beyond. And Tor is dead. So . . . welcome to your kingdom, Lord Sarazin!'

435

Then Sean Sarazin was plunged into one of the busiest times of his life. While Jarl planned the defence of X-zox with help from Fox (but with no help from Heth, a willing fighter but no military genius) Sarazin got to work.

First he had to absorb at least the bare outlines of Hok's recent history so he could properly understand his position. As Sarazin already knew, the ogre Tor had once been king of Stokos. When driven from his kingdom by the worshippers of a new religion — that of the Flame — Tor had eventually settled in Hok.

Half-hearted attacks by the Harvest Plains had failed to dislodge Tor from Hok. Then the ogre had launched a campaign to recapture Stokos from the adherents of the Flame. Unfortunately, the Flame worshippers had leagued with pirates, and had defeated Tor and had killed him.

Not all of Tor's men had died with their king. Some, notably Heth, had retreated back to Hok. Heth, the most senior of Tor's surviving officers, had done a deal with Epelthin Elkin, who had let him rent most of the Lesser Tower and use it as a castle. Thanks to Elkin's assistance, Heth had eventually become master of all the various refugees who had taken up residence in Hok.

After Tor's death, Stokos itself had been ruled by the pirates of the Greater Teeth. However, the strength of the pirates was broken at Androlmarphos, when the water thieves — then allied to Elkor Alish — had suffered a terrible defeat at the hands of Morgan Hearst.

The pirates thereafter proved unable to dominate Stokos.

The result had been civil war. The losing faction — which included many pirates — had withdrawn to Hok. The adherents of the Flame had finally won a conclusive victory, establishing themselves once again as rulers of Stokos. As a matter of principle, those victors had long wished to destroy Heth and all his followers.

For Heth was a sometime henchman of the evil ogre Tor, and a sworn enemy of the Flame. Heth's men were for the most part ogre-followers, or pirates, or religious dissidents, or escaped criminals, hence richly deserved death as far as the rulers of Stokos were concerned.

To Stokos, the destruction of Heth and all his people was a matter of religious duty. And Heth's people were now Sarazin's people.

Once Sarazin had finished his history lessons, he had to go forth and meet those people, to show himself, to make speeches, to accept oaths of fealty, to raise morale and rouse hopes in his troops. He proclaimed — and the claim was true — that the rule of the Flame on Stokos was not unanimously accepted.

'Many hate this religion,' said Sarazin, an instant expert on the subject thanks to detailed briefings from Heth and others. 'If we can break the strength of Stokos in battle then there are many on the island who would rally to our banner if we dared invasion.'

So spoke Sarazin.

But knew the breaking of the strength of Stokos might prove well beyond his capabilities.

Six days after Sean Sarazin learnt that he himself was the true ruler of Hok, warriors from Stokos struck at the Eastern Passage Gate. At the time, Sean Sarazin was defending the gate. Thodric Jarl was supervising the fortification of the Lesser Tower itself while Fox was lecturing junior commanders from his sickbed.

The raiders from Stokos did not come in great numbers, for this was not a full-scale invasion. Such an invasion

437

would follow shortly, but this was but a probing raid —
a reconnaissance in force.

The raiders were charged with establishing:

(a) whether Sean Sarazin had reached Hok alive;

(b) and, if he had, whether Jaluba could be used as a
hostage to compel his surrender; and

(c) if the Words revealed by the wench Jaluba would
truly open the Passage Gates.

The raiders landed unopposed on the coast of the Willow
Vale, for Hok lacked the strength to fortify and defend that
shore. Observed at a distance by scouts, the raiders
marched inland to the Eastern Passage Gate. Short of that
gate they were stopped by defenders under the command
of Sean Sarazin.

Lord Sarazin consented to parley with the raiders in
front of the hastily erected earthworks which now guarded
the Eastern Passage Gate. He told them to be gone. And,
when Jaluba was produced, weeping and wailing, he told
them they could butcher the bitch and eat her for all
he cared.

Sudden responsibility and the prospect of death at the
hands of a remorseless enemy had brought out the harshest
aspects of Sean Sarazin's character. And he was truly
furious with Jaluba. For, if she had only kept her mouth
shut, the enemy would not have learnt the secrets of the
Words, and would not be standing in armed strength
before his gates.

Rebuffed, the enemy retreated. But Epelthin Elkin,
standing beside Sean Sarazin during the parley, had
read them, and warned Sarazin to expect a night attack.
For the enemy, while they had the answers to questions
(a) and (b), still lacked an answer to (c).

'A mind search tells me they have the Words for certain,' said Elkin. 'They know how to command the gates
and indeed to open the Lesser Tower itself. But as yet
they cannot be certain that they know. Therefore they will
attack tonight, pressing their assault to the Eastern Passage
Gate to test it with a Word.'

Sarazin tried to think of something intelligent to say, failed, and so contented himself with saying the obvious:

'Then we must keep them from the gate. Can you help us?'

'By night,' said Elkin, 'I will conjure an illusion for your troops.'

'What illusion?' said Sarazin.

'Our own troops will see the enemy glowing scarlet in the dark. The enemy will not share the illusion, hence will think themselves night-shrouded.'

'Is that the best you can do?' said Sarazin.

'That,' said Elkin heavily, 'will be a sore trial of strength. It will suffice to exhaust me for a month.'

Sarazin hoped he was exaggerating.

That night, while Sean Sarazin waited for the enemy to attack, he realised he was not afraid at all. But then, he had little cause to be. His position was strong; he had experienced troops under his command; he had a wizard fighting on his side.

When the enemy finally attacked, they were massacred. Elkin did as he had promised. Sarazin's men saw the enemy glowing scarlet in the night. Many were shot by archers as they crept towards Sarazin's position, thinking themselves invisible in the dark.

Soon the enemy retreated, and Sean Sarazin thought the battle won. But the enemy attacked again. And a third time. A fourth. A fifth. That night, Sarazin learnt something about the nature of religious fanaticism.

However, by the time dawn came, the enemy's strength had been truly broken, and the enemy were in full retreat. Calmly, Sarazin ordered the pursuit. He led that pursuit himself, hoping to kill out every single enemy survivor before the foe could reach the shores of the Willow Vale.

And hoping, also, to capture Jaluba.

CHAPTER SEVENTY-ONE

Two days later, Sean Sarazin returned to the Eastern
Passage Gate with many scalps and three prisoners. One
of whom was Jaluba. Sarazin was determined to put her
on trial. But, on reaching the gate, he found he had a more
urgent duty demanding his attention. The Rovac warrior
Thodric Jarl had that day assaulted Epelthin Elkin at the
gate, and had tried to kill him.

Elkin himself was waiting by the gate to tell Sarazin of
this. The old wizard had escaped without serious injury,
but was exhausted. He had been forced to use his special
powers in self defence.

'Where is Jarl?' said Sarazin.

'We're holding him here,' said Elkin.

'On whose instructions?' said Sarazin.

'Mine,' said Elkin. 'If we'd carried him back to the Lesser
Tower as a prisoner, all of X-zox would know of it by now.
If you can persuade Jarl to behave himself, I'll not press
charges against him.'

'Let's go and see him,' said Sarazin.

'No,' said Elkin. 'You go alone. He almost starts frothing
at the mouth when I come in sight.'

'Is he mad?'

'Fanatical,' said Elkin simply. 'Like the rulers of Stokos.'

'I'll see what I can do,' said Sarazin.

This was serious.

Jarl was a seasoned campaigner, a greater warrior than
Heth, Fox and Sarazin rolled into one. Sarazin could not
afford to lose him. He knew the victory he had just won
was nothing — a skirmish, no more. The real invasion was

yet to come. And when it did, then his own life would really be on the line.

Sarazin was glad Elkin had kept Jarl's arrest as quiet as possible. Dissent in the highest ranks would be disastrous for the morale of the defenders of X-zox.

When Sarazin came to him, Jarl was being guarded by two hefty Stokos-born swordsmiths from Stokos.

'What's going on here?' said Sarazin, as if he didn't know.

'Let me go!' said Jarl. 'I'll kill him!'

'You'll kill me?' said Sarazin, faking amazement.

'No, fool! Elkin! He's a wizard.'

'So he is,' said Sarazin. 'But what of it?'

Jarl screamed with incoherent fury and struggled all the harder. Unable to escape, he settled.

'Whatever Elkin is,' said Sarazin reasonably, 'he's been a mutual friend for years. Your friend as well as mine.'

'By the knives!' said Jarl. 'If I'd known he was a wizard I'd have killed him when we first met in Voice.'

Elkin was right. Jarl was a fanatic. But what was the source of this fanaticism?

'I fail to see,' said Sarazin, 'why Elkin's death is so important to you. I've heard you mention a feud between wizards and Rovac, but surely this is neither the time nor the place to pursue such a feud.'

'I am not free to think likewise,' said Jarl.

Thodric Jarl, son of Oric Slaughterhouse, blood of the clan of the bear, warrior of Rovac and leader of men, was a man who disdained all compromise. Particularly when principle was at stake.

'Look,' said Sarazin, 'be reasonable. Elkin's just saved all our lives.'

'Saved our lives?' said Jarl. 'He may have helped you with a skirmish, but you could have won it in any case with both hands tied behind your back.'

'The point is,' said Sarazin, 'Elkin is fighting. On our side. He may do so again if we let him live.'

Sarazin pursued this line of reasoning at length, to no avail. What to do, what to do? Sarazin began to sweat. This was a life or death decision. Who was more valuable? The wizard or the warrior? The warrior, probably. But . . . Jarl was the guilty party. Jarl was the aggressor. What would Fox say if Sarazin moved against the innocent?

Sarazin, unable to bear the thought of Fox's condemnation, gave Jarl an ultimatum which served the purposes of justice. The Rovac warrior must swear to keep the peace while he remained in Hok, or he would be killed on the spot.

'Who will you get to do your killing?' said Jarl bitterly.

'I'll do it myself!' said Sarazin, exasperated beyond endurance. 'I'll kill you like a mad dog if you insist on behaving like one!'

He suddenly felt that he had had quite enough of these crazy Rovac warriors. They were a blight on the world. Whatever mayhem was going on, a Rovac warrior was sure to be at the heart of it. First there had been Elkor Alish, who had wrecked Sean Sarazin's conspiracy when he leagued with Qolidian of Androlmarphos. Then Morgan Hearst, who, unless Sarazin was very much mistaken, had doomed all civilisation in Argan North by destroying Drangsturm with the death-stone.

And now Thodric Jarl, acting like a madman!

'I mean it!' said Sarazin. 'Unless you come into line, you're finished!'

Finally, with his death thus confronting him, Thodric Jarl swore himself to keep the peace. Then Sarazin ordered Jarl to be released. The Rovac warrior stumped away in the worst of tempers imaginable.

'Come back!' ordered Sarazin.

'What do you want?' said Jarl.

'An apology.'

'To you?'

'No. From you to Elkin. For trying to kill him.'

'I did but my duty,' said Jarl.

Sarazin opened his mouth to remonstrate with him — then closed it again. He had been lucky to persuade Jarl to keep the peace, even when death was the alternative. There was no point in starting a contest of wills over the trivial matter of an apology — particularly not when Sean Sarazin would surely be the loser in such a contest.

'Very well,' said Sarazin. 'But . . . would you do me a favour?'

'That depends,' said Jarl.

'I sit in justice here and now on a criminal case,' said Sarazin. 'The charge is treason. I would like you to be my instrument of justice should the verdict go against the accused.'

Jarl considered, then said:

'I will serve as an instrument of justice.'

Sarazin smiled to himself, and forthwith convened the trial of the traitor Jaluba.

Jarl had agreed to something. Jarl would be his instrument of justice. There was an old trick Jarl had once taught Sarazin — get a man to obey you in a small thing and he will later find it hard to resist you in a greater matter. Sarazin complimented himself on his strategy.

The Rovac warrior would take careful handling, but Sarazin was confident that, in time, Jarl would prove an obedient instrument of his will. A lot of time, perhaps — but it would happen one day.

The matter of Jaluba's trial was swiftly disposed of. Sarazin was hungry, and eager to push on to X-zox. Besides, he wanted to have Jarl doing his bidding as soon as possible. Serving as an instrument of justice — an executioner in fact.

It all seemed very simple until Sarazin actually had Jaluba in front of him. He told himself:

—*She is but a whore.*

But she looked as beautiful as ever, despite her tears, her fear, her helpless heartbreak. She was still the luscious Jaluba, mistress of the thousand voluptuous perfumes,

443

queen of the lubricous arts, mistress of the pink lips and the bedroom eyes.

—And a whore, a thief, a traitor.

So thought Sarazin, steeling himself to his duty.

He outlined the charges against her.

'Jaluba, you stand before me charged with treason. You and you alone possessed the Words to the Gates and to the Lesser Tower. You and you alone could have given them to the enemy. You and you alone have brought disaster upon our land.'

Jaluba refused to speak, refused to plead, but simply wept and wailed. Sarazin, speaking over her grief, outlined the case against her, asked her to defend herself — and, when she did not, pronounced her guilt.

'The sentence is death,' said Sarazin.

And nodded to Jarl, who dragged Jaluba away.

She was screaming by now.

And Sarazin wished, then, that he could have cancelled his sentence. But it was too late. For he had spoken, and could scarcely unspeak himself, not under the circumstances.

CHAPTER SEVENTY-TWO

By the next day Farfalla had learnt all, and went hunting Sean Sarazin. When she caught him, he flinched from her scathing wrath, and tried to flee. But there was no escape.

'What have you done?' said Farfalla.

'What's on your mind?' said Sarazin.

'Jaluba! Have you had her murdered?'

'She had a trial,' said Sarazin coldly.

'For what?' said Farfalla.

'She gave the enemy the keywords which allowed them to attack,' said Sarazin, now trying to sound injured. 'She betrayed us.'

It sounded weak even to himself.

'Who gave her those Words in the first place?' said Farfalla, with fury and disgust mixed. 'You! Gods, what have I bred?'

'That's only part of it,' said Sarazin defensively. 'There's more. Jaluba's treachery goes way back, oh yes, right back to Selzirk. There she betrayed my trust. She stole from me. A bard, a book — documents as well. Thanks to that bitch, I did the most dreadful injury to a man of honour.'

'You don't know what you're talking about,' said Farfalla in fury.

'She's a thief,' insisted Sarazin. 'The day Plovey raided my quarters—'

'Gods!' exclaimed Farfalla. 'You fool! You bungling dolt! Were you born stupid, or do you have to work at it?'

Sarazin, stunned by the strength of her anger, made no answer. So Farfalla went on:

'You know why Plovey raided your quarters? Because I tipped him off. Yes, me! You know why? Have you any idea? To set him up! It worked, oh yes, it worked.'

Sarazin did not answer. Could not. Was speechless. His mother? At the heart of all this trouble, his mother? Could it be possible?

'Do you know why I set him up?' said Farfalla. 'Because he was getting close, oh, very close to you, Sean Sarazin. You and Jarl, conspirators! You were like big clumsy babies. I knew what you were up to! Worse, I knew Plovey knew, though I don't think he knew that I knew.'

'I don't see what this has got—'

'Listen! I decided to kill off Plovey. Dangerous — but leaving him alive was more dangerous yet. So I set him up. I tempted him into a crime which carried a death

445

penalty. Forging a warrant, oh yes — not to mention false arrest and a dozen lesser crimes. I could have finished him.'

'You could have finished me too!'

'Sean Sarazin, I meant to finish you. At least, I meant to scare you so badly that all your conspiracy nonsense came to an end. So I removed your precious documents. Your prophetic book and your bard as well.'

'What do you mean, you removed them? I was with you all the time. I remember that day. I'll not forget it for a lifetime.'

'Bizzie took them for me,' said Farfalla. 'She was mine, my creature, my agent. You knew that, surely? Didn't you? Wasn't it obvious? I gave her to you. Why, if not to watch you? Didn't you ever guess? Sean, are you really so stupid?'

'You're my mother! I never thought you'd—'

'What? Go to such lengths to keep you alive? Sean, that was what it was all about. Keeping you alive. I warned you when you first reached Selzirk, but you never listened. It was one crazy thing after another. So I wanted to shock you, frighten you, leave you guessing. To end your conspiracy. It worked, didn't it? After a fashion.'

'After a fashion,' said Sarazin sullenly. 'But Jaluba?'

'When Bizzie cleared out your room she cleared out your whore as well. Jaluba was held incommunicado until I could get to work on her. I put the fear of hell into her, believe you me! When I was finished with her, she was more than happy to flee to the Rice Empire. I made it possible for her, of course. Escorts, gold . . . oh, it was all taken care of.'

'What about my bottle?' said Sarazin.

'Your bottle?' said Farfalla.

'I had a magic bottle,' said Sarazin, 'a kindle of dragons within.'

'You had such stolen from you?' said Farfalla, in pitying tones. 'I wouldn't worry too much about it. Much is sold in Selzirk that is not what it seems. Maps

446

of treasure cities, magic rings, enchanted lamps and such rubbish. All trash, as you would doubtless have found out in due course.'

'You're right,' said Sarazin, 'it wasn't what it was cracked up to be. But it wasn't stolen, either. At least, not permanently. I got it back. From Glambrax. How come he took it from my quarters? Was he your creature too?'

'Oh, he did the odd job for me,' said Farfalla. 'We had some interesting conversations. But he wasn't my creature, no, I'd not call him that. He's your servant if he's anyone's. What happened was this. First Bizzie hustled Jaluba away. Then Bizzie took bard, book and documents from your room. Then she got hold of Glambrax and swore him to secrecy.'

'Why?'

'I'm telling you, aren't I?' said Farfalla. 'Don't be so impatient! She got an oath of secrecy from him, oh yes, a solemn oath, a binding oath. Then she told him Plovey would be raiding your quarters. If anything was hidden within, Plovey would likely find it. So Glambrax was to uncover it first and yield it up to Bizzie. We judged your dwarf privy to most of your secrets, even those few hidden from us.'

'And he did? He gave you . . . things from my room?'

'He didn't. He refused. He said he was sworn to secrecy but not to her service or mine. But Bizzie is a formidable operator, Sean — more than you'd ever guess! She forced another oath from Glambrax. He could take anything from your room, but he was not to give it back to you unless your life depended on it.'

'And he agreed?'

'His life would have been forfeit had he refused.'

'And Bizzie? Where is she now?'

'She's gone. She sailed for the west in the same ship which took Celadon, Peguero and young Jarnel. And Benthorn. Why do you ask, Sean? Do you want proof of my tale? Look! Here's proof!'

And, from round her neck, Farfalla took a bard.

447

'This is the bard, Sean. The one which was taken from your room. You can have it back, now.'

Sean Sarazin took the bard into his hands, then put it round his neck. Then said, in cold anger:

'You've used me. You've manipulated me. You never played straight with me. Thanks to you, a prince of the Favoured Blood was tortured, for we thought him guilty of theft. Thanks to you, Jaluba's dead.'

'Jaluba is dead,' said Farfalla bluntly, 'because you ordered her killed.'

'But I thought—'

'You set yourself up as judge, jury and executioner,' said Farfalla. 'You took upon yourself such responsibility. So why blame me?'

'I was not executioner,' muttered Sarazin.

'Who was?'

'Jarl.'

'Then you might,' said Farfalla, 'find what he's done with the woman's corpse, and see that it's decently buried or burnt.'

Then she turned on her heel and departed, leaving Sean Sarazin crushed, shaken, devastated. And alone with his guilt. Which was nearly unbearable.

Sean Sarazin sought for Thodric Jarl in the environs of the Lesser Tower of X-n'dix, but he was not there. So Sarazin went back through the underground passage from X-zox to the Willow Vale, and asked after Jarl at the Eastern Passage Gate.

He was told that Jarl had taken Jaluba to the shore, swearing that he would sacrifice her to the sea gods.

Sarazin took to horse and followed. Along the way he asked after Jarl and Jaluba. Yes, they had passed this way, riding together. Then, when he reached the shores of the Willow Vale, he asked after Jarl—

And was told that the Rovac warrior had commandeered one of the few fishing boats operating from that coast, and had sailed away in it.

'But what did he do with the woman?' said Sarazin.

He described the woman he was interested in.

Jaluba.

His description was a good one, and there were several
witnesses who could vouch for her fate. Thodric Jarl had
married her there on the shores of the Willow Vale, and
she had departed with him as his wife.

CHAPTER SEVENTY-THREE

It lacked but three days to Midsummer's Day, but Sean
Sarazin was sure he would never live to see his parents
properly wed. He would be defeated, executed — burnt
alive, perhaps. And those who remained loyal to him
would die at his side.

It was inevitable.

The enemy had followed up their raid with an invasion
in force. The invading forces had marched up the Willow
Vale to attack the Eastern Passage Gate. After brutal
combat, the enemy had stormed the fortifications defending the gate.

Now the enemy were in X-zox. They had won precious
little so far, for Sarazin had burnt all the villages of X-zox
rather than let them fall into enemy hands. All stocks of
food had been brought into the Lesser Tower, or had gone
with the noncombatants whom Sarazin had sent into the
mountains.

If the consequent disappointment had dampened the
enemy's spirit, their performance showed no sign of it.

They had assaulted the Lesser Tower three times already,
and three times they had been beaten back. Epelthin Elkin
had encompassed their defeat. The wizard of Ebber had

thrice surpassed himself — but at a cost. Elkin now lay unconscious in bed, struck down by a stroke.

They would get no more help from him.

And, when the enemy attacked for a fourth time, Sarazin was sure that the Lesser Tower would fall.

Sarazin remembered what Lord Regan had told him so long ago in the Sunrise Gardens in Voice:

'Remember, we create ourselves. Always remember that. We have free will so we are entirely responsible for ourselves. Everything happens to us by our own choice. Never forget that.'

He wondered.

—*Did I choose this?*

And realised that he had.

That was a bitter irony indeed. He now had everything he had once longed for, fought for, struggled for. He was ruler of his own kingdom, master of his own castle, head of his own army, liege-lord of valorous men. And this was going to prove his death.

For he lacked the strength to hold it.

Thodric Jarl must have seen as much, otherwise why would the Rovac warrior have fled? Surely not just out of love for Jaluba.

—*Though I once thought the world would have been well lost for such a woman.*

True, Jarl had hated Elkin bitterly. But Sarazin doubted that either love or hate could have compelled him to flee.

—*It was doom, that was what drove him.*

—*He never swore himself to my service. My error. I never demanded an oath of loyalty.*

—*But would he have given it had I demanded?*

Somehow, Sarazin doubted it.

The enemy would conquer then Sean Sarazin would die, his mother would die, his father would die, those who trusted him and honoured him would die. All dead, all slaughtered, all doomed.

What was the alternative?

450

There was none.

But a few could perhaps escape. Yes. A fighting retreat over the mountains might do it. Pursuit would be difficult.

—Besides, it's me the enemy want.

Sarazin thought it through.

At last, he realised he had no alternative. He sought out Heth, judging Heth to be the man to lead the retreat. Sarazin himself would stay, fighting a rearguard action.

—Fox and Farfalla at least may live. If they live, then not all is lost.

So Sarazin thought, trying to be brave. But when Heth came into his presence, Heth saw his despair at once.

'What now, my lord?' said Heth.

'The end,' said Sarazin.

Then, to his shame, burst into tears. Heth called for a little mulled wine and a little bread, and made Sarazin settle to eat and drink.

Then Heth said:

'You're tired, as are we all. For you, the fatigue must be worse, since these burdens have come upon you suddenly. Sleep, and you'll feel better on the morrow.'

'On the morrow I die,' said Sarazin. 'I'll tell you how.'

Then he told Heth his plans.

'But this is terrible!' exclaimed Heth. 'We can't do that! We can't surrender, not just like that!'

'What do you suggest, then?' said Sarazin.

But Heth had no answers. While he had been at war for a long time, Heth was no military genius. Besides, what could even genius have done in their position? They had only held against the enemy before thanks to Elkin. Surely they could not hold without him.

'My lord,' said Heth, 'sleep, and surely you'll think better of it tomorrow. Surely victory will come to you, for you are, after all, of the Favoured Blood.'

'But I'm not!' cried Sarazin, anguished. 'I'm not royal,

451

I'm no prince, no child of the Blood. I'm but a peasant's bastard with pretensions above my station.'

'You're man enough for me,' said Heth.

Which was a comfort, yes, good to hear, but:

'It's no good,' said Sarazin, miserably, tears again squeezing from his eyes. 'If only, oh . . . but it's no use. I only wish we had a real prince to lead us.'

'None could be better than you,' said Heth, trying to soothe him. 'What could others do that you have not?'

'No real prince would have ended up like this,' said Sarazin, in self disgust. 'Sitting bawling like a baby with the enemy without his gates.'

'What real princes have you met?' said Heth.

'Tarkal, that's one,' said Sarazin. 'Oh yes. But Douay was the greatest prince I ever met.'

'Douay?' said Heth. 'That's my family name.'

'Yours?' said Sarazin.

'Yes. I'm Heth Douay. It's a name common on Stokos. Was it someone from Stokos you met?'

'Oh no,' said Sarazin. 'This Douay was from the Scattered Empire, a seapower realm of the Central Ocean. Drake was his name.'

'Drake?' said Heth, startled.

'That means something to you?'

'In the language of Stokos it means pumpkin,' said Heth. 'It's short for Dreldragon.'

'Strange!' said Sarazin. 'This Douay I knew was also known as Lord Dreldragon. He was lord of the Gates.'

'Lord of the Gates?' said Heth. 'The gates of time? Of hell? Or what? Is this a god you speak of?'

'No,' said Sarazin. 'This is a man. The gates in question are those of Chenameg, where Drake Douay rules in grandeur.'

'This is passing strange,' said Heth, 'for I had a brother so called. I thought him dead years ago, yet perhaps . . .'

'You must think your brother dead still,' said Sarazin,

'for the lord of the Gates is not of Stokos but of a seapower empire, as I have told you. I met him first through a sad dispute over a bard.'

'You quarrelled for love of a singer?' said Heth.

'No,' said Sarazin. 'We disputed possession of a magical amulet which possessed the power of voices.'

'An amulet?' said Heth. 'Was it black, mayhap? A black as shiny as sea-washed shell with stars set upon it?'

'Yes!' said Sarazin, startled.

'And it could be made to speak, in a man's voice?'

'Yes.'

'And this Drake was — what? Blond like me? But short?'

'Yes. You — you know him?'

'But of course,' said Heth. 'It's my brother, as I've told you already. Cheeky, was he? A devil with his tongue? A cocky young sod in trouble as much as out of it?'

'He was a master swordsman,' said Sarazin. 'More than my match, that's for certain.'

'How else would he have survived for so long?' said Heth. 'Or has he died?'

'He was alive when I left him,' said Sarazin, 'and I expect him to be so still.'

Then Heth finally gave way to emotion, and whooped with joy, and cried:

'He lives! He lives! My brother lives!'

He grinned, whooped again, punched left hand with right fist, then jigged around on the spot slapping his thighs, then embraced Sarazin and hugged him tight. Then kissed him.

'Man, this is great news!' said Heth. 'Drake lives! My drunken bum of a brother is alive, alive!'

Sarazin extricated himself from Heth's grasp then said, slowly:

'I think I may have to disappoint you yet. What makes you so sure your brother lives?'

'Name, description and bard,' said Heth. 'My brother showed me such a charm when we met on the Greater

453

Teeth at a time when King Tor was leagued with pirates. Depending on his mood, he claimed he won the thing from the dragon Bel, or from Guardian Machines in combat.'

'When was this?' said Sarazin.

'Why, it was well back in time,' said Heth. 'Before the alliance of the pirates with Elkor Alish. The bard proves all.'

The more certain Heth became, the more reluctant Sarazin was to concede him victory. Surely it could not be true. Could it? Sean Sarazin had humbled himself before Drake Douay at the Gates of Chenameg. Surely it was a prince of the Favoured Blood he had knelt before. Not a — a bum. A lawless pirate. The brother of a thick-witted peasant from Stokos.

'Possession of a bard proves nothing,' said Sarazin firmly, 'for there are many such in the world, though some think in ignorance that there is but one.'

'The bard that Drake carried,' said Heth, 'was marked by a knife cut. That was where it saved his life in a bar brawl in Narba, if we can believe what he says.'

The final detail.

The truth could no longer be denied.

'It was him,' said Sarazin heavily. 'He lives now as I have said, ruling the Gates of Chenameg. Was he . . . was he really a pirate?'

'Oh, a pirate, yes,' said Heth. 'Pirate, drunkard, lecher, brawler, gambler, liar, thief. I love him, you understand, but such is brotherhood. As a stranger I might find him hard to bear.'

'And I wanted to swear myself to his service!' said Sarazin, shocked at the way Douay had fooled him.

'You see your error, do you?' said Heth. 'Oh, he must have told you a pretty story!'

'Gah!' said Sarazin in disgust.

Then Heth started to laugh and laugh. He collapsed to the ground, writhing. He laughed so much he cried. He laughed till the sobbing pain in his chest became unbearable. Then, slowly, he sobered himself, and asked:

'Pray, my lord, what could my fool of a brother do that you could not?'

And Sarazin answered:

'Nothing!'

He was furious. He had been suckered by a low-bred common criminal. Drake was a pirate after all! He did deserve to be tortured to death! He had behaved like the worst of criminals, too. Had humiliated Sarazin at the Gates. Had beaten him up. Terrorised him. Lied to him.

—I'll kill him!

So swore Sarazin.

Drake was a liar, cheat, pirate, oppressor, torturer and tyrant, a criminal whoremaster, scum from the streets, the lowest of the low, a murderous delinquent, an overgrown dwarf debauched by a debased appetite for power at any price.

And he had humiliated Sean Sarazin, and, worse, undermined his confidence in his own abilities.

—Gods. If a fool like that can master the Gates of Chenameg, then I can master X-zox.

'My lord,' said Heth, as Sarazin stormed from the room, 'where are you going?'

'To parley!' said Sarazin, for the way to save his people and his pride had already become clear to him. 'To parley with the enemy, now!'

CHAPTER SEVENTY-FOUR

Sean Sarazin was still burning red-hot with anger when he went forth to parley with the enemy with Glambrax at his side. There was nothing original in the offer he made to the enemy, and he should have thought of it before. Would have, had he not been so depressed, so overwhelmed by thoughts of doom.

Sarazin displayed not the slightest fear as he walked among the enemy's ranks, which was only natural, for he felt none. He was totally consumed by his anger.

Sarazin's offer to the enemy was but a variation of the one which had been made to him by foreign marauders when he had led an army to defend the lands of the Harvest Plains round the headwaters of the Shouda Flow.

This time, however, there was somewhat more at stake.

'This offer I make to you,' said Sean Sarazin when he was face to face with the enemy commander, a tall man built like a battleaxe. 'I will meet you in single combat to decide the possession of this castle. If you win, my people will surrender the castle to you, and you of course will claim my life.'

'And if you win?' said the enemy commander. 'Are you so extravagant as to expect us to surrender to you?'

'No,' said Sarazin. 'Merely to bring this campaign to an end, to march away to the Willow Vale then sail to Stokos and leave us in peace for another year.'

A year, that was all he needed. A year to fortify X-zox properly, to train men, to make alliances, to put spies ashore on Stokos.

'Let me think on it,' said the commander.

But Sarazin had already guessed his answer. For he had seen the fear in the commander's eyes.

Sean Sarazin knew himself for a bungling fool and a second-rate soldier at best. But to the enemy commander he was something else altogether. He was the lordly Watashi, a mighty warlord of the Harvest Plains, whose penchant for battle was proved by the scars on his face.

The enemy was not to know that those scars were but scratches which had been diligently enlarged by salt. The enemy was not to know that rumours of Sarazin's military success were at best misleading — since he had never won victory without Thodric Jarl at his elbow.

The enemy commander would not meet the great lord Watashi in single combat.

Sarazin was sure of that.

But, nevertheless, he was in high spirits as he made his way back to the Lesser Tower. For, while Sean Sarazin was not one of the world's military geniuses, he had been around soldiers for most of his life, and had been taught to use his eyes. He knew what to look for and how to interpret what he saw.

His foemen had endured summer rain, summer storms, threefold defeat, and onslaughts of nightmare and illusion courtesy of Epelthin Elkin. They were cold, hungry and dispirited. Sarazin had seen no evidence of tents. Also, if he was any judge, the enemy was right out of rations.

Logistics, that was the thing!

Sarazin had been general enough to deny all comfort to the enemy, burning villages rather than let the enemy have them. The invaders had exhausted their rations. They were cold, wet, hungry, defeated and frightened. In contrast, those in the tower were warm, dry and fed.

He said as much to his commanders when he got back to the Lesser Tower and assembled them in conference.

'If we can hold out for but a few days more,' said Sarazin, with enthusiasm, 'they're done for. Finished.'

'Good stuff to tell the troops,' said one of his commanders, 'but don't expect us to believe it. We're finished.'

'That's treason!' said Heth the loyal, Heth the thick-witted.

But he was shouted down, and Sarazin finally brought the conference to an end lest it end in mutiny. Yes, Sean Sarazin had been around soldiers long enough to know when mutiny threatened.

He brooded for the rest of the day.

He had been ready to abandon all hope because he thought the enemy sure to conquer. Then he had tried the single-combat ploy, but had failed. But had discovered, in the process, that the enemy were on the point of breaking. If he attacked, the enemy would break and run. He was sure of it.

But he was equally sure that his own men would not attack if he ordered them to. Rather, they would mutiny.

—But Douay would have managed it, damn it!

Sarazin was sure of it. Douay was a piece of low-bred trash, but he was a wily survivor. He would have found a way to motivate his men to attack.

—Kill someone?

No good. That would mean mutiny.

—Call for volunteers?

He would not get any. Except Heth.

Night came on. A stormy night of windhowl and thunderclap, of lightning startling. Sean Sarazin peered through an arrow slit and saw lightning writhing around the dragon of the Greater Tower of X-n'dix. Almost persuaded himself he saw that dragon move.

Outside were the enemy. Cold, by now. Chilled to the bone. Any fires extinguished for certain by the driving rain. No tents, no food, and doubtless little sleep under the conditions. Fear eating at their bones. Fear of the magic of nightmare which had thrice been used against them. Fear of the warlord Watashi.

Many would be sick, all homesick.

And their commander was afraid.

That doomed them for certain.

—One attack. That's all it takes. Something to rouse the troops out to battle. Fear or temptation, need or desperation, pain or . . . or . . .

—Magic?

Sarazin went looking for Glambrax, and, at midnight, found him. Glambrax was happily toasting half a dozen centipedes over a fire. A midnight snack.

'Glambrax,' said Sarazin, 'have you by chance the remains of my magic candle?'

'Of course,' said Glambrax, and produced it.

Moments later, Sean Sarazin was rousing the Lesser Tower with a battle-lung voice.

'Gather gather gather!' he shouted. 'Gather to me, for I have great news, great news.'

Slowly, grumbling and cursing, men began to wake. A few stalwart souls like Heth set themselves to kicking those who pretended to be asleep. It took a long time to get them all together, for sleeping men were scattered in rooms and corridors throughout the Lesser Tower, and even on stairwells.

As they gathered, bringing their weapons with them from habit, Sarazin had a little wine issued. They would be glad of the warmth of the liquor once they were out in the rain. And, fondling the stub of magic candle which was left to him, he knew they would soon be glad to be escaping to the rain.

The rest, of course, is history.

THE END

THE WIZARDS AND THE WARRIORS
by Hugh Cook

CHRONICLES OF AN AGE OF DARKNESS. 1:

'I ask all of you here today to join with me in pledging
yourself to a common cause,' said Miphon. Elkor Alish
laughed, harshly: 'A cimmon cause? Between wizards and
the Rovac? Forget it!'

And yet it had to be. Though Alish never accepted the
alliance, his fellow warrior Morgan Hearst joined forces
with Miphon and the other wizards. The only alternative
was the utter destruction of their world.

The first volume in a spectacular fantasy epic to rival
THE BELGARIAD and THE CHRONICLES OF THOMAS
COVENANT.

0 552 12566 0

Also available

THE WORDSMITHS AND THE WARGUILD

0 552 13130 X

THE WORDSMITHS AND THE WARGUILD
by Hugh Cook

CHRONICLES OF AN AGE OF DARKNESS. 2:

'Thanks to the wizard of Drum,' said the Brother, 'we know where to find these boxes. The nearest is in the bottom of a green bottle in Prince Comedo's Castle Vaunting in Estar. A monster protects the bottle from those who would acquire it.'

'Charming,' murmured Togura.

Togura would not have chosen the profession of questing hero, but in the end he had no choice. He was caught between The Wordsmiths and The Warguild, the two organizations which vied for power within the dismal kingdom of Sung, a land famous simply for being so often and so richly insulted.

Besides, if he did not find the *index*, the key to the magical treasure chest known as the *odex*, he would never be able to claim his love from its mysterious depths.

0 552 13130 X

THE WOMEN AND THE WARLORDS
by Hugh Cook

CHRONICLES OF AN AGE OF DARKNESS. 3:

'Lord Alagrace said you'd help.'

'Any oracle can give you a reading,' replied Yen Olass.

'I told Alagrace an oracle couldn't help me,' said the
Ondrask. 'I told him I wasn't interested in a reading. But
he told me you'd do better than that. He told me you'd
fix it.'

'What?' said Yen Olass.

She was genuinely shocked, and it took a lot to shock her.

So begins Yen Olass' involvement in the life-long feud of
the warlords of the Collosnon Empire. She was to witness
war, madness and wizardry, and would play a greater part
in the events of her time than a mere oracle had any right
to expect.

0 552 13131 8

THE WALRUS AND THE WARWOLF
by Hugh Cook

CHRONICLES OF AN AGE OF DARKNESS. 4:

The king drank some more blood. A little dripped from his lips to his leather trousers.

'You're right,' said King Tor. 'Those were but boyish pranks. So I'll let you off lightly. We'll have you birched in public today. You spend tonight buried to the neck in the public dungheap. Toward morning, we'll put you on a boat. Three leagues from shore, you'll be thrown overboard. That is my justice!'

Drake new he had got a good deal.

What he didn't know was that this was only the start of a long journey which would take him far from his home and his love — and that he would have to endure far worse before either could be regained.

0 552 13327 2

A SELECTED LIST OF FANTASY AND SCIENCE FICTION AVAILABLE FROM CORGI BOOKS

☐	12566 0	THE WIZARDS AND THE WARRIORS	*Hugh Cook*	£3.99
☐	13130 X	THE WORDSMITHS AND THE WARGUILD	*Hugh Cook*	£2.99
☐	13131 8	THE WOMEN AND THE WARLORDS	*Hugh Cook*	£3.50
☐	13327 2	THE WALRUS AND THE WARWOLF	*Hugh Cook*	£3.95
☐	13017 6	MALLOREON 1: GUARDIANS OF THE WEST		
			David Eddings	£3.50
☐	12284 X	BOOK ONE OF THE BELGARIAD: PAWN OF PROPHECY	*David Eddings*	£2.99
☐	12348 X	BOOK TWO OF THE BELGARIAD: QUEEN OF SORCERY	*David Eddings*	£2.99
☐	12382 X	BOOK THREE OF THE BELGARIAD: MAGICIAN'S GAMBIT	*David Eddings*	£2.99
☐	12435 4	BOOK FOUR OF THE BELGARIAD: CASTLE OF WIZARDRY	*David Eddings*	£2.99
☐	12447 8	BOOK FIVE OF THE BELGARIAD: ENCHANTERS' END GAME	*David Eddings*	£3.50
☐	13106 7	MORT	*Terry Pratchett*	£2.99
☐	13105 9	EQUAL RITES	*Terry Pratchett*	£2.99
☐	12848 1	THE LIGHT FANTASTIC	*Terry Pratchett*	£2.99
☐	12475 3	THE COLOUR OF MAGIC	*Terry Pratchett*	£2.99
☐	13325 6	STRATA	*Terry Pratchett*	£2.50
☐	13326 4	THE DARK SIDE OF THE SUN	*Terry Pratchett*	£2.50
☐	13101 6	SERVANTS OF ARK I: THE FIRST NAMED		
			Jonathan Wylie	£2.99
☐	13134 2	SERVANTS OF ARK II: THE CENTRE OF THE CIRCLE		
			Jonathan Wylie	£2.95
☐	13161 X	SERVANTS OF ARK III: THE MAGE-BORN CHILD		
			Jonathan Wylie	£2.99